THE ENFIELD CONNECTION

A Civil War Novel

By

John M. Kevin Jr.

WHITE FOX PUBLISHING

THE ENFIELD
CONNECTION
A Civil War Novel
by John M. Kevin, Jr.

All major non-historical characters in this book are products of my imagination. Any resemblance they bear to persons living or dead is pure coincidence.

White Fox Publishing
P.O. Box 372
Red Hill, Pa. 18076

White Fox Publishing,
P.O. Box 372,
Red Hill, Pa. 18076
(215)679-9477 e-mail slverfx@fast.net

ISBN 0-9656450-2-9

Original publication date: October 1997

Second edition published 1999

10 9 8 7 6 5 4 3 2

Printed on acid free paper

Printed in the United States of America

Cover design by Robin Hepler Photo by Cinda Sites

This book is dedicated to

*The brave men of the Bucktail Brigade, especially
Sergeant Samuel Pieffer, the heroic color bearer of
Company I*

and

My father, a Navy Corpsman

TO THE READER

The idea for this book began in 1988 in Gettysburg during the 125th anniversary of the Battle of Gettysburg. Reading Regimental Histories about the battle can be interesting for the history buff; but for the average person they can be very drab. I felt that I would try a novel approach that all could read and enjoy. At the same time the reader can learn a little about the history of this great battle. In this story historical facts are interwoven with fiction to draw the interest of the reader. My main objective was to point out the great courage of the Bucktail Brigade of the First Corps. This was in no way to take from the other Brigades in the same Corps. They all fought bravely on that first day. The Confederates lost the battle through leadership problems, not lack of courage. What I have tried to convey to you, the reader, was the confusion and fear felt by the ordinary soldier through modern eyes. These re-enactors didn't have any idea what was happening around them, only what was happening to them directly. I hope I was successful. Enjoy.

ACKNOWLEDGMENTS

I would first like to thank my wife, Jane for her patience for all these years that this book was in progress.

Many other people assisted me and gave me encouragement on this endeavor. My daughter Deborah, my son John, both gave me pointers on how to improve my writing style.

Jim Durkin, Mike Santeralli and Don Gallagher were a great help in proofing and how to improve the book.

Ed, Margaret, Nathan and Aaron Zifra had some very good ideas on what would make the book more interesting.

Tom Smith, Cdr. of the Burgwyn Chapter of the Sons of Confederate Veterans and David Adams, G-Grandson of the last Colonel of the 26th NC, supplied information on that regiment.

Anthony G. Mollo of the 14th Brooklyn gave me information on the Red Legs.

Mike Dallas of Meadville, Pa. for information on the 150th PVI.

Thanks Elsa Boorse, for Crackers.

Many thanks to all my comrades in the 150th PVI, Co. C & F. Also the 149th PVI and the 1st Penna. Rifles, all bucktails who posed for various pictures for the new cover. Cinda Sites and Dianne Conroy for their help with the pictures which are part of the cover and inside the book.

To my friends in the 5th Alabama Battilion for your support.

Thanks to my friends and comrades in the 7th Tenn. Co. B, you taught me the school of soldier.

Many thanks to my proof reader and editor.

ABOUT THE BOOK

Have you ever thought, I wish I could go back and relive history?

Three Civil War re-enactors wished this many times. During a re-enactment their wish comes true. The men are thrust back into history and the epic Battle of Gettysburg with all its' horrors.

Can they use their knowledge of the past to survive without changing history?

What effect does the mysterious Enfield have on these men, and will it make the full circle?

Now that they are actually fighting the Battle of Gettysburg in all its fury, will they live? If they are killed, how will their families ever know? If they survive, do they return to the future or will they stay in the past?

How do their families in the present cope with their disappearance to the past? Do they know what happened to their loved ones? Will they ever know what fate befell them?

This book crosses market lines and will interest science fiction, mystery and Civil War enthusiast alike.

NEVER, NEVER say or think, "I wish I could go back in time and relive history..." You may just get your wish!

CHAPTER ONE

Thick, sulphurous smoke covered the battle ground and made breathing difficult, while crashing volleys and roaring of artillery numbed the senses. The field was littered with the casualities of earlier intense combat. Company A of the 150th Pennsylvania Bucktail Regiment stood shoulder to shoulder awaiting the next attack from the Confederates to their front and also from their right. The earlier attacks on McPherson Ridge, along with the horrendous cannon fire had decimated their ranks. The 150th Pennsylvania Volunteer Regiment had won their honor this day still standing against overwhelming odds. Now the time had come. They were about to meet their greatest challenge. Before this fight was over, this Regiment would lose many more men. Everywhere one looked, bodies lay strewn over the field where the men had fallen in earlier attacks. Some of the wounded were trying to crawl to the rear, but for the moment no one could help them.

George Murray could see a Confederate regiment coming toward them and the order was shouted above the rattle of musket fire, "Forward. . . march!" The men stepped off shoulders touching and George could feel his best friend, Jack Meyers, on his right. As they moved over the uneven ground, the Rebels fired a volley into their ranks and over a score of men went down, including Jack. His friend raised a hand up to George, their eyes meeting for a second, as Jack silently pleaded for help. There wasn't anything George could do to help his friend as the file closers screamed, "Close it up, close on the colors!" At last they were brought to a halt and the order was given by officers and repeated by sergeants, "Fire by company . . . Fire!" At last they were able to return the deadly fire into the Rebels, who were now only seventy-five yards away.

When the smoke had cleared, it appeared that the whole front rank of the Confederates had gone down. A huge cheer went up and down the ranks. But it was short lived as someone shouted, "Cannon to our right about to fire!"

George looked quickly and he could clearly see the cannoneer. He was wearing a brilliant red shirt and leaned sharply to his left as the firing lanyard went taut. The last thing George saw was the cord ripping loose and a small wisp of white smoke shooting up from the vent. The blast which enfiladed the Bucktail line, ripped and tore gaping holes in the ranks. George Murray and his file partner Tim Fretz were part of the pile of Union dead on that hot and sunny afternoon. The fighting ebbed back and forth for another fifteen minutes. When it was over and the Confederates had carried the field.

Cheers filled the air as the victorious Confederates discharged their muskets in the air. As George Murray and the other re-enactors stood up, spectators all around clapped and cheered as the first day's battle was done.

As Tim freed himself from the jumbled pile of men, he remarked to George, "That was utterly fantastic, the way we went down when that cannon fired."

"Tim, for a split second I was scared to death. I think I went through the bubble."

"What do you mean?"

2

"As I saw the lanyard tighten on that cannon, I thought I was about to die. It was too real."

"So that's what the bubble[1] is like that everyone talks about. Well, I haven't been through the bubble yet," Tim confessed.

When Jack Meyers joined the two men he remarked, "Man, I was so hot back there, I decided to take a hit. These damn wool uniforms are hot as hell."

Tim replied, "Well, you are kinda outta shape. Hey, you missed it when that cannon fired. It was so realistic the way everyone went down. You should have heard the spectators clap when we got up."

"What makes you so all fired sure they were clapping for you? I did a hell of a somersault when I took my hit. Anyway, anytime you want to go one-on-one, we'll take a little run, say five miles. Then we'll see who's in better shape!"

George interjected, "All right you two knock it off. You sound worse than a couple of kids always arguing about something."

"Up yours!" Tim replied, "Who in hell died and left you boss?"

Their Captain yelled for the Sergeant, "Form up the men, so we can pass in review for the spectators."

The men gladly fell in, marching back to camp and an ice-cold brew. Following that would be a dinner of grilled chicken simmering over the aroma of an oak wood fire, cooked by the women.

---

[1]Bubble-Most re-enactors at one time or another go through the bubble- that period in which they actually feel they are back in time. It can last for a split second or for several seconds.

* * * * *

George Murray was born and raised on a small farm in upstate Pennsylvania near Jersey Shore. Their farm was small, but self-supporting for the family. They farmed the land, raised chickens, a couple of cows and some hogs. This land supplied all their needs, but there was never any money to have their wants. The only money they made was from the Saturday trips to Williamsport. Here they would sell butter and eggs at the farmers market. Cash earned from their produce would buy gasoline for the tractor and fabric for clothing. When George turned eighteen he joined the Navy. It was better than waiting to be drafted into the Army. His parents were apprehensive but his father understood that this may be his chance for a better life.

Thirty years later, George Murray's grey hair was the only indicator that he was in his late forties. He stood almost 6 feet and still had the trim muscular look of a navy corpsman when he served in Vietnam with the Marines. His steel blue eyes gave away the horrors he had seen and felt during that war. His first taste of combat changed his life forever. He vividly remembered hearing the bullets crack around him, clipping off branches and leaves. The screaming of wounded men calling, "Corpsman," prompting George to crawl to render first aid. The first wounded man he went to help, died before George could reach him. An exploding Viet Cong rocket propelled grenade had ripped open his neck, spewing blood six feet in all directions. It was then that he realized how human he was. All his training did no good whatsoever. He could only save the men who God willed to live. As he crawled across a trail to render first aid to another wounded Marine, something bumped into his leg. To his horror, a Viet Cong grenade lay next to him, hissing and smoking. George fought off the urge to run, picked up the grenade and threw it back up the trail just before it exploded. Four Viet Cong were on the receiving end as the grenade sent its deadly shards of steel into their bodies. This action broke up the ambush the Marine patrol stumbled into. George killed four men, which tore deeply into his soul. He never wanted to kill, just save lives. Thank God those days were behind him.

His hands were large and rough from working on his small truck patch. Despite his massive hands, he was quite nimble. He had proven this many times in the service, suturing and probing wounds. Now he just worked his small farm to feed his family. His one hobby was reading and researching the war of rebellion. George had become very interested in the Civil War while he had been stationed in Norfolk Virginia and had since become an avid Civil War buff. He even wrote and published a few short stories on different regiments he had researched. George started re-enacting and skirmishing the same year, the year after he retired. It suited him very well. With the re-enacting, he experienced the marching, battlefield drills, camp life and to fight in battles of that war. And with the North-South Skirmish Association, he also learned how well these muskets shot. The skirmishers formed units of actual regiments both North and South that fought in the war between the states. They also dressed with the same uniforms of the regiment they were portraying. The men fired in competition in eight man teams. With skirmishing, George learned different problems they faced during the Civil War. Trying to load, aim and shoot accurately. Then reloading and shooting against time.

He and his wife, Jan, were now empty nesters, with their daughter and son grown. George met Jan

5

when he was first stationed in Norfolk, Virginia in the early 60's. She was a southern belle and it was love at first sight. Jan was a strong woman, and during the long absences while her husband was overseas took complete charge of the family. Their first child came two years after they were married. Their daughter Denise, initially, and two years later a son, James. Even though she was in her mid forties, she kept her figure and with her shoulder length brown hair, looked to be in her early thirties.

They enjoyed their laid back life on the small farm. Their spread consisting of twenty acres was located at the base of the Blue Ridge mountains in Southeastern Pennsylvania. The house, barn, summer kitchen and pond occupied seven acres while the rest consisted of mature woods. The original house with several additions and summer kitchen was built in the 1700's of fieldstone which was readily available. The Murray homestead was out in the country, but, the city of Allentown was only 20 miles away. They didn't go to town often as the urban area seemed too closed in. George set up a small range near the base of the mountain so he could practice firing his Civil War muskets for competition shooting. On days off, his friends and their families would come up for a lively weekend of camping and shooting. At night they would sit around a campfire cooking hot dogs and toasting marshmallows. During the day George would instruct the men and their wives, how to load and fire the muskets, which helped them learn more about that war's firearms.

* * * * *

Tim Fretz was an electronics technician in a factory which manufactured computer components and lived south of George, in the suburbs of Philadelphia, Pennsylvania. He was in his early thirties, almost 6' 2", with a slender build. Tim had piercing dark eyes and a dark complexion, giving him the appearance of middle east ancestry. In fact, both his grandparents had emigrated from Germany. Although Tim was slightly better-than-average intelligence, he had bypassed college to serve his country in the Navy for four years. He had been fortunate that he didn't go to Vietnam, however duty on that desolate island, Diego Garcia, as a radioman had been quite boring. In his spare time, he had become an avid reader and since he had an interest in the Civil War it was natural for him to focus on that topic. After he was discharged from the Navy, he married Marge, his childhood sweetheart.

Marge was a very petite blonde with captivating blue eyes. With her fair complexion, she had to be careful not to get sunburned. Her father had been killed in an automobile accident when she was seventeen and she missed him very much. Her mother had never recovered from the shock of her husbands' death. Unfortunately her mother contracted Lyme disease three months after his death and was not diagnosed correctly in the beginning. By the time the doctors realized the correct diagnosis, it had attacked the valves of her heart. This is an insidious malady that mimics many other illnesses. Her mother died a month later. Marge knew her mother had simply given up and died of a broken heart. The double loss devastated Marge, but Tim had been her hero, prodding Marge to get on with her life. He knew she wanted to go to college and insisted that she do it. Her parents would be watching from heaven and would be proud of her.

While she waited for Tim to finish his time in the Navy, Marge had completed college. After graduation, Tim and Marge were married and she started working as a dental assistant. The couple were blessed with two boys early in their marriage. They also bought an old house which seemed to need constant repairing. Tim hated the Lansdale area where the factory was located. The traffic was terrible, especially in the morning and evening rush hours. You had to cope with these pressures just to have a decent job.

To help relieve the stresses, he started re-enacting after meeting Jack Myers at an event three years earlier. He knew Jack casually, since he worked in the same factory. He didn't know at the time that Jack was interested in the Civil War. Tim took his family to a re-enactment and recognized Jack who was there as a Union soldier along with George. Later, he talked with his co-worker during a lunch break at work. It didn't take Tim long to decide to try it and he was soon hooked. Marge also joined in, making her own Civil War Era dresses. She made simple ones to portray the average woman of that time. Their two boys, Daniel and Matthew, were too young to be riflemen, however they dressed in period clothing and joined on as a drummer and a fifer. They were anxiously waiting for the day when they could re-enact as soldiers. One of Marge's favorite past times and weaknesses was shopping and sometimes went on shopping sprees. This upset Tim and on more than one occasion he had threatened to cut up her credit cards.

Jack Myers was the shortest member of the group, had a stocky build and was all muscle. He was highly intelligent and when looking at you with his sky blue eyes, gave the impression of seeing into your soul. He had just turned thirty and had gone to Drexel College, graduating with an electrical engineering degree. Jack also had a minor in history and his interest in the Civil War started with Professor Kaufman, whose great-great-grandfather had fought in the Civil War. The professor had brought a diary from those war years that his forbearer had maintained for four years. It had been amazing reading about Frederickburg, Bull Run and of course Gettysburg by someone who had actually been there. The most enjoyable time spent in this class were the weekend field trips to Gettysburg where they studied the battle in great depth.

When Jack graduated, he started working at the same factory as Tim. Two years later, Jack married Katey. They had met and dated while in college. Katey was the outdoors type, having camped with her family all over the country when she was growing up. Her hair was dark auburn, worn long and was just showing the slightest tint of gray. Her dark blue eyes accented her heart shaped face, and while she was only 5' tall, she carried herself with great poise. Katey caught Jack's eye in the same history class they shared. Her large smile and infectious laugh just swept him off his feet. She had developed a keen interest in the Civil War from the same instructor. Their relationship was solid but in his characteristic way, he could not commit to marriage until he had figured every angle. His mind was that of an engineer and no decision could be made without verifying everything. His behavior sometimes irked Katey, like when she asked her husband to wash the car. First Jack would check the temperature, the weather forecast, read all the labels on the soap bottle, the car wax can and so on. However, for some reason Jack abandoned his methodical ways when it came time to join the re-enacting fraternity. It was as if some unseen force drove him. Katey shared her husband's love of the Civil War, making her own clothing and joining in as a camp follower. For her it was a natural thing, because she taught history at the High School in Lansdale.

Jack had met George at a re-enactment in July of 1985 and Jack immediately told Murray that he would like to join up. George had been playing with an idea to start a new group for over a year. Between the two men, they managed to recruit some more men. They formed a loose organization and called themselves Company A of the 150th PVI BUCKTAIL Regiment. They always stood out, because of the Bucktails that they wore on their forage caps. George could never figure out what mysterious force drove him to form a new company. He had been quite happy with the unit he had been in. And why in the world did he pick one of the Bucktail Regiments. It had just happened or so he thought.

* * * * *

The exhausted soldiers marched back to their camp which was located on the side of a hill. The re-enactment had been held on a farm located in Adams County several miles outside of Gettysburg. It was still a working farm and the group organizing the event had convinced the farmer to use his hay fields after the harvest. The ground was very rocky and rough just like most of the land in Adams County. This made for very hard walking and the men had to be very careful not to sprain or break an ankle. Their march up the hill to the camp was hard and the men were hot, dusty and tired by the time they reached the company area. The temperature was very warm this first weekend in July and the humidity was high. This was typical for the area this time of the year. At last they halted in front of the Company streets and the colonel gave the orders to all the officers to dismiss their men. George and his two friends ambled slowly back into their camping area and looked for their wives, but they were nowhere to be seen. George asked one of the ladies, "Mary, did you see our wives? Did they watch the re-enactment?"

"Yes, they were at the re-enactment, but said they and the boys were going to the sutler area to do some shopping."

"Damn, I knew I should have taken Marge's credit cards away," Tim groaned.

Jack just laughed and said, "Tim, you should have trained her better. Maybe you can send her to obedience school."

"Go pound sand. Don't try to tell me how to train my wife. It seems to me that when Katey tells you to jump, you always ask how high."

"Can't you guys ever talk to each other without bickering," George interjected? "You haven't learned the finer points of marriage yet. Just give it a few years and it will all fall into place."

Both men glared at George, but for once they were at loss for words. So they let it drop for now. They would get even later. It was always a running battle among the three men, and all in good fun. The first order of business was to shed the leather

11

accouterments and those damn hot wool jackets. At last they were sipping cold beer as they sat around with the other men, swapping tales of the days' battle. The next order of business was to scrub their musket barrels to remove the black powder fowling. This was a very dirty job. Tim really didn't care if his gun was ever cleaned, but peer pressure from George and Jack pushed him into doing it. The job was completed, just as the wives came back to camp.

Jan came over and gave George a loving peck on the cheek, then whispered, "I bought you a surprise, guess which hand."

Pointing at both sides at once, he replied "Both of them."

"You never play fair, now you won't get your surprise," Jan pouted.

"OK, OK I'll guess this time." Tim standing behind Jan pointed to her left hand. George knew Tim was setting him up, so he said, "It's in the right hand." Sure enough, Jan bought her husband a new vest. He wanted one for some time, but felt they were too expensive. He hugged his wife, "Thank you very much. You didn't have to buy it, but thank you again. Can I try it on now?"

George tried on the vest which fit perfectly and even had a pocket for his pocket watch. Proudly he showed the other men in the company.

Jack turned to his wife, "See what a good wife Jan is. Why don't you learn from her?"

"Well I did buy something for you, but it'll be a cold day in hell before I give it to you now!" With that slavo delivered, she went into the tent and pulled the flap closed.

Turning to George, "Now look what you've done. I'm in hot water with my wife."

"What do you mean, what I did? It seems to me you just shot yourself in the foot again."

Jack went to the tent to plead with his wife, while the other men jeered and called him hen pecked and showered him with other derogatory terms. The ice was broken when someone called out, "Come and get it, before we throw it out to the hogs." One thing everyone learned quickly in camp, when the call went out for food, you didn't dally. It was like a swarm of locust descending on a wheat field. Katey left the tent still not talking to Jack, but cooled down after dinner. Everyone loved the grilled chicken that the women made, not to mention the corn bread cooked in the dutch oven.

After dinner and cleanup, everyone found a spot around the fire and sat down. All but the young boys and girls, who were filled with energy. They played roll the hoop and other Civil War era games. Most of the adult conversation centered around upcoming events and which ones they would attend. They considered the Gettysburg event for the next year. It would be the 125th anniversary of the Battle of Gettysburg and it was already being touted as the biggest event ever. There would be a lot of planning for this re-enactment. For one thing there would be three days of events for the spectators instead of the normal two days. Many re-enactors would be spending the whole week at the site drilling and marching.

The beautiful evening was accentuated by a full moon, and it lit up the camp. It was so bright that lanterns weren't needed. The group sat around the camp fire for hours and sang Civil War songs while Jack played the banjo. Soon, families from other camps wandered over and joined in the singing. A rather large fellow named GG (Gentle Giant) from the 90th PVI, brought his guitar and his deep baritone voice added to the sing along. It was one of the most enjoyable evenings they could remember. George finally had enough and asked Jan, "It's one in the morning. Are you ready to turn in for the night?"

"Yes, I'm worn out tonight. Even the hard ground will feel good."

As they stood up and announced they were going to bed, Tim remarked, "Yea, you old folks better hobble to your tent, it's after 8 p.m."

George fired back, "OK wise ass, I'll sure as hell make sure you're up tomorrow morning by six, then we'll see who hobbles around!" Before Tim could answer, George and Jan left the campfire and went to their tent. They were the first to leave and the mass exodus started, leaving only a couple people at the fire. As the night wore on, the sky clouded up, promising a change in the weather.

The next morning a storm front moved through and the rains started at day break. Soon the ground turned to mud and everyone was up, grumbling as they broke camp. The forecast called for heavy rains all day and the re-enactors had to leave before their vehicles bogged down in the mud. Several still had to be towed out, thanks to the Adams County clay and mud. Everyone said their good byes as they departed. In two weeks they would meet again at the next event in Leesburg, Virginia.

CHAPTER TWO

The sunlight reflected off the calm water of the lake while the cool breeze shook the leaves, damp with the morning dew. Tom stood mesmerized, hands deep in the sudsy water as he attempted to wash the morning dishes. It's amazing how calm the morning can be after such a rotten night, he mused. Ironic that his last assignment - that damned unsolved case - should continue to haunt him, especially in this place where the calm of the mountains had always eased his pain. This particular case was the only one, in his long years of service, that really bothered him. Even after he retired, this case consumed him with a passion to find the truth, which still eluded him. He wondered if he would ever know for sure what actually happened.

Tom Gallager was now in his early sixties, his hair had long since turned a silvery white. At 6'2" he carried his 190 lbs. very well. He ran every morning and loved to ride his bike all over the roads that criss crossed the perimeter of his beloved lake. Tom still looked to be a man in his forties, and his mind was always working, a carry over from his Secret Service days. He was an honest, straight forward compassionate man, who would never waver when duty called. Tom would always do what was expected of him and more. If called upon, he would sacrifice his life without hesitation.

Tom was the son of a coal miner and had grown

up on the outskirts of Mahanoy City, in the heart of the coal mines of Pennsylvania. He probably would have been destined to work in the mines, except for the Korean War. He was drafted into the army in 1949 and went through basic training at Ft. Dix. Due to severe cutbacks in the military by the Truman administration, basic training was cut from twelve weeks to eight weeks. Tom remembered how this lack of funds affected him in training. There was very little live fire on the rifle range due to shortages of the basic components for the infantry, rifle ammunition. When he finished training, Tom was held at Ft. Dix doing menial jobs because there was no money to assign him to a unit. At last in early June 1950 Gallager received orders to the 19th Infantry Regiment on occupation duty in Japan.

This was a cushy set of orders, Tom told his parents before he left and not to worry about him. Duty in Japan would be uneventful and he would be home in a year. The 19th Regiment which was assigned to the 24th Division had a distinguished past. During the Civil War it earned the name of "Rock of Chickamauga." The men in the regiment were affectionately known as "Chicks."

Tom arrived in Japan on June 20 after a long flight on a C54 transport. He reported to his unit which was located in the Honshu training area. Tom was appalled at the condition of the regiment. Nearly one third of the primary tools of the soldier were out of service. Many M1 rifles were inoperative due to lack of spare parts. He was glad they were on occupation duty and not going to war.

Gallager remembered the morning of June 25, 1950 very well. At morning inspection, they learned that the North Koreans had invaded South Korea. At least they would stay in Japan. Nobody in their right mind would send a regiment in this condition into combat. Not so, on June 27 the regiment was put on high alert, to be ready to sail for Korea. However the navy was suffering from the same severe cutbacks and the 19th Regiment did not sail with the rest of the 24th Division. They didn't board ship until July 6, over a week since the 24th had sailed. By the time the Chicks arrived and off loaded at Pusan, the 24th had been bloodied at the Kum River line. The 19th Regiment was rushed to help the 24th in repulsing the North Koreans.

Tom remembered vividly the heat and high humidity of the Korean summer. While sailing to Korea an unusual cold wave and rain had hit the troops then in South Korea. However, when the 19th arrived, the weather changed to the typical summer. One of the first things that hit the Chicks was the stench of the rice paddies, they smelled of open sewers. That was a smell he would never forget.

Life on the Kum River line was horrific for the inexperienced Chicks. While the enemy stayed on the other side of the river, Tom and his comrades were under incessant artillery, mortar and machine gun fire from the North Koreans. All this changed on the 16th of July when the enemy launched a heavy attack across the river. The 19th was forced to fall back because their left flank gave way. During the melee that followed, this regiment lost over half of their men by the time they reached the next line of defense at the Yongdong staging area.

During the retreat an incident happened to Tom which was a precursor of his future. As they moved down the road among all the refugees escaping the war, a jeep came along side transporting a bird colonel sitting next to the driver. As the vehicle drew along side of Tom, a North Korean disguised as a refugee pulled a pistol and aimed it at the officer's head. Without

17

thinking Tom jumped on the man and wrestled him to the ground before he could shoot. In the struggle, the pistol went off and the bullet just missed Tom's head, burning his face from the muzzle flash. Gallager reached for his combat knife and dispached the enemy infiltrator before he could fire again. As Tom stood up, shaking, the colonel thanked him for saving his life and asked his name and unit. He would recommend a medal for heroism for the soldier. Later as Tom was plodding along, he came upon that same jeep, everyone was killed from a mine sown by the enemy. Oh well, he thought, so much for that medal.

Tom thought of those days following that retreat. They would attack but the North Koreans would flank them. The army for some reason stayed on the roads while the enemy used the surrounding hills to flank them all the time. It was retreat, attack, retreat then attack again. He knew that only by the grace of God that he had survived that year in Korea. He remembered the promises, "You'll be home for Thanksgiving," then "You'll be home for Christmas." In December of that year, the United Nation troops made a push to the Yalu River, to crush the North Korean Army once and for all. The harsh reality of the Korean winter was setting in just as the Chinese Army entered the battle with over whelming force. He remembered the retreat and fighting in the bitter cold. The U. S. Army was so complacent and smug that the war would be over soon, the soldiers still had summer uniforms. He would never forget that winter for as long as he lived. Tom was sent back to the states when his tour was completed and was asked if he would re-enlist. In no uncertain terms, he told the recruiters he wanted a discharge. Never would he serve in the military again, not after what he saw in Korea.

Tom was able to go to college under the GI bill

after his return to the United States. This was his ticket out of the coal mines and he made good use of his opportunity. He majored in accounting, finishing at the top of his class. In his senior year, two monumental events changed his life forever. He met his intended wife, Nancy and the Secret Service recruited him.

Tom thought back over the years when he and Nancy had bought this bare land on the forested shores of Lake Walenpaupak. It was an ideal area away from the hustle and bustle of the cities and only 20 miles east of Scranton, Pennsylvania. The lake was man made, which had many uses besides generating electricity and flood control. Lots were sold around the lake over the years and now it was a bustling community year round. Tom felt a little sad, it wasn't quiet anymore. The lake was becoming a booming tourist attraction with all the problems of a transient population. They were fortunate to have water front property, however the boats choked the lake most of the summer. The one thing that Tom loved about the lake was the crystal clear waters. On a still day you could see down 15 to 20 feet. Many a day was spent fishing and even if no fish were caught it was total relaxation. At night the gentle breezes stirred up the waters to cause tiny waves to slip on shore. These sounds of water lapping put a tired soul to rest in the evening.

Nancy was born in Arlington, Virginia, a daughter of Senator Chandler from Iowa. Even though being a Senator consumed most of his time, Nancy's father insisted on being with his family at every opportunity. He always stressed the importance of family to his daughter which she carried all her life. Her mother had been a down-to-earth farm girl. Even though she didn't care for the social circles in Washington, she always accompanied her husband to social events. Her mother taught her self reliance and honesty. When Nancy was eighteen, it was off to State College in Pennsylvania. In her Junior year she had noticed a handsome man in her accounting class, but he never paid attention to her. She was too shy to approach him and in those days, a nice girl just didn't do that. In her senior year, Nancy was getting ready to open the door to the class room, when Tom, remembering he left his notebook in his locker burst out of the room. The force of the door knocked her on the floor scattering books and papers all over. Tom had been apologetic as he helped her pickup the scattered belongings. He had felt badly and tried to make it up to her by buying her lunch. Over the years he always laughed about how he had swept Nancy off her feet at first sight. The years had been good to Nancy. She was still petite and only her grey hair suggested that she was a grandmother. Nancy kept in shape by running and riding with her husband.

"Hey, hon, better get a move on," the cheery voice of his wife roused him from his revelry. "The kids should be here soon."

Thank God for Nancy, he thought. In spite of all the tough years when the Service had to come first, she was always his beacon in the night. "I'm hurrying. If you hadn't used every dish in the house to make breakfast, I'd have been done by now," he teased.

Nancy made a face, gave him a quick hug and moved along to fluff the pillows thrown on the couch. She had the special touch that made even a vacation home seem comforting and welcoming. Thank God for her, he thought again.

Tom Gallager wasn't a religious man but the incident in '88 that had shaken him to the core, made him question all the "knowns" in the universe. He retired from the Secret Service in 1989 because he reached that magical retirement age of sixty. Before becoming a man of leisure, Tom had the case of a lifetime, one that continued to haunt him because it remained an enigma that seemed to have no beginning or end.

"Oh, well, Tom, old boy, enough of this," he mumbled, pulling the drain plug and rinsing the sink.

"Pop-Pop!" a young voice called from outside the cozy cabin. "We're finally here." Screen door banging, a tow-headed twelve year old appeared. "If Dad drove any slower, we'd have been going backwards! Hey, whatcha doing? Is it going to rain? Dad said it was going to rain. It sure is cold, Pop-Pop."

Laughing, Tom tousled his grandson's hair. "Just finished doing the dishes to answer your first question and yes, I'm afraid that is what the forecast is calling for. I think I told you last time we talked, Tad, that you were to stop growing. Now, how come you didn't listen? I thought you liked your old Pop."

Tad smiled, his freckled face crinkling. "I'm taller than Em! Can we fish if it rains?" At twelve, Tad was already beginning that adolescent sprouting, as evidenced by his thin, gangly body, currently enveloped in jean cut-offs and a Nirvana t-shirt. "How come it's so cold here? It's nearly July. Guess how hot it was at home?"

"Tad, stop rambling! You'll drive your grandfather up a wall," Betty laughed, as she followed her youngest child into the cabin. "Go help your dad carry in the luggage. Even Emily is helping." Her taunt had the desired effect as Tad ran off to prove his "manliness" to all who would be witness. Betty kissed her father-in-law on the cheek as he followed Tad out the door. "Nancy, are you here? Did you run off with a handsome lumberjack 'cause your husband has been driving you crazy?"

Laughing, Nancy entered the great room, wiping her hands on her slacks. "Oh, so you've heard about the curses of retirement, have you? If Tom doesn't stop

21

tossing and turning in his sleep, I may just consider that lumberjack."

A concerned wrinkle crossed Betty's forehead. "Is dad still consumed by that last unsolved case? I really hoped that being up here would help him come to grips with whatever it was that happened. No dice, huh?"

"His one passion, now that he is retired, is to find the truth of that case. It is always the same thing. I know he isn't supposed to talk about service-related cases, but I'm beginning to wonder if all this holding back is healthy." Nancy just finished her sentence when Tom, Tad, Emily and Matt, arms loaded with backpacks, pillows, and suitcases, came banging on the door. "You'd think that among all those brains, there'd be one working enough to realize that you'd need one hand free to open the door! What would you do without Mom?" With a tender smile, she held the door as the gang tramped on through.

"Gramma, can we go fishing? Did you make brownies? Can I sleep on the sofa-bed?" Tad began his barrage of questions once again.

Nancy explained with the greatest of patience that he'd better get all his stuff put away quickly if he wanted to get some fishing in before the weather turned for the worse. "Brownies? It's only 9 in the morning-who do you think I am-superGramma? As for the sofa bed, I think you'd better sleep in the loft. Your parents, Pop-Pop and I will end up staying up pretty late and we wouldn't want to disturb your beauty sleep."

Amidst grumbles about sharing a loft with his "gross" sister and not needing beauty sleep-what did they think he was-a girl? Tad reluctantly carried his bags upstairs. Emily followed to make sure her "slimy" brother didn't touch her bed.

At fourteen, she was at that awkward age between being a little girl and a woman. Too old to sit on my lap, Tom thought, and yet, too young to tell dirty jokes to. It was the first time he felt a little uncomfortable around his granddaughter. Gee, I hope she still likes to fish, he thought.

"Dad, it sure is good to be here. As much as I hate that drive, I am always glad to see the old cabin again. How are you guys doin," Matt asked? "I sure am looking forward to this vacation. Things were pretty crazy at work and I suppose they will be even worse once I get back."

"Matt, you promised you wouldn't talk about work, think about work, nor attempt to call your voice mail the whole time you're here," Betty admonished. "Dad, you've got to keep him so busy that he won't be able to spend one second thinking about work. Promise?"

Tom hugged his daughter-in-law and agreed without hesitation. Matt had a tendency to worry about everything. The leaves don't fall far from the tree, he thought to himself. "Now how about that fishing. The weather channel is calling for thundershowers in the early afternoon, which means we'd better get a move on if we are to satisfy young Tad. I'll go gather up the bait and rods. Meet me at the dock when you are ready." Kissing Nancy and grabbing his windbreaker, Tom headed out into the sunshine.

"Mom, Dad seems a little preoccupied. Is he okay?" Matt voiced the concern that had been plaguing Nancy all morning. "Maybe Tad will keep him occupied so he won't be able to worry."

"Let's hope so, Matt. I'm growing more concerned each day. He is actually talking about taking a drive to Gettysburg over the fourth. I can't believe that's a good idea, especially when you are only here for the week." Nancy shook her head and looked at her son, the worry evident in her eyes.

"Don't worry, Mom. We didn't drive six hours to take a little jaunt to Gettysburg. I'm sure that Dad will see that. It's not like its right around the corner or anything."

"Well, thank the good Lord for that!" Nancy laughed. "Otherwise, we'd be there every day, trying to unravel the big mystery! Go on-leave the unpacking to Betty and me. Your father could use the diversion of fishing." Reassured, Matt followed Tom outside.

As he walked down the path to the dock, Matt felt himself relaxing for the first time in ages. He shared the love of nature with his father, and understood the healing effects that these mountains had on him. If only Dad could let go of that Gettysburg incident, Matt thought as he pushed back the bough that protruded from a large pine next to the path. The sunshine helped lift his concern slightly as he approached the dock. Matt had learned the finer arts of fishing and swimming on this dock in his youth.

Kneeling, Tom prepared his old fiberglass rod. Sensing his son's approach, he said, "I remember when you learned to dive right off this dock. You couldn't have been more than ten years old at the time. When I look at Tad, I see you again. I'm glad you made it, Matt."

"I remember the first time I tried to dive off this pier and instead of landing gracefully, I did a completely ungraceful belly-flop, barely missing the dock," Matt laughed. "I don't know which hurt more-my aching belly or my aching bottom from the licking you gave me!" Pushing his dark hair off his forehead, he looked out onto the lake. "It's beginning to get cloudy. Do you really think we'll get some fishing in before the storm hits?"

Tom sat back and looked out onto Lake Wallenpaupak. "The cove might be okay for an hour or so, but I doubt that we'll get much more than that in

24

today. I'm really only going out because Tad will be disappointed if we don't."

The black clouds swirled and rolled in from the west and the fishing for the day was over. The boat raced ahead of the storm and they made it to the dock just ahead of the first rain squall. Everyone jumped out of the boat when it was tied, and ran for the cabin, amid flying leaves and dust, the storm chasing on their heels. Nancy held the door open as they burst through, laughing and falling to the floor of the great room.

"Gramma, you should have seen the big bass I caught, but Pop-Pop made me throw it back. It was huge," Tad exclaimed breathlessly. "And man did it fight. It almost pulled me in."

Behind his back, Emily showed with her hands, the size of the fish Tad was bragging about, and everyone started laughing. "Oh my, it was so big that it almost couldn't swallow the hook" she chided. Tad turned red, and raised his hand to hit his sister, when his father grabbed it and sternly warned, "You don't go around hitting people, especially girls, young man!"

Nancy broke in, "OK, everyone, the rules of the house during vacation are, no fighting and no pouting. We're going to have a great week. Now all of you get to the kitchen for some homemade vegetable soup and grilled cheese sandwiches your mom and I made while you all were fishing."

After they finished lunch and the kitchen was cleaned, everyone retired to the great room. With Tad's help, Tom and Matt started the fire in the fireplace. It quickly warmed the great room as the teeming rain pounded on the roof, promising to be a dreary, damp afternoon.

Tom sat in his lazy boy and sipped on his coffee, as everyone settled down in their favorite chairs. Tom asked, "What story do you want to hear today? The time

I saved the President from falling down the steps of Air Force One or the time I had to lie about the size of the fish the President caught and got away?"

His son, Matt looked at him and said, "Dad, mom told us about that incident at Gettysburg and how it has totally consumed you. Maybe that's the story you should tell us."

Tom thought for a minute, then replied, "Well, Son, maybe you're right. It's a long story and it's going to rain all day. Maybe I can get it off my back, if I tell the story. Anyway that portion is not classified any longer so I can disclose it. You know, I'm a good investigator, but I can tell you, this one has me stumped. Matt, you're an FBI agent, and you know about gathering evidence, putting everything together for a case. But what I'm about to tell you, will blow your mind. You'll say it can't be, but I've checked and rechecked the facts. So with that behind us, the story begins."

Tom started slowly, as his mind was trying to sort out the facts. "I still haven't figured where the story begins, either in 1863, 1950 or in 1988."

Tad looked at his grandfather confused and asked, "Pop-Pop, how can you have three different beginnings in a story?"

"Well Tad," his Grandfather said, "After you hear this story, you tell me where the beginning is. In fact, you can ask your father the same question when I'm done, because I think he'll be as confused as I am. It's almost like the age-old question, Which came first, the chicken or the egg?

In early April of '88, I was called into the superintendent's office and asked if I would like an assignment in my home state of Pennsylvania. After I accepted, the boss told me that President Reagan would be going to Gettysburg to rededicate the peace memorial. This would be the 50th anniversary, of the dedication by President Roosevelt. I was against the whole operation because of the security problems expected that weekend. But the President was adamant about going and I lost out. I went to Gettysburg and set everything in motion for the President's visit. I stressed to the local police, the state police, the National Park Service, and everyone who would be involved, that anything out of the ordinary should be reported to the command center immediately. I alone, would be responsible for determining if further action would be required.

Considering the complexity of the operation, and the hoards of people streaming into Gettysburg for the 125th re-enactment, things went fairly smooth. Except for one incident that started on the 24th of June. It seems that three re-enactors had simply disappeared in front of a group of spectators. I thought that it was either a hoax or the spectators were suffering from the heat. However, the chain of events that would envelop me, the re-enactors, and many others, would change us all forever. The odd thing is, the whole Secret Service operation came to an abrupt end on the morning of July 3, 1988. The President's trip was canceled, because a civilian Airbus was shot down by a U.S. Navy ship in the middle East. And by then, although I didn't know it, this story was moving toward a climax, with another strange occurrence that afternoon near the high water mark."

"What's the high water mark? What happened at the high water mark?" Tad asked, in rapid fire.

"I won't go into that right now Tad, but switch over to the actors in this story and I'll tell you what they told me of the chain of events. I'll also tell you my involvement, then you all can decide what happened. Maybe after you hear the account, you can tell me, because I can't comprehend what occurred. What I can tell you for sure is the fact that I checked every aspect of what happened and I can assure you that it was no hoax." And in front of his spellbound audience he proceeded with the incredible story.

CHAPTER THREE

It was the beginning of a warm, sultry day in July 1950 in the small town of Landis Corner, just west of Spartensburg, South Carolina. Bill Sloan Jr. was on his way to his father's general store where, in a month he would start running the business, after his father retired. As a youngster, he had helped in the store on Saturdays and all week during summer recess from school. Sundays were reserved for church in the morning and catfishing in the afternoon. Those were the enjoyable years just before World War II. As he looked back, it seemed strange, how his father always talked about the World War when he fought in the trenches of France. Little did they know that there would be another World War, needing numbers to keep track of them. Bill joined the Marines in 1940, going through boot camp at Paris Island. His first duty station was Marine Barracks, Pearl Harbor. On the morning of December 7, 1941, Bill was on his way to the chow hall for breakfast as the first wave of Japanese warplanes streaked out of the sky, bombing the sleeping U.S. Fleet. Running to the armory, Bill, with the aid of two other Marines, carried a fifty-caliber water cooled machine gun to the roof of the barracks. The men fired on the aircraft as they swooped over the barracks and managed to hit two aircraft. They never knew if the aircraft that were hit actually crashed, they were too busy trying to stay alive.

When Navy Intelligence learned that Midway

would be the next Japanese target, he was sent to that island to bolster it's defenses. Two weeks before the attack, Bill flew in on a C-47 with the rest of his light anti-aircraft unit. The intervening time was spent digging fortifications and filling sandbags. This was an un-nerving time, not knowing when or if an attack would come. The only thing they knew for sure, they were expendable.

On that fateful morning as Bill was manning his water-cooled fifty calibre machinegun, he watched the Brewster Buffalos, P-40s and Wildcats take off on morning patrol. An hour later a droning noise could be heard over the ocean. Next the air raid sirens sounded out their moanful warning of imminent danger. Soon small dots on the horizon grew larger as the Japanese air armada swiftly approached. The attack came with a vengence and bombs were smashing the airfield and entrenchments. Bill and his men were firing at swooping aircraft constantly, with the tracers reaching out as in slow motion. Suddenly an enemy Zero was bearing down on them in a shallow dive. Bill fired at the rapidly closing aircraft and he could see his tracers passing all around the plane. Flashes of light from the cowling and wings spelled out impending disaster for the anti-aircraft crew. Bill remembered twisting and turning in the air before crashing to the ground unconscious. The other four men in his crew were killed in the strafing. Bill was severely wounded in the left leg and spent the next year in hospitals undergoing numerous operations and learning to walk again. His left leg was 1/2" shorter than his right leg and he walked with a noticeable limp.

When he arrived at the store, his father was already there. While enjoying a cup of coffee together, his father said "Bill, this is the inventory list of the hardware section. I'll go over the appliance list next." Picking up several large catalogs, his father continued,

"Now these are the catalogs you'll use, and make sure that when the order comes in, you count each and every piece."

"Yes dad. Do you remember how you always made me count even the nuts and bolts? So, don't worry about counting, I've had a good teacher."

His father chided with a twinkle in his eye, "Now you listen here, you young whipper snapper, you're still wet behind the ears and you better listen to what I tell you. And one thing for sure, you'll have a hellava time trying to ask me questions later because I'll be out fishing." The store wouldn't open for another half hour and he wanted to pass on as much as he could in the next few weeks.

Bill Sr. knew his son could run the business and would not squander the money. His son had worked closely with him and he had instilled a good work ethic in him. They worked hard and played hard, always keeping both in the proper perspective. His son had graduated from college with high honors in business administration. He was the first in the family to go to college and Bill Sr. was proud of his son.

When Bill Jr. went to unlock the front door, he noticed old Clem Akers with a dour expression on his face outside waiting for the store to open. Clem always wore the same thing, bib overalls, straw hat and long sleeve flannel shirt, no matter how hot it was. Over the years Bill could never remember the old man ever smiling. As he came through the door, Bill noticed a long object rolled up in an old army blanket carried under his arm. "Good morning Clem, how are you today?"

The grizzled old gentleman mumbled something as he brushed by Bill and went to the counter where his father was standing. He could barely hear them talking, so he walked up just as Clem was unwrapping the object in the blanket. It was an old Enfield musket that Bill had seen before at the local Turkey shoots. He watched as his father gave the man $20 and then Clem left, leaving the old musket on the counter.

After Clem had gone, Bill went to his father and asked "Why did you buy that old Enfield? Don't you have enough Civil War muskets in your collection?"

"Clem is on some hard times and needed some money," his father explained. "Anyways, I've always admired that old Enfield that Clem's father had taken from a Bucktail at the Battle of Gettysburg. I don't have one quite like that in my collection from the war of yankee aggression. I gave him a fair price for it, I'm happy and so is he. Believe me, if Clem didn't need the money he would never sell that old gun. That was one of the last things he had that belonged to his father and he knows he can come to the house and look at the musket any time."

"Dad, may I take it apart and inspect it? I'm just curious about why you would buy it for $20. I know you only paid $18 for the last Enfield you bought."

"Go ahead, just be careful. It's pretty old. And anyway, if I want to pay $20 for a musket, I will. So don't question me again" His dad scolded as he laughed.

Bill was amazed at the good condition of the musket, but he was perplexed by the manufacturer of the Enfield. It was Parker-Hale of London. He had seen a lot of the Enfields in his father's collection and didn't remember seeing a Parker-Hale. Bill disassembled the musket and to his amazement, the stock was inlayed with some material over the wood which was smooth, and had the appearance of that new material on the market, fiberglass! No wonder old Clem won those matches, he thought. This gun was accurized. Imbedded on the inside of the stock where the barrel laid, was some lettering and it was backward. He then looked on the barrel itself and read the lettering. "Dad, can you come here for a minute? I want to show you something."

"What is it Bill? Is there something wrong with the musket?"

"This couldn't have been used in the Civil War. You've been hood winked!"

"Why do you say it couldn't have been used in the Civil War? Don't you believe old Clem?"

"Look Dad, at the lettering on the underside of the barrel, it says USE BLACK POWDER ONLY! Dad, during the Civil War all they had was black powder and this was only put on guns after the invention of smokeless powder. Also, I've never heard of a Parker-Hale Enfield."

To which his father simply replied, "When I was a young man, I personally saw Clem's father with that musket. In fact they had also seen the writing on the barrel and wondered what it had meant and what the material was lining the inside of the stock. And that was at the turn of the century. So I know that it is authentic, even if I don't understand how the writing got on the barrel. Son, we don't have time to talk about it now, but tonight, stop over to the house and I'll tell you the story about that mysterious musket."

That night Bill went to his parent's house for dinner and to hear the story about the Enfield. His mother was small in stature, but a strong pioneering woman who never seemed to run out of energy. She was without a doubt, the best cook in the county, no, the whole state. While Bill and his father worked at the store, his mother ran the house, cooking, cleaning and doing all the other chores necessary for a family. She had been the disciplinarian in the family, but had also taught her son compassion.

In his mother's usual fashion, the table was piled high with hot steaming food. Bill was always amazed how his mother could have everything ready at the same time. Nothing was ever cold. How many times had he drooled at the thought of these meals, while sitting in a foxhole eating cold "C" rations.

After he gorged on southern fried chicken, with gobs of mashed potatoes covered by her famous gravy and polished off with large hunks of corn bread smothered with homemade butter, came the "piece de resistance." Homemade apple dumpling covered with cinnamon.

When the meal was finished his mother washed the dishes as Bill helped by drying and putting them away. Some things never change. In his younger years this was one of his chores, but he didn't mind.

Bill joined his father at the kitchen table, "OK dad, I'm ready to hear the story of that musket."

"Well son, I'll tell you the story just as it was told to me by Clem's father, Josh while he was still alive. I was a young man at the time, a little younger than you now."

After his father finished the account of the Enfield, Bill sat there with his mouth open, trying to fathom what his father told him. He laughed and said "Boy Pop, you really had me going there, I was beginning to believe that yarn."

The father looked at his son and let out a sigh, then said "Son, that is the God's truth, even though I don't know how it happened. I know that musket was around long before they had smokeless powder and that Clem's father owned that gun!"

Bill thought long and hard. This can't be possible. There is no possible way this musket could have been around during the Civil War. But he also knew he saw this same musket when he was a young lad. And if his father said he saw the gun in the 1890's, then it had to be possible. It just didn't make any sense. "Dad, what you're trying to tell me is that musket somehow has passed through time, right?"

"Well son, I guess you could say that, and I don't understand it either. Didn't that Einstein fella say something about time and space? Seems I remember reading about that in the Life magazine a while back."

"Yes Dad, I remember reading something like that too, but don't forget, that was theory only. It hasn't been proven yet."

"Son, someday that Civil War collection will be yours and you better keep a close eye on that musket. Maybe in your lifetime, you may solve the mystery. From what I know, something will happen with that Enfield in the future, but for the life of me, I have no idea what that will be!"

Bill left his parent's house and as he was driving home, his thoughts were going round and round trying again to comprehend what his father had told him. There's no way possible that a physical object could travel through time, no matter what the scientist claimed. One thing that bothered him though was the mention of the black box with the bright flash Josh claimed blinded him when they encountered the Bucktails. It sure sounded like a flash gun on a camera, but cameras were too bulky and would never fit in a haversack. He knew it couldn't be feasible, but he also knew that his father was dead serious and would never lie. As soon as he had some spare time, he would try to find out about Parker-Hale of London!

Re-enactment: To re-create or re-enact a time in the past.

CHAPTER FOUR

Early in June 1988, George and Jan invited the re-enactors and their families for a picnic. This was a busy weekend for most of the members in the group, as many of them were starting their vacations. Only two of the families were able to come and with good weather promised, it would be a grand outing. George was looking forward to the picnic and the gathering of the families. One of the reasons for the event, was the upcoming 125th anniversary of the battle of Gettysburg. The group signed up several months before and had to figure out what equipment they would need for camping. George had been very busy having just returned from the Spring Nationals of the North-South Skirmish Association. The Skirmish consisted of live firing of Civil War weapons in competition wearing period clothing. Since this event was first, he had devoted most of his time to the Skirmish. Now he had to get serious about the planning for the re-enactment.

"Yo, Jan, did you make up the ice tea yet?" George asked his wife.

"Of course I did dear. I made it a couple of hours ago. Did you fill the coolers with soda and beer yet? You know that Tim likes his beer ice cold on a hot day." Jan fired back.

"Of course, both coolers are full of ice. One has beer, the other soda. And the charcoal grill is ready to light. I also put up the volley ball net, but remind me not to put it back in the barn again. A damn mouse made a nest in it and chewed a couple holes in it. I think we're just about ready for the crew to get here."

Jan chided, "Dearest, don't be pulling any pranks today. Remember what happened at the Wilderness re-enactment in '86."

George feigned a look of hurt, "Me, pull a prank? Now why would you ever think I would do something like that?"

Their playful bickering was interrupted by a horn blowing, as a car came up the dirt driveway spewing dust behind it.

Tim Fretz and his family showed up first. As the car came to a halt, Tim got out and stretched and George called down to him, "Tim, what are you trying to do, blow away my whole driveway in dust?"

"If you weren't so cheap, you would have it macadamized," Tim retorted.

"You damn city folk, if it looks like dirt, cover it with that damn blacktop, that's all you know. You even cut down the trees so you don't have to rake leaves."

Jan broke in, "OK you two, knock it off, we'll have none of this today." Then looking sternly at George, "Remember what I just told you about pranks!"

Both Tim and George started laughing at getting Jan all fired up again. She was always breaking up their mock fights.

Marge and the children exited the car and along with Tim, went up the steps that led to the deck beside the farmhouse.

Daniel and Matthew were both excited as they asked in unison, "Can we go fishing now? We brought our fishing rods and dad said we could."

"I don't know, the last time you fellas were here, my fish population almost disappeared. I'll tell you what. You tell your dad that since he said you could, I'll only

38

charge him a dollar a fish for every one you catch."

"Since you're gonna charge me a dollar a fish, then I'll charge you a dollar for every can of this lousy beer that you have the nerve to serve."

"If I serve such lousy beer, then why do you bother drinking it?"

Looking serious, Tim replied, "It's my sworn duty to dispose of this crappy beer so that some other poor wretch doesn't have to suffer. It's a dirty job, but somebody has to do it."

They broke into laughter as George turned to the boys and said, "Go on, get us a bunch of fish! But stay out of the water and stay away from the weeds at the far end. A pair of geese has a nest there."

Another car whisked up the drive way in a swirling cloud of dust, parking next to Tim's car. Jack Myers and his wife Katey had arrived. Jack always seemed to be the "tail end charley." Always the last to arrive.

Jack and Katey came up to the deck to join the others proudly announcing, "We're here. Where's the food? And none of that Civil War shit either!"

Katey turned sharply and scolded her husband, "Watch your language, the kids are here!"

He started to protest, but thought the better of it and didn't respond.

They all sat and chatted for a while before starting their annual horseshoe match with husband and wife teams. Of course with all their practice on the home range, George and Jan had won every year except for one.

"OK," George called out, "Are you all ready for horse shoes, or are you willing to concede defeat before we start?"

Taking up the challenge Jack answered, "Not only are we ready, but today we are going to give you the worst whupping you ever had!"

"This time, don't put the sun in our eyes. Play fair," Tim chimed in.

George looked at him incredulously, "But we change sides after each match, so how could the sun always be in your eyes?"

"Yea, but each time you move, the sun does too!" Tim defiantly countered.

Everyone broke out laughing and George knew he couldn't match that one.

"If you men would quit yapping so much maybe we could start the games," Jan interjected.

"Yea," Katey added, "If you didn't flap your jaws so much, maybe you could carry your weight in the games. I get tired of making all the ringers."

Not to be outdone Marge chimed in, "You always cry foul when someone beats you, quit complaining before we even start."

"OK, OK enough of that, let's see if everyone can throw horse shoes as well as they can talk," George answered.

After several hard played matches, Jack and Katey were the overall winners. Their ultimate win came with Tim's help when he distracted George by making faces at the most inopportune times, as George was shooting. George swore revenge, but it fell on deaf ears as the boys came back with a stringer full of fish. Of course they wanted to cook them for lunch, which sounded like a good idea to everyone. Hamburgers and hot dogs were included on the menu. After they cleaned the fish, George started the grill, then cooked the picnic meal which turned out to be quite a feast. The fish were delicious and everyone enjoyed themselves. After the meal, the entire group joined in the volley ball match with jungle rules being followed. They played the games hard and after four exhausting games, the sweating participants retired to the deck to discuss the upcoming re-enactment.

They reminisced about different events that they had attended, especially the good times partying in camp. Everyone had a good laugh, about the time that it was George and Jan's turn to supply the meal at the one re-enactment. George being a practical joker, had told everyone not to worry about supper, as he would cook up a splendid Civil War meal that they would never forget. George made up a large batch of hardtack, just like the authentic hardtack of that era (a hard biscuit made of flour and water). He went to a local farm market and bought fatback that was mostly fat. At the re-enactment he fried up the fatback, crumbling up the hard tack in the greasy mess. As George was cooking it up, he had slipped some brown rice in with the meal. When he served it, he told every one that they were getting an authentic Civil War meal.

"What are these brown things in the food," Jack asked?

George was laughing so hard, he almost fell down. With tears in his eyes, he told them, "I told you it was an authentic meal. They're weevils!"

Several people had felt queasy before they realized a joke had been played on them. The victims put their heads together to get even with the master jokester. They quickly decided the punishment and the whole company started running after George. Quite a ruckus was raised, as he was chased through several camps before he was caught and brought back to the scene of the crime. By the time they brought in their hapless captive, there were several hundred re-enactors gathered around as they exacted their vengeance on George for his prank. Someone brought out an old feather pillow which they ripped open, and the closest thing they had to tar was molasses. While he begged for mercy, they stripped him down to his pants, then sprinkled George liberally with the molasses and feathers. After they finished with the feathers, the group paraded him through many of the camps. Everyone laughed, except George, who was being taunted by re-enactors he didn't even know. Someone yelled out, "You surely are a purty chicken!" Another jeered, "My, look at them thar thighs!" As he suffered, he was already planning his next move.

When it was all over, George retreated to the water buffalo, washed and scrubbed until he finally got cleaned up. George told them, "I had a terrible time getting the molasses off and as sure as the sun comes up, I will retaliate. You will never be able to sleep in peace. You'll always have to look over your shoulder, and rest assured, I will strike, swift, sure and with malice!"

That night, they all sat around the fire, talking and having a good time. But of course, to rub salt in the wound, they also brought up the tar and feathering of the day. George finally had enough and he drew himself up tall, proclaiming, "You can laugh now. But one day, your teeth will be gnashing, and you will pray to the great father of re-enactments to deliver you from my wrath, but this will be of no use to you. I will pick the time and the place to wreak havoc on your miserable excuses for bodies, I will triumph!"

Someone yelled, "Where's the tar and feathers, let's get him again!"

With that, George decided that discretion was the better part of valor, and beat a hasty retreat into the darkness, while the group laughed. Later he returned to the campfire and kept a very low profile. The evening was damp and someone had heard a weather forecast calling for showers the next day.

Sure enough, the next morning just as they were

preparing breakfast, a heavy downpour hit which quickly put out the cooking fire. This had a detrimental effect on everyone, as they also missed the morning coffee. It took them another hour to get the fire going and just as the coffee was ready, a drum roll announced morning drill. Other than the inconvenience of the rain and no coffee, the re-enactment was good for most, except for the tar and feathering George suffered. But now it was time to quit reminiscing and get to the business planning for the Gettysburg event.

As they sat on the deck, George told them, "I'll be going out a couple of days early and if you like, I'll set up your tents for you."

They all thought it would be a great idea, but Jack warned, "Don't plan any reprisal by putting our tents over ant hills or anything else, like horse apples."

George promised, "I won't do any thing just yet, that would be too easy, anyway, what I'm planning will be the grandaddy of all reprisals."

The group decided on other equipment to take with them. George made canvas covers for their coolers as they were not to be visible in camp, and also made his own tent. In fact, he made most of his equipment and uniforms, except for his Enfield musket. He bought the musket over ten years ago brand new and still in the box.

They were having such fun that the hours had slipped quickly by, and it was time for everyone to go home. They planned to get together one more time, to bring all of the equipment to the farm, for George to take to Gettysburg. As everyone was leaving, George had a strange premonition that something was going to happen to them that would forever change their lives. For the life of him, he couldn't put his finger on it.

While he and Jan were cleaning up George told his wife, "You know what? As they were leaving tonight, I had the weirdest feeling about this re-enactment. It sent shivers up and down my spine."

"It's nothing to worry about, you're just tired."

George deep in thought said slowly, "No, this feeling, was just like one I had many years ago, the day the Tet offensive started and we had been zapped really bad. In fact we had taken over fifteen casualties in less than five minutes, and that feeling was the same, and it scares me."

Jan told him, "You're just letting your imagination run away with you! What could possibly happen at a re-enactment?"

CHAPTER FIVE

Tim's loud snoring caused George to wake up, his back sore from sleeping on the ground. Although he had put down ample straw, it wasn't the same as his soft bed back home. George arrived two days earlier, setting up the tents in the area assigned to their regiment. The parking area for the re-enactors was over a mile away. He was only given a half hour to unload all of the equipment at the camp site, then he had to park his truck over near Route 15 and walk back. The walk wasn't too bad, but the fields were heavily rutted and you had to be careful not to turn an ankle. Tim, Matthew, Daniel and Jack had arrived last night after dark and were thankful that their tents were set up for them. Tim wasn't worried that George may have done something to get even since they were sharing a tent. But Jack checked all around his dog tent, looking for ant hills, horse dung or anything else the outraged re-enactor could have done to even the score for the tar and feathering.

George had assured him, "I haven't done anything, yet. That would be too easy. When I retaliate, it will be a true classic that can't be topped!" In reality he hadn't planned anything yet, but he would just let them sweat for the whole re-enactment.

As George started to get up, he heard a drummer somewhere nearby beat out the reveille call so he nudged Tim and told him, "It's time to get up, laddie! It's a bright and beautiful day out there."

Tim swore at him, "Go to hell with your beautiful day, I'm tired, leave me alone!"

So George climbed out of the tent, grabbed him by the ankles and drug the groggy Tim into the middle of the company street. Tim continued to curse him and questioned his ancestry back to the apes. Several men and their wives were sitting by the company fire. They were laughing as the embarrassed Tim, clad only in his undershorts, beat a hasty retreat into the safety of the dog tent, all the while swearing and threatening retribution to George, up to and including castration.

The ruckus woke up Jack who hollered to Tim to "Shut up or I'm going to stuff a dirty sock in your mouth."

"You can go to hell too, garbage for brains" Tim sharply retorted.

Captain Dubois, who had his tent at the end of the company street, was still trying to sleep and bellowed out to, "Shut up or the whole bunch of you will be walking post tonight." The camp grew quiet and everybody outside stood up. They faced the captain's tent and gave him the fickle finger of fate, then broke out laughing. Since it was obvious that nobody was going to get any more sleep, they all got up and gathered around the campfire and drew some coffee, brewed earlier in the big company coffee pot.

Captain Dubois who looked as if he had been, "Drug in by the cat," thought to himself, He would not go over to the reb camp tonight to see his friends again. The beer and white lightning bout the night before was too much. Damn, how his head was pounding. The sun was now above the horizon with a few clouds in the sky and a slight wind blowing. He told the group, "We'll fall in at 8 a.m. for musket and uniform inspection. And don't forget to have at least one full canteen of water whenever we fall in."

Tom, George and Tim's wives were staying in town at a motel. The heat and humidity in the camp this time of the year could become unbearable. Their wives would be able to get a good night's sleep in the air conditioned rooms. They would be in camp later that day, but they had decided to stay in town so they could shop. The soldiers would have preferred to sleep in the comfort of the motel. However they would miss too many of the activities in camp and on the battle field. Not to mention the heat they would take from the other members of the regiment.

There was a large area set up for sutlers, and the men decided that after morning inspection and battalion drill they would go and see what was for sale.

As they gazed around the camping area, George remarked to the others, "I'm totally amazed at the amount of tents. As far as you can see, there's tents. And to think that this is probably only ten percent of what was actually the size of a Civil War encampment is unbelievable!"

All around the edges of the forty acre camping area were horses in make shift corrals of rope and posts which belonged to the calvary units and general staff. Smoke was rising from hundreds of campfires and the smell of burning wood was like a tonic to the nose. If it wasn't for a few spectators starting to arrive, one would have thought it was back in the Civil War times. At 8 a.m., a drum call sounded assembly. All the participants grabbed their equipment and fell in on the first sergeant. The captain ordered the lieutenants to open ranks and prepare for inspection. The officers inspected each man for proper equipment and plenty of water. They checked their muskets carefully to insure they were in proper operating condition and not loaded. After their muskets were checked, the inspecting officer placed a round green sticker with his initials on it, on the stock just below the lock plate. This showed that the musket was checked that day. There was a different colored sticker for each day of the re-enactment so that any musket used during that day, could be spot checked.

While they were in formation, but at rest, the officers were planning the morning drill. They could see other regiments going through their maneuvers and practicing firing in volleys.

George saw a rider come up to the officers and just as the messenger was about to dismount, a regiment nearby fired a volley. The horse reared up, throwing the courier. Then the horse stepped on the man's shoulder and kicked him in the groin. The soldier screamed in agony and as the captain grabbed the horse's reins he called, "George, come over quickly. Check this man out and see how badly hurt he is.

The former corpsman carried medical supplies in his haversack. When he saw the accident, he broke ranks and was over the injured man before the captain could finish his command. George checked the man's shoulder which was badly bruised, but no broken bones. The thigh was a different story, the courier had a compound fracture. He told the soldier to lie still while he put a compress bandage over the open wound to keep out infection. He shouted to the captain, "Call for an ambulance and get me some blankets for a splint! I need to immobilize the break and to cover him, to keep him out of shock!" He checked the injured man's vital signs and he appeared to be stable. It didn't seem long before the ambulance arrived, and he told the emergency medical technician what procedures that were done. When they finished their exam, they loaded the injured re-enactor into the vehicle. Turning to George, the technician said, "You did a nice job of first aid and a fine splint job!"

After the ambulance left, George retrieved his musket and fell back into formation. Everyone told him he did a really good job to which he simply replied, "I've had a lot of experience in that sort of thing and I've seen a lot worse. This was a piece of cake. In Vietnam the mines were the worst, with soldier's legs and arms being blown off. You can't imagine the gory mess you had to work with trying to tie off bleeders and dressing those terrible wounds, all the while knowing the poor man would never have use of those limbs again."

While George was standing in the front rank, he noticed an old man talking to the captain and pointing to their rank. Dubois came over to the formation and addressed the unit. "Men, this is Bill Sloan from South Carolina. He asked if he could look at your muskets. He's looking for a particular Enfield and not to worry, it's not about anything being stolen."

As the old man was walking down the rank, George noticed that the man was limping, as if one leg was shorter than the other. One could hear the whispers going up and down the ranks of men, "Wonder what he's looking for? Is he looking for a stolen musket? Who is that guy?"

As Bill Sloan was looking at each musket, George noticed he would look only at the lock-plate and occasionally on the other side of the barrel.

When he came to George, Sloan asked "Do you have a Parker-Hale musket?"

George replied, "Yes, I have a Parker-Hale which I bought new over ten years ago."

"Do you mind if I look at it?"

George gave him the musket and watched as Bill Sloan looked at the area where the serial number was found.

Suddenly, the man turned white and his hand

started shaking. Sloan looked at him "Could I talk to you in private? It's very, very important!"

He could tell the man was earnest, but couldn't begin to imagine for the life of him, what Sloan wanted with his Parker-Hale. George asked the captain, "May I break ranks for a few minutes?"

Captain Dubois replied, "No problem, as long as you have passed inspection."

He followed Sloan off to a small clump of bushes not too far from the regiment, but out of hearing range.

When they stopped, Bill Sloan looked at him, "I know you're trying to figure out what I want. Trust me, after I tell you, you won't believe me."

"Mr. Sloan, I know that this has something to do with my musket. But I bought it brand new, back during the mid-seventies."

Sloan replied "I know what you're implying and I'm not here to claim that the musket is stolen. I know it wasn't. I will tell you that musket with the serial number 4733 was in my collection in 1950, until it disappeared in 1975!"

George was stunned by what the old man was saying. Then he stated, "There is positively no way this musket was in your collection in 1950. It wasn't manufactured until the mid seventies and I bought it brand new in the original box."

"Look, I know you're upset because you think I'm trying to claim that musket, but it isn't true. Let me tell you the story about that Enfield, as I know it."

George interrupted him first, "If you look around, you'll notice thousands of re-enactors. How did you narrow in on our particular regiment?"

Bill Sloan looked at him and simply said, "Your hat."

Dumbfounded, George asked, "My hat?"

Laughing Bill Sloan, replied, "You have a Bucktail on your forage hat. There weren't any other units that I saw with a Bucktail on their hats. So it was quite easy."

The old man laid out the whole story to George, who listened intently not able to believe a word that he said.

"You're right, I don't believe a word of what you're telling me because I know it's impossible," George countered.

"I know it sounds far fetched, but it is possible because what I've told you is the absolute truth. My only reason for being here is to warn you about what may happen to you and ask you to not do this re-enactment!"

Becoming irritated, George remarked, "There's no way I'm not doing this re-enactment. I've waited a long time and I won't let down my friends, period!"

Sighing, Bill Sloan looked at George sadly, "Sir, I've tried to warn you, but I sort of knew that it would be this way. I didn't tell you the entire story-there's not enough time. I have a train to catch back home. But I do have one question, do you have a small black camera with a flash in your haversack?"

Confused at the question, George answered, "Yes, but why do you ask that?"

Shaking his head he simply replied, "It just confirms my suspicions and I would suggest that you keep that camera on you during the re-enactment. I must run along now. You take great care and I wish you all the luck in the world. Sir, I have a feeling you're going to need it. I've done all I can and only hope you heed my warning. But if you don't, maybe you'll be better prepared."

With that Bill Sloan limped off and left George standing there with his mouth half opened. As his mind was trying to comprehend what the old man had told him, he held back the urge to call Sloan back for more explanation. Then he said out loud, "The hell with it, that story can't be true. I came here to have a good time and I'm going to do just that."

George walked back and rejoined the regiment and went through all the different movements and firing by volley and by files. After they had finished the morning drill, they broke and went back to camp. Everybody wanted to know what the old man had wanted.

"Oh it was nothing. I have to sort out what he said and try to figure his angle. When I know more, I'll tell you the preposterous story he told me."

George sat by himself still trying to understand what the man had told him. Thinking back over the years to when he bought the Enfield, he remembered something that had been forgotten. He had gone to buy a musket with the intention of getting a Springfield but for some reason saw this Enfield in the box. When he had picked it up, a strange feeling came over him for a moment. George had a brief glimpse into the past. He could actually see a battle going on and felt he was there. Just as quickly as it came the feeling was gone. Shaking his head as if to clear it, he knew immediately this musket would be his even if it cost more than a Springfield. Now, years later, this musket is claimed to have been in somebody's Civil War museum. It wasn't possible to have been in that War. When he bought the Enfield it was brand new. Something didn't make sense about this whole story. After this re-enactment George would retire the musket to gather dust over the mantel of the fireplace. Even though he didn't believe Sloan's story, George would not tempt lady fate.

Later they all went to the sutler area to do some shopping. The street was mobbed by re-enactors and spectators making it almost impossible to get close to most of the sutlers. They milled around for an hour or so then made their way back to camp. The day was getting hotter and muggier. After lunch, they fell in again for some more drill. Everyone was hoping the captain wouldn't keep them in the hot sun too long. All around them they could see regiment after regiment marching, with rising dust, to drum beats and fifes. Meanwhile, people were walking in droves down the hill from Frogtown road. George said to nobody in particular, "I bet there's going to be 50,000 spectators the way it looks."

A man in the ranks grumbled, "Damn't how long are we going to stand around in this sun and wait. You'd think the officers would know what they're going to do before we get out here."

Another voice answered, "I'll tell you one thing for sure. This Fall I'm going to vote for someone else to be the captain. Hell, my dog has more sense than Dubois."

"Yea and your dog is better looking too."

Amid the laughter, Captain Dubois called them to attention. "Men, today we're going to do some Battalion drill on how to retire from the field without chaos under fire. This afternoon during the re-enactment, we will be driven off the field just as in the real battle. The lead company will fire a volley, then divide in half, with each half running to the rear of the regiment down each side. We'll leap frog in the reverse, with a company ready to fire as soon as the lead company clears the front. As soon you get to the rear, start loading to be ready for your turn to fire."

At last the captain gave the orders to march over to the rest of the battalion. The regiment marched off amid the rising dust which clogged their nostrils. The sun beat down on them as they went through the maneuvers. Each and every man was drenched as he loaded, fired and ran to the rear, getting ready to fire again.

After an hour of drill they were called to a halt as everybody grabbed for their canteens to drink heavily of the tepid water. As they stood there waiting, someone called out, "Damn I don't know how they do that, always marching us uphill. Can't we march down hill just once?"

No one answered this time. Everyone was exhausted and sweat soaked. Finally they were told to break ranks and get a little rest before they fell back in at 3 p.m. for the first day's battle. The group went back to camp and crashed. They couldn't find any shade except in the tents which were like ovens. They just sat there and poured water over themselves to try to cool off. Tim was thinking to himself, about how the soldiers in the Civil War could wear wool clothing in the summer time, but he guessed they were used to it.

The re-enactor's wives came back into camp, with all of their loot they bought from the sutlers. George looked at them, "We thought you may have been in the sutler area, but there were so many people, we never saw you."

They all sat in a group and hardly talked, as even talking made them sweat. A gentle wind started blowing, helping them to cool off and rest better. George, Tim and Jack told their wives about where they would be in the field.

George said, "You better go soon, so you can find a good place in the shade to watch the battle. Afterwards we'll go to the motel and take showers so we can feel human again."

They agreed to meet back in camp after the event, then wait until the traffic died down before they tried to depart.

As their wives were about to go look for a shaded

spot to watch the battle, George told Jan, "You take the larger camera and I'll keep the small camera with me. I may be able to get some unusual pictures as long as no spectators can see me." So he gave Jan his larger camera, which wouldn't fit in his haversack.

Finally, 2 p.m. came and Tim's boys started the drum roll for assembly. They formed in two ranks and counted off by ones and twos so they would know who their file partner would be. This would be important for unit cohesion as they would be marching in Civil War style, shoulder touching shoulder. This way, during all the noise of battle, if they couldn't hear commands, they would know what to do by body contact. During the maneuvers, each soldier had to know where his file partner was, so they would be in proper position. After they fell into ranks, it was just like the present day army-hurry up and wait all over again. George never did get used to this. Even during his time in the navy, it had always been the same. If there was a personnel inspection at two p.m., the ranks always fell into formation at least an hour early and then waited for the inspecting party.

Over by the ridge on the Bucktail's right was Bullfrog Road. They could see masses of Confederates marching off to the left, with drums beating out a marching roll. They could hear bands playing Dixie and other Civil War tunes. Even at that distance, almost a mile, they could hear the clank of tin cups and the like. The sun light glistened off their bayonets and muskets. The forward elements of Confederates passed from view behind a tree line, however the rising column of dust gave away their position.

Captain Dubois told them that they would be marching out soon. The company would be behind and to the right of the Iron Brigade. They would wait until the battle was heavily engaged, then would move up as if going into battle on the McPherson Ridge. Their ultimate position would be on the right flank of the Iron Brigade.

A rider came up from the general's staff and talked to the captain, motioning with a gloved hand toward the woods to their front. And just that fast, the courier was gone, galloping off to another regiment with their orders.

Turning to the first sergeant, the captain shouted the order, "Left face, forward march." The company went from a double rank, into a column of fours and marched forward. Marching in formation was difficult because of the ruts in the field. When they entered the woods, the trees and rocks broke up the formation, but then like a Civil War regiment, they were back in formation marching toward the sounds of battle. Morning and afternoon drill helped refresh their memories of the maneuvers, as they didn't practice every day as in that long ago war. After the soldiers marched for fifteen minutes they stopped and waited. Regiment upon regiment could be seen marching up, some moving forward, but most waiting all around them in small groups. The captain had them drink plenty of water, but he didn't have to urge them as the heat was almost unbearable. He had the company snap caps to clear the oil and also make sure there were no obstructions in the barrels. Next he had them load their muskets, capped and put on half cock.

Abruptly, five or six cannons fired, but the Bucktails couldn't tell if they were Confederate or Union cannons, as they were in a hollow. More artillery opened up and the whole world seemed to shake by the concussions blasting out of the barrels. In front of them could be heard the fierce crackle of muskets sounding like the pop-pop-pop of Chinese firecrackers exploding. Nearby there was a loud CARUMP as a volley was fired by a regiment. Soon the firing of cannons and muskets was continuous. The noise was so intense, orders couldn't be heard, the troops had to watch the regimental colors, and close on them. The smoke started filtering in around them and soon it would be difficult to even see the colors.

Their colonel screamed while waving his sword forward, "By companies into line! March!" This order was repeated by the company commanders and first sergeants. The Bucktails went from a column of four, immediately into battle formation of two ranks. The order was given, "Double quick, march." This movement was pushing their endurance as they were going up the hill to the ridge, trying to keep in formation, while dodging rocks and various debris. When they made it to the ridge, there was firing all around them; but they couldn't see any rebs yet. Just like a mirage the Confederates appeared out of the smoke in front of them, only about 75 yards away.

George heard an order to fire a volley but had no idea who gave it. Everyone was scrambling to reload before the Confederates over ran them. When each man finished loading, he brought his musket to the ready. As soon as the men were ready they started firing by files, down the line. After they had fired five rounds, the rebels had enough and quickly melted back into the dense smoke.

Captain Dubois ordered the company to cease fire. The men rested as best they could in the sweltering heat. The barrels of their muskets were so hot you couldn't touch them.

"The smoke is so thick in here I can't even tell if that regiment on our right is Union or Confererate," Tim remarked.

As the unknown regiment fired a volley into them, George responded, "Well there's your answer.

They're rebels!"

While the Confederate regiment on their right was reloading, the colonel shouted, "Wheel right and fire!" The regiment swung around changing the front to the right and fired a murderous wall of fire into the rebel ranks. They kept reloading and firing by ranks again and again until the rebs had fallen back, leaving many men lying on the field. But the cost had been high for them as the captain, a lieutenant and two sergeants and 10-12 men were down. Many of the men had taken hits because they were exhausted by the heat and needed rest. The others took hits because earlier they had been given numbers, which, when called out the re-enactor would fall as if killed or wounded. Spectators who were in full view off to their left would see the impact of what happened when a volley or a cannon fired into the closely packed regiments.

They immediately reformed ranks closing on the colors and started falling back to their original position at the start of the battle. Soon they were attacked from the front, this time by two screaming regiments of rebels. The pressure of this overwhelming attack caused the line to sag backward. Everyone was firing as fast as they could load and Union troops were falling back on their left. The plan was to fall back with each front rank firing, then they would run to the rear of the second rank while loading. Each rank would do this so it covered the regiment in retreat. This was working fairly well as they fell back slowly. Off to their left, the Union troops appeared to be total confusion and retreating. Everything seemed to be going according to the scenario until WHAM,CRASH as two rebel regiments fired point blank into their right flank. This wasn't supposed to happen, in a split second the regiment was in total rout, not knowing what transpired. They found themselves moving to the rear as fast as they could, only stopping to fire after they had loaded. It was too late George, Tim and Jack, were surrounded. The men simply turned their musket's upside down in a surrender gesture common to the Civil War. The trio was glad they were captured, because they had reached the end of their endurance and would get some rest. If it had been a real battle in that War, the men would not have been happy as Libby prison or Andersonville would have been bad choices. Suddenly, cheers and yelping announced the Confederates were everywhere! They couldn't understand how it happened. They weren't supposed to be overrun, but that's how it goes in battle.

Tim asked the other two, "Did you see the boys as prisoners?" But they were nowhere in sight. Being too young to carry muskets, they were the drummers and had been held back to carry ice for the re-enactors. Tim wasn't worried, because they knew that if they were separated, they were to go straight back to camp. Plus there were other men in the regiment who would look after them.

They sat in the shade, breathing deeply, sweating profusely, drinking heavily from their canteens, then pouring water over their heads, trying to cool off.

Tim remarked, "It seems like we've been running and fighting all day."

Jack spoke up, "Yea, but in fact it has only been a half hour or so."

The sound of the battle was moving away from them, as the rebels pushed the Union troops back relentlessly. The cannons were still firing from both sides and they could see an occasional air burst from the fireworks display set up. There were more gray clad regiments moving by them on the double quick.

George said, "I'm glad we're captured, because I don't think I could run another step, and those rebs there, have a lot of running to do yet. In fact we had it easy today, considering the rebels had to cover over a mile in the attack."

Tim agreed with him, "You're right about that, I'm completely soaked! I can't wait to get that shower tonight."

Soon the firing started dying down, then a few sporadic shots as men were downloading their muskets. Suddenly, a huge rebel yell went up from thousands of men in unison, as they celebrated their victory. The battle was over for the day!

The three of them started walking slowly, back toward their camp. They were surprised at how much ground they had covered and realized how far camp was from the re-enactment area. After walking slowly for ten minutes, they came to a gully, which was about 100 yards from the reviewing stand used for the filming crews and dignitaries. The ravine had a small stream meandering through it, shaded by several large trees. Many spectators and re-enactors were using the small trail leading to the Union and Confederate camps where ice cold drinks were waiting.

George suggested, "Why don't we sit in the shade for a little while, until the crowd dies down, then we can take our time getting back."

Everyone thought it was a good idea. The three of them laid down, relaxed and in short order, fell sound asleep as only fatigued men can do.

As they were dozing by the bank of the stream, a spectator with a video camera started filming them. As he was filming, two rebel re-enactors came by and the spectator asked them, "Would you fix your bayonets, and pose like your taking those yanks as prisoners. It would make a good movie."

The one rebel replied, "We ain't allowed to fix no bayonets on the field, but we will be honored to take them chicken thieving yankee scum prisoners!"

The Confederates posed holding their muskets as ready to capture the sleeping yankees. The spectator was busy taping, when he realized that something was wrong with the scene. For some reason a fog appeared in the area where the re-enactors were laying. He took the camera down to locate the Union soldiers, but nothing was there, not even the fog! The spectator looked at his lens and it was clear as a bell, there was no fog on the lens.

Both rebel soldiers had a look of bewilderment and disbelief on their faces. Frantically the one cried out, "What the hell, them yanks plum disappeared, as if they were never there! That strange fog appeared and when it was gone, so were they." Turning to the other rebel re-enactor, he asked, "Did you see that? And did you feel that cold, clammy breeze when that fog appeared?" The other man just nodded his head yes, in stunned silence.

Everyone started looking around in the bushes, but nothing could be found. Meanwhile, a crowd started forming. The spectator and the rebel soldiers told the people how, "The three yankee soldiers with Bucktails in their hats, had simply disappeared before their very eyes." Of course no one believed them! The three of them kept looking, but no evidence could be found of the missing soldiers.

State trooper Alex Stone was at the controls of the police helicopter and was flying over the re-enactment below him. He had flown a Big Muther[2] Helicopter in Vietnam, rescuing pilots shot down behind enemy lines. After he had left the service, he had joined the Pennsylvania State Police. Because of his flight experience, he managed to get assigned to fly the state

---

[2]Navy Rescue Helicopter

police helicopters. Trooper Stone and his co-pilot Sam Felton's assignment was to be aerial traffic control for this re-enactment. The two were glad they weren't part of the ground units, as it appeared to be a nightmare down there. Returning, after flying around the perimeter of the re-enactment area, they had a birds eye view of the battle going on below. Finally the battle was over and they were making a pass near the trailer set up for reporters, when they noticed a group of people by a gully, waving frantically at them. The Trooper went into a hover, off to one side about 700 feet high. People were gesturing at the ground, but he couldn't see anything wrong and couldn't imagine what their problem was. Pushing the mike button on the stick, he said to his co-pilot, "Sam, get on the horn to one of the ground units to see what the hell has all those people excited? I can't see anything wrong." His co-pilot simply hit the button twice, to signal that he understood, then cranked in the frequency for the ground unit. He then contacted a team, which was in the vicinity of the state police trailer, to go see what the problem was, since the copter couldn't land with all the people around.

A short while later, two troopers interviewed the spectator and rebel soldiers. Troopers Collins and Wells didn't know what to make of the disappearance, the witnesses seemed earnest. But, people don't just disappear! They remembered that the Secret Service, which had a command post set up in Gettysburg, had directed everyone to report anything out of the ordinary. So they took down all of the information, names and addresses of the rebels and spectators who witnessed the disappearance. Trooper Collins asked the spectator, "May we borrow the video film and view it, and see if we can find anything on the tape, to solve this alleged disappearance?"

The spectator agreed and said, "I don't mind, as long as you make sure I get it back."

Trooper Collins called the pilot of the helicopter and said to him, "Alex, this sure sounds like a hoax or there was some sort of mass hallucination. We do have a video, which supposedly shows the disappearance. I don't believe it! People don't just vanish into thin air!"

* * * * * *

The wives had gone over to an area which had some shade to protect them from the hot sun. It wasn't too far from the reviewing stand, in an area where a small stream meandered through. They wouldn't be able to see the whole battle, but it was better than being in the sun on this hot muggy day.

Jan was dressed as a common housewife of the period. She had a straw hat with a large stick pin, her Garibaldi blouse, and a ankle length cotton skirt with a binding on the hem. During the Civil War, fabric for dresses and skirts was very expensive so a disposable binding was used to protect the fabric. Boots that were laced above the ankle finished off her outfit.

Trying to portray a well to do lady of the times, Katey's dress was much fancier. Her outfit was layered, with a corset, pantalets, petticoat, hoop and another petticoat over top of the hoop. A one piece day dress made of printed cotton with pleated flounces and decorative ribbons covered everything. A blue velvet hat with ostrich plume covered her head and she carried a parasol to ward off the sun.

Although Marge was dressed very similar to Jan,

she wore a snood[3] instead of a hat.

Jan was fanning herself, just trying to cool off, then said out loud, "One thing for certain, tomorrow I'm just wearing shorts! This clothing they wore, is just like being in an oven."

Katey quipped, "Amen to that, I don't care if the other women frown on it or not, it's just too damn hot for all these clothes."

They settled in to watch the battle and according to what Jack had told them, their regiment should be fighting their way back, right in front of them. The ladies had also brought some ice-cold lemonade which would be shared with the men and boys after the battle was over. It surely would be a sight better than the horrible water from their canteens, thought Marge.

Turning to Katey, Jan asked, "Are you going to stay for the ball tonight over at the barn?"

"No way, as soon as I can get back to the motel I'm going to turn on the air conditioner full blast then jump in the shower. I can't believe how hot and dusty it is. Why look over there, you can see the dust rising above the trees where the Confederate troops are marching. And that's over a mile away. Nope I'm heading for the comforts of the motel. Anyway we have to get in shape for tomorrow. You didn't forget we're doing some serious shopping? The shops will never be the same after we rip through them. Remember, we hold up our credit cards and yell charge!"

Jan and Marge laughed, then Marge fired back, "The good news is, Tim and I finally paid off our charge cards, the bad news is, he took my charge cards away."

"Oh you poor dear how will you ever manage." Katey said in mock pity.

---

[3]A small netlike cap worn by women during Civil War

A distant muffled BOOM announced the opening of the battle of the first day at Gettysburg. Off to their left a Union cannon opened up with a deafening roar while the ground shook.

From their vantage point they could see small groups of Union troops hidden by the tall grass, in a ravine in front of them. Marge asked, "Jan, are they the Bucktails in front of us?"

"No, none of them have Bucktails in their hats. Our men are up there where that white flag with a blue circle on it is moving."

They all looked over to a ridge on their left where they could see the battle flags and the 1st corps flag moving toward the fighting. By now the smoke was getting thicker and thicker all over. An aerial burst went off over head and they could hear the "oohs" and "ahs" of the spectators all around them.

Soon the firing increased in front of them, but because of the trees, they could only see shadows of men moving through the smoke. Shortly, there was firing off to their right as Confederates ripped into the flanks of unseen Union troops hidden by the trees. Next they could see the Federals falling back, stopping to fire, then moving back again. The Confederates appeared out of nowhere as they swept forward to scoop up the retreating yankee troops. To the rebels surprise the Union troops, who were hidden in the tall grass stood and fired a volley into the attackers! The rebels immediately fell back to figure out what happened to their easy victory.

Marge shook Jan's shoulder and pointed, then shouted, "There's the boys right in front of us!" Jan looked and sure enough, the drummer boys with Bucktails in their hats were moving as fast as their little legs would take them. The Confederates swarmed down the hill on two sides and the Union soldiers realizing it was over, turned their musket's upside down signaling surrender. A loud rebel yell went up as men discharged their muskets into the air.

The boys heard their mother yelling their names. "Daniel, Matthew, over here, got some ice cold lemonade!" Finally they made their way up to Marge. As their mother poured lemonade into their tin cups, she asked, "Where's your father and the others?"

Daniel replied while trying to catch his breath, "I don't know, things got awful confusing back in the woods and the rebels came out of nowhere. Everyone was running, trying to get away. I didn't see anyone from our regiment after that."

"Well never mind, we'll go back to camp and wait for them there like we planned," Marge stated.

They gathered up everything and started back to the camp amongst the throng of spectators.

As they made their way back to the camp, Daniel started talking up a storm, "Man that was awesome, you shoulda seen all those rebels, they was everywhere!"

His mother cut him off, "Daniel, use correct English, you sound like you've never gone to school. Anyway it's too hot to talk now, wait until we get back to camp then you can tell us the whole story."

As they were approaching the camp, a helicopter could be heard behind them and all turned to look.

"Look at that," Jan stated, "That helicopter is hovering, over near where we were sitting. I wonder if someone is having problems because of the heat. And look at that crowd of people. Wonder what's going on?"

"Maybe someone is lost or something," Katey replied. " The men will probably tell us about it when they get back."

"Yea, you're probably right," Jan agreed, "And if I know George, he'll be in the thick of it."

Little did Jan know that her words would prove

very prophetic!

After they had settled in at camp in some shade, they broke out the lemonade again which helped to cool them down.

Turning to Daniel, Marge said, "Tell us now what happened and remember to use correct English."

Daniel started right in where he had left off earlier, "While we were out there, the lieutenant had me use the drums to tell the men when to fire. Boy was that neat. I would do the rolls and after the third roll, we did three thumps and everyone fired a volley. Then after the fourth roll of the drum they would recover arms."

"That's good but I don't understand what you're talking about, the rolls and such."

Daniel was about to explain to his mother what it all meant when the other men started straggling into camp and the women all stood up to see where their husbands were.

"Did you see George or the others come back with you?" Jan asked the sergeant.

His face beet red from the heat, the sergeant replied, "I didn't see them since those rebs over ran us back in the woods. I think they were cut off from the rest of us. But I imagine they will be along in short time."

"Sergeant, what was going on over there when the helicopter was flying around?"

"Don't rightly know, but I heard some one say some re-enactors disappeared right in front of some people. It must be the heat or something, people don't vanish!"

Jan felt like she had been kicked in the stomach. Her mind immediately flashed back to the story her husband had told her earlier in the day about the old man and the Enfield. And there was also that strange premonition Jack had right after the picnic. Out loud she exclaimed, "Oh, that's just hogwash, they'll be back in no time."

"What did you say?" Katey asked puzzled.

"It's nothing, I was just thinking out loud."

Just then a horse and rider rode up and the courier dismounted, went to the captain's tent at the end of the company street. He talked briefly to Dubois, then with his horse in tow went to the next camp.

"Daniel and Matthew, drum out assembly immediately!" Captain Dubois ordered.

As the men started getting up, from where they were sprawled in the shade, they were grumbling. "What the hell are they doing now? We just got back into camp. They better not think of doing any more drills today!"

"Just do as you're told, we may have some missing re-enactors! The general staff wants a roll call of every unit, to see if anyone is missing," the corporal answered.

After they had called names, they were short five men. "Do any of you know where the missing men might be?" Queried Captain Dubois.

"I know Bob and Dennis went to the sutler area to buy some new shoes. But I don't know where the others are," a voice answered from the back rank.

Again he asked, "Did anyone see, George, Tim or Jack, since we were in the battle?"

No one answered and he turned to the three wives, "Do you know where your husbands' are?"

The wives shook their heads, no.

"Sergeant, send a runner over to the general staff with their names and tell them if they show up, we'll send another runner. And while he's over there, have him find out what this is all about."

"Jan, you look awful. Is there something

bothering you? Do you know something, about what's happening here?" Marge asked.

"No, there's nothing I can put my finger on. Let's just wait for the men. They'll be back shortly. They probably stopped at the sutler area and you know how crowded that place is."

After an anxious hour had passed, Jan, could no longer keep her fears to herself. Turning to the other two wives, almost tearfully, "Marge, Katey, why don't we go somewhere by ourselves, so I can tell you what George told me."

A look of grave concern swept over Marge and Katey's faces as Jan told them about George's premonition and the encounter in the morning, with the man from South Carolina.

"So what you're trying to tell us, there is a possibility of a connection between our husbands being missing and that old man with the story of the missing musket," Katey repeated. Now really, don't you think that's carrying it a little far?"

Marge broke in, "There's a logical explanation to this whole thing. They are probably over at the sutlers' at this very moment. This is the twentieth century and we no longer believe in this kind of hysteria. Let's not talk about this anymore, and just wait until the three of them get back."

"Look over there at the captain's tent," Jan pointed. "There's a state trooper talking to the captain. Now I wonder what that's all about?" Jan felt her face flush as the captain turned and pointed out the three wives to the trooper, who started walking toward them, accompanied by the Captain.

When they had joined up with the wives, "Ladies, this is Trooper Collins and this is Jan Murray, Marge Fretz and Katey Myers. Trooper Collins wants to ask you a few questions, so I'll leave you all alone."

69

After the captain left, the trooper asked, "Do any of you know where your husbands are?"

All answered "No", as they started a barrage of questions.

Putting his hands up he said softly, but firmly, "Ladies, ladies, I don't know where your husbands are. But I need you to answer a couple of questions. Now describe your husbands to me, and what they were wearing, especially their hats."

When they had finished, Trooper Collins wrote down everything they said, but when Jan described the Bucktail in the hat, his head jolted up, "Did you say, they all had Bucktails in their hats?"

"Yes!"

"Ladies, I think you had better come with me over to our command center. We have a TV and a VCR there. We have a video that I think you may want to see. After that we can go from there to figure out what has happened!"

CHAPTER SIX

The three re-enactors woke up, after they had fallen asleep on June 24, 1988. The rain hitting their faces startled them and they sat up at the same time. All that was visible were some cows around them, but no people.

Looking around Tim exclaimed to no one in particular, "Where in the hell are we and where are all the people that were here?"

Jack's mind was working furiously and he felt completely disoriented. He wondered how long they were asleep. "This is weird, it looks familiar, but then again, it doesn't. The terrain looks the same, but there's hardly any trees. George, what do you know about this? Is this your idea of a joke to get even?"

"Honest to God, I'm not playing any jokes. I'm not sure what's happening but I do have a very bad feeling."

His head snapping around Tim asked, "What do you mean, you have a bad feeling?"

"I don't know, maybe we're dreaming."

"Oh shit!" Jack exclaimed as he pointed to the area where the trailer and camera crews had been.

The other two re-enactors turned to where Jack was pointing. Tim gasped, "How in the hell did that get there?"

"Are you both seeing what I'm seeing?"

Jack and Tim replied in unison, "Yes!"

"Weren't there thousands of people here and wasn't there a trailer and metal barn over there?"

Again "Yes!"

"Then, how in God's name, did that new farm house, barn and all those outbuildings get there?" George asked.

Before them, was a fairly new farm house with smoke curling out of its chimney!

"This can't be the same place where we fell asleep, no way!" Replied Jack.

"The ground looks the same, but look around you, it's all corn, wheat and pastures where the woods were," Tim mused.

George countered. "It's almost like we're looking back through time at this place. Why don't we walk over to that house and find out just where we are?"

As they started to walk toward the house George pointed, "There's somebody coming."

They looked toward the house, where a farm wagon could be seen being pulled by two large dray horses approaching them, being driven by a farmer. The wagon creaked and bounced as it went over the ruts. The men could see there were no springs on the axles. He appeared to be in his late twenties with a full black beard and was wearing cotton pants with suspenders, a calico shirt and straw hat.

As the wagon stopped abreast of them, the man announced, "Good day gentlemen, my name is Mark Shultz. What are you doing here on my farm? Is the Union Army nearby?"

"My name is George Murray, this is Tim Fretz and Jack Myers. We're lost and what happened to all the people?"

Looking puzzled, Shultz replied "I don't know what people you're talking about, but I did hear that General Lee was invading Pennsylvania and is nearby."

72

This guy is playing the part well, thought Tim.

Looking at the farmer George asked, "What day is it?"

"The 24th I think."

"What is the whole date?"

The farmer thought for a few seconds and said, "June 24, 1863 I think, yes, that's right, Wednesday the 24th. Why in tarnation, are you so worried about the date?"

Slowly, the date sunk into their minds, but they didn't really believe him. "One more question, what time is it," George queried?

Looking around he replied, "Well it's nigh on 4 O'clock in the afternoon I reckon."

George said to the farmer, "Would you excuse us for a minute, we have to talk."

"Sure" replied the farmer, suspiciously.

The three stepped away to talk among themselves. Tim started, "Someone is playing a joke on us. I don't know how they pulled it off, but that is the only explanation I can think of." Jack agreed, however George was strangely quiet, which made Tim ask, "George, you're not saying anything. Do you know what's going on here? Is this one of your tricks?

"No, I'm not sure what's happening but for the time being lets go along with this charade and see where it takes us."

The other two decided to go along with the gag for the time being and wait to see what would happen.

Walking back over to the farmer, George told him, "We're just confused and lost. We are looking for the Union army but we have no idea where they are. Maybe you can help us?"

"Why don't you soldiers come over to the house, to get out of the rain and dry out? Then we can talk. Jump in the wagon, I'll give you a ride."

"Thank you, but we'll walk, if you don't mind."

The farmer simply shrugged his shoulders, "Suit yourself."

While they were walking to the farmhouse Tim asked the other two, "Do either of you know how this gag is being played out? How did the pranksters get rid of all the people and tents? Where are the electric lines?"

"Maybe we were transported to an Amish farm, while we were asleep," Jack offered.

"No way," answered Tim, "I don't sleep that sound, I would have woke up, unless someone drugged us."

"George," Jack asked, "Is this your revenge, that you planned for us, since we tarred and feathered you?"

"Tonight when we're alone I'll tell you something that happened this morning that just may explain what's happened."

Pressing him for the answer Tim asked, "Did it have anything to do with that fella looking at muskets this morning, ah, or whatever year that was?"

"I can't tell you right now but I'll tell you later when we're alone. It's going to take awhile. But in the meantime, watch what you say, just play along with the gag."

As they approached the farmhouse, they saw a young girl in her early teens on the roofed porch churning butter. She wore a full length cotton dress, with a tight collar, a bonnet and had bare feet. George also noticed an unlit lantern hung at each end of the porch. In the barn yard, a young boy who looked to be nine or ten years old, was spreading corn around for the chickens. He was wearing bib overalls with a long sleeved calico shirt and he also was shoeless. Mark had pulled the wagon by the barn and hitched the horses to a rail, then came over to the men.

74

Mark introduced the three visitors, "This is my son Luke. These folks are some lost Union soldiers, Mr. Murray, Mr. Fretz and Mr. Myers."

Luke's eyes got big as he exclaimed, "Are you real soldiers? Wow, can I see your gun?"

Mark scolded the young boy, "Luke, leave the men alone. They're tired and wet. Don't you have some chores to do?"

"Yes, papa." As he went back to feeding the animals. Later he would unhitch the horses from the wagon in the barn and stable them for the night.

As they went on the porch, Mark introduced them to his daughter, "This is my daughter, Tilley. This is Mr. Murray, Mr. Fretz and Mr. Myers. They are Union soldiers."

The young girl curtsied, blushed, then simply said, "Nice to meet you."

They went into the house where they were introduced to farmer's wife Mildred. She was a young woman with blond hair and fair complexion wearing a full length cotton dress, with a white apron over it and a snood covered her hair.

"Ma'am we're sure glad to meet you."

As they looked around, they marveled at the hand made furniture.

"Did you make all of this furniture?" George asked the farmer.

"Of course, store bought is too expensive and hard to come by. It's a good chore during the long winter." Even though it was summer, they had the cast iron cook stove going in the kitchen and it did feel good as they were soaked. And because it was overcast and dismal outside, there were several lanterns lit in the kitchen. One, which had a reflector plate, hung by the door, one over the stove and one on a chain over the kitchen table. The lantern with the reflector helped lighten the shadows cast by the other lanterns. In addition, it was easily removed and used outside as you would a modern flashlight.

"How old is the house and who built it?" George inquired.

"We had a house and barn raising some ten years ago, when all the neighbors came over and helped." Then Mark looked at them long and hard then said, "You must be city folk to ask a question like that, or very rich because that is how it's done around these parts."

"Yes, we're city folk from Philadelphia, before we joined the army."

"Why don't you have electricity?" Asked Tim.

"What is that?"

Glaring at Tim, George whispered, "Remember what I said earlier!"

Caught off guard by George's hostility Tim answered, "Oh nothing."

"Millie, do you have enough food in the making? I would like to invite our guests for supper."

"Yes, but you'll have to get another jar of beans from the cold cellar, some more lard and go to the spring house and fetch in some more milk and butter."

"Mrs. Shultz, what are you making?" Jack asked.

"Smoked ham, green beans, gravy, mashed potatoes, fried potatoes and fresh bread"

Smiling Jack replied "That's what smells so good."

"Well thank you and I hope it tastes as good," Mildred replied, as she blushed from the complement.

Later when dinner was ready, they all gathered around the table. Mark said the blessing and as he ended he added, "Dear God, watch over my brother Matthew, cousin Jake and all the other soldiers in the Army of the Potomac, Amen."

All three of the re-enactors thought the same thing, Boy, these people are really playing this along good!

While they were eating, George asked the farmer, "What have you heard about the rebels in the area?"

"My neighbor Herman, stopped by this afternoon and he had been in Gettysburg yesterday. He said the whole town was in an uproar. The Confederate army was nearby. They had been in Chambersburg a couple days ago. Mainly they were looking for shoes which they didn't find. Herman was upset because nobody would buy his eggs and butter. Seems like everybody was taking everything of value out into the countryside and hiding it from the rebels in case they came. Herman skedaddled out of town and came here to give me the news. What do the three of you plan to do?"

George answered, "I suppose we'll look for the Union army tomorrow, but we do need a place to sleep tonight since it's raining."

"You're more than welcome to sleep in the hay loft in the barn. We don't have much room here in the house.

"We certainly thank you for your generosity and we accept," replied George. Turning to Mildred he said, "We thank you for the delicious meal. I don't know how we can repay you."

Again Mildred blushed, "Why, thank you. You don't have to repay us. It's an honor to serve such brave men of our army!"

It was beginning to get dark and Mark lit the lanterns on the porch. When he came back inside he turned to Mildred and said, "We are almost out of coal oil and I should go into Gettysburg with eggs and butter. Maybe I can get the cans filled at the general store."

Mildred looked frightened and replied "You'll do no such thing. If we run out of coal oil we have some candles and they'll have to do. We can wait until we're certain that the rebels have left the area. I'm too young to be a widow! Anyway, Herman couldn't sell his, so what makes you think you can sell yours?"

Sheepishly Mark replied, "Yes ma'am, you're right." He turned to Tilley and said, "Go fetch three blankets for these soldiers. Then to Luke he said, "You take them out to the barn and show them where to sleep and also where the outhouse is."

After they had gone to the barn and settled in, Tim and Jack pressed George for some answers.

George asked them, "Do you remember that old man who talked to me this morning, while we were in formation for inspection?"

In unison they both replied,"Yes."

Jack asked, "Want does this have to do with what's going on now?"

George replied, "He asked if he could examine my musket, so I let him look at it. After inspecting it, he asked if I would talk to him in private. So I asked the captain if I could fall out for a little bit and he said yes, just as long as my musket had passed inspection. The old man told me his name was Bill Sloan, from Landis Corner, in South Carolina. He told me a story which I found impossible to believe at the time. In fact I just thought the fellow was a con man, trying to talk me out of my musket. Mr. Sloan told me that the Parker-Hale, serial number 4733, which I have, was originally in his gun collection, which his father had bought from a son of a Civil War soldier in 1950."

Jack held up his hand to interrupt George, "Are you saying that your musket you have here, is the same one?

"Yes, that's exactly what I'm saying. Look here at the serial number."

"Well I'll be damned, it is the same serial number! Is there any way that fella could have known the number?"

"Not that I know of. I've never met that man before in my life."

"Ok, go on with the story. This is getting very interesting."

"Well, Sloan said that the rebel soldier had taken it from a Union soldier at Willoughby Run on the first days battle of Gettysburg. I politely told him, that it was impossible, because this musket wasn't made until the mid 1970's. What's weird is, he agreed with me, but wanted to warn me, that something out of the ordinary, may be about to happen. He went on to say that this particular gun was in his collection until 1975, when it just simply disappeared.

Because of the extensive collection of original Civil War firearms he and his father had collected over the years, there was a security system installed both in the home and the collection room. There was no way that particular musket could have been taken, without setting the alarm off. In fact he had been watching that gun because of what his father had told him. And the more Sloan talked, the more the hair on my neck stood up.

The fella went on to tell me that when his father had bought the musket from old Clem Akers in 1950, he had field stripped it, and much to his surprise, the stock had been fiberglassed. On the barrel and embossed in the fiberglass was the following statement, "FOR BLACK POWDER ONLY." Mr. Sloan told his father, that at the time of the Civil War, the only powder available was black powder. And the statement on the barrel was not put on until after the introduction of smokeless powder. Futhermore, there was no record of Parker-Hale being made during the Civil War. His father had told him point blank, that when he was a young lad, Clem Akers father had this very same Enfield. In fact he used to win every turkey and ham shoot he entered, to the point where no one would shoot against him. Bill suspected that fibreglassing of the stock may have given Clem the edge needed to win. He often told the story of how he had gotten the musket from a Bucktail on the first days battle of Gettysburg! Now you both know, I did fiberglass my stock on this musket to accurize it."

Tim looked at him and asked, "Is that all that he told you?"

"Basically yes, I tried to get him to tell me more. But he said he had talked too much already. Sloan did tell me to take great care and that he didn't know if I was the one who would lose the musket. He also suggested strongly, that I not do the re-enactment. After the fellow left, I started to think of what he said, but it didn't make any sense until a little while ago."

Jack chimed in, "If this makes sense to you, how about enlightening us."

"Well," George replied, "It seems that what the old man was trying to tell me was that an object can only occupy one space in time according to the Einstein theory. And when my musket was manufactured back in the seventies, the Parker-Hale musket in his collection disappeared. This means, somehow we've passed backward in time and I'm going to lose this musket very soon. My only fear is, I may be killed in the process and that's what the old man was trying to warn me about. Although what worries me more, my family will never know what happened to me. So that's the story, which may explain what's happening now."

In the light of the lantern, George could see Tim and Jack as they stared at him dumfounded.

Finally Tim said, "George, that's a good story, but I know you would go to great lengths to pull a prank and I think that's exactly what is happening."

George thought for a second, then replied, "I swear to God, this is no prank. I don't know how or why, but somehow, we have been transported back in time. The thing that has me wondering is, how can we die before we even exist?"

They all started to talk at the same time, then Jack put his hand up to shut every one up. He said "Look, from what I've seen tonight and from what George has told us, let's, for the time being say we have gone back in time and plan accordingly. Our first priority will be survival. We should try to avoid getting caught up in the fighting, and not do anything that could affect the future. Just try to act as if we don't know what will happen. And don't forget Tim, don't ask about electricity again, it doesn't exist!"

George laid out a plan, "Tomorrow, we'll head toward Gettysburg and see what's going on, then once we know absolutely it is 1863, we'll have to take it from there. Maybe we can get away from the area before the shit hits the fan."

Tim told George, "I'll go along with you for now, but tomorrow we'll find out for sure. If you did pull a gag on us, I swear, that tar and feather trick will seem like a walk in the park when I get done with you!" Jack agreed whole heartily with Tim. The three men were extremely tired so they turned out the lanterns and went to sleep buried in the hay loft.

* * * * *

Early the next morning they awakened, hearing the horses and cows becoming restless below them.

81

Soon, young Luke, hollered up to them, "Breakfast is in a half hour iffen yer hungry!"

George opened his eyes. It was pitch black and he yelled down to the boy, "What time is it?"

"Don't rightly know, but I reckon the sun will be up shortly."

Tim and Jack stirred and sat up looking around. All they could see, was the young boy going out of the barn with a lantern. "I thought when we woke up, that this nightmare would be over. I have a feeling it's just beginning," Tim said to no one in particular.

George rummaged around in his haversack and found some matches, then lit the lantern.

"Be careful with that match George or the whole barn will go up," Jack warned.

Sarcastically he answered, "I was playing in hay lofts with matches, when you were wearing diapers."

"Yeah, and how many barns did you burn down?"

"Only two!"

After sharing a hearty laugh, they crawled down from the loft and went out side. A false dawn was starting in the east. The young boy was busy doing his chores, slopping the pigs and feeding the chickens. They looked over toward the house and could see several lanterns lit on the porch and one in the kitchen. George looked at the chimney and noticed that the smoke from the cooking fire was leaving the chimney and going straight to the ground. He remarked, "Well there's low pressure today, so I guess we'll get wet for sure."

As the trio entered the house, the farmer said, "Good morning gentlemen. I do hope you slept comfortably last night."

"We certainly did and we appreciated a dry, warm place to sleep," George answered.

"Good morning," Milley told them, "Breakfast is ready, I hope you brought your appetites with you."

"Good morning to you and that sure does smell good." Tim answered. "I feel like I could eat a horse."

Finally Luke came in and they all sat at the table, Matt saying the same prayer as the night before, except for the ending, "And dear God, watch over these brave men today!"

They had a delicious breakfast of ham, bacon, fried potatoes, eggs, flapjacks, bread and fresh milk. This was the first time that Jack and Tim had tasted fresh milk almost at room temperature. Both wished for ice cold pasteurized milk. George didn't mind the milk, as he had drank it as a young boy and it brought back childhood memories.

"You are the perfect hosts and we can't thank you enough. I wish we could pay you, but we have no money." George told them.

Mildred just blushed and Mark replied, "We don't want any money. It's our patriotic duty to our country and the army. You are defending our homes and lives. What are your plans? You are welcome to stay as long as you like. It does appear that we will have some heavy rain today. Stay another day then it should clear."

"Well, it does look like we're in for a downpour. Maybe we could stay another day." George continued, "We would be willing to help with any chores around here to help pay our room and board."

"You don't have to do anything, but if you would like, I could use some help in the barn cleaning up and we do need some more kindling wood split. Won't be able to work outside, I can smell the rain acoming."

"You have a deal, we'll gladly give you a hand around here. Jack, you can take care of the kindling, while Tim and I help in the barn."

"Luke, show Mr. Myers to the wood shed. Get the axe and give him a hand," the farmer told his son. Turning to George, "We can go to the barn and get

83

started. Have to clean out the stalls, put some straw down, and work on the wagon and equipment. Good day to do inside work, curry the horse and the like. Don't have to milk the cows, Luke did that earlier."

Jack went with Luke to the wood shed which was piled high with all the wood logs stacked neatly around three sides. In the front of the shed which was open to the outside for ventlation, stood a large log which had a dual purpose. It was used for splitting logs into kindling and also used to chop off chickens heads. Dried blood and pieces of feathers could be seen lodged in the wood from the axe blows. Luke handed the logs to Jack while he split the wood into smaller slivers, so they would burn hot in the cooking stove.

As they were working, Luke as any inquisitive young boy, asked a lot of questions. "How long have you been in the army?"

"Well I've only been in the army a short while."

The young boy queried again, "Did you see the Elephant yet?"

Jack looked at Luke, "Now how do you know about seeing the Elephant at your age?"

"My Uncle Matthew is a soldier and he told me that you see the Elephant whenever you get afighten with the enemy. He's seen the Elephant lots of times. He's a real hero, he told me so.

"Yea, I suppose you're right, he's a hero. But no, I've never seen the Elephant and I really don't care to see it.

Luke looked at him, like only a young boy who doesn't understand how bad war is, "What, are you scared of fighting? My uncle ain't scared, he told me so."

Jack really didn't feel like talking much anymore so he just let Luke ramble on and answered as little as possible.

The two worked all morning and Jack felt the

muscles in his arms and shoulders cramping up. Fortunately, his hands were hardened from doing carpenter work around his house, but he could still feel the blisters beginning to form. Finally, to his relief, they heard the dinner bell ring around lunch time. They had quite a pile of kindling stacked, which he figured would last the summer of cooking.

George and Tim worked in the barn stalls while the farmer pulled the wheels on the wagon one by one, to grease the axles. When he finished that job, he hauled harnesses to a workbench which was lit by a lantern. The harnesses needed repairs where they were chaffed or ripped from the hard work of pulling plows and wagons. This was necessary work, to be accomplished when the outside chores couldn't be done.

After Tim and George cleaned out all the stalls, they moved the soiled straw outside, placing it on a large pile of manure which would be spread on the fields later. After they were cleaned out, the stable hands hauled fresh straw and covered the stall floors with it.

As they were working, Tim told George, "Don't do me any favors again. This is a stinking, lousy job. I don't know if I'll ever get this smell off me. Don't you ever volunteer me again. I can pick my own jobs."

George countered, "This is the real life. If you hadn't lived a sheltered life this wouldn't bother you. This is a good experience for you. Back to the basics."

"To hell with your basics, I've seen it, don't like it and ain't going to do it again. Enough said!"

"You're a real wuss. What are you going to do if we stay in this time. Remember this is their way of life, there is no other way, period."

Tim looked at George, and for a moment he was at a loss for words, replied, "I don't know what I'll do.

85

But I'll only do what I absolutely have to, nothing more, nothing less."

Finally the bell rang calling them to lunch, and Mark came over announcing, "You two did a right nice job here, I might just take you on as hired hands," as he looked at George, he gave him a knowingly wink of the eye.

Tim didn't say anything but felt himself blush as he knew that Mark had sent a friendly barb in his direction.

The lunch meal was as big as the supper the night before. The table was piled high with ham, fried potatoes, corn, mashed potatoes, ham gravy, bread, jam, a large bowl piled high with fresh made butter and fresh milk in a large pitcher.

After lunch they all went back to the barn and worked all afternoon. Young Luke, curried the horses, fed the cattle while the others did various chores around the barn. The re-enactors helped Mark fix plow points, grease wheels on all the farm implements, and do general maintenance on all the equipment. The afternoon chores were easier than the morning. Before they knew it, the bell rang again and although the lunch had been huge, they were all famished.

After they had finished dinner Mark told the visitors, "We don't take our baths until Saturday night. But since you will be leaving tomorrow, I had Mildred heat up some water and Luke will bring in the tub. I'll leave it up to you who goes first and last.

The three re-enactors gathered in a corner whispering. First Tim, "What did he mean by first and last."

With a gleam in his eyes George replied, "We all use the same water, it's not like our time, with showers and the like. So we'll all draw straws. I have three lengths, the longest goes first and the shortest goes last."

Jack drew the longest. Tim was not happy at all, drawing the shortest. He knew better than to complain. Despite being last, maybe he could wash off some of the barn smells.

When they finshed their baths the trio went to the barn and fell into an exhausted sleep, snuggled in the hay loft.

After the re-enactors left for the barn to sleep, the farmer and his wife sat at the kitchen table talking. "Millie I don't know what to make of this coin you found on the floor." He held it up to the light of the lamp and squinted at both sides of the coin. "That sure looks like President Lincoln's likeness on this side. Look at the date, I swear it says 1976. It just couldn't be, why it's 1863. The coin does say United States of America. The other side has some kind of a building with a man sitting in a chair. What do you make of it Millie?"

"I don't know. Do you think it's real? I do know they have acted very strange since they've been here. Remember that question Tim asked about e...city or something and Jack got real funny like and told him to shut up?"

"Yea, I remember and while we were working in the barn, I overheard them arguing about some weird things. The one odd statement one made was...in our time... what ever that means. Something else I thought of, isn't it true a President's likness isn't put on until after he dies?"

"I believe that's so," Millie replied.

"We can't stay up all night fretting about this. There's a lot of work to be done tomorrow. When they leave I'll give it back to them. Maybe they'll tell us more, maybe not." The farmer along with his wife retired to their bedroom just off the kitchen settling in for the night snuggled in their soft feather bed.

*****

Early the next morning George awakened first, then woke the others. Tim grumbled, "It's not time to get up it's still dark outside. I'm going back to sleep, leave me alone!"

Sitting up Jack groped for his pocket watch, opened it and lit a match to see what time it was. "Yep, it's time to get up. It's a little after five a.m. and we'll have a full day ahead of us. Turning to George he asked, "Do you remember what happens in the area today?"

"Well if I'm not mistaken, Early's Confederates go into town today to look for shoes. If we can get there early enough we may be able to confirm we really are back in time. So Tim, whether you like it or not it's time to get up. Anyway the farmer and his family will be up by now."

The three re-enactors climbed down from the loft and trudged outside where it was still dark, including the farm house. The sky had cleared, the stars were out, the partial moon was setting.

Tim asked Jack, "Let me look at that watch, you can't be right about the time." He looked at the watch and sure enough, it said 5:15 which confused him, as it was too dark.

Suddenly it dawned on Jack, "Aw shit. This watch is set on daylight savings time. They only had standard time in the Civil War, it's really 4:15 a.m..

Protesting loudly Tim shouted, "Damn it you got me up for nothing. I'm going back to sleep!"

George interjected, "No use going back to sleep.

Your loud arguing woke them up." Looking to the farm house the trio could see a lantern being lit.

Coming out on the porch holding the lantern up the farmer asked, "Is there a problem out here?"

Appologeticlly George answered, "Sorry we woke you up, but we thought it was later than it was. We have to be on our way soon."

"I was just about to get up anyway so before you go we'll feed you some breakfast. Come on in the house."

After another big breakfast the three travelers gathered up all their belongings, readied themselves for the day.

The farmer told the three, "I know you have to go, but George, could I talk to you alone for a minute, in private?"

Nodding his head yes, George and the farmer went out to the porch.

"I do have the feeling that you don't belong here, in our time, I mean."

Shocked George asked, "Why do you say that?"

Motioning George over to the lit lantern Mark opened his hand, which revealed a Lincoln penny with the date 1976.

"Where did you get that coin?"

"One of you must have dropped it last night in the kitchen while you were taking baths. Now some of the questions you asked yesterday make some sense. Also the odd way you were acting. Why is there a likeness of Lincoln on the coin? I do have a feeling that you know what's going to happen. If you would share it with me I would be forever beholding."

Slowly George answered, "I can't lie to you, we are not of your time. Somehow we are here now. I can't tell you what's going to happen or why Lincoln's likeness is on the coin. If you and your family stay here you will be safe. We owe that to you for your kindness and hospitality. I would ask for the coin back and that you never tell anyone about this."

"I do understand. The good Lord doesn't want us to know the future and the coin doesn't belong to me." Mark pressed the coin into George's hand then said, "May God be with you and guide you, through whatever you are embarking on."

Going back inside, George told the other two, "It's time for us to try to find the Union army." As they turned to leave, George looked at Mark and saw a look of understanding, to which he just nodded his head in acknowledgement.

As they left Mark gave them some coffee beans, sugar and some salt which they graciously accepted. George then thanked them again and the three soldiers left heading across the field.

CHAPTER SEVEN

The re-enactor's wives spent the afternoon their husbands had disappeared, frantically searching for their spouses to no avail. After leaving notes in the tents just in case they showed up, they and Marge's boys went to Gettysburg and their motel rooms to plan their next step. After they told the boys to stay in the motel room, the trio immediately went to the Gettysburg police station to file a missing person report.

As they entered the station, a police officer who sat behind the duty desk asked, "May I help You?"

Jan spoke up, "Yes we would like to file a missing person report on our husbands."

"I'm Officer Brooks, please give me the details."

When Jan had finished, with both Marge and Katey interjecting comments, they waited for him to respond.

"Ladies we have a couple of problems here. First you have to wait 72 hours before a person is considered missing. Second they aren't missing in our jurisdiction. Anyway the state police have already filed a report with the U. S. Secret Service. We have the bulletin already so the best I can do, is have our officers be aware that they may be missing."

Angrily Katey answered, "Do you mean you won't help us?"

"Mrs. Myers I didn't say that. Our hands are tied,

we can't mount a search for them. Don't you realize we have tens of thousands of visitors this week? If it were our jurisdiction, it would be different, however we will be on the lookout for them. I have your phone number and if we hear anything at all, someone will contact you."

Jan told the other two, "He's right. At least they will be looking for them so let's go back to our rooms."

After they arrived back at the motel, Jan told the other two, "It's after 10 p.m. We better get a good night sleep and then tomorrow we'll go out to the re-enactment and look for them again. There's not much else that we can do for now. If they go back to camp, we left notes there and the others there will tell them that we're worried about them."

Jan and Katey went to the room they shared, while Marge went to the room next door which she shared with the boys. Daniel and Matthew had protested. The boys wanted to stay at the re-enactment. Marge would not allow that given the circumstances. Everyone listened to the news, hoping to hear something about their husbands. Nothing was said about the disappearance. They went to bed and fell into a very restless sleep. All the women were too tired to think any more.

Saturday morning they were all up early. The only place to get a cup of coffee was at the stop and shop. They also picked up the morning papers, hoping to find something about their husbands. Nothing was in there, not even a mention that their loved ones were missing. As they sat in the motel room drinking their coffee Jan mentioned, "You know something is bothering me about what the police officer said. About the secret service I mean. Why would they be involved?"

Marge replied, "I don't know why. Jan, is there anything else you can tell us about what George told you?"

Jan shaking her head no replied, "I've told you everything. It still doesn't make sense. That video showing them disappearing, along with what George told me, gives me a very weird feeling. I know it's not possible. But what if it is true?"

"Let's not deal with science fiction," Katey spoke, "Lets go out to the re-enactment and see if they showed up or if anybody knows what happened to them. We can check with the state police out there. Maybe they know something by now."

"I already called them this morning and they have no news at all." Jan replied.

The women spent the next two days searching at the camp for their husbands to no avail. Sadly on Sunday, they packed their husband's tents and gear into their cars. They picked up George's truck and went back to the motel to wait.

Monday morning the frustrated wives decided to contact a local lawyer just in case they would need him. Marge, the boys and Katey would have to leave and go home, leaving Jan there to wait and search. They had all agreed there was no reason for them to stay there. Two of them had to go to work plus there was a chance their husbands might show up at home. Also they had no motel rooms, with no chance to get one during this busy week. Jan had been lucky just to find a room at a bed and breakfast. Someone had canceled out at the last minute. Jan promised them both she would call every day. If she heard anything at all, she would call immediately. Also, she would check the motels for at least one room for the following weekend. The Gettysburg police had been kind enough to contact the motels asking for priority for the wives in case of any cancellations.

By the time the three travelers went outside, it had become overcast with a light mist as they started out across the field toward Frogtown Road. George remarked, "I thought it was going to be a nice day, here it's raining again."

Jack answered, "That's the way it is in this part of the country. The weather can change quickly."

As they were walking, Tim asked, "George, when you went outside on the porch this morning, what did you and the farmer talk about?"

"Someone dropped a penny last night in the kitchen. Mark found it. He knows we're from the future however he's much more intelligent than you think. He fully accepted it. I told him I couldn't tell him what was going to happen. I only told him that he and his family would be safe if they stayed put. We are going to have to be extremely careful from now on. In the next few days we'll have to go through all our belongings and get rid of anything from the twentieth century."

As they approached Frogtown Road, there was a stone farm house with a large stone bank barn and several outbuildings. Just down the road from the farm house, stood a new brick one room schoolhouse. The trio plodded onto Frogtown Road, where they turned left and followed the dirt road, knowing it should take them to Route 15. While they were walking, the re-enactors had been thinking about what happened the last couple of days. It was slowly sinking in that, indeed they had been cast back in time and they had no control over their lives in their present circumstances. They still had to be absolutely sure. So the group would head toward Gettysburg to see what was happening there. The mist had grown heavier and their wool clothing felt like it weighed a hundred pounds. Surprisingly they weren't cold and the walking made them perspire.

After fifteen minutes of traveling George broke the silence, "You know, this is completely unreal. There's no way this can be happening to us, yet here we are. Would you believe, many re-enactors would give their right arms to be here right now? In fact, I've imagined it many times during a re-enactment. But now that I'm here, I don't like it one bit! Maybe, it's the uncertainty of not knowing what's going to happen to us."

Tim agreed, "I know what you mean, I'm scared to death of the next few days and what could be in store for us."

Jack didn't say anything, but just nodded his head in the affirmative.

After another half hour of walking, the trio finally came to what they thought was Route 15 or Emmitsburg Road. It was a dirt road, muddy from the rain and mist. The center of the road was raised slightly and had a little grass growing on it. They started north and tried to keep on the raised portion of the road, to keep out of the sticky mud. The only problem with the center of the road, were the horse droppings, which they tried to avoid. Sometimes they weren't successful and someone would say "Aw shit," lightening the heaviness of their thoughts. After a while they tired of it and simply grumbled. The men passed several houses and were starting down a hill toward what they knew was Marsh Creek.

George put up his hand to signal everyone to

stop. He whispered, "I hear something coming. Get off the road and out of sight. Just follow my lead."

They melted off the road and hid in the wet underbrush, waiting to see what was approaching. It sounded like a wagon and they could hear metal striking stones from the rimmed wheels and horses snorting. Soon they could see a lone, dull green wagon with red trim being pulled by two large horses. The wagon had a white canvass, covering something in the back and had no springs on the axles. It was being driven by a young man in his early twenties. He was wearing a blue forage cap, which had obviously seen a lot of use, a poncho to ward off the rain and blue wool pants.

As the wagon grew abreast of George, he leaped out and grabbed the horse's reins as the other two jumped out and covered the young man with their empty muskets. George commanded, "Don't move, keep your hands where I can see them!"

The young man had a look of fright on his face at first, then relief as he exclaimed, "Damn you scared me to hell, I'm glad your Union and not those damn secheesh."

George asked him, "What do you have in the wagon?"

The young man replied, "Hams and such. I'm taking them to my uncle's farm down the road. We're going to hide them in the caves because the rebels are in the area taking everything that ain't tied down."

George asked him "You're wearing a Union uniform. Why aren't you with the army?"

The soldier didn't say anything. He just lifted his left leg, which was just a stump. Then he answered, "I lost this at Antietam last year, when a reb minie ball got me before I even had chance to fire. In fact, I hardly seen the Elephant. Now I'm home on furlough from the Invalid Corps."

"Do you know where the rebel army is right now?"

"A bunch of rebels went into Chambersburg a couple of days ago, took everything in sight, then headed in the direction of York. They didn't go to my uncle's farm, but they may be back any time now. So I took everything of value to hide until we're sure they're gone. What are you doing here? Are you pickets or are you deserters?"

George replied, "We're neither pickets nor deserters. We joined the army in Harrisburg, requesting to join a Bucktail regiment and now we're trying to find them. We know they are close by."

The young man said "Thank God the army is near. The whole countryside is in an uproar with the rebels being just about everywhere. I suppose that old Hooker will whip up on Bobby Lee when he gets him cornered."

George knew that in a couple of days, Meade would take over the Army of the Potomac, but he didn't say anything. "Can you spare any extra food? We don't know when we'll catch up to the army."

The young soldier answered, "I would be honored to give some food to fellow soldiers and my uncle won't mind." He climbed down from the seat and with the help of a crutch, hobbled to the rear of the wagon and untied the canvas, then pulled it back. They saw that it was loaded with barrels of flour, some smoked hams, slabs of bacon and canned vegetables, plus an assortment of tools and household items. He gave them each a slab of bacon, and they thanked him.

They helped the young veteran retie the canvass, then he climbed back up in the wagon seat. George told him, "You're free to go. Be careful. And thanks again for the food."

The young man replied "You're quite welcome. May God protect you and give Bobby Lee a good whupping for me. I do wish I could still fight and repay them rebs for what they did to my leg."

They watched as the wagon rumbled down the road and out of sight around a bend in the road. The men now knew for sure that they were indeed reliving the past. No one said anything for a while as they slowly walked up the road. After they had crossed Marsh Creek, they came upon a small country store on their right. There was a covered front porch, which had two lit lanterns, two rocking chairs and a large barrel between them. A bay horse and buggy were tied up to a hitching post in front of the store. Through the large front window, the men could see a glass enclosed display case. The room was lit by several lanterns and every inch of the walls had full shelves of various goods. The store owner, who was rather short and stocky, was listening to a tall slender man who was talking rather excitedly and gesturing wildly with his hands.

Jack whispered, "I bet you he's talking about the rebel army being in the area. We had better move on and not talk to them."

Quietly, they passed the store without being seen. Soon the trio saw another house on the right and just past the house on the opposite side of the road, stood another brick schoolhouse. The inside was dark and it was obvious that school was out for the summer. George broke the silence, "I recognize that schoolhouse, it is still standing in our time, but it's in much worse shape."

A long lane on their right led to another stone farm house sitting a quarter of a mile off the road.

Next came a brick farmhouse on their left, sitting fairly close to the road. As they approached this house, they could see it looked almost new, had a front porch and white picket fence in the front yard. Behind the house was a stone bank barn and a chicken house.

Beyond the barn, there was a small apple orchard and on both sides of the road were corn and wheat fields.

George thinking to himself, It must be a good year as the corn is chest high already. The wheat is ready for harvest, however if these poor people don't harvest it soon they'll never get the chance. In a couple days it will be trampled by the armies.

"You know what," Tim remarked, "I remember seeing that house but it is really run down. The front porch is gone and the barn roof caved in. This house really looks good now. It appears to be almost new. It's a real shame it was allowed to deteriorate. Just look at all the colors around us. The reds, greens, yellows and the other vibrant colors. I always had the impression that life during the Civil War was drab and dreary. Those old photographs that we see are all black and white."

"You're exactly right, it always seemed like it was so dull then," George replied.

Suddenly a dog started barking and a pretty young woman came out the front door. She started yelling, "Maw, Grandma, Grandpa, come quick, there's Union soldiers out in the road!"

As the re-enactors stopped at the front gate an old man and woman slowly came out of the house. He was dressed in dark blue pants with suspenders over a dark shirt buttoned at the neck, but no neck wear. The older woman, who was quite robust, wore a dark full dress with a white bib and a dark bonnet on her head. Finally a younger woman came out, dressed similarly to the older woman with a light blue dress and bonnet.

The old man stepped gingerly down the steps while the women stayed on the porch. He shuffled to the fence, back bent from years of hard toil, until he was close to the strangers. Then he looked up and down the road and asked, "Where's the rest of the army?"

"We're lost and are trying to find the army

ourselves," Jack answered.

As the farmer cocked his head to one side, he looked at them sternly, "Jumpin Jehosaphat! Do you mean you're alone and there ain't no army around? The whole reb army is here stealing and taking everything in the area. Who's gonna protect us? The damn army sent our militia to Washington a couple weeks ago and now we have to fend for ourselves. In fact, my daughter Amy's husband is in the militia and he ain't here to work the farm or protect us and the wheat is ready for harvest. And all there's between us and the rebels is three mangy Union soldiers." They listened to the tirade and watched the old man gesturing with his hands. For some reason this old guy was visibly upset and taking it out on them.

Finally, George put up his hand, to quiet the old man, "Sir, I don't know why you're troubled, but we'll be on our way, sorry we bothered you."

As they started walking along the road, they could hear the old man shouting at them, "You can tell Mr. Lincoln we ain't happy with him around here and he better protect us!"

Finally they all had enough and as if all were thinking the same thing, whirled around, flipped the old man the finger and shouted in unison "Asshole!" They watched as the women put their hands to their mouths in shock and ran back into the house. The old man just stood there.

They kept moving up the road talking among themselves trying to figure out what had upset the old grouch. George told the others, "Maybe we better try to avoid these farmers around here. That farmer was obviously frightened and angry and the last thing that we want is an altercation."

Jack agreed, "You're right about that. I think that old fella was upset because his wheat is still standing and with this rain, it's probably ruined. He obviously can't do the work and with his son-in-law gone, the work doesn't get done. I guess I would be upset too."

"That is very true, but that old man must have made some enemies around here. Other farmers would have pitched in to bring in the wheat harvest, unless he pissed them off. But it doesn't much matter now, in a few days, it will all be flattened by the armies," George stated.

The rain started to slack off and gave promise that it would soon stop. Soon they came to another farmhouse. This one was white clapboard with a bank barn and a white outhouse in back. They stopped and looked to see if anyone was outside before they would pass in front of the house. They couldn't see anyone, but they could see lantern light in the one front room. In the rear of the house was a summer kitchen and smoke was coming out of the chimney.

Tim exclaimed "Damn, I smell blueberry pies cooking and I sure could eat a whole pie myself."

Jack, who hadn't said too much all day, told him, "Didn't you learn anything with that old farmer back there? You don't know what these people are thinking and how they are going to react."

They walked quickly and quietly past the house, hoping that no dogs would bark. The trio passed several more houses the same way and no one else challenged them. It was mid morning when they came to a dirt lane which appeared to go to the Round Tops to their right. These hills would be crucial in the battle ahead. Whoever held the Round Tops would control the battlefield. As they stopped to look toward these large hills, they observed a peach orchard on their right and on the left corner of the road was 1 1/2 story log house.

Tim was the first to speak, "I guess you know we're at the peach orchard and that log house is the

Wentz property."

Standing with their mouths open, George exclaimed, "Damn, that log house isn't there, just the foundation and I always figured it was a stone house. This is really neat, seeing how the area looked during the battle."

Looking around Jack remarked, "It looks like it's going to clear up. The clouds are thinning out. We better keep moving if we want to get to town before the rebels get there. We can sight see later."

"How far do you figure we've walked by now?" Tim asked.

"Oh I'd say five or six miles give or take," Jack answered.

The men moved on passing several more houses before coming to the Codori house. Tim spoke, "Man, that place really is well-taken care of."

"All these houses we've seen are well cared for." George answered, "It's a shame that some of them were not kept up. Look over there at Cemetery Hill and the Copse of Trees. That is the focal point of Picketts charge in a few days. It looks strange with no monuments or the Cyclorama."

On they walked toward town as the sun came in and out of the clouds. Something caught their attention in the distance toward the west, where the Confederate lines would be in a couple of days. Before them was a sight which they would probably never see again.

Jack was the first to point, saying, "Look at that huge flock of birds coming this way."

Looking to where he was pointing they couldn't believe their eyes. Never did they ever see such a large flight of birds at one time. Tim asked as the birds flew nearby, "What kind of birds are they?"

Studying them intently Jack replied, "Gentlemen, I do believe that we're looking at a flock of passenger pigeons. I've read about them and how they could block out the sun. Seems hard to believe with that many birds in just that one flock, they could become extinct. Those birds are coming from the West. I wonder if the Confederate Army stirred them up?"

The three re-enactors just stood there watching in awe for 15 minutes listening to the rustling sound of wings cutting the air, until the last of the pigeons passed by heading east.

When the flock had moved on, the men started walking toward town again. As they passed under where the birds had flown, the ground was covered with fresh pigeon droppings. George told the others, "Well I can understand why they shot those pigeons. If this flock passed over a town, it would make one hell of a mess. Worse yet, if they decided to roost in the town, think of the stench."

After another mile the trio started down a gentle incline into the outskirts of the town. Tim spoke, "Sure could use a hamburger and fries right now, however, nothing's there. That's the house where they took General Reynold's body and there's the Dobbin's School just beyond. My God is that the Wagon Hotel on the right?"

George could see a carriage tied at the hitching post and horses tied there also. "Yep, that it is. There's several men on the porch there and they've seen us. So just keep walking. Maybe they won't say anything to us."

As they drew abreast of the hotel one of the men called down, "Hey soldiers come on up here on the porch and sit a spell."

Reluctantly, they climbed the steps up to the porch where three men were sitting on rocking chairs. They were all dressed as farmers. Not what they would have expected in town.

The re-enactors pulled some small kegs over and

sat with the three men. "Good morning soldiers I'm Abner Zook, this here is Nathan Stoltzfus and he's Aaron Schmidt," as he pointed to the other men. "And what might your names be and what are you doing in town?"

George gave the men their names then added, "We're trying to find the army. We've been dodging Confederates in the area the last few days. You men look like farmers. Why are you here at the hotel?"

Aaron, who looked to be in his early twenties, was a large man with a tawny beard spoke first, "We're hired hands for whatever farmer needs our help and willing to pay. So we live here then go to the town square by the railroad in the morning. Any farmer who needs help goes there and picks out hired hands. Today no sense going down there. Ain't no work when it rains. Where's the rest of the army?"

"Like we said, we're looking for the army ourselves," Jack answered. "What have you men heard about the rebels in the area?"

The older of the three farmers, Abner Zook appeared to be in his early thirties and small in stature, wiry, with a long black beard. "Wal, there's been all kinds of goings on the last few days. First the Union calvary rides in and out. Then some rebels wander in town and leave. Did hear there's a bunch of rebels up yonder in Chambersburg justa helpin themselves to anything they want. Sure hope they don't come to town here. Ain't got much and can't afford to give up anything."

George asked, "Did you see any rebels in town this morning?"

"Naw, none this morning. Mostly what has been going on the last few days was everybody taking everything they can outta town in wagons to hide. Even their horses and cows. All the freed coloreds have left for unknown parts. Ain't nary a one to be found in these here parts. Don't rightly blame them. Heard that any coloreds the rebs find, they send back South into slavery, papers or not."

"I have a question," Jack stated. "What was that large flock of birds that flew by awhile ago? Do they roost in this area?"

Replying, Abner told them, "They were those damn pigeons, passenger pigeons! You don't see them around here much anymore, cause when they come, every farmer goes out with his shotgun. You never seen such a mess as when they decide to land in a wheat or corn field. Faster then you can hitch a horse, they can strip fifty acres bare. We shoot them on sight. As for that there flock, they was just passing through. Something had them riled up cause we don't see them much. Thank God for that. Strange that you don't know about them pigeons."

"Oh we know about them, we just couldn't tell what they were since they were in the distance," Jack replied.

Standing up George told them, "Thanks for the information. We're going to take a look around town. If you happen to see any rebels, you never saw us."

"You soldiers take care. Don't worry we never saw you. Godspeed."

Leaving the porch, they started down the street. Tim who had been quiet asked the other two, "Don't you think you should have told those men to hightail it out of town. Before the rebels come and rob them?"

Replying sharply Jack said, "Listen shit for brains we can't do or say anything that can change history."

Tim fired back, "Oh yea. If you're so damn smart, you tell me one thing. Just us being back in time, doesn't that change history in itself?"

Thinking for a while Jack replied in a very subdued manner, "Tim, I have absolutely no answer to that. I don't even know how we can be back in time at all. It makes no sense and it should be impossible. Although, here we are and we have to make the best of it."

As they moved up Baltimore Street, much to their surprise, the three men were walking on a laid brick side walk which was slightly lower than the dirt street. They passed a long low building with a large chimney on their left when George remarked, "If you notice to our left sitting back behind those houses is the Tannery."

"Well I'll be damned, so it is," Tim replied.

The re-enactors traveled a couple more blocks marveling at how few houses there were on Baltimore Street when George suddenly put up his hand to stop and remarked, "Something is not right here. Nobody is outside and at several of the houses I saw people peering out between the curtains. We better take it nice and slow like. The hair on my neck is standing straight up."

They stood close to a house as a young barefooted boy ran down the sidewalk toward them. Running by them he shouted, "You'd better git. There's rebels up yonder acomin this way."

George exclaimed, "Oh shit we're right in the middle of the block. Lets cut through between some houses and find a place to hide."

The three men ran like frightened rabbits down a dirt alley between two brick houses, trying to find some place to hide where the Rebels weren't likely to look. As they ran behind the one house, they realized they were trapped. There was a tall wooden fence around the back yard. There was a small chicken coop, a wood pile, a small garden and carriage shed. These were too obvious to hide in. Time was running out. They could hear loud banging on doors and southern accents demanding entry just down the street.

Jack heard a loud "Pssts" and turned toward the rear porch of the house. He could see a young girl maybe fifteen years old, motioning for them to come to the house. The men made a mad dash to the house and ran in.

"Follow me quickly. I'll hide you upstairs in the attic. The rebels are right down the street. We don't have any time to waste."

They ran upstairs to the third floor attic. There were two small windows, one at either end of the house. In the one corner next to a chimney several large chests were piled up.

"Hide behind those chests, they probably won't look there. I'll come back for you when it's safe," and the girl disappeared down the steps closing the door quietly behind her.

The three men huddled behind the chests and waited in the stifling heat of the attic. Tim started to complain, "This was a bad idea coming to town. This damn place is like an oven."

"Just shut up and be quiet!" George whispered angrily.

Several minutes went by before there was banging on the door downstairs. A door could be heard being opened. A loud voice exclaimed, "Ma'am, we have to search your house for anything of use."

The trapped re-enactors could hear men rummaging through drawers and cabinets being opened and closed. The commanding voice was heard again, "You all heard General Lee's orders. Don't take any thing except what we need, but we pay for anything we take. Be quick about it. General Early wants to move on quick like for York."

Soon they could hear the men searching the floor below them. Another voice could be heard, "Young Lady, what's up on the third floor?"

"We don't have much up there. Just some old trunks, Mama and Papa use when they travel abroad. They're empty now."

Footsteps could be heard coming up the steps, next the door opened. The three re-enactors didn't move a muscle and held their breath as they heard the footsteps moving toward them. The loud clicks of the latches snapping open scared the hiding men, but they managed not to move. They could hear a hand sweeping around inside the trunks. A voice which sounded like it was on top of them, "These here trunks are empty all right. Damn it's dark up here and hot as hell."

More footsteps could be heard retreating toward the door. It squeaked closed and the rebel headed downstairs.

Another voice could be heard questioning the young girl, "Where is you're Mama and Papa?"

"They went to my Aunt Hattie outside of town. She's real sick. They'll be back tonight."

Shortly they heard the same voice state, "Thank you young lady. Sorry we inconvenienced you. Good day." Finally the door could be heard shutting behind the departing Confederates.

George told the other two, "Stay here, I'm going over to the window and have a look. Be right back."

Creeping to the window, he peered out cautiously. Below him could be seen a score of Confederate soldiers. Most wore dirt clogged tattered butternut clothing. None had shoes. All the men that he could see wore all sorts of hats. Most were in tatters also. Several of the men were carrying chickens and two were wrestling with a rather large pig that had no intention of joining the Confederate army. Shortly an officer rode up and shooed the men back to their regiment. As quickly as they arrived, they were gone.

George returned to their hiding place and told them, "The rebels appear to have left the area. We'll wait here until the girl tells us it's safe."

Jack asked, "Did you see the rebel soldiers?"

"Sure did. And they were the most motley looking crew you could imagine. A couple of them were rolling around in the street with a pig. It looks like the pig may have won!"

"Could you see anything else down there," Tim asked?

"No that window is pretty small and I had to keep back a little so no one could see me from below."

They hadn't heard anyone ascending the steps while they were talking. The sudden light streaming in from the opening door startled them and they feared they were captured. It was a relief when they heard the girls voice, "You can come down now. Those soldiers are gone."

As the three men followed the girl downstairs, they could feel the rush of the cooler air. It helped revive them from the heat of the attic. George thanked the girl for saving them and introduced his friends to her.

"I'm Thea Scheib. I didn't want to see you men get captured or worse. Anyway I'm no secesh. I'm for the Union and so are my parents."

"You took an awful chance," Jack told her. "There's no telling what they would have done to you had they found us. By the way, where are your parents?"

"My parents did go to my Aunt Hattie's farm. They were taking everything of value including most of our food. So the rebels wouldn't take it."

Tim asked, "Out of curiosity, just where is your Aunt Hattie's farm?"

"Oh they live just this side of Harrisburg. My

parents left two days ago and should have been back yesterday. I hope they are well."

George thought quickly, This poor girls parents probably ran straight into the Confederate army and lost everything they were trying to hide. Lying, he said, "Oh they're probably all right. Maybe your aunt really is sick and they decided to stay for a couple of days. Is there anyone to watch out for you while they are gone?"

"Oh dear yes, my Uncle Frederick just lives two doors up so I'm perfectly safe here. Is the Union army nearby, are you scouts? I know you're not cavalry because you don't have any horses. The cavalry has gone through town several times the past few days."

Loud banging on the door startled them as they heard a voice ring out, "Thea are you in there, are you Ok?"

Thea started for the door, "That's my Uncle Frederick."

When she opened the door, a rather small man with a large handle bar mustache entered the house. When he spotted the re-enactors he asked his niece, "What are these Union soldiers doing here? The rebels were just here. Are you crazy or something," as his voice got louder and louder?

"No Uncle Frederick. I was just hiding them so they wouldn't get caught."

"That was a dumb thing to do. Your parents would never forgive me if something happened to their only daughter."

George interjected, "Now hold on there. This young lady saved our lives. She's a heroine as far as I'm concerned so if you have anything to say, say it to us."

The man who had sallow skin, reminded George of what they would have called a dandy. He was wearing a frock coat made of gray wool with velvet trim and black planters hat. He wanted to say something more to prove his manliness. Her Uncle backed down as he looked at the three re-enactors who were much taller than he.

George could tell that the man was cowed so he tried to smooth things over, "Look she didn't do anything wrong and her parents will be very proud of her. I know you're worried about her. Believe me she can take care of herself. She's quick witted."

"Anyway Uncle Frederick, I knew you're close by to protect me so I wasn't worried."

George thought, Not only is she brave, she's a politician too.

Her uncle started to leave and said, "I'll be at the house if you need me. I'll check on you later."

George turned to the pretty young girl who had dainty features, rose red cheeks and coal black hair, which set off her smooth skin. "Miss, I think we'll be on our way just in case those rebels come back."

Thea looked at the three men, "I wish you didn't have to leave. I hardly even talked to you yet. Don't be afraid of my uncle. He's really quite meek you know."

"Oh we're not afraid of him. We just have to try and find our new regiment. Anyway it's tempting fate if we stay here. The rebels may not take kindly to you if they find us here."

"Do you think they'll be back here?"

Jack answered, "Thea if they're in the area, you don't know when they'll just show up. George is right. We do have to leave and find our regiment. After all we are soldiers."

Satisfied she replied, "We don't have anything to give you. I can fill your canteens with cool well water and give you a couple biscuits I have hid, to help you out."

George answered, "We would be ever grateful for

111

that as long as you have something left to eat."

"Oh we have a few biscuits and when my mother gets back she'll do some baking."

As they were about to leave Tim spoke, "Thea, if I wasn't a married man you would be the perfect wife for me. You're beautiful, brave and a considerate person. I wish you all the best in life and thank you from all of us for what you did. We'll never forget you."

Thea just blushed, then curtsied as each of them kissed her hand as they left.

The trio headed back down Baltimore Street not talking, just heading out of town quickly. People were outside now, some wishing them well while others just glared at them. But they didn't stop to talk to anyone. They just wanted to get the hell in the cover of the woods. The encounter with the rebels had shaken them.

After they crested Cemetery Hill George stopped and took his camera out of his haversack, turned and took a picture into the town. "I need some pictures so if we go back to the future I can prove to myself that I was here."

Jack spoke sharply, "You idiot. What the hell are you doing? If anybody sees you no telling what could happen. Keep that camera out of sight! Better yet, get rid of it."

"I'm not getting rid of this camera. It has something to do with whatever happens to me later. I'm going to get some good pictures. Can you just imagine the value of those pictures in the twentieth century?"

The re-enactors left the road and headed for Culps Hill which was wooded. This would afford them some cover for the night and they could start a fire to cook. Later George spoke, "That was too close back in town. We better lay low and try to figure things out."

They found a sheltered area in some rocks and

started making camp for the night. George broke the silence, "Now do you two believe me. This is no joke. We are back in time and it's no dream."

Jack answered, "You're right, we are indeed back in time. I don't know how but here we are. I do have a question, is there any way we can avoid the fight that we know is about to begin?"

"No, somehow we are destined to be in the fight, at least I am," George answered. "Maybe you two won't be in it but I know I will be. Don't get me wrong. Right now I don't want any part of it."

Tim broke in sarcastically, "If I remember right, aren't you the one who wished he could go back in time to see what it was really like? Well I don't appreciate you bringing me along."

Glaring at Tim, "Listen pea brain, you've said the same damn thing. Just like any other re-enactor. So don't give me any crap about that and don't blame me for you being here."

Jack stepped in, "OK you two just settle down. No use fighting amongst ourselves. We have more to worry about like cooking something to eat. We have those two biscuits to divvy up and we can fry up some bacon. That'll hold us over until tomorrow. George, can you set up some snares tonight so we can get some rabbits?"

"Sure no problem. We'll have fresh rabbit for breakfast. I think that tomorrow we should sort of ease over toward the Round Tops but take it real slow. We don't want to be seen by anyone. There could be too many questions. I suggest that after we eat we douse the fire and get a good night sleep. I don't know about you two but the strain of today has worn me out."

Tim and Jack agreed, they too were exhausted and when they finished supper everyone found a soft spot and slept soundly through the night.

* * * * *

Tim felt something crawling across his neck waking him up. Taking his left hand, he flicked a spider off. He laid there for a minute with his eyes closed and tried to remember where he was. All he knew for sure, was the realistic dream that they had traveled in time. Opening his eyes Tim could see trees towering over him, That's strange, he thought, Where's my tent? Sitting up he rubbed his eyes and looked around, saw his two friends still sleeping and they were in a strange place. Damn this was no dream, he thought, We really are back in time. How he wished that this had been a illusion. Slowly the other two stirred. Both sat up and rubbed their eyes looking around them as Tim had done.

George spoke first, "I slept soundly, never even moved last night. I was hoping that when we woke up this would have just been a nightmare."

"Man, I'm still tired. Yesterday was harder on us than I thought," Jack replied. "Since we're not at the re-enactment, I guess that means we are still back in time."

"I'm afraid that's true," Tim replied. "What do we do today, stay here or move on?"

After thinking George said, "Let's see, today is Saturday, the 27th, that means we have four more days. Maybe if we're lucky we'll go to the future before then. Today maybe we should stick to this hill. We'll find a place where we can see the town, the roads and just watch."

Nodding his head Jack answered, "Sounds good to me. Guess we should start a fire to make breakfast.

George you gonna check the traps for some rabbits?"

"Yep, I'm going right now. Be back in a minute." George checked and found he had caught two rabbits in the snares he had set last night. Good thing I had survival training in those SEAR[4] schools while I was in the navy, he thought. After he went back to the camp, they cleaned the Catch of the Day. After cleaning the rabbits they wrapped strips of bacon around them, then roasted the meal over the fire. Tim and George took turns rotating the meat while Jack stood watch just in case someone would smell or see the smoke. After they ate their breakfast, the three went further up the hill until they could see the town and roads. Throughout the day they could see carriages, wagons and people on horse back, going to and from the town. The day was cool and lightly overcast. At least it wasn't raining. It was a lazy day, however the day before had been strenuous. A hard walk of eight or nine miles from the farm to the town didn't help. The re-enactors didn't talk very much. Each was in deep thoughts, trying to fathom what was happening to them. Toward evening, the men went back to their hiding place. After starting the fire again, another rabbit was roasted. George had managed to snare another one during the day. They went to sleep early figuring on moving at first light the next day.

---

[4] .SEAR-Survial Escape And Rescue

*   *   *   *   *

The three men were up at dawn the next morning and George went out to check the snares and collect the traps to be used later. As he went back to their camp he announced, "Well boys today is going to be lean."

Tim looked over, "Do you mean you didn't catch anything?"

"I caught two more rabbits. Only problem is, it looks like a fox helped himself to our breakfast."

"Well, no problem, we still have plenty of bacon left." Jack replied, "We'll just have to ration it out so it lasts awhile."

After breakfast the trio went up to their lookout one more time to check the area out. There was a steady stream of carriages heading into town which puzzled them for a moment.

George said, "It's Sunday and all the farmers are going into town for church. I bet in a few minutes we'll hear the church bells."

Sure enough, bells from all the churches started ringing about the same time.

"I have an idea." Tim spoke, "See that farm down there. Let's go down there quickly. Maybe we can get a chicken or something while they are away."

George fired back, "We'll do no such thing! That would be stealing and we aren't starving. We'll get some more rabbits later. These people will suffer enough in a few days."

"Up yours," Tim replied, "Two strips of bacon is not a good meal in my book and I'd rather have a

116

chicken instead of rabbit."

"Tim," George countered, "You go right down there and get your chicken, by the time you get back we'll be long gone. If you want to steal, you'll do it on your own."

There was complete silence for a few minutes before Tim replied, "I guess you're right. That would be stealing and I was wrong for suggesting it."

"No problem, let's get out of here and see what's below."

Carefully they made their way down the hill. At first pushing through thick underbrush, the blackberry bushes and creeper vines tearing at their uniforms and tangled their legs. Soon they came to a well-used game trail, and followed it down hill. They still had to push through some brush and climb over downed trees and branches, but it was much easier walking. The trail led them directly to a spring which had been widened and deepened, then lined with rocks. To their surprise there was a well used narrow dirt road crossing the head of the spring.

George whistled, "I do believe this is Spangler Spring boys."

"I think you're right. Look over there," Jack replied.

They all looked toward where Jack was pointing. A cup hung on a nail for weary travelers to use to drink from the cool waters. They filled their canteens which were almost empty and drank deeply from the clear pool of sparkling waters. After they had their fill, the men headed south through some more woods before entering into cleared fields. The rolling fields helped hide them from the different farms they encountered. The men always tried to go in a southern direction aided by George's pocket compass.

Tim spoke to no one in particular, "There are

more farm houses than I imagined were here. And now that we are out in the open there's hardly any trees. We can see Cemetery Hill with no problem from here. In fact, the only way we can tell where you are on the battle field in our time, is the National Tower."

"You're right about that. And some people think it is an eye sore." George agreed, "Maybe it is, but it really is a good marker. Maybe if they tear it down, they'll figure another way to make a readily recognizable landmark. Did you also notice? We can see the Round Tops from here, in fact they can be seen from almost anywhere today. This place really looks different. You just don't realize, however now it makes more sense that the battle developed as it did."

Tim asked, "What do you mean?"

"Well, think of it this way. If we can see the Round Tops and Cemetery Hill from here, they can see us. It made it difficult to move troops around on the field without being seen. We assume in our time that this area was all grown up, just because that is what we see. We can't understand why they had such trouble moving unobserved, however now it makes sense. And if you look over there a ways, where that distant line of trees and brush is. That's probably Rock Creek," as he pointed to the east.

Tim and Jack both agreed with George's observation.

After walking for some time the men came to a small shallow creek which they crossed with no difficulty and soon came to a road which appeared to head in the direction of the Round Tops. Behind them stood Cemetery Hill in full view.

George remarked, "I think this is Taneytown Road so maybe we should get off the road and hide in that brush for a while and take a break. If we angle a little to the right we can come up on the back side of Little

Round Top where it's wooded and will hide us from prying eyes."

While they rested, several carriages came out of town. The farmers and their families were heading back to their farms. One wagon came by with the parents sitting on the seat while in the back, two young boys sat with their legs dangling out the open back. They didn't appear to be very happy, being all dressed up in their sunday best. One boy kept tugging at his neck where the string tie was too tight.

As the soldiers prepared to move on, it started raining again, lightly at first, then steadily. After checking to make sure no one was on the road, the men started trekking toward the hills in front of them. After going a short distance they wound up in marshy ground which was littered with cow manure, in green patchy wallows.

Tim complained, "Dammit, I just went in over the top of my shoes in this stinky crap. Can't we go up on the road?"

"No," countered Jack, "We can hide easier here than we can on the road."

After a short 20 minute walk they came to another dirt road which was narrower than Taneytown Road. The men picked this road heading to the Round Tops. It didn't appear to be as well used, so they just kept watching behind them as they traveled the lane. A brick farm house appeared on their right which had a very large barn and several other outbuildings including a separate summer kitchen.

George remarked, "If I'm not mistaken, that is the Weikart farm right there."

"Well I'll be jiggered. Now I know where I am," Jack replied.

"Yea, it's pretty obvious, with the Round Top right in front of us. Instead of going around the back side, why don't we go around the front, I'd like to see what it looks like without any monuments."

Jack answered, "Sounds good to me."

The re-enactors soon encountered the rising slope of the Little Round Top, gently working their way around and up. They noticed at once there were very few trees on the side facing them and it appeared to have been recently logged. The men started climbing the stone hill to the top.

"It really looks different with no monuments on the Round top," George noted as he snapped a couple more pictures.

Tim and Jack agreed with him, not saying anything further, as their breath was labored and chests hurt from the climb over the rocks. Eventually the men came to some large boulders. The area was littered with toppings from the logged off trees. The trees which had not been logged off, began near the large boulders. The ground dropped off sharply from the boulder line down to the valley separating the two Round Tops.

George told the other two, "Look at that flat boulder over there. That is the future site of the 20th Maine monument."

"Yeah, I believe you're right. Everything looks different, no land marks and no roads," Tim agreed.

The group scouted around and decided to build a shelter at the base of that boulder for the night. After several attempts they were able to start a fire with the wet wood. Being careful, they built the fire in the group of boulders which shielded it from view. Hopefully no one would see the fire and investigate. While Tim and Jack finished setting up camp, George went out and set up several snares on the many game trails crossing the round top. In a very short time George had snared three rabbits. The trapper made sure to beat the fox to their meal this time. After cleaning the rabbits, the hungry men slow cooked them over the fire as they had done before. The fire took away the numbing cold of the rain and wet clothing. Soon the heat warmed their wool uniforms and steam started rising with a fragrance of a clothing press in a dry cleaner.

After they had eaten dinner, the trio started talking about their plans for the next few days. George spoke first, "We probably should have done this before, we have to check our belongings for anything modern and get rid of whatever we find. One thing we can't be for sure, is a Farb!"[5]

Lucky for them they didn't have much cash. They had left their wallets in camp and had only brought their credit cards for use in Robbers Roost.[6] So between them they only had a few dollars in coin, a wrist watch and George had a small pocket compass. They threw their credit cards in the fire and watched them burn and melt.

Tim said with sadness in his eyes, "I probably should have done that a long time ago. I wouldn't be so much in debt."

George had some change in his pocket which amounted to four quarters, four dimes, one nickel and three pennies. He decided he would put them in a small cotton bag along with his pocket compass and carefully bury them. George did this in case they did return to the present day, he would be able to retrieve them. Carefully he counted off forty-five paces toward the south from the 20th Maine rock, to a boulder which had a flat side facing north. He buried the bag under the southern side of the boulder and in the crevice he piled

---

[5]A re-enactor term for someone who doesn't dress and act authentic

[6]Re-enactor's slang for Sutler Row

121

two flat stones to hide the bag. George kept his camera since he knew it would be involved somehow. The old man had asked him if he had a camera with a flash. There was no way he could have known about the camera unless someone told him. It almost had to be that Clem Akers he talked about. His haversack also contained some compresses and antiseptic salve which he carried for first aid.

George told them, "I have some first aid supplies. These supplies could possibly save our lives should we get hurt or wounded."

The other two agreed with him about the medical supplies, but were very upset with the idea of keeping the camera. Jack looked at him in the light of the dancing fire and George could see his piercing eyes boring through him. Damn he hated when Jack looked at him like that.

"You know George, if someone finds that camera, not knowing or understanding what it is, they could come to the wrong conclusion. In this time they can act irrationally about something they don't understand. What I'm trying to tell you is, they could kill us."

"That camera has something to do with that Confederate soldier," George argued, "So I've got to keep it and take my chances. Somehow that old man knew I had the camera. So far what he said has come true. Also, under no circumstances can I help anyone outside our group with first aid, no matter what I or any of you want."

"What do you think we should do tomorrow, stay put or move on?" Jack asked.

"Well, I think we should stay put for a couple of days. No matter where we go we'll run into Union or Confederates. Either way it wouldn't be good. Tomorrow is the 29th. If we go to the cleared off side of the Round Top, we'll probably be able to see the cavalry on Emmitsburg Road. We still have two days to kill. Just maybe we'll pass back to our time before the battle starts. At least I hope so."

Tim interjected, "I don't think we should stay here. We should move on and get out of the line of fire, so to speak."

"And where do you propose we go," Jack asked?

"I don't know. You guys are so smart, tell me."

George countered, "Well just think about it, if we go north or west, we run into Confederates. East or south we run into the Union Army. Don't forget, we are dressed as Union soldiers. The Confederates will either shoot us or send us to Libby prison, which I really don't care for. If the Union catches us, we could be arrested as deserters. If I'm not mistaken, they have the habit of shooting deserters. No, I think we stay put for now and on the 1st of July we try to find the army."

"Are you crazy?" Tim shouted, "Why do you want to find the army? Do you have a death wish or something?"

"No, we are here, trapped." Jack added, "We can't stay up here. If I'm not mistaken, it gets pretty hot and heavy on the 2nd of July. So we really don't have any options open right now. We just sit tight and just see what develops."

"I don't believe this! You're both out of your minds," Tim fired back.

"Let's quit arguing tonight." Jack responded, "We're staying put, period!"

Tim glared at them, not saying any more. He didn't have any answers either.

George stood up and stretched, "Well, it's getting dark now. I think from now on we should take turns on watch, while the others sleep."

"Yeah, you're right, I'll take the first watch. Tim, you take the next one and George the last. I'll pass on my pocket watch to Tim and you pass it onto George."

"Sounds good to me. I'm exhausted tonight so I'll crawl into the lean-to first, since Tim is the next on watch."

Jack went over to a large boulder setting the first watch of the evening. The boulder afforded a fairly good view of a foot trail passing below him. It would be a long watch, as it was pitch dark, cold and quiet. Clouds were hiding the moon and stars. At least the rain had stopped for the time being.

* * * * *

Early the next morning the sky was overcast and the temperature cool. The three re-enactors ate rations of bacon cooked over the fire along with their coffee. They had to crush coffee beans between two rocks since the farmer gave them whole beans, not ground. The day was a restful one. No one felt like talking. Each was enmeshed in their own thoughts, some of home and their families but not all of them.

As Tim sat by himself, he started to plan his future. To hell with the others, anything I wanted to do, they both went against me. I will make the best of everything and at least I'll be very comfortable. As far as changing history, what do those two idiots know? Nothing at all. I have no compunction about changing history and if it makes it easier on me, then I'll use my knowledge to my advantage. The first opportunity I get, I'll slip away and hide somewhere until the battle is over.

Jack thought of his lovely wife and longed to see her one more time. It saddened him to think she would always wonder what happened to him. She may have to wait seven years to even declare him dead. God, he wished this would be over. What was going to happen in the next few days to him and his friends. He could only pray to God to protect him and his comrades and watch over his wife.

Why didn't I listen to Mr. Sloan, George thought. If I had sat out that re-enactment, maybe this nightmare wouldn't have happened. Somehow I involved my two friends in this mess. Maybe if they went their seperate ways, only he would be caught up in the battle. After all, it seems like the musket is what's driving these events. No, that couldn't be the whole story. Why didn't just he go back in time? For some reason, they were meant to be involved. What could the reason be? It didn't make sense to him at all. He hoped that his wife would know and understand what happened. George prayed with all his being, that she would get on with her life if anything happened to him.

Later in the day, the trio ventured to the other side of the hill and watched Emmitsburg Road. No cavalry was seen traveling on the road. Only travelers seen were the wagons and horsemen moving along the busy road. They retired back to camp in the evening and the night passed uneventfully and turned into the new day, the 30th of June 1863.

* * * * *

George was the first up. It appeared the day would be decent. The sun was just appearing over the trees however there were still some clouds. Thinking to himself, Well this will be the last quiet day. Gettysburg will never be the same again. The birds were singing and squirrels could be seen running about foraging for breakfast. Tim was just coming down from the lookout boulder as Jack was beginning to stir. They all looked bedraggled. No one had shaved for days and their clothing was covered with mud. Also their clothing was ripped in several places from the brambles they had pushed through on their odyssey of the last few days.

As they sat by the fire cooking their breakfast Tim spoke, "I was thinking, why don't we go back to the Mark Shultz farm and see if we can hide there? The battle doesn't happen around his farm. That way we'll be out of danger."

"Quit thinking about yourself." George answered, "If we hide there and the provost happens to stop there and find us, think of that good farmer. They will not look kindly on him for hiding deserters. They could take everything and burn him out. That is totally out of the question."

"OK how about this, why don't we go into town and buy some farmers clothes at the general store. We could blend in with the local populace."

Jack, who was getting annoyed at Tim sharply replied, "Listen dummy, what are you going to use for money? They don't take credit cards. And if they did, you burned yours a while back. Today we are going to plan for the next few days as best we can."

Knowing he had been beaten again, Tim decided to wait and see what would happen.

After their breakfast the trio went back to their outpost to watch the roads. This day they did see the cavalry passing by.

In astonishment Tim said, "Just look there. That's a hell of a large force of cavalry. They've been riding by continuously for a half hour and there's more coming. Here comes the horse artillery up the road now. Man this is neat."

After an hour the riders finally passed out of sight. There was very little traffic on the road the rest of the day.

As the afternoon wore on the clouds increased and a light rain started again. The travelers worked their way back to camp to get the fire started and try to get out of the rain.

After dinner the three huddled around the fire to plan for the next few days. George started the conversation, "The only thing that we can do is get a couple hours of sleep and head back down to Emmitsburg road. We have to try and link up with the First Corps. Otherwise, if we get caught by the provost, we could wind up being shot as deserters. If I have to die, I would rather go as a man facing the enemy. How do you two feel about that?"

"I guess you're probably right. There's no way out that I can see either. I've always wanted to know what it would be like fighting in the Civil War. I guess we'll sure as hell find out very soon."

"You're both demented. Hell George, you of all people should never want to fight after what you went through in Vietnam," Tim replied.

"Tim, you're absolutely right. I don't want to fight. In fact many years ago I swore I would never try and kill a man again. Remember, I told you how I hated myself for throwing back a Viet Cong grenade. Even though I didn't try to kill them, it was a matter of survival, but they were still dead. Now I'm faced with survival again and I don't know if I'll be able to do it all over. Somehow we have to survive. Do you have an idea how to get out of this mess? If so, please tell us. No matter what we try, it won't really make any difference. If what that old man told is true, we are destined to be involved in the battle."

Tim didn't reply at first, his mind was racing a mile a minute. "I don't have any ideas at all. In fact, I guess I might as well get used to the idea of fighting

tomorrow and hope that I, or we will survive somehow."
To himself he thought, I'll get out of this mess on my
own. Tomorrow morning I'll slip away from the other
two and find a place to hide.

Next they planned out the watches for the night.
George would take the first watch for two hours and
the other two would do the same. Everyone would get
some sleep, this may be the last sleep any of them
would get for a while. The next order of business was to
make up a story which was plausible, in case they found
the Union Army in the morning.

George had an idea, "We joined the army in
Harrisburg, with the understanding from Governor
Curtin, that we would be assigned to the Bucktail
Brigade under Colonel Stone. They had given us orders
and a military pass signed by Adjutant General Russel.
However, since we left Harrisburg, we have been
dodging the Confederate Army. We had to abandon
camp one night, when rebel skirmishers discovered our
site. We left in such a hurry, all we could grab was our
muskets and leather accouterments. Everything was left
behind, including our orders and military passes which
were in our knapsacks. How does that sound?"

Jack and Tim agreed that it was probably the
best story they could come up with. George asked Jack
if he could borrow the pocket watch, so that he would
know when his two hours were up. He would pass it
onto Tim for his turn on watch. Tim and Jack laid down
on the ground by the fire and promptly fell into a fitful
sleep.

George left camp and went about 20 yards, sat
on a log and watched the trail they had used earlier. As
he sat there, he started thinking of the trouble they
were in. How would he react if they went into battle
tomorrow? He knew for sure that under no
circumstances would he be able to use any of his medic

training to save any lives, unless it was his or one of his friends. He could not do anything to change history, even though he knew, how the Union doctors practiced medicine, would cost lives. Even if it went against his beliefs, he could not use his skills as a medic. The cloud cover was starting to break now and the almost full moon cast its light down on the camp. George pulled out the old pocket watch and peered at it intently to try and make out the time in the light of the moon. It was almost 11 p.m. and time to get Tim up for the next watch. George had been so intent on trying to see the time in the moonlight that he never saw the brief glimpse of two shadowy figures silently cross the soggy trail below him.

On July 1, 1863, the 1st Corps of the Army of the Potomic had casualities of over 6,000 out of approximately 9,400 engaged.

CHAPTER EIGHT

Josh Akers was born in 1845 on a small farm in Anson County, South Carolina. His parents were very poor tenant farmers and lived in a ramshackle cabin with their six children. He was the youngest of three boys, being the terror of his older brothers. He made up for being smaller, by having the tenacity of a cornered tiger. Josh carried this trait through his whole life. This probably saved his life on many occasions during the upcoming Civil War. He was fortunate also, because he had been able to go to school for six years, while his older brothers helped farm the land. Josh was a good student and enjoyed learning. His mother and father encouraged him to study. Josh's parents knew that education would be his only chance for a better life. His older brothers had no interest in school and only went through three grades. It was more fun to play hooky and go fishing for catfish in the nearby Pee Dee River. Their father decided that if they had time to fish when they were supposed to be learning, then they had time to work on the farm.

The time went quickly by for young Josh and before he knew it, he was sixteen years old. Years of hard work on the farm had made him wiry and strong. He only stood 5'8" tall, and looked much older than he was. Fuzz on his face gave his age away with a couple whiskers sprouting here and there haphazardly on his chin.

The whole area was talking about the South firing on Fort Sumter several days before and there was going to be a war between the North and the South. Josh was excited and decided he would join up as soon as possible. His parents weren't too happy about that idea. He was too young and they had already lost their oldest son and youngest daughter to yellow Fever two years ago. Their other son had joined the local militia two months earlier when there had been a call to arms. Josh felt he had to join as soon as possible, because everyone was saying the war would be over in a couple of months and he was afraid he would miss the whole thing. His parents were adamant and told Josh, if he tried to join, they would reveal his age and that would be the end of that.

After several weeks had gone by, he heard that North Carolina had seceded and he knew he had to join the army. Josh figured his parents wouldn't think of him joining a regiment in the neighboring state. He had tried to leave several times but he couldn't bear the thoughts of leaving his parents. Several months had gone by and the lure of earning his glory in the army finally overpowered him one night in August. That night after everyone had gone to bed, he crept out of the house and walked up the road. Just before he came to a bend in the road, he turned and looked back to the cabin, which was lit by a full moon. He knew he couldn't turn back now as his destiny lay somewhere up that road. As he gazed at the old cabin, he wondered if he would ever see it, or his family again. Then with a heavy heart he turned quickly up the road and disappeared into the shadows of the trees.

Now two years had passed and he was in the 26th North Carolina Regiment. Josh had gone to Crabtree in

Wake County, North Carolina, arriving there as the recruiting officers were signing up men for the 26th NC. The recruiting officer asked Josh if he was over 18. Earlier Josh had been talking to a boy who didn't look over 14 years old. He asked him if he lied about his age to join the army. "Hal no I didn't lie." The young boy took off his one shoe and showed Josh a piece of paper in it which had the numerals' 18 written on it. "When they asked me ifn' I was over 18, I shure was."

Josh immediately wrote 18 on a piece of paper and put it in his shoe. So when the officer asked him if he was over 18, he replied, "Yes sir."

After the regiment was formed, they drilled every day all day. First as companies, then as a regiment. Marching, drilling in the school of soldiers, musket loading and firing drills until they did everything automatically. After a month of intense training they were on the move, marching almost every day, setting up camps at night. During this time they only had a few skirmishes. This went on until they went into winter camp just before Christmas. The year 1862 saw this regiment fight in five battles and many skirmishes. The next year would see two more battles before the Army of Northern Virginia would invade the North.

They had been marching for almost a month with General Lee's Army. The soldiers had passed into Pennsylvania the day before and Josh was tired of the dust, mud, heat and sun. He also wasn't happy about invading the North, he joined to fight and defend the South. His tent mate, Paul, whom he campaigned with for almost a year, felt the same way. It was unusual to have a tent mate this long, as he had gone through three the year before. One had died in winter camp of the dews and damps and the other two had been killed in some small skirmishes. Now they were in a small town that someone called Chambersburg, looking for supplies.

133

Paul and Josh had both talked of going home again, as they were tired of fighting and seeing all the wanton killing that took place in every battle and skirmish. So they both decided that when the opportunity presented itself, they would skedaddle while the regiment was dispersed in town searching for anything of value. When the chance came, the two men left town with every intention of going home to South Carolina.

Paul and Josh were lost the first night, trying to dodge Provost Guards, who were looking for stragglers and deserters. For the next three days they hid out in any available woods, only moving at night. They sneaked up to different farms to snatch whatever they could find to eat. The first night they managed to liberate a German farmer's big fat rooster which they roasted over their camp fire. Another night they snatched a blackberry pie cooling on a window sill of a summer kitchen of a farm. They almost got caught when the farmer's dog started barking in the house and the farmer gave chase until they were lost to the darkness.

Every time the two rebels had started out for home, either a Confederate or Union Cavalry patrol would show up, and they would have to go back into hiding. Finally, on the fourth night they headed toward two hills, one about half the size of the other. It had been raining off and on all day and they hadn't eaten since the night before. The night was very dark and dismal, but hunger and cold kept them moving. Josh and Paul passed a swampy area and a farm house on their right. Just as they were about to sneak up to the building to find something to eat, the farmer's dog started barking and a man came out of the house with a lantern. They simply kept on and soon came to a large slope on their left, which had been logged off. The Rebels started climbing over the extremely rocky and steep hill.

As they approached the far side of the knoll, Josh stopped and grabbed Paul. "I smell wood smoke and I don't reckon that there's a house up here, so let's go real quiet like and see what's here."

The two rebels moved cautiously, they could see trees and a lot of brush, but walking quietly was easy because everything was so wet from the rain. They followed the smell of the wood smoke until they could see the glow of the camp fire. Near the fire, the Josh and Paul could see one man moving toward two others sleeping on the ground under a makeshift lean-to.

Josh whispered to Paul, "Well I'll be jiggered if that ain't some yanks there! I'll bet they got some vittles and coffee. We'll just go in there and jump them!"

"It may be a trap, I don't aim to become target practice for some yanks."

Josh countered, "If there were more yanks around, there would be more fires too. Anyway, if there were more around, they would have pickets all over. Naw, I bet they're just like us and just skedaddled from the Union Army."

* * * * * *

George had gone back into camp, went over to the sleeping form of Tim, and started to bend over to wake him up, when suddenly he heard the unmistakable loud click of muskets being cocked behind him. He spun around and in the soft glow of the campfire, he could make out the two most bedraggled soldiers he had ever seen. They almost reminded him of the newsreels of Japanese soldiers finally surrendering in the 1950's in the Philippines. But they were holding the meanest looking muskets and looked like they knew how to use them.

135

The commotion woke the two sleeping men, who sat up and rubbed their eyes in disbelief. "What the hell is this?" Jack exclaimed.

Josh who stepped back into shadows, hissed, "Shut up and don't move!"

"Do you have any vittles or coffee?" The other man questioned.

"I have some fresh coffee beans here in my haversack, you're more than welcome to," George offered.

"Get them out real slow like," Josh ordered, "Don't make any fast moves or you'll be eating a Richmond musket ball!"

George reached into the haversack and felt for the lens opener on the camera, slipped it open, then fumbled for a couple of seconds so the flash would charge. He pulled it out slowly and held it toward the two unsuspecting rebels and pushed the shutter release. In the bright flash he could see their eyes get as big as saucers.

Both men put their hands to their eyes and screamed in unison, "I'm blind!"

It gave George and his friends time to grab their empty muskets, cock them and cover the two rebels. The surpised soldiers rubbed their eyes and as their sight came back, they saw the three muskets pointed at them and realized the captives were now the captors. They simply turned their muskets upside down, in a gesture of surrender. George motioned the two sullen rebels over to the fire and in a commanding voice said, "Lay your muskets on the ground, step back five paces and turn around!" The two Confederates promptly obeyed.

"What are ya'll yanks going to do with us, turn us in as prisoners?" Josh asked. "Are ya'll deserters yourselves?"

"We're not deserters." George answered, "We are trying to catch up to the army, it sure does sound like you deserted. Let me introduce you to my comrades. This is Tim Fretz, Jack Myers and I'm George Murray. What are your names?"

"Wal, yes, we sort of tired of soldiering and hankered to head home, we didn't join to fight in the North."

"What are your names?"

"Sorry, my name is Josh Akers and this here is Paul Sanford. We're from the 26th North Carolina Regiment."

When George heard the name, the hair on his neck stood up and his mouth dropped open. His mind was awhirl, this is the same name that the old man had told him about. Everything was coming true!

Regaining his composure, he called to Tim over his shoulder, "Pick up their muskets!" To the rebels, "Sit by the fire and cross your legs." Slowly, while watching the re-enactors, the two rebels did as they were told.

"Man look at these 1855 muskets, they are really in good condition," Tim exclaimed.

"Watch what you say," Jack whispered.

"We're not going to hurt you, turn you in or anything like that," George told the men. "But on your word of honor, we'll have a truce with you tonight and share our coffee and as you say, our vittles. Do you agree with that?"

Both of the rebels nodded their heads in agreement, however they still showed distrust in their eyes.

"Right now I want you both to give us all your ammunition," as he motioned for Jack to get the ammo. After they emptied their cartridge boxes, the two captives had a look of total apathy in their eyes, as they knew for sure, they would soon be sitting in some yank prisoner camp.

"After we eat and have some coffee, we'll give you back your muskets, not your cartridges. And then you can be on your way. My suggestion is for both of you to try and rejoin your regiment, as there are Union and Confederate troops all over and there is no way out."

"What was that bright light in that black box that blinded us?" Josh queried

"I can't tell you. You would not understand anyway. So don't ask again."

Both rebels feasted on smoked and salted rabbit along with some bacon left over from dinner. As the rebels wolfed down the meat, Josh said, "That's the first meat we've had in several days and we're surely beholding to you yanks." The coffee, which had been brewing in their cups on the fire, washed down their supper.

"It seems like you have some education." George stated to Josh.

"Wal yes, in fact besides the captain and other officers in our company, I'm the only one who can read or write. When we're in camp, I write letters home for the men and read their letters from home for them."

As they sat drinking their coffee George looked the rebels over closely and noticed how badly their clothing was torn, worn and extremely dirty. He thought to himself, If these men would be shot and wounded in the days to come, they would have dangerous infections. He knew from experience that a bullet would punch pieces of the dirty cloth deep into a wound, causing serious and many times, mortal wounds. George also noticed their shoes were badly worn and had pieces of leather tied around them to hold them together. But their muskets were well oiled and in extremely good condition, as any modern soldier would keep their tools of the trade.

"See their bedrolls wrapped around their shoulders?" Tim whispered, "I remember reading somewhere that soldiers kept extra ammo in there. Maybe we should unwrap them."

Nodding his head in agreement George told the rebels, "Take off your bedrolls and unwrap them!"

Sure enough wrapped up in some oilcloth were an extra forty rounds apiece packaged with musket caps. He looked at one of the packages and it said, 'Richmond Arsenal, 1862' and thinking to himself, These would bring a good price at a Civil War sale. Turning to Josh and Paul, "Do you have any other ammunition on you?"

The two rebels shook their heads no, with a look of helplessness in their eyes.

"We're going to discharge your muskets and give them back to you," George informed them.

That's when Josh and Paul started laughing so hard that they almost fell on the ground.

"What are you laughing about?"

With tears in his eye's Josh replied, "Hell, our muskets weren't loaded nohow, as it was too wet!"

Then it was the re-enactors turn to start laughing, "Our muskets weren't loaded either!"

The whole group had a good laugh. This would probably be the last time any of them would laugh for some time to come.

"I didn't have chance to ask before, but wasn't that Josh fella the same name as the old man told you about?" Jack whispered.

"I'm afraid it is!"

"Damn, this is the worst case scenario!" Jack exclaimed out loud.

Turning to the two rebels George said, "You're free to go, but you should head toward the west and rejoin your regiment."

"I'd rather head home," was Josh's reply.

"You'll never make it, between both armies, there's nowhere to go." George replied. "You'll either wind up dead or in a yankee prison!"

Finally, Josh and Paul believed them and decided to head back to their regiment. Josh spoke for both of them, "We thank you yanks for being kind to me and Paul. I surely hope that we won't meet on the battlefield!" Out of the blue, Josh looked at George's Enfield and exclaimed, "But if we ever meet in the field, I'll surely relieve you of that musket. As I aim to have it."

That statement sent chills up George's spine, as the old man's words came back to him. With that, they all shook hands and George bade them goodbye, "May God be with you in the upcoming days."

The two rebels simply disappeared into the brush silently and were gone.

Tim and Jack started a barrage of questions to George, wanting to know if this was part of what the old man had told him.

George's mind was confused, as thoughts kept crashing into each other. One part of him was saying, this can't be happening and the other side simply saying, yes it is. Finally he put up his hand, for them to stop talking. Then after a pause, he told them in a measured voice, "Everything the old man told me is coming true and it has me scared to hell. Now look, we only have a couple of hours left before we have to start moving. So I'll stay on watch and you two can sleep until it's time to go."

"It's my turn on watch," Tim protested "And I want to hear the rest of what the old man told you."

"Look, after what happened tonight, I could never sleep and I have to sort out my thoughts, so you guys get some sleep. I swear, I'll tell you the whole story tomorrow morning, while we walk. Now before you sack out, we'll divide up the ammo. Make sure you keep it dry!" After they had divided up the ammunition, George repeated, "Now off with you and get some rest. You're going to need it in a couple of hours."

Begrudgingly, Tim and Jack agreed. George went back up the trail to take up the watch again. Tim and Jack put more wood on the fire and laid down to try and get some sleep. Strangely enough, even with all the excitement of the evening, they both fell into a deep sleep as a strange mist closed around them.

* * * * * *

As George sat on watch, he tried to sort out everything that happened since that first day at the re-enactment and that damned old man with a limp. Everything was coming true so far and he felt utterly helpless. If events continued happening as the old man had said, then he and his friends were going to be involved in the ultimate re-enactment in just a few hours. And he couldn't figure any way out, which bothered him more. Throughout his life he had always been in control of events which could affect his life. Even in Vietnam, he had volunteered to go with the marine division as a corpsman. But this time, it was as if the supreme draft notice had been served on him and he would be involved in the Battle of Gettysburg along with his two friends. Now he felt a pang of guilt. Maybe if he had told them what the old man had said before the re-enactment, they may not have been near him when he slipped back into time. But then again, it must have been meant to happen to them also. Damn, if I gave that musket to that rebel, Josh, when they were in camp, maybe lady time would have been satisfied and we would have gone back to the twentieth century. Well too late for that as he could never find them now. Damn, that was dumb.

The mist seemed to be getting heavier and he felt a chill go through his body. That was a weird feeling, he thought. But then everything was weird and he huddled trying to stay warm. Thoughts about the morning started flooding his mind and he wondered if he would be alive at the end of the day. His thoughts turned to the camera, in fact he had a photograph of two live rebel soldiers and of the town. And somehow he would try to get some pictures of the battle, just to prove that he went back in time. But it would only matter if somehow he would be transported back to the future.

George's mind turned to his family and wife Jan. She would be worried sick and maybe somehow, she would know the truth about where he disappeared to. After all, he had told her the story about the old man, even though she didn't believe it. Well anyway, he could hope she would believe it now. And what if he would be killed, how would that affect the future? It was hard to comprehend, in fact he had no idea how it could be. The other possibility was he would survive the war and stay in this time. What would happen to him? Hell, he could be a great soothsayer and predict all the major events down to the day and year. But he never heard of anyone in the 1800s' doing that. Maybe, just maybe, he could advance the medical field. Wasn't he better trained and knew medicines better than any doctor of this time? But, there wasn't anyone who made a major medical break through in that period right after the Civil War. No matter what he thought of, he couldn't remember anything in the history books that would point to someone from the future being back in Civil War times. Another thought crossed his mind, if he had to fight for his life in the days to come, could he take a life. George honestly didn't know, he would have to cross that bridge when he came to it. His mind wandered back to his wife and family. George felt great sadness, knowing he may never see them again. Not to mention the loss they would feel and the uncertainty of his fate if he should be killed or stay in this time.

The sentry brought himself back to reality and looked at the watch. It was hard to see in the darkness, even though the moon was breaking in and out of the clouds which seemed to be thinning out. He finally struck a match and it was just a little after three in the morning. Well, he thought, It's time to get them up and figure out how we're going to meet the army. George crept back into camp. The fire was almost out. Damn, they must have been sound asleep and allowed the fire to go down. George sensed that something was wrong. What was it? Gripping the musket tightly and with every nerve in his body wound tight, he looked intently at the scene in front of him. Even though he was chilled from the mist, he immediately broke into a sweat. George crouched down, wishing that he had loaded his musket, knowing that in this dampness it wouldn't make much difference. Slowly he looked around and in the dim light from the dying fire, it was what he couldn't see, that had heightened his awareness. He couldn't see the sleeping forms of Tim and Jack by the lean to. In a whisper he called out, "Tim, Jack, where are you?"

Finally Jack's voice in the dark answered, "Yo, George, I'm over here, I had to relieve myself."

As Jack came back into camp George asked, "Is Tim with you?"

"No, he was still asleep when I went out to relieve myself. Didn't he go up with you?"

"He didn't come up with me."

"Well, his equipment is gone too. That's strange. Why would he take his musket and stuff just to take a leak," Jack pondered?

"We better look around for him. He can't be very far."

The two men looked around the camp, put more wood on the fire and called out Tim's name. Still no answer came from the darkness.

"Maybe he slipped on the wet rocks," Jack suggested.

The two remaining re-enactors took firebrands from the fire and started searching for their lost friend. They had to return every few minutes to get another firebrand. As hard as they looked, no trace of Tim could be found. George said in a concerned manner, "Maybe those rebs sneaked back into camp and took him!"

"No. I don't think so, they wouldn't have had the time. I was only gone a few minutes," replied Jack with distress in his voice.

They sat by the fire and tried to figure out what had happened. Later George spoke, "We'll have to wait for dawn and try to find him. The brush isn't that thick here, mostly trees and rocks. And if he went out to take a leak, he couldn't have gone very far. He would have probably gone in a northeast direction where its reasonably level, as the ground drops toward the south."

Jack shook his head in agreement. One thing bothered him though, "George, I wonder if maybe Tim slipped back to the future while I was gone?"

"After everything that has happened, I wouldn't be surprised at anything right now." George replied. "However, when we came back in time, we were together. I don't think he would go to the future by himself. Anyway, I still have the musket. No, I think he may be just lost or hurt. Like you said earlier, it's odd that all his equipment is gone too. At first light, we'll look real hard for him." They sat in the light of the warming fire and didn't speak. George and Jack were both engrossed in their own thoughts. When it was light enough to see, the two stranded soldiers built up the fire so they would have a reference point. The men started searching in an ever widening circle, calling out Tim's name, to no avail. After an exhausting search, they returned to the campfire. Their options were shrinking and where was Tim? If the rebels had him, he might be on his way to Libby prison. And if it was the Union, then maybe he was on his way to the army or under arrest for desertion. However, if he went to the future, they were on their own.

"What the hell are we going to do?" George said. "If someone has him, we don't even know where to look. We're running out of time. We'll have a one third chance of finding him if we head to the Union army. If he were picked up by the Provost Guard, they would probably take him to the Bucktail Brigade, as long as he kept to our story. If somehow he went to the twentieth century, we have no chance of finding him, given our present circumstances."

Jack agreed, "You're probably right, we do have to get moving soon. I still have a gut feeling that Tim may have left this time somehow. I have no idea how it could be though. I just hope Tim is safe, wherever he is!"

CHAPTER NINE

After searching around the camp one last time, the two men put out the fire and half heartily started down the round top. When the two men started out, they kept slipping and half falling over the many rocks and downed branches that littered the hill. Now it was easier to walk now as dawn was in full bloom. Both George and Jack spirits were very low with the disappearance of Tim. Worse yet, they were powerless to help him. George told Jack, "I have to share the blame our friend being missing. I was on watch. Damned if I know how someone slipped into camp without me knowing it. However, that's the past now, we have to pull ourselves together and think of our survival."

"You're not to blame, hell I was laying right next to him, just before he disappeared. We're both victims of circumstances beyond our control. So don't think about it, Tim is a big boy and can take care of himself."

George willed himself to think only positive thoughts as he started planning on what to do in the coming battle. He looked at the watch and saw it was nearly 7 a.m., when they were off the round top and back on the dirt, or more accurately, the mud road. The next thing George noticed as he plodded along the road, was the lack of clouds. There were some wispy clouds, but he knew that today they would be of no relief. With the rising humidity his wool uniform felt like it weighed a ton.

"George, did you notice that the rain has stopped

and it's getting awfully hot."

"Amen to that!" George replied. "How in hell did they stand the heat in these uniforms?"

"Well," Jack retorted, "We'll damn soon find out today."

As the two wanderers headed west, they soon passed the Trostle farm, but no activity could be seen around the house. George thought this was unusual. Shortly after they left the farm, the two men came upon a wheat field on the left. The field was golden yellow and ready for harvest. God, George thought, That is the Wheat Field that will become the whirlpool of death tomorrow. As they were approaching the Peach Orchard, the re-enactors heard horses galloping down the Emmitsburg Road. The two men waited for a few minutes before moving on. The sun was getting higher in the sky now and there were some clouds moving lazily along. Not like the past few days, when it was gloomy with rain and mist. Over at the Wentz farm, George could see smoke coming out of the chimney. A man could be seen moving about in the farm yard, spreading feed for the chickens who were running to and fro pecking as if they hadn't eaten in days. Out in the field, the merry tinkling of cow bells could be heard, as the animals foraged for grass in the pastures. George figured it had to be close to 8 a.m. and they had been walking for an hour. The two men were slowed down due to their constant searching for their friend, Tim.

As they stood on the Emmitsburg Road, a very faint crackling noise could be heard off in the northwest, then a rapid succession of rattling musketry. While neither one spoke, the re-enactors knew that the battle had just opened and soon there would be cannon fire. Sure enough, in about ten minutes the booming of the guns followed. Puffs of white smoke could be seen above the trees on McPhersons Ridge. People were gathered in the road looking and pointing toward the rising smoke. If only they knew what the future held for them, they would be packing and getting out of there, George thought.

The two were so engrossed in the start of the battle, they never heard the horses ride up on them!

"Hey soldiers, what are you doing here?"

Startled, they both turned around quickly and the first thing they saw were four Union cavalry soldiers pointing Smith carbines at them. At the outset George was at a loss for words, then he stammered, "Damn, you scared the hell out of me, we're looking for the First Corps."

One of the horsemen edged forward, keeping them covered with his carbine, "Why aren't you men with your regiment? Are you deserters or maybe you're Confederate spies, now which one is it?"

George answered quickly, "We're neither. We've been ordered by Governor Curtin to join the 150th Bucktail Regiment. We've been dodging rebel patrols the last few days. I know the First Corps is in the area. Are you men provost?"

The trooper who had closed on him replied, "Hell no, we ain't no provost, we're couriers from Buford's Cavalry. We just left the First Corps a bit ago. They're back down that road a ways," as he motioned with his gloved hand toward the road intersecting Emmitsburg Road. He lowered his carbine and said, "We ain't got time to mess with you. We have to get back to General Buford real quick like. So we're going to let you go, but as soon as we see some damn provost, we'll tell them about you. If you ain't with the Bucktails when they find you, they'll shoot you down like dogs. So you best be heading down that road to the First Corps or the crows will be picking your bones come tomorrow!"

With that the four horsemen brushed past them

and galloped toward Gettysburg, scattering the civilians who were standing in the road. George and Jack immediately headed west on a dirt road.

"We better stay alert or we'll never make it through the day." George told Jack.

"Shouldn't we be going down Emmitsburg Road, I thought the First Corps came up that road?"

Nodding his head George replied, "I thought so too, but that trooper was very emphatic about them being down this road, so we'll just go that way."

The two re-enactors walked for less than an hour, interspersed by jumping off the road and hiding as mounted couriers rode furiously up and down the road delivering messages. Soon they could smell the smoke of many fires. This meant the First Corps camp area was close by. They crossed what they knew to be Willoughby Run, over a fairly new wooden bridge. After about twenty minutes, they came to a red-covered bridge crossing the Marsh Creek. The two men hid in some brush, as the sounds of approaching troops could be heard. The unmistakable sound of clanging cups, stamping of feet and shouting of orders, filtered through the bridge. Soon the Iron Brigade marched into the covered bridge, with their colors furled. The noise of marching feet was amplified by the confines of the bridge. After about ten minutes, the troops had finally passed. George and Jack jumped back on the road making a mad dash across the bridge before more troops came up.

The two hadn't walked for five minutes when suddenly, two sentries jumped out from behind trees and covered them with their cocked muskets. "Halt and identify yourself," one shouted.

"George Murray and Jack Fretz, Privates assigned to the 150th PVI of the First Corps," George answered.

"What are you men doing out of camp? Don't

move and ground your muskets."

George and Jack immediately complied as the sentry moved toward them while the other sentry kept them covered. "Where are your passes?" He demanded.

"We had passes and letters of introduction from Governor Curtin to proceed from Harrisburg to find the First Corps and the 150th Bucktail Regiment," George told them. "We were jumped by two rebels and lost our knapsacks, which held our passes. Later our one friend disappeared. Maybe he has passed here before us?"

"No one but couriers have passed here. Stand fast and don't move. Jeb over there is real nervous and has a hair trigger." The sentry called up the road in a loud voice, "Corporal of the Guard." Shortly a squad of men double-timed up the road accompanied by a very young corporal. One of the sentries spoke to him and motioned toward George.

The soldier wearing corporal chevrons came over and picked up their muskets. "We're going to march you both over to the Bucktail brigade. They are standing by, ready to march out. We'll see if their colonel will accept you. If not we'll turn you over to the Provost Guard. Now march smartly. Forward march!"

The squad of men fell in around them as they marched toward the camps. As they were being escorted, George saw artillery batteries lined up along the side of the road. The horses were excited and seemed anxious to head toward the sounds of cannon fire. Masses of men in blue uniforms could be seen as far as the lay of the road would allow. In the fields on both sides of the road, Union troops were feverishly breaking camp and loading hundreds of wagons. Soon they came to the head of the waiting column and they were forced to squeeze between the artillery units and the regiments on the road.

After they passed the first regiments in the

column, the group came to the Bucktail Brigade and the corporal approached the first officer he could find and spoke to him. A middle aged officer accompanied by the corporal approached the prisoners. George saluted the officer and identified himself. Jack, following his lead, did the same. The officer returned his salute saying, "I'm Captain Jones of Company B, 150th PVI. If I understand correctly, Governor Curtin sent you. Is that right?"

George replied "Yes sir," and repeated the story he had told the corporal.

Captain Jones questioned the two, "Aren't you two just a bit old to be soldering?"

George replied, "Sir, it was Governor Curtin's intention, that at Colonel Wisters' discretion, we could be assigned to Company K[7] in Washington to free up younger men. But I'm in good shape and I came to fight sir. I would be honored to help in the fight to come." As he finished, George thought to himself, Boy, what a bunch of nonsense I just fed him. I don't want to fight!

The captain turned to the corporal, "Give them back their muskets and I'll take charge of these men."

After saluting the officer, the corporal turned to George and Jack, handing their muskets back,and wished them, "Good luck!"

Captain Jones turned to the new men and simply stated, "Wait here, while I go to Colonel Wister to see where he wishes to put you two."

As George waited, he had a chance to look over some of the troops nearby and it struck him, that most of the men were awfully young. In fact most of them didn't look older the sixteen or seventeen years of age.

---

[7] Co. K stayed in Washington throughout the war as security and body guards for President Lincoln at the Soldiers Home.

That's why the officer had asked them if they weren't too old to fight. Although the captain looked to be in his mid to late thirties.

Captain Jones came back shortly, accompanied by a colonel, who looked to be in his late thirties, was short and thin with a full dark beard laced with a tinge of gray. His piercing eyes commanded immediate attention. George had enough experience in the military to know that this man knew what he was doing and could lead men through the toughest fight. George and Jack came to attention and saluted the colonel, who returned it.

He asked George in a gruff voice, "The captain here said you men were sent by Governor Curtin, and you want to fight and that there were three of you. Is that right?"

"Yes sir," George replied, "Our comrade is missing."

"I'm Colonel Wister and we can use all the help we can get, so I'm going to put you with Captain Jones in Company B. Do you know skirmisher drill?"

George replied "Yes sir."

"Very good, because Co. B is our skirmish company."

He turned to Jack and said "You'll be in Co. A. Captain Widdis is your Company Commander." Turning to Captain Jones, "Take charge of these men. After the fight, we'll get this all straightened out with Governor Curtin, as soon as we establish the telegraph." With that, the colonel was gone and as he made his way up the regiment, George could hear the men cheering him.

The captain turned to the sergeant and told him, "Assign this man a spot in the company. Take this other man to Company A for assignment as per Colonel Wister's orders."

The sergeant shook George's hand and said, "I'm

Sergeant Dickinson and I'll be turning you over to a corporal. I hope you've had some soldering, because I don't think we'll be doing much training today. I've heard that the whole rebel army is just up ahead!"

After George was placed in the ranks, they were called to attention and Sergeant Dickinson said, "We've got a newcomer in the ranks so let's count off by twos." After the count, they were grouped into fours and they became comrades in arms when they formed a skirmish line.

An order was given by an unseen officer, "Stand at rest, men."

The sergeant told everyone, "Drink all the water in your canteens and we'll send runners down to the creek to refill them." As they were resting, everyone started introducing themselves to George, he would never remember all of the names. He made it a point to remember the men in his squad. His file partner was a young lad who introduced himself as "Skeeter." He didn't look much older than sixteen and was really scrawny. Skeeter was trying to grow a beard, but it was laughingly patchy. George hoped this young man would live long enough to grow a real beard. Another man in his squad, who was known as "Sully," was tall and lanky, looked to be nineteen or twenty, with long brown hair which was matted and dirty, freckles and a full dark beard. The other man's name was "Bull." This was understandable, as he was short and stocky, barrel-chested. He had black hair and beard and looked to be in his mid 20's. This was clearly a very powerful man and George was glad he was on his side. Later, George learned that Bull had worked on the wharves in Philadelphia.

Skeeter interrupted George's thoughts, "I'll be behind you and if'n I see you doing something wrong, I'll push you in the right direction. Now you best be getting ready to do some hard marching, drink lotsa water."

Just about that time another sergeant came up and George recognized the chevrons of an Ordnance Sergeant. He grabbed George's musket and looked it over, then stated "First time I've seen a Parker-Hale Enfield musket. When did they start making Enfields?"

"Sergeant that came from a batch of new muskets received by the state."

"Danged, it makes no sense, there's nothing wrong with the other Enfields," the sergeant complained. "Why do they buy the contract muskets? How many rounds do you have?"

"About 40 rounds sergeant."

The non-com reached into his haversack and took out two packages of cartridges and caps and gave them to George.

Turning to the corporal, "Where is that other new fellow?"

Corporal Terry pointed over his shoulder to the front of the regiment, "Company A."

The sergeant left and started toward Company A, threading his way through men and equipment.

Jack meanwhile, had joined Company A, but wished that he could have stayed with George. Maybe later they would be able to get together if they both survived the day. As he looked around he was totally amazed at the amount of men in the fields, horses, wagons and cannons were everywhere. After being put into the ranks, the company counted off by two's and Jack was a two. Since he was "fresh fish," he was in the front rank. His file partner introduced himself as Dean. This young man didn't look older than fifteen or sixteen, had long blond hair, which was unkempt. Dean had a poor excuse for a beard and what surprised Jack most, was his teeth. Although he was young, his teeth were

154

terribly rotted except for his front teeth. Other men came up and introduced themselves to Jack, but his mind was awhirl, he would have had a hard time even remembering his own name at that moment. Looking through the ranks, Jack just saw very young men, even the officers and non-coms looked to be in their early twenties.

The Ordnance Sergeant came up and demanded, "I want to inspect your musket!" The Sergeant looking intently at the reproduction Springfield, exclaimed, "Now I've seen everything, USE BLACK POWDER ONLY! What other kind of powder is there? Come with me to the ordnance wagon and I"ll issue you an Enfield. I don't want any problem with ammunition jamming on the field. I don't like the looks of that musket, mighty poor workmanship, yep, mighty poor."

While at the wagon, the sergeant asked him how much ammunition he had, then gave him enough rounds to make up the required sixty rounds the colonel had directed each man carry this day.

As Jack was going back to his company, his heart was racing a mile a minute. In his hands he was holding an honest to goodness original Enfield!

Around 9:00 a.m., the word was passed to get ready to move out. They waited and waited. "Just like the army, hurry up and wait," George lamented.

Skeeter laughed and replied, "Don't worry, before long you'll wish we were just standing around. One thing for sure in this brigade, no grass will grow under your feet!"

At 9:30 a.m., the regiment started marching up the road toward Gettysburg. Jack could see that the colors were furled and the drummers were beating out a cadence only. As they moved, the heat of the sun, coupled with a lot of moisture in the air, caused them to sweat profusely. Especially George and Jack, they were not used to the heavy wool uniforms. Earlier in the morning the road was muddy. Now the marching feet, rolling wagons and prancing feet of the horses dried up the mud and now choking red clay dust filled the air. The regiment crossed a road, which George knew would be called West Confederate Avenue later. They stopped briefly at a stone farmhouse where runners came through each company to gather canteens which had been emptied. These runners went to the well next to the house, filling them with cool water. As the canteens were passed out, everyone took deep swigs of the refreshing water to help wash out the dust.

While they were resting, George watched as another Division of the First Corps turn and started at the double-quick up West Confederate Avenue, toward the sound of the fighting.

After the brief respite, the officers issued orders and the regiment started marching again, on the same road the two re-enactors had passed over earlier. Soon the regiment turned left on the Emmitsburg Road moving relentlessly toward the sound of battle. Cannons could be heard booming in the distance and increased in volume with every passing yard. While they were advancing, terrified civilians were streaming down the road in wagons, carriages and on horseback. However, as the columns of soldiers approached, they had to pull to the side and wait for the army to move on. George noticed they didn't speak to the soldiers. They appeared to be in shock, terror showing in their eyes. George saw a young farmer and his wife sitting in a wagon waiting for the troops to pass. The wagon was piled high with everything they owned. A cow and a calf were tied to the rear of the wagon. George wondered to himself, If these people would ever have a home to return to. The musket fire was increasing rapidly in the distance, interspersed with the louder reports of cannon fire.

Both George and Jack knew they were about to relive history. Even knowing the dangers facing them, they were both excited only as a soldier can be, when entering combat. Several times they had to move off to the side of the road to give the cannons and caissons the right of way. When they were about a mile from Gettysburg the column stopped, while a mounted staff aide conversed with the officers of the division. This officer was sitting on a beautiful chestnut mare, with a diamond shaped white spot on its' head.

Jack while looking at a stone farmhouse thought to himself, Well there's the Codori house again. He could see one of the staff officers pointing to the left toward the fields and talking to the Brigade Commander, Colonel Stone, but he couldn't hear what they were saying. Colonel Wister left the impromptu meeting and told the men, "We'll leave the road here and quick time across the fields toward the fight over yonder!"

An area of fencing had been torn down earlier and you could easily see where the Iron Brigade had trampled down the corn and wheat fields. As they were double timing across the undulating fields, Jack thought he was going to fall down. His legs hurt bad, and they felt like rubber, but he willed himself to make it.

Being much older, George wasn't faring as well, his legs were holding up OK. What finally did him in, were the side stickers. He doubled up in pain and somehow found himself off to the side, as the regiments went rushing by. As he lay on the ground even the act of breathing hurt, that tears came to his eyes. The fatigued soldier knew that he had to drink a lot of water to avoid heat exhaustion. But the side stickers hurt like hell and he had great difficulty even reaching his canteen. After about ten minutes and a long swig of water, he managed to look around at the troops still double timing past him. Wherever he looked,

George could see men on the ground, some just lying there breathing deeply, others had the dry heaves and some were trying to get up but stumbling and falling. The former corpsman wondered how many of these men would be dead soon, from heat stroke. With the help of his musket, George managed to get up on wobbly legs and start walking. A rather young, stout officer with a Bucktail on his hat approached. He was gathering up stragglers, which were many and shepherding them toward the sound of battle. George fell in with them and hobbled along with the rest. He hurt everywhere despite thinking he was in such good shape. Now he was eating humble pie.

* * * * *

Meanwhile, Jack was struggling to keep up, every muscle in his body was screaming in agony. He kept drinking water as he was double timing, but it streamed out of his pores and his uniform was completely soaked, even his leather accouterments. The sounds of musket fire were getting very loud and heavy smoke could be seen rising from the woods to their front left. Cannon balls could be heard hissing overhead, which Jack knew would be coming from Herr Ridge. Then he heard another shell pass overhead, this one made a weird noise that was half screech and half moan. What the hell was that, he thought to himself. He remembered something about breech loading cannons the rebels had. They were still about 500 yards from the Seminary, but he knew he would make it. All along the way he could see discarded knapsacks and bed rolls. The men who had passed earlier had rid themselves of the extra weight, probably from exhaustion. As he was double timing, Jack saw his first dead men, the first of many he would see this day. There were three of them and they looked like rag dolls thrown in the field. Passing them, he could see the effects a Civil War solid shot to a human body. One man had no chest at all, just a head and arms being held together by shreds of clothing. Another man had no lower torso and the third had no head. There was blood everywhere, which was turning black and already the flies were swarming over the corpses. Jack started to upchuck, much to the dismay of the man ahead of him, fortunately just missing him.

"Damn you sunvbich, if your going to heave, do it to the side, or I'll tear your heart out with my bare hands."

Several men started laughing and one shouted, "You should've puked on Mac. He ain't had no bath in a month."

Mac yelled back, "I'll tear your arm off and shove it!"

A Corporal yelled, "Knock it off, we've got work to do just ahead. Save your fighting for the rebs."

As they approached the Seminary, more bodies could be seen scattered around the fields toward the McPherson Ridge, including several horses and a caisson which had been shattered by a cannon ball. One wheel was gone and white cylindrical packages were scattered all over. The brigade stopped at the base of Seminary Ridge and the officers shouted for the men to stack their knapsacks and everyone who still had them, gladly did. Jack was thankful they had stopped, as he couldn't have run another yard. He drank heavily of the warm water in his canteen. Jack looked for George, but couldn't see him anywhere in Company B. Jack's uniform was wringing wet, including his shoes and the sweat running in his eyes burned like hell. His mind was in a whirl, Jack was about to relive history first hand.

Colonel Wister shouted, "Unfurl the colors, Bucktails. Forward at the double quick. March!"

Quickly a chorus of voices went up, "Say colonel, shouldn't we load up?" After the laughter died down, the colonel told the men to load.

Jack started loading with shaking hands. After getting the powder down the barrel, he started the Minie ball down the barrel. Without thinking, he started to slap the side of the stock. It occurred to him, Damn, I've got to use the ram rod and push the bullet down. Jack managed quite clumsily to ram the bullet down the barrel, almost dropping the ram rod. Unfortunately for Jack, a corporal had noticed his awkward attempt at loading, "Before this day is over," he snarled, "you'll know how to load your musket or you'll be dead!"

* * * * * *

As Jack went into action, George was moving up the ridge with the other stragglers and he too could see the effects of the cannon fire. Several dead horses lay by a wrecked caisson and he could see several men taking the harnesses off them. Bodies lay scattered around the field. Some of them looking just like lumps of rags. George noticed four men carrying a body on a litter, moving slowly from the area of Herbst Woods. What caught his attention were the men carrying the litter. They were wearing bright red pants! Following slowly behind the litter bearers were a horse and a rider. George saw the horse had a blue saddle blanket with a border of gold and gold stars. This told George it belonged to a general officer. But it didn't appear to be a general riding the horse. It had to be General Reynold's horse, he was the only general killed on

McPherson Ridge. George couldn't stop to find out and soon the horse and men were out of sight in a gully.

When they reached the Seminary, he could see piles of personal equipment where the regiments had stacked them by companies. Each company had assigned a man to guard them. He knew that by the end of the day the Confederates would have the knapsacks. Off in the distance he could see large puffs of white smoke as the cannons on Herr Ridge opened up on them. Next George heard the whirring of cannon balls flying closely overhead. Looking up toward the sound, he could actually see the ball in flight, trailing a faint stream of smoke. WHAM, CRASH, the one shell exploded right behind him while it was still 20 feet in the air. Immediately he heard the whirling of shrapnel which just missed his head and then a blood curdling scream. Instantly, the soldier in front of him had no left arm or shoulder and blood was spurting everywhere. The man fell to the ground screaming and thrashing around in agony.

George instinctively ran to the man to render first aid, when an officer screamed at him, "You can't help him, keep moving up."

Damn, you've got to forget you were a corpsman or you'll screw up history for sure, he thought to himself.

The officer yelled at the men to keep moving as they advanced across a shallow ravine, then up the hill. When they topped the hill, McPhersons farm, lay just in front of them. George could see the Bucktail Regiments forming in their front and on the right. Across the rolling fields to the right he could see regiment upon regiment lined up toward Oak Hill. Heavy firing could be heard in the woods to his left, where he knew the Iron Brigade lay. Great palls of smoke was rising above the trees and the cannon fire was intense from in front of him and from his right. Soon he would be caught up in the maelstrom of battle and God willing, he would survive. He started praying to himself, "Dear God let me live out the day and somehow, don't let me take a life!"

* * * * *

After Josh and Paul left the re-enactors, they had moved down a rutted logging road. They went around the base of the Little Round Top as the moon broke through the clouds. In the light, boulders could be seen scattered on the small hill.

Neither said any thing for a while. Then Paul spoke, "Josh, do you reckon we oughta go back there and jump them yanks and get our ammunition back? Maybe take them prisoner. That way if the provost get us, we can say we were out getten yanks?"

Josh thought for a moment, "Naw, them bluebellies were all right. I would want them no harm. I don't know why I got so all fired up about that yank's gun. It ain't no different than any other musket. But I just had the funniest feeling I ever did had, like it was the Holy Grail or something." The rebels walked silently from there on, each deep in his own thoughts of what was going to happen to them in the coming days. The two men walked west, cutting through pastures and unharvested wheat fields. As they started climbing a small ridge, they heard several horses galloping by, just ahead of them. The two soldiers crouched down in some bushes as the riders passed them only ten feet away. In the moon light, they could see they were cavalry, but they couldn't tell if they wore blue or grey uniforms.

162

"Damnation, ifn that weren't close," Paul whispered, "I couldn't tell ifn they were yankies or our boys."

"Them were federals for sure, their uniforms were too dark to be grey. We best be movin real quiet like and keep headin fer that yonder ridge. Thems probably part of a cavalry screen for the yank army, which means they are mighty close."

So they moved across the road and down the hill, crossed a stream, then up the next hill. They kept skirting small groups of men scattered all over, who were talking in low tones. They could see the glow of pipes as some of the men smoked. The wet grass helped to quiet their footsteps and they managed to get by unobserved, past the yankee troops. After they had passed Herr Ridge, they crossed a couple streams and by this time dawn was starting to break. They saw very few houses, but corn and wheat fields were abundant. The scattered houses were interspersed with pastures and grazing cattle, horses and sheep.

The rebels were just passing one of the farm houses, which had smoke curling out of its chimney. The front porch door opened and a man came out with one suspender over his shoulder and one hanging loose at his side. He was walking toward the outhouse and was just about to open the door when he spied the two Confederate soldiers. His eyes opened wide, his mouth dropped open, then without a word, he ran for the house, disappeared through the door and slammed it shut.

"Did you see the look on that fellas face, it was as if he saw a ghost," Josh chuckled. "Sure do hope he don't hafta clean a mess out of his pants."

Josh and Paul hiked about a half mile past the house, when they were surprised by four men who had their muskets leveled on them.

"What are you two doin here? Are you shirkers or what?" One of the soldiers asked.

"Naw, we're just lost and trying to find the 26th North Carolina," Josh answered. "Who are you boys?"

"We're skirmishing for Archer's Division and they be right behind us."

"Why have you skirmishers stopped moving?" Demanded an officer who came up on the group.

"Sur, we jest found these two men thar," and motioned toward Josh and Paul.

"You men pass through this line and turn yourselves into the provost back yonder, I don't have men to spare to send you back, there may be yanks up ahead," the officer told them sternly.

"Sir, we just slipped through the enemy lines . . ."

Raising his sword, the officer screamed at them, "Damn't I told you men to move and don't you ever speak to an officer without permission, now move!"

So Paul and Josh moved through the skirmish line and when they were out of hearing range of the officer, Josh just said, "What an uppity mule's ass, some good men are gonna be killed because he ain't got no horse sense. And I ain't turning myself in to no provost, we'll just try to find our regiment."

Paul nodded his head in agreement. They went about 100 yards when they heard a single shot ring out behind them. Turning, they couldn't see who fired the shot, but they did see the skirmishers start firing over toward the nearby road. Well, they knew something was about to start and they moved more quickly toward the line of troops coming toward them with their colors floating in the breeze. The two soldiers moved quickly through the lines of Archer's Brigade and in short time came upon their regiment.

CHAPTER TEN

Tim woke up slowly, he felt groggy and completely worn out. He lay there for a few minutes trying to sort out what was happening. He noticed that it was dawn and it wasn't drizzling any more. Something wasn't right and Tim rolled over to nudge Jack, however no one was there! The puzzled soldier immediately realized the lean-to and fire weren't there either. What the hell is going on, Tim thought to himself? Did he wander off in the night? Slowly he got up and looked around in the gathering light and there was the rock they had slept by the night before. The area didn't look right. There were too many trees, also they were much bigger. Tim left his musket and his accouterments lay on the ground and eased back down the hill from the rock, slowly turning around. He rubbed his eyes and said out loud, "What the hell is that?" There, less than 100 feet away, was a macadam road! Tim turned back to the rock and another shock awaited him. There was a monument on top of the rock! Abruptly he stopped, then sat on a small rock. His knees felt like they were going to buckle. His mind was in total pandemonium, what was happening or maybe he was having a bad nightmare. This was the Little Round Top, but why was he here and where were his friends? Maybe he was dreaming. If he were dreaming this, why wasn't he back in camp? Yesterday or whatever day it was, Tim had been back in 1863 with his friends or so it seemed. God, what have I done? Did I come back alone because of what I planned to do? Maybe they are here somewhere. Again he looked around and the monument was still there, so was the road and what looked like a horse trail nearby.

Finally Tim said out loud, "Get yourself together, you've got to find George and Jack. They must be close by, then maybe you can figure out what is happening." Slowly he walked back up to the rock and looked around intently. He could find no evidence of the camp fire or the lean-to they had built. "Jack, George where are you," he shouted at the top of his lungs. There was no sound except the birds singing and squirrels rummaging through the leaves. Tim wandered around for over a half hour, calling out the names of his friends. The confused re-enactor had a sinking feeling in the pit of his stomach. If this wasn't a dream and his friends weren't here, then what had happened to them? Maybe, just maybe, they were back in camp and this all could be solved.

Suddenly, he heard a sound of some one approaching and feeling greatly relieved shouted out, "Hey, Jack and George, I'm over here!"

* * * * *

Ranger Janet Bullock enjoyed the early morning hours in Gettysburg Park, especially during the summer months. When she worked the day shift, she would rise at dawn and jog around the Little Round Top before going to work. The early morning work-out cleared her head and the silence of the park allowed her to prepare for another busy day in the park. As she jogged, Janet couldn't help but think how lucky she had been, landing this job three years ago. To work in Gettysburg National Military Park was a prime assignment.

Although Janet enjoyed her present assignment, there were the occasional problems caused by visitors to the park. Most of these problems were inconsequential, however, on occasional there would be vandalism or thefts of plaques from the mounuments. Like the time three enterprising youths who removed items from several regimental markers and tried to sell them to an antique dealer a few short miles away in Maryland. For the most part, the visitors were good, and Janet enjoyed the challenge of answering the thousands of questions about the park and the battle. She also knew that no matter how well she answered the questions, some of the visitors would never fully comprehend the reality of what took place on the battlefield. Even she couldn't fathom the full reality of how they fought here. Sure, she knew all the troop movements by heart, but she really couldn't imagine thousands of men battering themselves to death against the mass of lead and iron that rained down on them as if in a violent thunderstorm of hell.

As she jogged past the 20th Maine position, she heard someone shouting from the heavily wooded area beyond. As she scanned the area, Janet couldn't locate the source of the noise, so she decided to check the underbrush in the area. It was now past sunrise and she noticed there were no cars parked in the area, and there were no vehicles riding through the park. As she continued to investigate, Janet thought that maybe someone was lost or injured. Because she jogged in the early morning hours, she always carried her portable radio and a snub-nosed revolver in her fanny pack. Believing that someone was in trouble, Janet called headquarters on her radio and requested back-up rangers and park officers respond to assist in the search.

After calling for her back-up, Janet continued to survey the area. While she searched, a person could still be heard calling. She edged up to a rock, stopped and listened, trying to pinpoint the direction of the shouting. As she paused, Janet heard the voice exclaim, Damn it, George and Jack, where in the hell are you?" Janet was struck by the obvious hysterics of the caller. Slowly, she edged around the rock, all the while trying to be quiet. However, she stepped on a branch, which snapped. In the silence of the early morning, the crack sounded more like an entire tree falling.

Again Janet heard the voice call out. This time the caller seemed more relieved saying, "Hey! Jack and George, I'm over here!" The ranger continued the rest of the way around the rock, and much to her surprise, she saw what appeared to be a re-enactor in a muddy and torn Union uniform. Janet called out, "You there, what's the problem?"

"I'm looking for my friends. I can't find them."

"I'm Ranger Bullock and I want you stay right where you are! Turnaround and place your hands on the back of your head. You're breaking park rules by being on park property after hours."

Tim started to protest, "I don't know what's happening, I lost my friends."

The ranger replied, "What are you doing here and what about your friends?" Janet stayed where she was, keeping her hand in her fanny pack grasping her pistol. She didn't know what this was all about and she wasn't taking any chances.

"Ma'am, I lost my friends. When I went to sleep last night, my two friends were with me. When I woke up a little while ago, they were gone."

Janet heard the park vehicle arrive, she called down and told the officer that she was below the 20th Maine boulder.

Park Officer James Hamilton walked to the side of Janet and asked, "What's going on?"

Pointing to the re-enactor, Janet replied, "When I found him, he was calling out for his friends, who must be around here."

"Come over here and keep your hands where I can see them," Hamilton instructed Tim.

Janet maintained the cover position as the officer frisked Tim. When he was satisfied that Tim had no weapons he asked the re-enactor what his name was and what was he doing on park property at this time of day.

The displaced re-enactor recounted the story to the policeman on his trip to the past and back.

"Do you expect me to believe that story? You said you have a musket and real Civil War ammunition? Where is it?"

"Sir it's up there by the 20th Maine rock, right where we were sleeping."

"Janet, will you go up to the rock and see if his equipment is up there like he claims?"

Hamilton motioned for Tim to sit on a rock, "What are your friends names and addresses?"

While the park officer was questioning the suspect, Janet Bullock went over and picked up Tim's musket, leather accouterments and bayonet. As she walked back, she started looking in the ammunition pouch and it appeared he did have Civil War era cartridges.

Tim asked Hamilton, "Can you have someone look for my friends? I've told you the whole story, but I'm scared for my comardes."

Janet walked over to Jim and talked to him in a low voice and showed him the contents of the ammunition pouch.

"Mr. Fretz, it does appear that you have live

ammunition and primers with your equipment. Don't you know it's illegal to have these on park property along with your musket and bayonet?" Officer Hamilton asked Tim.

"Sir, I've told you the absolute truth about what happened. If you find my friends, they will tell you the same thing."

"Mr. Fretz, we have to handcuff you and take you in. This is procedure and we must do it. Turn around and put your hands behind your back."

"Does this mean I'm under arrest?"

"Yes you are and I'll read your Miranda Rights to you now." After reading Tim his rights, Hamilton informed the prisoner, "We're going to take you in for further questioning shortly. What is your full name and social security number?" After writing down the information, the officer said "Stay here with Ranger Bullock."

Turning to Janet, "I'll put his equipment in the trunk and run him and his friends through NCIC to see if there are any warrants on them."

A few minutes later he returned, "Janet this man matches one of the missing men from the re-enactment last week. Also before we take him to HQ, the Secret Service would like to talk to him since he was armed. Some more men are coming out to mount a search for his two friends. The Secret Service is sending out two K-9 teams to help out."

In a pleading voice, Tim asked, "What about my friends, I can't just leave them out here."

"If your friends are out here, we'll find them, so don't worry about them."

Turning to Janet, "Take the prisoner to my vehicle. We'll wait for the search teams to get here, just in case his friends show up."

Janet took the prisoner down the dirt trail to the

park vehicle and put Tim in the back seat.

"Ma'am, why am I under arrest? I didn't do anything wrong."

"We'll talk about this later, so just be quiet."

Janet thought to herself, In two days, the President of the United States would be here to rededicate the Peace Memorial. This so-called re-enactor has live rounds in his pouch, plus two friends he's looking for, possibly they are assassins.

Tim was in total shock. He couldn't believe this was happening. He was under arrest, he had lost his friends and nobody was going to believe his story. How would he explain the live ammunition. They won't believe that he traveled in time. How did he manage to show up here? This is the worst nightmare he had ever endured and now handcuffed like a common criminal. Hell he didn't even know what day it was. He wondered where his wife was. She must be frantic at his disappearacnce, or what happened to his friends. Surely, they came back too, but where were they. Maybe they were back at the re-enactment camp or in town at the motel. Tim's mind was in total chaos and his thoughts were jumbled together. When he was seated in the back seat of the vehicle he tried to ask Ranger Bullock, "What day is it?"

"I told you not to say anything, you'll get a chance to talk later."

Damn, Tim thought, They won't even tell me what day it is, what the hell is making them so nervous. It can't just be that they found me on park property with live rounds. No, it has to be something that has happened, or about to happen. But for the life of him, he couldn't imagine what. Meanwhile, he could see Officer Hamilton by the left front of the vehicle, looking around intently with binoculars as Ranger Bullock was standing by Tim's door looking to the rear. Soon he saw three vehicles tearing up the road with their emergency lights flashing. They pulled into the small parking area and Tim could see five additional officers talking with the arresting officer while Janet Bullock kept guard over him. He could see Hamilton pointing to the area around the 20th Maine monument gesturing to the right and the left.

Jim Hamilton came over, opened the drivers door, looked in at Tim, "Tell me where your friends are, it may go a little easier for you. We have canine units enroute, and they will be searching the area and if your friends are out there, the dogs will find them."

Tim, in a wavering voice replied, "Look, I don't know what's going on and I have no idea what happened to my friends and that's the honest to Gods truth."

Hamilton stared at him, shrugged his shoulders and turned to Janet Bullock, "The others can handle the search, hop in"

After entering, he started the vehicle and called in to notify HQ that he was proceeding as per his instructions.

Tim heard the conversations between HQ and the car, but didn't understand all the codes they were using on the radio. Still he had a terrible feeling that he was in big trouble and he would soon know what was happening. The ride back was uneventful and soon they drove down a long stone and heavily rutted driveway. Up ahead he could see a large stone farmhouse, with a trailer along one side and a satellite dish mounted on top. There were at least two dozen antennas of various sizes mounted on top. Also, there were several cars, vans and a helicopter. As they were driving, Tim had been so engrossed in his predicament, that he hadn't paid attention where they had gone and now had no idea where he was. As they stopped by the house, two men came outside on the porch wearing dark suits. This seemed strange to Tim at this time of the morning.

The car lurched to a stop and Hamilton jumped out of the car, opening the door by Tim. Reaching in, he helped the prisoner out of the car by his arm. This hurt Tim like hell, since his hands were still handcuffed behind him. Tim started to complain but thought the better of it. He was lead up to the porch and presented to the two dark suited men.

"This is the suspect we found up on the Little Round Top and I believe he had live ammunition on his person." The park officer informed the older of the two men.

The older man nodded, then motioned to another man in a dark suit to take Tim inside. Tim was lead into a small room which looked like it had been a sitting room. There were several file cases and a long folding table. A map hung on one wall, with colored pins stuck all over and several folding chairs scattered around the room. Tim was placed in one of the chairs as the agent stood guard over him. The room was lit with banks of fluorescent lights, which made the room extremely bright. From another room, Tim could hear the ticking and whirring of electronic equipment. He could hear the chatter of several radios, as police and other agencies had their usual early morning banter between cars.

"Officer Hamilton and Ranger Bullock, I'm Special Agent Tom Gallager. Did the suspect make any verbal threats on the President while you had him in custody?"

"No sir, nothing at all," Hamilton answered.

"Ok, you can wait outside while I question the man."

"I don't think so," the park officer replied, "He's my prisoner."

"He may be your prisoner, but this matter could

be national security. So like I said, wait out here."

"Like hell I will. I want my prisoner back, now!"

The older man glared at Hamilton, "If you value your career, backoff. I just envoked Presidential Security. Enough said. You wait here!"

Heading for the vehicle, Hamilton said to Janet,"Come with me, I'm calling for the superintendent, I don't buy this security bullshit. That man is my prisoner and I won't have anyone screw up this arrest, not even the Secret Service. Those people are pompous assholes!"

After reaching HQ on the radio, Jim was informed by his supervisor that the superintendent was away at a meeting and couldn't be disturbed. He would be back later in the morning. The supervisor told him that he was on his way out."

"I'm Special Agent in Charge Tom Gallager of the U. S. Secret Service, and this is Special Agent Bob Muncy" he informed Tim. "What is your name and address?"

The re-enactor felt the blood rush to his head as he heard the word Secret Service. He was totally disoriented, as he answered the question like a robot.

After Tim had given his name and address, the agent continued, "I understand you were found on park property with a musket and live cartridges, so how about telling me what you were doing."

Tim was totally confused, he knew from the way the rangers had acted, that he could possibly be in some very serious trouble. But he couldn't figure out why the Secret Service was involved for firearms violation in a National Park. If his friends were really hurt, he couldn't risk their lives. Anyway, he didn't do anything wrong and somehow the truth would come out. He would put his faith in God and tell them the whole story.

He asked Agent Gallager, "Shouldn't I have a lawyer present?"

"Mr. Fretz, I only want to know what happened out there on Little Round Top. There are other factors here that need my undivided attention. All I want to know is what transpired this morning.

Tim laid out the whole story as he knew it, from the beginning to the end. As he told them what happened, the looks of disbelief was quite evident on the faces of the agents. When he finished, Agent Gallager motioned for the agent to stay with Tim, while he went and talked to the park personnel.

Tim looked around the room, trying to find something that would give him a hint of why the Secret Service was involved. There was a large map on the wall which was very detailed, showing the entire park, roads, houses, woods, trees and just about everything an army would need to know for a battle. He thought to himself, Damn, if Lee had a copy of that map, the battle may have turned out very differently. But as he looked at the map something wasn't quite right, then it dawned on him! The location on the map depicting the Peace Memorial was marked with an X, with ever widening circles eminating from the X. Handwritten notes were scattered throughout the map. That's strange, Tim thought, What in the world was so important about the Peace Memorial. Try to think! Damn, he thought, I can't think of anything. Wait a minute, that's right, the President of the United States is supposed to rededicate the monument on the third of July. That's why they're so nervous. Once they find out, I'm telling the truth, everything will be OK. Anyway, by now my wife has notified them I'm missing.

Hamilton's supervisor, Sergeant Larry Huff flew up the driveway spewing dust and stones from the tires. He stopped behind the other park vehicle and jumped out as Jim and Janet went to meet him. "What's going on here? Did they let you back in with your suspect

175

yet?"

"No, the Secret Service have him inside right now and I have no idea what's happening."

"OK, let's go to the house and try to get in."

The three of them approached the front door which two Secret Service agents were guarding. "We want to get our prisoner back. Let us in right now!"

"No one goes in until the agent in charge says it's Ok," the one agent informed them.

"This is bullshit. No one screws with my officers and their prisoner. You get that asshole agent in charge out here right now, or I'm going to walk right over you."

The hostile confrontation was defused as Gallager came outside.

"I'm that asshole, Special Agent Tom Gallager. Just settle down and listen. My only concern with your prisoner is to make sure that he doesn't pose a threat to the President. You can come in now, but I will ask all the questions for now. I'm not trying to infringe on your turf. But just bear with me, this is a very interesting story and I have some additional information which may shed some light on this episode.

The sergeant cooled down somewhat, "Sir, we'll go along with you for the moment, but don't forget, he's our prisoner."

"How could I forget? You keep reminding me."

The group went inside and entered Gallager's temporary office. Agent Gallager settled himself into his chair, behind his portable desk, as the others grabbed chairs and sat down in a semicircle around his desk. Tom spoke first, "I'm not sure what to make of this story. I know it's bogus, but I can't figure out what the angle could be. This does seem to tie in with the disappearance last week. Did they find his buddies yet?" He asked of nobody in particular.

One of the other agents answered, "No, we sent

two teams out and they have two dogs out there right now. We haven't found anyone else, but there is something a little strange. They tried to get the dogs to backtrack on that guy, just to find out where he started out from. However the dogs just keep working in a very small area, just as if he just appeared out of nowhere. This doesn't make sense, because the dogs will follow the scent of the person, as well as the vegetation that is crushed as the person walks. The K9 handlers have never seen a situation like this before."

Agent Gallager turned to Hamilton and Bullock asking them to tell him everything that transpired. He listened intently, then asked for the musket and ammunition pouch. He looked at the musket and saw that it was made in Italy. Opening the ammunition pouch, he took out one of the white packages and embossed on the label was Richmond Arsenal 1862. He turned the small package over, then slowly and carefully opened up the package. Inside there were ten loaded paper cartridges and a smaller package about the diameter of a pencil and as long as the cartridges. Opening the smaller package revealed copper percussion caps.

"If I didn't know better, I would say that you have in your hands, original Civil War cartridges and percussion caps in pristine condition," Ranger Bullock said. "But it's not possible, as the copper caps would be discolored and those are shiny as the day they were made. Why don't we open one of the cartridges? Maybe there's no powder in them and they are just dummy cartridges."

"Sounds like a good idea," Tom agreed as he tore open one of the cartridges and poured out the contents. There on the table was what appeared to be coarse black powder.

"I've seen modern black powder and I've seen

black powder from the Civil War, from our collection," Ranger Bullock told them. "I'll stake my reputation on that being identical to the Civil War powder, just by its texture."

"We can easily tell if its modern black powder, just by burning it," Tom replied. "All modern black powder has tagging agents incorporated, which will leave some residue, like little colored balls. And if it's old powder, it won't have any tagging remnants. Take some outside and burn it on a piece of glass or something. It won't be a scientific test, but just a field test to see what we have here."

Jim Hamilton went outside with two agents, and after a few minutes came back inside and brought the piece of glass over to Tom to look at. As hard as they looked, there was no evidence of any tagging agents in the residue.

Ranger Bullock turned to Tom and said, "This doesn't prove anything, maybe they came across some old powder somewhere. There's still a lot of original powder around in private collections." Meanwhile Officer Hamilton had been fingering the opened cartridge and had squeezed out the Minie ball from the paper. He spoke in a low voice "Janet, I want you to look at this Minie. If I didn't know better, I would say that this is an original Minie ball!"

Tom came over as Janet was examining the object and asked Janet, "What's wrong with the bullet?"

Janet didn't say anything at first, then held the bullet up for the agent to see, replying, "What we have here, is a swaged Minie. This was made by forcing lead through a swaging die. If you look in the base you will see a star-like pattern. This was made by the tool which pushed the lead through the swaging die. Many of these type minies were issued to the troops. It looks freshly swaged." Janet continued, "I can't believe that an original minie would be in as good a condition as these. Today, I don't know of anyone who swages minies just like the original, but they pour them in molds."

Tom sat there for a minute running his hand over his chin, deep in thought. Then he turned to one of the agents and said "Bob, we have a missing person report last week on three re-enactors from the re-enactment last weekend. Pull that file and any updates. As of the last night, they hadn't found those guys and possibly he may be one of them." He turned to the rest of them and said, "OK, now let's now lay out all the facts we have. I want to get this settled quickly, we have a lot of work to do in the next three days. If this fellow turns out not to be a threat, we'll turn him over to the park service to do what they want with him."

The other agent came out of the back room used as a file room, holding a large bulging envelope with papers and a video tape. He took material out of the folder spreading everything out on the table. The contents included a sheaf of stapled papers compiled by the Secret Service. The folder contained information about the missing re-enactors. Tom took the report and glanced through it quickly, as he had gone over and over the report during the past week, urged on by some unseen force. Tom spoke slowly, "I don't know why, but this missing person report has had me intrigued for a week now. Now we only have two missing, this fellow matches Tim Fretz to the 'T'. These people supposedly vanished in front of witnesses last week and at the same time a fellow videotaped the supposed disappearance. The FBI analyzed the tape and as far as they could find, it was authentic and not tampered with. One thing that was odd on the tape, was the appearance of fog, but it only lasted about thirty frames, just when they disappeared. The FBI analyst indicated that this was very unusual, when a lens fogs over, it won't clear up that quickly."

Gallager was still perplexed, he couldn't figure out how one re-enactor could reappear and show up five miles away on Little Round Top, while his two companions had not reappeared. This was really getting to Tom. As he continued to run the events through his mind, he reached into his pocket and pulled out a pack of antiacids and popped two into his mouth. The stress of this problem in conjunction with Presidential security had caused Tom's stomach to churn.

Tom continued, "Gentlemen and lady, on the third I have the President of the United States coming for the rededication of the Peace Memorial and I'm still missing two re-enactors. Now what the hells going on around here? Anybody have any ideas?"

Bob, the agent who had retrieved the file, started the impromptu briefing on what had transpired since the original disappearance. "The state police originated the report, followed up by interviews with all the witnesses, the tape and a general search of the entire re-enactment site for two days. Also, the Chief of Police in Gettysburg has been pulling his hair out with the irate wives of the re-enactors. One of the wives was still in town, constantly calling everyone who could possibly help them. Thank God they hadn't gotten our phone number!"

At that point Tom broke in, "On the 27th, I interviewed the wives and the one wife told an interesting story that her husband relayed to her on the day of his disappearance. I also have some agents in South Carolina trying to track down a gentleman who may or may not have some part in this story. Unfortunately we don't have a name of this person yet, however we know he owns a general store. Somehow the gentleman told the one re-enactor that the musket he was using, had been in his collection some years ago.

Mrs. Murray said her husband didn't believe the story, because his musket wasn't even manufactured when it was in that supposed collection. I don't know what the significance of the discussion was, but I'm sure we'll know soon."

One of the agents asked, "Do you want me to call the suspect's wife, to see if she can identify him?"

Tom looked at him with a look that made the agent realize that he had made a mistake. Tom with obvious anger in his voice said, "The one thing I don't need right now is a high-strung wife out here screaming at me. No, we'll keep him here out of sight until we can figure the possibilities. In fact we'll try to keep him from calling for his lawyer, as long as possible. It's not that I want to deny his rights, but his lawyer will want to contact his wife right away and I don't want this to get out until I've figured out what's happening."

Another agent stuck his head around the corner, "Boss, I've got Agent Stoner from the Spartenburg office on the horn and he has that information you wanted."

Tom sprang from his seat and quickly crossed the room in a couple of long strides and went into the communications room. When he answered, the voice on the other end spoke in only a way that close friends would talk, "Tom, this is Bucky Stoner, how in the hell are you and the family. I haven't spoke to you for several months, and if I remember correctly, you and the missus were coming down to visit."

Tom sighed, "Bucky, I don't want to cut you short, but I may have a crisis here. Do you have anything on that guy down there?"

"Tom no problem, I'll get to the point. I found that fellow, his name is Bill Sloan Jr., and he is a retired general store owner, over in a small town known as Landis Corner. And he says he did go to Gettysburg last week to warn a re-enactor about a musket that had been in his collection and had disappeared in the mid 70's. Now the story he told me, about that musket, will make your hair stand up. Don't think for a minute, that I believe any of this hogwash. I'll lay out the whole story and what I have been told by the locals that really makes this story sound believable." He spent almost an hour on the phone before he finally finished.

Tom sat at the desk looking over the notes he had scribbled and didn't know what to say to the agent. Finally he spoke softly, "Bucky, I appreciate what you've done, but I have a gut feeling about this. I want you to go back to Mr. Sloan and see if you can dig up anything else. There's something missing, but I can't put my finger on it. Give me a call back when you finish and let me know if you found anything else. Also I promise, that after I've wrapped up this detail, the wife and I will come down to visit. I need a break. So take care and tell Katey I said hello and miss her." Wearily, he hung up the phone.

He just sat there completely engrossed by what his friend had told him, trying to grasp a hold of something that would tell him that this was all a ruse. But no matter how he looked at this, nothing in what the suspect had told him, nor the evidence gathered so far, could point to this whole story being anything but the truth. Worse still, the information gathered by Bucky made the story more believable. From his years of experience he did believe the suspect, his demeanor and the way he spoke didn't fit the profile of a potential assassin. But there was another thing he could do right now. Turning to the door, he called out, "Bob, come in here for a minute and bring in Jerry."

Jerry was the first one to enter and by most standards, he looked too short and gave the impression of an English professor rather than a Secret Service agent. But looks were deceiving. He had been a Green

Beret before he had gone to college. Now, besides being an agent, he was widely known to be one of the best lie detector analysts around. Tom said quickly, "Jerry, I've got to get this cleared up in a hurry. Take Bob with you and set up your equipment and we'll run a test on this guy."

"Boss, I don't think he is a good applicant for the lie detector test. In fact he would be the worst possible polygraph candidate you could ever find anywhere. I don't feel that the test would even show one conclusive answer."

Tom looked at Jerry, "Do you mean to say that the test would be a total waste of time?"

"That's exactly what I'm saying. Maybe in a few days, after he settles down we could run it, but not now."

"Well that won't do me any good at all. I'll go back over all the physical evidence we have and make a decision. I do have a feeling that he's telling the truth or what he believes is the truth. We need to clear this up now and get on with other business. Thanks anyway Jerry."

"Sorry I couldn't help you boss."

Meanwhile Tom got up and went into the room with Tim, who by this time, looked like the most severely depressed man he had ever seen. This was a man who was beaten, just awaiting his fate and Tom almost felt sorry for him. But until he knew for sure, he would treat him as a danger to the President. He sat across from Tim and said, "How are you feeling?"

Tim replied in a faltering voice, "I feel like shit to be honest. I have no idea what is happening here, but I do know I've told you the truth. And I know my wife is worried sick by now and I sure would like to see her. I'm concerned about my friends. I may have left them back in time and I can't do anything to help them. And not only that, I don't have the foggiest notion what day this is."

"What day do you think it is?" Tom asked.

Tim thought for a minute, trying to figure out the days, then replied, "I think it must be July 1st, because we fell asleep on the 24th. We spent several days walking and spent a couple days on the Little Round Top. So it must be the 1st of July. I remember we saw the cavalry on Emmitsburg Road yesterday, er, what ever day that was. We got jumped by the rebs that night, later we went to sleep. When I woke up I was on the Round Top where they found me. So as far as I can guess, it is the first.

"Well, it's Friday, July 1st and I find your story beyond belief.

Tim's mouth just dropped and he thought to himself, Damn, if this is the 1st and I left them on the 1st, those poor bastards may be still stuck back in time. What would he tell their wives? What could he tell them? These people won't believe him no matter what he said. Hell, if he were in his shoes, he wouldn't believe the story either.

Tom arose from the chair and told the other agent in the room, "I'll be back shortly, stay here with him." He went back to his office to sift through all the information he had on the man.

Bob came in with a cup of steaming coffee and placed it in front of Tom, "Boss, here's some Java for you, anything else you need?"

"Yes, there is," he replied, "How 'bout getting on the horn and see what the search party has found. Thanks for the coffee, I need it pretty bad right now."

The agent left the room leaving Tom engrossed in his own thoughts, trying to figure out what was next. He couldn't see any reason to keep this man. He really didn't fit the profile of an hit man and his instinct told him that this man was not dangerous. Other factors to consider were the report from Bucky, the state police report and the video tape he just viewed. The video clearly showed this man and the two other missing men. The actual Civil War ammunition and percussion caps were hard to interpret also. No, this may be a hoax, but it didn't involve the president. As far as he was concerned, this was a matter for the park service and the local Police. When the agent came in and told him that nothing else had been found on Little Round Top, he told him to send the park personnel in.

Ranger Bullock, Sergeant Huff and Officer Hamilton entered the room and sat across from Tom, waiting for him to finish writing on some papers. When he finished he looked up, "I don't see any reason for me to hold him, so I'm going to turn him back over to you. Do you have any plans to charge him with anything?"

Jim Hamilton spoke first, "He broke the law and we'll have to charge him with firearms and ammunition violations in a National Park."

Tom looked at the officer long and hard. Then in a measured voice, replied, "I know I can't tell you what to do, but I want you to think about extenuating circumstances in this case. From everything I know about this fellow, I have a very strong feeling that we are dealing with forces that we have absolutely no knowledge about. I would seriously consider backing off, or at least reducing the charges. I think, if you pursue this, it just may jump up and bite you. Another thing to consider, a constitutional lawyer will have a field day with this, not to mention all the publicity that will be generated. We could all wind up with some serious black eyes."

"You've had your interrogation and from here on, this is no longer your concern," Hamilton answered, "We'll have to take this up with the Superintendent of the Park, but we will pass on your reservations."

Tom glanced at the two and thought to himself, These people are young and full of idealism, but I hope they use common sense in this case. Or they may be better off being in a phone booth with a pissed off Bobcat. Then he said out loud to them, "Suit yourself. But before you leave, I want to talk to that fellow for a few minutes alone."

Sergeant Huff started to object, "He's our prisoner..."

Gallager cut him off, "I said alone! I'm not going to interrogate him further. I have to satisfy myself about this strange occurance."

Tim, who was sitting in the front room with the one agent, attempted to start a conversation, but was met with stone silence. Now that he had time to think a little, he had become more composed and thought of what had transpired in the last few days. True, he didn't understand most of the events of his reliving the past. But he did know, that he had to get himself out of this predicament. Somehow, through no fault of his own, he faced some serious charges, however he may have an ace up his sleeve. They may have tricked him by talking him out of having a lawyer present during his interrogation. Maybe, all along, they had his friends and they were just playing on his fears. After all, he had been gone several days. There was no telling what has happened that he didn't know about.

His thoughts were interrupted when another agent came in and said, "Come with me. The Special Agent in charge wants to see you." Tim rose up from his chair and followed him to another room. As he was entering the room, he heard Tom tell the ranger and park officers to wait outside while he talked to the prisoner.

Tom motioned for Tim to sit in a folding chair

across from the portable desk. The desk had several piles of papers neatly stacked in groups. Tom sat, then told the re-enactor, "I'm releasing you to the custody of the park service because I haven't found any reason for me to hold you on. I will warn you though, not to say anything to anyone, about what has happened here this morning. This is a matter of national security."

Tim was starting to get very angry. This agent and the rest had put him through hell and were not even sorry about inconveniencing him. However he thought, Discretion may be the better part of valor, he wasn't a free man yet. "Sir," he replied, "I still don't understand what's happening to me, and I don't feel I've been treated very fairly here. In fact, your so called national security crap doesn't give you the right to trample on my rights. My only concern right now is to find my wife, my friends and gain my freedom. I'm not guilty of any crimes, yet you are treating me like a common criminal. And I don't care if you believe me. I have no idea what has gone on in my life the past few days. However I do know that something extraordinary did happen. As long as you and those rangers don't screw with me anymore, I won't go blabbing to the newspapers."

Agent Gallager glared at him, and gave Tim the unpleasant feeling that his eyes were burning right through to the back of his skull. He spoke with a very level, stern voice, "I won't offer you an apology, I'm only doing my job here, and the President's safety is paramount in my book. If you feel uncomfortable about that, well tough. I did what I had to do. If you feel that you have a case against me and you feel froggy, then leap. Before you leap, you better keep one thing in mind. Your story won't hold up in the papers, maybe in the tabloids, not the press. You'll be a laughing stock and who knows, maybe they'll put you in the hospital.

In fact, if I hear any bullshit out of you, I can have you put in a mental hospital for observation for a few days, just because I may think you are a menace to the President. Do I make myself perfectly clear?"

Tim felt like he had been kicked in the groin again. He knew this agent would play hardball, if forced in the corner, but he had to get his freedom. "Sir, I'm not trying to threaten you in any way, but you have to understand where I'm coming from. I swear to God, I haven't done anything wrong and I'm no-threat to the President. I'm just a re-enactor who, for some reason, went through that black hole in time and back again. I don't care if you or anybody else believes me, I know it's the truth. I do have a question for you. Have you found my friends yet?"

Tom felt a little relieved, he thought for sure this man was going to get combative and threaten him with lawsuit and the like. But he wasn't that worried about it, no one would believe him anyway. Finally he answered, "Your friends have not been found yet, but there is a missing person bulletin out for them. That's all I can tell you. I am curious about one thing though. Something seemed to be bothering you when I asked why you came back alone, you said you didn't know. I believe you do know. Can you explain that?"

"Sir, it's what I was thinking while I was back in time. I'm very ashamed of those thoughts. I was thinking only of myself and to hell with the others. I don't know if that is the reason for me coming back and not them. But I don't feel good about myself at all."

This answer satisfied Tom, he knew the young man was being honest in his soul searching. "Now, if you have nothing else to tell me, I'm quite busy, you may leave with the park police."

Tim rose up from the chair slowly, he wanted to say more, but thought the better of it, no use pushing his luck. He went out of the room to the waiting officers. He looked at Hamilton, "I hope you're not going to put those handcuffs on me again, I'm not going to give you any trouble."

"Rules are rules, now turn around and put your hands behind your back," The Park Officer instructed him. After he was handcuffed, they led him out the door without saying another word.

* * * * * *

Jim Craig was in his motel room and it was now almost seven in the morning. He was sipping a cup of coffee and flipping through his notes, as he listened to his scanner. The scanner always went with him on his assignments away from home. He came to Gettysburg last week to cover the re-enactments for his hometown paper, "The Daily Dispatch." He was supposed to go home for a week then come back this weekend to cover the President's rededication of the Peace Memorial's 50th anniversary. President Roosevelt had dedicated the Memorial on July 3, 1938. Over the years, his mother told him how she had been there, as a little girl, and had seen President Roosevelt from a distance as he dedicated the monument.

Jim planned on going back home for the week, except for the commotion over at the re-enactment on the first day. It seemed that some re-enactors had disappeared in front of a bunch of people and they were missing ever since. It just smelled of a good story and he couldn't let it go. He interviewed one of the wives during the week and she was extremely agitated. Two of the wives had to go back home because of family and work, but one wife stayed in Gettysburg, just in case something turned up on the missing husbands. He was just plain intrigued by the story. Even more so after she told him the wild story about the old man and the musket. He knew it couldn't be, however, so far he couldn't find anything to prove it to be a hoax. He wanted to be there, when and if these men showed up. Maybe he could get an exclusive story about how the deception was pulled off, especially the disappearing act. He was in touch with Jan Murray every day and stuck close to her hoping to get the scoop on the story. He had to admit she didn't appear to be a person who was a hoaxer, she was visibly upset, but then again, maybe she was a good actress.

His thoughts were suddenly jolted by something he heard on the scanner and he turned it up, listening intently to the transmissions back and forth. Jim heard something about a re-enactor being found on Little Round Top. The reporter could only get bits and pieces of the transmission, some other station was skipping in and drowning out the voices. He did pick out something about searching for two more men and a request for dogs. Then he heard something about the Secret Service, however it was very garbled. A few minutes later he heard that they were transporting a suspect back to headquarters. Hot damn, maybe this wait was worth while after all. He would get over to the park headquarters and maybe be able to interview someone. In fact, he would stop by the bed and breakfast where Mrs. Murray was staying and tell her what was going on. He had to hurry to beat them, so that he could see who they were bringing in. He started to grab his note pad, pocket tape recorder and camera as another transmission came over directing the rangers to go to the Secret Service headquarters. Now where in the hell is that, he thought, he had gone to a small office near the courthouse the other day for his press credentials.

He knew that couldn't possibly be the headquarters, as the Secret Service never traveled that light. His best bet would be to get Mrs. Murray and go stake out the park headquarters. If anything was happening, it would probably wind up there.

He hurried outside and jumped into his Chevy Blazer, fumbled with the keys, started it and tore out of the parking lot. Jim managed to go the wrong way in the one way parking lot, but time was of the essence here. He screeched to a stop in front of the bed and breakfast, where Jan Murray was staying since the other wives went home. Jan had just opened the door and stepped onto the porch. This was her morning ritual since the disappearance. She would go to the corner stop and shop to pickup a morning newspaper. Jan would read through it, from front to back, for any hint of anything that might help find her husband and friends. Jan heard the vehicle tires squeal and the driver yelling something to her about the missing re-enactors. She bolted to the passenger side and looked in, where she saw the reporter who had been talking to her every day since the disappearance. He was visibly upset and was babbling something about the park rangers and the Secret Service.

"Slow down, I can't understand a word you're saying." Now what is it with the rangers and the Secret Service?"

Jim caught his breath, then told her, "Get in quickly. We have to get over to park headquarters. Something is happening, concerning re-enactors, I will explain everything on the way over." When they arrived in the parking lot, he parked as close as he could to the main entrance and the single steel door located about 50 feet from the main entrance doors. He knew that if they wanted to take someone in without the tourists seeing them, it would be through that steel door.

After stopping, Jan Murray started bombarding him with one question after another. He had enough and shouted, "Damn it lady, just shut up. I don't know anymore than I've told you so far. I'm not even sure what they were talking about. It seems funny that the Secret Service would be involved. Now our best chance is to wait and hopefully they will bring that person to this building sooner or later."

As Jan started to get out, he asked her where she was going. "I'm going in to ask the rangers what they've done with my husband and where the Secret Service is."

He grabbed her arm and stopped her, then in an sarcastic tone said, "Lady, do you think they are going to tell you where they are? Why do you think they call them the Secret Service? Now get back in here and settle down, believe me, right now it's our best chance."

His tone and answer made her laugh and it helped settle her down. She knew he was probably right. After a few minutes she said to Jim, "I don't know what's going on, but if they have them at the Secret Service office, I really should call the lawyer we hired. There must be more to this than meets the eye. He told me I could call him any time."

Jim looked at his watch and figured that wherever the re-enactor was, they had him almost an hour now. He may need a lawyer, in any case it wouldn't hurt to put the counsler on notice. Jim turned to Jan saying, "There's a phone booth by the building. I'll keep watch for you. Just tell him we think they found a re-enactor."

Jan walked quickly to the building and took the phone off the receiver with shaking hands. In fact they were shaking so badly, she dropped a hand full of change before she was able to put the right amount in for the dial tone. Shortly, she came back and entered the car saying to the reporter, "He said to sit tight. As soon as we see or hear anything, to call him immediately and he can be here in five minutes."

"That's good, it wouldn't do any good for him to be here while we wait. Every minute he spends with you would cost money."

They waited for almost three hours and the tension was building. Jim knew what he had heard that morning. He was sure that one of the re-enactors had been found. Which one did they find and where were the other two men. Damn, he thought, It had been dumb running out this morning without my scanner. If he had the scanner, maybe they would know what was going on, if nothing else by the amount of radio traffic. They couldn't take the chance of leaving now. With his luck, they would come while he was gone. Here he was, a reporter for over twenty years and he never had a blockbuster story in all those years. He was probably chasing a red herring trying to follow this event. His instincts told him it would be worth the wait.

Meanwhile Jan had her own misgivings. Here it was six days since her husband and his friends had disappeared and she was depending on a perfect stranger. True, he had some ulterior motives. He had told her up front, he would help her find her husband as long as she gave him exclusive rights to the story. She had wished she hadn't made that promise, but she was as good as her word. Anyway he had been very helpful. The other wives had gone home because of obligations, but she had no reason to go home until her husband was found. She also thought about the weird feelings her husband had and what that old man had told him about that damn musket. She had to find her husband. He was her sweetheart and the love of her life. He had always been a good husband and friend. Jan would never be able to live, not knowing what happened. With all her being, she hoped for his safety wherever he was.

CRASH! They looked to the sound and a van had backed into a red sports car. The driver of the car jumped out, screaming, "You idiot, why don't you look before you back up. Look what you've done to my car!"

Something told Jim to look back toward the building. "Damn, while we were looking at the accident, a park police car came in. They're taking someone inside."

Jan looked over, recoginized the man in the Federal uniform and yelled, "Tim is that you? Where's George, is he being held somewhere else?" "

Jim could see the man who was wearing an extremely dirty uniform and damn if he didn't have a Bucktail on his hat!

The two of them started off at a run toward the building, trying to get there before they took Tim inside.

As they approached the building the single steel door opened as if someone was watching. As the officers whisked Tim through the door and into the building, they heard Tim's plea, "Help me, get a lawyer" then there was silence after the door slammed shut.

Jan was beside herself, "Dammit, what the hell is going on around here," and she kicked the brick wall with her foot out of frustration. As Jan started to run for the phone, she realized that her purse was in the car. She turned to Jim and asked "Can I borrow some change to use the phone?"

After calling the lawyer, Jan had time to think about Tim being found and not the others. Her knees felt like jelly and she just sat down on the sidewalk. Damn, she wasn't going to cry and let the world see her weakness. Tim was alive and if nothing else, he would know where George was and if he was OK.

The reporter woke her from her thoughts, "Mrs. Murray, we better go to the parking lot and wait for the lawyer. We can't do any more here and I feel quite sure they won't let us see your friend."

They went to his car where she retrieved her purse. Jim exclaimed, "Those people just went to the car and took out a musket and some equipment from the trunk."

Sure enough, Jan saw the two park police racing up the sidewalk carrying a musket and what looked like an ammunition pouch and belt with a bayonet. Before they could react, the officers passed through the steel door and it slammed shut again.

Ron Dustin was in his office reviewing a case he had been working on for almost a year. All the depositions were completed and he was ready for the court date next week. His morning had been interrupted by the frantic phone call earlier. It was the woman who had hired him for his services just a few days earlier. In fact, it was the three women whose husbands had disappeared at the re-enactment the past weekend who had hired him. He hadn't done much yet on the strange case but, if what the woman had said earlier was true, then he may have his work cut out for him. Ron was a lawyer for almost thirty-five years and he would soon be retiring and turning his modest practice over to his son. Over the years, he had his share of different cases. Everything from murders to divorces with fights over who gets the cat. He had agreed to take this case because he wasn't carrying a heavy case load, leaving most of the work to his son. Anyway, this probably wouldn't turn out to be much of a case and he could get ready for some serious fishing. Just then the intercom clicked on and he heard the secretary say, "Sir, you have a call on line one. It's Mrs. Murray."

Both Jan and Jim saw the old Ford Maverick pull into the driveway and stop in the parking lot. They didn't pay much attention to the old car, as they thought a lawyer would be driving a flashier one. However, when the man got out of the car, Jan recognized him and called out, "Mr. Dustin, over here," as she waved her arms. Jim looked toward the lawyer and saw a tall, slender man, with a short flattop that was completely gray. He was wearing gray slacks, short sleeve white shirt and tie which set off his deep tan. He would have never recognized him as a counselor if he had met him on the street.

The lawyer walked up, "Hello Mrs. Murray."

Jan introduced him to the reporter. Quickly, both Jim and Jan explained what had happened, then Jan was ready to charge into the building.

Ron Dustin cut in and told them "I can get in and see this Tim Fretz fellow, but they won't let you anywhere near him. So it is better for you to wait inside by the information stand, and don't talk to anyone until I know what's happening."

Jan felt a little depressed. She was so close, yet so far away from finding her husband. "Try and find out where my husband is," she asked the lawyer.

The Superintendent called Ranger Bullock, Sergeant Huff and Officer Hamilton into his office after they put the re-enactor into a holding room. After they sat, he asked them what happened that morning. He listened intently and made notes as they talked. When they finished he didn't say anything at first, just looked over his notes for a minute. Then he looked up and started his questions, "I see you allowed the Secret Service to interrogate the suspect. Is that right?"

They three nodded in the affirmative.

"Of course you did allow the suspect to call a lawyer. Right?"

Hamilton could see that this wasn't headed in the right direction and nervously replied, "No sir, but I thought that the Secret Service should know what was going on and anyway they asked to talk to him."

The Superintendent looked at them both and asked in a very low voice, "May I ask, whose prisoner was he? Did the Secret Service arrest the man?"

Officer Hamilton could feel the blood rushing to his head. He knew that all hell was about to break loose. How many times had the Superintendent talked about making a good arrest and keeping within the rules. He had hammered it into their heads the importance of constitutional rights and now in their haste, they had botched up this arrest big time. Sheepishly he answered, "I was the arresting officer, however under the circumstances, I felt the Secret Service should be involved."

The Superintendent who was visibly upset fired a salvo into the Officer, "Sir, I don't question your decision to involve the Secret Service. But what in the hell was going on in your head when you allowed them to interrogate the suspect without you being there. Of course you know that they maneuvered that man into a position of not having a lawyer present. You may have jeopardized this whole case. Now, I don't know who the lawyer will be. If he has half a head, this case will be thrown out before it goes to court and we may have one hell of a lawsuit on our hands. The other thing that bothers me is the two friends of the re-enactor. They are still missing and no-one knows where they are. Now I don't know what is happening, there's something here that doesn't meet the eye. Do either one of you have any ideas of what is happening here?"

"Sir, for what it's worth," Hamilton answered, "I do believe something extraordinary has happened here. Everything I've seen points to this story being true or what he believes is the truth."

Ranger Bullock agreed, "Sir, I was the one who found him and he was filthy and strangely, he was covered with fresh mud. It hasn't rained around here for days. I agree with Hamilton, something very weird has happened."

A buzzer rang on the phone. He picked the reciever up, listened, and said, "I'll be right out." As he got up, he said to them, "Well, now it's time for damage control and just in case it may interest you, we have the worst case scenario. His lawyer is Ron Dustin who happens to be one of the best lawyers in the state. If you were figuring on advancement in the next few years, forget it. Feel very lucky if your next assignment is Adak, Alaska."

The trio went inside the building and walked to the information booth. The lawyer looked at the ranger on duty announcing, "My name is Ronald Dustin, Esquire and I have reason to believe that my client, Mr. Tim Fretz, is being held in this building. I want to see him."

The ranger didn't say anything to the lawyer. He simply picked up the phone, punched in a couple numbers and spoke quietly into the receiver. In a matter of seconds they heard a voice say, "Hello Ron, I see you've finally came over for a visit."

They all turned and saw the older man coming down the hall. After a brief round of introductions, Ron said, "Superintendent, you know why I'm here, and I would like to see my client right now."

Superintendent Jackson was suave as he replied, "Sure, no problem. Your friends can wait in my office while you talk to him. I'll have some coffee sent up for all of you."

Ron could sense that the Superintendent was feeling very uneasy and was trying to smooth something over. They probably fouled up the arrest somehow. Whatever it was, he would uncover the truth.

The lawyer was lead back to the holding room, while Jan Murray and Jim Craig went into the superintendent's office. When he entered the room, he saw a young man in his mid to late 30's, sitting on a plain metal chair. His hair was disheveled, his uniform was torn and his pant legs were muddy up to the knees. He thought to himself, That's odd it hasn't rained for days and he's muddy almost up to his rear. On the plain table sat a Civil War hat with a Bucktail pinned to the side. The man slowly stood up and the lawyer extended his hand as he said, "Hi, I'm Ron Dustin, your lawyer." He hardly got the words out of his mouth and Tim was hugging him, almost in tears. After he broke the bear hug, he stepped back and exclaimed as he wrinkled his nose, "Damn, when was the last time you took a shower. You smell like a barn yard!"

Tim settled down and at the lawyer's urging told him the whole story. The lawyer looked long and hard at Tim, then said, "I'm your lawyer and the only way I can help you is for you to tell me the truth."

Tim looked the Ron Dustin in the eye replying, "Sir, what I've told you is the absolute truth. I've done nothing wrong except, being in the wrong place at the wrong time."

"OK," the lawyer responded, "We'll go on the premise that your story is true, or what you believe is the truth. The first thing I have to do, is find out just what they intend to charge you with, then we'll go from there. The worst that could happen is you will be arraigned and held over for trial. In that case we'll get you out on bail. I believe we have a strong case here, since they maneuvered around your right to have an attorney present. You must not say anything more to them, period! You must remember that. The only way you say anything, is with me present and only if I say it's OK. Do you understand?"

Tim nodded his head yes and for the first time that day felt that there was some hope. Ron Dustin left to talk to the Superintendent of the Park.

Ron went into the office where the reporter and Jan Murray were talking to the superintendent. When the lawyer entered, Jan leaped from her chair, "Did Tim say anything about my husband? Did he say he was OK?"

Looking at her Ron said, "We'll talk about this in a few minutes when we're alone. Right now I want to talk to Mr. Jackson," motioning toward the superintendent. Reluctantly Jan and the reporter left the room closing the door behind them. Ron sat across from Richard Jackson and said "Dick, you may beat me at poker every Thursday night, but this hand I've been dealt is a Royal Flush."

The superintendent, his hands clasped at his mouth, looked across the desk at his old friend and knew beyond a doubt, that his position wasn't real strong. He also knew that his friend would hold nothing back in the fight for his client and that it would be nothing personal, just his job. For the time being he would play his bad hand and try a little bluff. "Sir, your client broke park rules and had a musket, percussion caps, live ammunition and a bayonet on park property. The live cartridges is the most serious of the charges. Coupled with the others, your client is looking at some pretty hefty fines and maybe jail time. So, I think you're only holding a small pair."

A smile crept across Ron's face, as he knew his friend was bluffing. He had seen that nervous scratching of the left ear every time his friend had tried to bluff at cards. Then he spoke, "Well sir, the first thing I want to see is the arrest report and interview the arresting officer. Also from what my client has told me, much of the evidence you have will be thrown out. You may have deprived him of his constitutional rights. I'm going to move that all the charges be dropped. Then I think a lawsuit will be in order. However, if you decide not to press any charges, then I believe we can convince my client to forget the whole thing."

Dick Jackson looked across the desk at the lawyer, he had a feeling that this whole case could blow up in his face. "While you review the arrest reports, I'm going to get the Deputy U.S. Attorney down here and see where we go from here. So if you'll leave me I can get started."

Ron stood up and before he turned to leave said, "I'll read the reports, then I'll be outside with my client Jan Murray. So let me know when you're ready."

When the lawyer went outside, he asked the reporter to leave him alone with Jan. Ron sat with her on a bench and told her everything that had transpired. "Did you call Tim's wife yet?"

"Yes I did, and she is on her way out at this very moment, along with Jack's wife.

"Do you believe any part of the story?" She asked the attorney.

Ron stared up at the sky for a moment then replied slowly, "This whole thing sounds far fetched, but what bothers me is the fact that everything points to it being the truth. Hell, a hundred years ago flight wasn't possible and here we've had men on the moon. So I can't say that anything is impossible anymore. The only thing I do know is, we will get Tim out of this jam somehow. Under the circumstances the park service would be very foolish to pursue this any further."

Jan felt relieved for her friend Tim, but what was happening to her husband. If what Tim had told the lawyer was true, then her husband could be in the distant past. At this very moment he could be over by the 150th monument facing possible death. How could that be possible? That would have happened long before he was even born. It just didn't make any sense.

This whole week had been a living nightmare and it didn't look like it would get any better. The lawyer left Jan and went back into the building. Meanwhile the reporter sat with her and started taking down notes. Ron Dustin went into the superintendent's office and sat with the group that had assembled there.

CHAPTER ELEVEN

George Murray had rejoined Company B and the men were glad to see him and the other stragglers. Soon every man available would be needed if they were to survive.

Several of the men came over to him and one asked "Are you all right? You look like your head is gonna explode, it's so red."

George replied, "Yea I'm OK, except for this lousy heat and the side stickers."

A couple of the men laughed and another one said, "You think it's hot now, take a look over yonder," as he pointed over his shoulder.

George looked toward Herr Ridge and gasped, "Damn," as far as he could see, there was regiment upon regiment of gray, moving toward them like a series of large ocean swells. Looking around, George could see that part of the company was posted in an apple orchard and the rest in an open field. There were some woods to the south of the McPherson house and to their front was a wheat field, which was golden ripe. Off on the ridge, he could see the cannons and the men loading them. Soon there was puff, puff, puff of white smoke as each cannon fired. He could see the solid shot hit the ground and skip like a flat rock across water. It was almost like slow motion as they bounced once, twice and then whizzed harmlessly overhead. He could hear and see leaves and branches snapping from the apple trees as the cannon balls swept through. George instinctively ducked, even though they weren't close to him. The noise was intense and yet the battle really hadn't started for them. He thought back to his days in Vietnam and the noise of battle there. This noise seemed different, as if it was in a lower frequency range, however it was just as fierce as twentieth century warfare. Suddenly, the firing slowed and he could hear officers giving commands above sounds of the groaning wounded men.

Suddenly it dawned on him that he hadn't loaded his musket. As he looked around, George saw the other men had their muskets primed. So he took out a cartridge and ripped it open with his teeth, but when he tried to pour the powder down the barrel with his uncontrollably shaking hand, he missed the barrel. On the third try, he managed to get most of the powder into the barrel then he gave the musket a slight tap. You dumb shit, he thought to himself, You've got to put the bullet down the barrel with the ram rod.

The man next to him, whom everyone called Corporal Terry, asked George, "Where do you hail from?"

George replied, "Oh I'm from a little town in Northern Lehigh County. Where do you come from?"

The corporal replied, "I'm from Philadelphia right near Germantown. I've been watching you and I can tell you ain't had much drilling. So you just watch me and follow what I tell you and what your file partner does. I told him to help you along too. I do hope you can shoot better than you load!"

George felt that he had been put down, but realized that they were just trying to help him along.

His file partner, Skeeter, said, "I think we'll call you Pops, cause you're old enough to be our Pa. Yep that sounds good. OK Pops?"

Several of the men around him laughed and

agreed, so George just nodded his head yes, knowing that he probably was the oldest man in the regiment. Looking around George spotted a soldier in another squad whom he didn't know and the man didn't look to be over fourteen or fifteen. He heard someone call him Bull Dog. Bull Dog looked more like the runt of the litter. He only stood about 5'4" and couldn't weigh much more than 100 pounds wet. He looked out of place with his frock coat and his musket which was almost as tall as he was. In fact he wasn't even old enough to grow whiskers. George knew that looks were deceiving. This young man was wiry and strong and George hoped that the soldier would live long enough to attain manhood.

As he stood there in ranks, a noticeable thing was the body odors of those around him. The exertion of long marches and lack of baths didn't help, not to mention that everyone was soaked in perspiration. George wondered, if he smelled just as bad, but what the hell, out here who cared. Around him many of the men while waiting for the coming fight, were trying to straighten out their uniforms as if getting ready for a parade. Most of the men spoke in low tones amongst themselves and the air of excitement was heavy. As he glanced around it occurred to George that he was one of the tallest men in the company, being about three or four inches taller than most. He looked as best he could toward the Chambersburg Road where Company A was posted, but he couldn't see his friend Jack. He hoped he was OK. If he had chance later he would go try to find him.

While the company awaited the order to move out, George looked around the area to their left. He could plainly see where the 14th Brooklyn had fought earlier. Broken muskets, knapsacks and clothing littered the ground, including some bodies with red pants. In fact all across in front of them the litter of the battle field attested to the fierce fighting before they arrived on the field.

George was shaken out of his daydreaming by orders for the skirmish company to move out by screaming officers and noncoms. A nearby corporal shouted at the top of his lungs, "Skirmish company. Forward march." George felt Skeeter gently push him ahead. The skirmishers hadn't gone ten paces, when the order was given to quick step. As they moved through the wheat field George could only think, Thank God we're going down hill. His legs feeling like rubber, still hadn't recovered from earlier efforts. Soon they were climbing a gentle incline and his breathing got harder as they broke into four man squads. They crested the small hill and started down through a pasture to the creek. At this point the skirmishers started double quick timing in a full charge. The men were making a 50-yard dash for a fence line and the heavy brush at Willoughby Run, each squad spreading out until the company covered the whole regimental front.

Continuing down the hill, George could see the smoke from the rebel skirmisher's muskets. He could hear the bullets whistling and whining over and around him. It dawned on him, they were shooting at him! And just that quickly they were to the fence right after passing a small quarry. To his surprise he could see the rebel skirmishers falling back and he nor anyone else hadn't even fired yet. However the rebel skirmishers didn't have time to re-load and the Bucktails were still loaded, prudence called for an immediate withdrawal. By the time he reached the rail fence on the near side of Willoughby Run, he was sweating profusely, his hands were trembling and he felt like his heart was going to explode.

An officer shouted "Fire independently" and the order was repeated by the sergeants and corporals.

Everyone started firing at the retreating rebel skirmishers.

George had only managed to get off four shots as his hands were trembling so bad. He had aimed over the head of the closest rebel who was retreating toward a fence line. He could see the man's face clearly. As the Confederate turned around to fire, George fired! To his amazement, the man dropped his musket, grabbed his chest and did a slow twisting fall into the tall grass. What the hell, he couldn't have hit him, he had aimed high, then he looked at his sights. They were OK.

He heard Skeeter yell over, "Hey pops. Did you see me dust that reb's britches?"

George felt a rush of relief as he called back, "I sure did Skeeter. Good shooting."

The order was given to cease fire and it quieted down around them. The rebels didn't return fire right away after they made it to another fence line up the field. George imagined they were just as hot and out of breath as he was. He knew where they were, but the gray uniforms blended in well with the brush in which they were hiding. Occasionally George would see a flash of light from a tin cup or the polished bayonets.

After a few minutes, the rebels started harassing fire and the bullets were coming very close. At one point, George heard a loud crack and felt a tug at his right shoulder. There was no pain and after feeling his shoulder for blood or a wound, he realized he wasn't hurt. He didn't have time to worry about that right now. He had to keep down and not draw fire again. The re-enactor took a long swig of water from his canteen, which didn't help clear the terrible taste in his mouth, which was a combination of black powder, dust, pollen and sweat. While he rested, George glanced towards Chambersburg Pike. He could see the skirmishers from the 149th and 143rd Regiments spread out all the way to the Chambersburg Pike.

George looked over at Skeeter and he almost laughed. His face was blackened, as a mixture of clay-like dust and black powder ran down the sides of his mouth as blackish/brown drool. George realized he probably looked the same way. He looked down at his hands and they were black also. Suddenly, he heard intense firing to his left. Because they were in a ravine, he couldn't see what was happening. Rising smoke showed where the Iron Brigade fought for their lives against the Confederates who were assailing them from the west. He couldn't see past the fence where the rebel skirmishers were posted. However he could tell from the rising dust that not too far in front of him, Confederate regiments were just waiting for the word to pounce on them. George knew that the closest regiments were only about 600 yards from them and once they started, it wouldn't take long to over run them. There was a fence row with brush, only about 300 yards from them where the enemy skirmishers had taken cover behind. At least for the moment they weren't shooting at them, it was the calm before the storm.

The re-enactor looked down to the water in the creek below him. At first he thought it was muddy, then he realized it was blood mixed in the mud. Damn, he thought, The water wouldn't be fit to drink. The bank down to the stream was muddy and he could see where the rebel skirmishers had scrambled down earlier when they had pushed them out. As he started down to the water, he slipped and slid, falling into the creek with a splash. He was up to his knees in the water before he stopped. But he didn't mind, it felt pretty good. George soaked a rag in the water and used it to wash his face to try and cool off. Knowing full well, the fight had just begun for him. After the events of the past couple of hours, he hoped he would have the stamina to keep up and make it to the Cemetery Hill later, where he knew they would retreat.

"What the hell are you doing down there? Get back to your post," shouted an angry Corporal Terry.

Pulling himself hand over hand, George climbed back up the slippery slope to the fence.

The corporal berated him again, "Don't you leave your post again! You're lucky someone with itchy fingers didn't shoot you with the commotion you made."

George just took the verbal chastising, knowing that he had been wrong. However it was humiliating to be chewed out by someone only seventeen or eighteen years old. But in looking at most of the officers and noncoms, very few were past their mid twenties. Just that fast the corporal was gone and George was left with his thoughts and bruised ego. As he waited, George couldn't get over how tired he was already. All he wanted to do was sleep. If he did, it would be the long sleep, so he forced himself to stay alert.

It occurred to George, This would be the perfect time to get his camera as no one could see him. He would take a picture of the rebel skirmishers in front of him. Reaching into his haversack for his camera, to his surprise, he pulled out a handful of plastic and torn up film. Son-of-a-bitch, he thought, Now I have nothing to prove that I was here in this time. George wondered how the camera had been smashed. Examining the haversack, he saw the small round black hole in the front and back of the haversack. He remembered the tug at his right shoulder and the loud crack, it was the force of the bullet pulling on the strap, as it smashed the camera. Suddenly it dawned on him. He had been only three inches from a terrible wound and he broke out in a cold sweat. George emptied out his haversack throwing the smashed camera and torn film into the stream in front of him.

Corporal Terry passed the word, "Any time reb skirmishers show themselves or shoot at us, fire at them!" For the moment it was quiet in front. To his left the Iron Brigade was still slugging it out. George could hear the constant crash as volley after volley was fired and the confused shouts of orders. It sounded like complete bedlam in the woods. Behind him the musket fire had died down and he could hear the heavy cannon fire from Oak Hill, seeing an occasional air burst. Not much different from modern warfare for the grunt, you only know what's going on in your immediate vicinity.

Someone yelled, "Here they come" and as he peered out from the fence, George could see the rebel skirmishers moving toward them. They weren't running, but in a crouch, relentlessly moving forward with their muskets at the ready. He cocked his musket, aimed just over the man closest to him, then he heard the corporal scream "Fire" and a volley of murderous minie balls reached out and staggered the line of skirmishers. George could see men falling everywhere and the stunned survivors turned tail and ran back to the cover of the fence. He could hear the groans and wailing of the wounded men and it went against everything he believed in, but he couldn't help them. Above all the noise, noncoms and officers were yelling, "Load quickly, boys. Load quickly!"

Skeeter called over, "Hey Pops, you OK?"

George called back, "Yea, so far. I'm starting to get tired and hot, though."

"Don't worry about falling asleep. From the looks of that dust rising in front of us, we're about to have a grand time. As far as the heat, it's gonna get real hot soon enough,"

George wondered what time it was and took out the pocket watch. It was 1 p.m. and he thought really hard, trying to remember what the sequence of the battle would be. If he were right, the rebs attacked from the north around 1:30 p.m. He had a little time yet to figure out what he could possibly do. He hadn't read the regimental history for over a year. There was no doubt that very soon he would be in the hardest fight of his life. Also, if he remembered correctly, when they were attacked from the west, some how they would be pushed over to the woods to his left.

George thought back to some of the re-enactments he attended. How many times had he thought, Boy, I wish I could go back in time and actually fight in the Civil War? Well, his wish had come true, and it wasn't fun at all! In fact, he was apprehensive not knowing what his fate would be. It still didn't make any sense, that this could be happening. The worst thing was his family and loving wife, might never know what befell him. His mind drifted back to his younger years in Vietnam. He was scared to death there too. If he had died there, his family would have known what happened to him. But here now, if he died, nobody would ever know what his fate was. This was almost too much to comprehend.

* * * * * *

Jack ran at the double-quick up the low hill and as they topped it, he could see the McPherson farm in front of them. They ran past a battery, which was on their left. After they had passed, the cannons fired toward Herr Ridge. The rebel guns there had been lobbing shells at them as they advanced. Soon they had passed the farm buildings and reached a dirt lane which had a post and rail fence on both sides. Many of the rails had been removed, to provide makeshift protection during the earlier fighting. Everywhere he looked there was the litter of clothing, haversacks, hats, wooden boxes, smashed muskets and other accouterments. His company moved to the right until it was about fifty yards from the Chambersburg Pike. To his amazement, there was a sunken road right alongside the toll road and he saw the 149th regiment take cover there. Just across the pike, he could see half a dozen dead horses, where the artillery had been earlier. He was glad his company was in position, so that he could get a little rest and a drink of water. His whole body was aching and it felt like every muscle was about to break. Every man was breathing heavy and several had knelt on one knee trying to catch their breath. One man, started staggering as if he were drunk, finally he collapsed to the ground. A couple of men went to him, carrying the unconscious soldier to the aid station inside the McPherson barn. It was obvious to Jack, this man probably had heat exhaustion or stroke.

Looking down the Chambersburg Pike, he could see the 149th taking up their position. They were lining up along the road, while the 143rd filled the area between the 150th and the 149th. The 149th faced toward Oak Hill while his regiment and the 143rd faced Herr Ridge. As he looked toward the Ridge, he was totally awed. All he could see were masses of Confederates everywhere. Herr Ridge and the tavern were very visible, this was due to the lack of trees. Regiments of rebels could be seen moving and maneuvering into position then stopping, waiting for the signal to advance. He couldn't get over how many men were out there. It dawned on him, just how small the re-enactments he attended, really had been.

Looking over to the McPherson farm house, it

occurred to Jack, It didn't look as neat and tidy as the other farm houses he had seen. In fact it looked run down and had a large chimney, which he imagined was for heat and cooking. He felt a little saddened, the house no longer stood in modern times along with the apple orchards, cherry orchards, and the scattered farm buildings. The only building still standing in the twentieth century was the barn. But then he reminded himself that for the time being, this would be his modern time and he would have to make the best of it.

Several of the Union cannons fired and Jack could see the cannon balls bouncing into the massed rebels, flipping bodies into the air. As soon as the Union cannons fired, the Confederates unleashed heavy counter fire from their massed guns on Herr Ridge. Jack could see the one battery behind them scurry around, hooking up the horses and pulling the cannons out as exploding shells burst all around them. They simply couldn't stand up to the overwhelming fire coming from Herr Ridge. It either was move quickly or die.

How is George doing? Jack thought. He hadn't seen him since they had joined the regiment. He wondered if George was able to keep up and hoped that he didn't have a heart attack from the exertion and stifling heat. The men around him were quiet for the time being. Everyone was just trying to catch their breath. They drank heavily from their canteens. They were drenched from sweating, their faces beet red and some had the dry heaves.

When Jack finally caught his breath and almost drained his canteen, he turned right to talk to the man next to him. Suddenly, he saw a tremendous amount of smoke billowing from Oak Hill. Immediately Jack could see several cannon balls streaking toward them and a couple of them had smoke trailing behind them. The solid shot was closing fast, while the smoking shells were coming in a little higher. There was complete bedlam as shells burst overhead with a tremendous boom and he could feel the heat and concussion. But these bursting shells took your attention away from the bouncing solid shot. They tore into the ground like a plow, tearing a furrow 6 to 8 feet long, then bouncing into the men. As if in slow motion, he saw soldiers and body parts flying into the air, then thud to the ground. Men were screaming, some were moaning while one man sat on the ground, looking at the blood pouring out between his fingers clutching his mid-section. The soldier simply fell to one side, let out a sigh and went limp. Jack was totally unnerved and just wanted to run and run anywhere, but away from here.

Above the noise, orders were heard, "File closers, close the ranks! Company left face. Forward march! Quick time to the barn!" A couple men stayed behind to tend their fallen comrades and help them off the field. As they were moving, he could see several men who had been hit, but only three or four appeared dead. As they approached the barn in columns of fours, they heard the rebel cannon balls whooshing overhead again. This time all of the shells missed their target with the exception of one, which burst directly over the lead company. Jack could see several men go down while others tried to help their wounded and screaming comrades. The officers and noncoms were shouting for the men to reform and keep moving. Soon they were in the safety of the stone barn. The barn was between them and those hated guns on Oak Hill. Because of the slight gully by the barn, they were also out of the sharp eyes of the gunners on Herr Ridge. The company formed up and they counted off by twos again.

"Your file partner Dean, is wounded! Go with your new file partner and take a bunch of canteens to that pump by the house to be filled," a Corporal screamed above the noise to Jack.

They each took as many canteens as possible and ran to the well pump. Jack pumped as fast as he could, while the other man, whose name he didn't know yet, held the canteens under the rushing water. Jack noticed that his hands were trembling too, then he introduced himself. "I'm Jack, one of the new fellows and your new file partner. What's your name?"

In a wavering voice, which almost sounded like it had a touch of puberty, replied "Name is Jedidah, but everyone calls me Jed."

Jack kept pumping the handle up and down. He would have liked to question Jed more, it would have to wait. He didn't have any more breath left, not to mention that his arms felt like lead from the pressure of the pump handle. When they had finished filling the canteens, they each took turns putting their heads under the cool well water while the other pumped. This seemed to revive them somewhat. They would have liked to stay there all day, except that other men appeared from other companies, demanding their turn at the pump. The two men staggered back under the load of the heavy canteens. After they had returned, the corporal assigned two more men to fill the rest of the canteens, while Jack and Jed passed out the full canteens. Jack and Jed simply waited in the shade of a tree. The cannons on Oak Hill were still firing on the Union line however, for the moment they were safe. The Union guns were returning the fire from Seminary Hill and another battery which they had passed earlier. From the sound, it appeared that the Union cannons were very much out gunned. Another young fellow came over and sat with him and Jed. This soldier didn't look a day older than fifteen and was pathetically thin but was taller than most of the other men. His uniform pants were ripped at the knees and it looked to Jack as if a piece of shrapnel had torn the pants.

Jed introduced him as his cousin, who was nicknamed "Crackers."

Jack asked, "Why the nickname Crackers?"

Jed laughed and replied, "That's because this sick lad likes hard tack, that's how he got that name."

And sure enough, Crackers started munching on a piece of hard tack. He offered Jack and Jed a piece which they accepted. Jack started eating his piece, Damn, he thought, I'd rather eat a piece of cardboard. It would have more flavor.

The conversation turned serious as Jed spoke to Crackers in earnest. "Crackers, if I'm kiltd, will you tell my Maw and Pa that I died like a man, facing the enemy?"

Crackers replied, "Jed, you ain't gonna get yourself killed, but will you do likewise for me?"

"Of course, you know I will," Jed answered, "And you have to promise to make sure I get a proper burial."

Crackers just nodded his head as he was writing his name and regiment on a small piece of paper. He pinned the paper on the inside of his frock coat. Jed did likewise, in hopes if they were killed, they would at least be identified.

The conversation ended as the officers started shouting for everyone to form up again. They marched back up to their previous position. There was a let up in the firing, but Jack knew that it wouldn't be long before the storm hit them.

As they marched up the farm lane, they moved closer to Chambersburg Pike than before. That's when Jack noticed that the 143rd had shifted to the right of the 149th, closer to town. He also noticed several men being carried to the barn and it was obvious that they were dead. Turning to Jed, "It looks like the 149th lost some men from the cannons."

Their attention turned to another company,

where they heard some catcalling and joking remarks, as an old man approached the center of the regiment, by the color company. Jack recognized him from accounts he had read, it was none other than John Burns, alive and in person. He was the civilian hero of Gettysburg. John Burns was 69 years of age and a veteran of the War of 1812. He saw him talking to a major then Colonel Wister approached them. While he couldn't hear the conversation, he could see the colonel pointing to the woods where the Iron Brigade was positioned. Soon, John Burns walked almost dejectedly, with his musket in the trail position, toward the woods and out of sight. God, how I wished I could have talked to that man in person, he thought, but he would have to be satisfied just to have seen him. The battle renewed as rebel forces attacked the 149th and 143rd from the north. He watched as the 149th advanced, then disappeared into the railroad cut. As soon as they appeared on the other side, the 149th opened fire on the approaching enemy. Bullets were flying thick and heavy all around Jack, hitting the ground then screaming off to the woods. The cherry orchard where they huddled, was taking a terrible beating from the bullets. Leaves, branches and unripened cherries falling like snow. Now it appeared that the other Bucktail regiment was in trouble. Orders passed down the ranks, "Advance, right wheel into line! Double quick, men!" They were coming to the aid of the 149th, which had fallen back under the onslaught. Some of the 149th were trapped in the steep railroad cut and by the time they had arrived it was too late to help them, they had already been captured.

Enemy fire was intense, from both muskets and those damn cannons on Herr Ridge and Oak Hill. The regiment was in a very bad position. Shells from Oak Hill were hitting them from the front, while the cannons on

Herr Ridge were enfilading their ranks from the left. But this is where they would stay and make their stand! Jack could hear musket balls striking home, men screaming, groaning and some crying. Several were down, including at least one officer. Jack saw the officer being hit, his head exploding like a watermelon. The officer just dropped like a sack of potatoes. Another order was screamed, "Charge bayonets!" The regiment made a full charge to the other side of a hay field, where they stopped and fired a volley into the foe. Jack didn't feel the kick of the musket as he fired at the rebel, the man just disappeared from his view. This volley staggered the Confederate formation, with many of the gray clad soldiers dropping where they stood. The remaining rebels stood there for a couple of seconds, looking around in bewilderment. Rebel noncoms along with the remaining officers could be heard yelling for them to reform. Before Jack's company could get off another volley, the enemy broke to the railroad cut and across to the wheat field beyond and disappeared. When it was apparent, they weren't coming back for a while, the Federals counter marched back, this time they stopped at the farm road and waited for the next attack. As Jack rested, he looked over the ground they had just marched over. He could see muskets, hats, clothing and even parts of bodies lying all over. There were several men helping to carry wounded comrades back, under constant musket fire.

A soldier who was helping a man with a shattered arm, passed just in front of Jack. At that moment, the soldier straightened up, with a quizzical look on his face. He dropped his human cargo and fell backward, dead with a minie ball in his back. Jack jumped up and darted out to help. As he was helping the wounded man, he could hear bullets whizzing by him, then he felt other hands help grab the injured soldier. Jack looked up and saw that Jed had come out to help him get to the cover of the trees behind the regiment. The wounded man, was white as a ghost, was breathing shallow and rapidly. Jack realized that the man's left arm was completely gone below the elbow. Holding the man's head up, he tried to give him some water. The dying man's eyes opened, he tried to say something, then went limp as his eyes glazed over. Jack knew the man was dead, by now Jack was completely numb. He had already seen enough of death. With shaking hands, he gently laid the dead soldier's head on the ground.

Many thoughts ran through Jack's head, This is what war is really like. It's not fun anymore. Never will I look at a re-enactment the same way again, if I have the chance to. That is, if I survive this day and go back home.

Turning to Jed, Jack said, "Thanks for coming out and helping me carry that wounded man back."

"Well you're my new file partner, since your old file partner was wounded a while ago. Anyways, the capt'n told me to watch out for you since you're a fresh fish."

It was then that Jack realized, he had just "seen the Elephant." As far as he was concerned, he didn't care to see it again. The firing continued, he and the others crouched down and took cover behind a small breast work of fence rails. He wished it would be large Oak trees instead of the thin split wood. Bullets were continually whining and cracking overhead and the smoke was so thick, it was difficult to even see Herr Ridge by now. The hardest part of the fight was yet to come, and he wondered if he would survive, despite the carnage all around him.

Jed said out loud, "Man those hornets are really thick today."

Jack turned and with a quizzical look, asked,

"Hornets, I didn't see any hornets."

Jed and several others laughed as Jed explained, "You don't ever see these hornets, causing if you do, you'll probably be dead. Listen fresh fish, hornets are those miserable minies whizzing by."

* * * * * *

George rested and cooled down a little after the last skirmish and was almost out of water. Corporal Terry came by with a soldier, carrying a whole load of canteens.

The Corporal told Skeeter and George, "Give this man your canteens so that he can go back to a spring back yonder and get fresh water."

As the man left, George heard Skeeter call out to him, "Hey Rody[8], make sure that water is sweet and cold."

George thought to himself, Damn that name sounds familiar, I know that name. Then it dawned on him. That was the fellow who went for water and never came back until after the battle. He was picked up by the provost in Baltimore. Well, he thought, I'd better pick up the first full canteen I can find.

They rested and waited for the attacks to start again. Occasionally a bullet would whine over head or could be heard smacking into a tree. For now, things had quieted down and the only firing were the cannons.

---

[8]William Rodearmel redeemed himself later and served with distiction the remainder of the war. He was promoted to Corporal on May 1, 1865.

They could hear the artillery rounds swooshing overhead going in both directions. As George and his company sought refuge in the ravine, they could hear the cannonading, but couldn't see the effects of the shell fire. Captain Jones was moving down the line telling the men, "You must hold your positions, no matter what happens. I want you to fire by squads, unless told otherwise."

Suddenly, to their right, CRUMP, CRUMP as volleys were being discharged. Heavy firing and rising smoke could be seen above the road, but they still couldn't see any of the fighting. It was evident that a major attack was unfolding from the north, and George couldn't remember who would be attacking. After about ten minutes, the firing slacked off. George could hear screaming and yelling from the direction of the road and knew that the rebels had just been beaten back. A few minutes later he could hear heavy firing coming near the McPherson farm and if George remembered correctly, the 149th was probably fighting by the Railroad Cut. As the fighting intensified, the cannon fire was also increasing, with most of it coming from Herr Ridge and Oak Hill. George heard a screeching noise that was half way between a moan and a whistle coming from Herr Ridge and heading down the railroad cut. "Damn if that didn't sound like modern artillery," he said out loud. Fortunately the noise was so loud no one heard him. This time the musket fire went on for almost fifteen minutes before it diminished again. The cannons kept up their heavy firing even during the lulls in the battle. George thought to himself, Thank God they aren't firing on us.

Looking around, he could see men building small

breast works[9] wherever they were posted and that seemed like a good idea to him. He gathered up some small logs and some of the smaller trees that had been cut down earlier by bullets and cannon balls. He knew that very soon the battle would open on them from the west.

"Hey Skeeter, can you tell what's going on?"

A voice fired back, "Naw, I can't see anything from here, except for the reb skirmish line in front of us. I sure hope Rody gets back with those canteens pretty soon. My mouth is really dry."

"Have you "seen the Elephant," before today Skeeter?"

"Naw. At Chancellorsville we was held in reserve. So this is the first time I've seen it and it ain't so bad."

"Skeeter, I don't think you've seen the worst of it yet!"

"Naw I suppose you're right. Lookin at all them rebs out there, it may get a wee bit uncomfortable kinda soon."

* * * * * *

While Jack and the rest of the regiment were back in line along the McPherson farm road, heavy firing could be heard over in the direction of Oak Hill. Huge volumes of smoke could be seen rising above the fields beyond the railroad tracks. Because of the 150th's position, they couldn't see the action, except the air burst of exploding cannon balls. At least for the

---

[9]Breastworks are hastily thrown up barricades of logs, fence rail or anything handy.

moment, no one was firing at them directly. They could clearly hear stray minies whistling overhead from the intense fighting off to their right as two armies smashed into each other head on.

The regiment counted off by twos again and Jack noticed that Company "A," was much smaller now. In fact, he wished he were in the second rank instead of the first. Just maybe his chances for survival would be better. Jack was thankful for his new file partner, Jed, who gently grabbed his cartridge box belt and guided him through the maneuvers. Jack, in fact, was getting better at changing position. At times, because of the noise, when he couldn't hear the orders he felt Jed guide him. Men around him were pulling up their cartridge tins which were divided into four compartments and refilling them from ammunition being passed out from several wooden cases someone had brought up. Jack grabbed as many packages as he could hold in his hands and stuffed them in his haversack. He knew, that before the day was out, he would run out and have to restock again.

There was very little talking now. The men were looking around as best they could, trying to see what was happening around them. They knew that soon they would be in the thick of the fighting again. You could feel the tension building in the air as the men waited their turn to join the fray. Over toward Herr Ridge, visibility was poor as smoke and fire belched from the cannons. Masses of Confederates could be seen eerily lurking in the smoky haze and they seemed to be on the move. Unfortunately they were moving toward them. The battle was about to begin! Above the din of the battle Jack could hear the weird screeching noise that appeared to be heading toward the Iron Brigade. He tried to think back to the action he had just been in. Everything happened so fast, all he tried to do was load and fire as fast as he could. He had been shaking so badly that several times while trying to reload, he missed the barrel completely, dumping the powder on the ground. Then he learned a little trick of resting his hand against the bayonet as he poured the powder. One problem persisted though, he still dropped two or three percussion caps before he could get one on the nipple. The one thing he didn't care for at all, was biting off the end of the cartridge paper. He always managed to get the black powder in his mouth which tasted salty and bitter. His mind wandered to that poor Reb, who was less than 50 yards out when Jack fired once and the man had dropped in his tracks. The hapless rebel was looking straight at him as Jack fired. There was no emotion in the man's eyes as Jack pulled the trigger. He imagined it happened so fast the fellow's brain never registered what the eyes saw. Jack had never taken a life before and it was not a good feeling. Jack felt that he had committed a terrible deed. However it was a matter of survival, either the reb or he would have died. He said a silent prayer for the man's soul, then praying that God would forgive him for taking a life. Jack also prayed that God would spare his life.

Startled, Jack jumped when a tremendous crash of musketry erupted from the other side of the Chambersburg Pike. Then another! And another! He realized that the battle had opened in earnest for the troops on their far right. Cannon balls could be seen bursting everywhere. The Union troops who stood between the Bucktails and Oak Hill were locked in a contest to the death. Jack knew full well, the Bucktail Brigade was next.

Suddenly, there was a blood curdling scream nearby as if from a hundred banshees! A large mass of rebels rushed toward the 149th. Volleys crashed from both sides and the whole scene disappeared in heavy smoke. Through the smoke, Jack noticed that the 149th colors were planted well in advance of where he knew the 149th was positioned, which he thought was odd. He wondered what was going on, usually the regiment would close on the colors. The fighting was intensifying and minie balls were whizzing everywhere. Above the terrible din of battle, he heard screeching and groaning of men being wounded and killed. For the moment they were just standing there, not doing anything and he couldn't figure out why.

Soon the officers shouted orders, "Forward march, double quick," which took them across the farm road. They went about 100 yards, when the next order was given. "Right wheel into line!" As their regiment was doing this maneuver, minies and cannon shells were taking their toll on the men. The noise was over powering and he was marching blindly, with Jed guiding him by his cartridge box belt. The smoke was so heavy, the acrid smell tore at his throat and burned his eyes.

To Jack's horror, they stopped about 50 yards from a regiment of rebels. Before the order was given to aim and fire, the rebels had their muskets leveled at them! The re-enactor thought, Oh God, this is it, I'm going to die, they can't miss. He put his head down so he wouldn't see the end come. It was the most terrifying sound he had ever heard! As the volley ripped into their ranks, the sickening thuds and thumps could be heard as the wicked minies struck home all around him. Wailing of wounded and dying men was gut wrenching and for a split second, his mind went completely blank, as his brain shut out the horrors around him.

Jack snapped back and to his amazement, he wasn't hit! Officers and noncoms were screaming "Close it up, fire a volley into them, quickly, quickly, boys!" He raised his musket and aimed at a rebel who was in the process of biting off a cartridge and at the command to fire, he felt the musket kick his shoulder. When the smoke had cleared, the man was gone, with many more gray backs replacing him.

Another order was shouted above the noise, "Charge!" Forward they went, shrieking at the top of their lungs as they pushed to the rebels with their bayonets. The remaining enemy turned, ran, and disappeared into the wheat field again. Jack was sweating profusely and shaking worse than before, when they stopped just short of the line where the Confederates had stood. He saw the carnage, they had rendered on that line. There was a long line of dead and wounded men. Jack didn't look for the man he shot, he really didn't want to see him. It was his mind's way of locking out the horrors of war. Jack thought, Thank you God for sparing my life.

"Load and come to the ready," was ordered as he loaded with trembling hands. As he looked around, noticing that the ranks had been thinned down severely as a result of the last rebel volley. While they marched back, Jack could see the line of blue clad soldiers lying where they had stood only moments before. Some men were trying to crawl. Others were hobbling; while many were just lying there groaning, crying and calling for their mothers. Jack had to close his eyes to block out the horrors of these dead and terribly wounded men, but he couldn't shut out the sounds.

Jack was like a zombie, as Jed guided him back to their original position. God, how he hoped that this nightmare would end soon and he could go back to the twentieth century.

* * * * * *

George was resting behind his small breast works trying to cool down and wishing he had his canteen because his mouth was dry as sand. His thoughts were interrupted by an order being passed down the line. "OK boys, here they come. Corporals, give the order to fire by squads when the captain drops his sword."

Standing, George could see the rebel skirmishers moving toward them. About 100 yards behind the skirmishers, he saw the first Confederate battle flags appear over the knoll. He counted three flags in a line, which meant that there were three regiments about to tear into their small band of skirmishers. Corporal Terry told them, "Hold steady boys," as they watched the enemy skirmishers close on them.

They waited until the rebels were only 75 yards out, when the their corporal ordered, "READY... AIM... FIRE!" Instinctively, George brought the musket to his shoulder, aimed at the chest of the nearest reb and fired. When the smoke cleared, the man was gone. George thought he was going to be sick. I just killed a man and I did it without thinking.

Men were screaming everywhere "Load and fire, load and fire." Reloading, George placed a percussion cap on the nipple and fired at the next man he saw. The rules had just changed for him. George was fighting for his life. The re-enactor was numbed by all the intense noise around him. Volleys being fired, bullets whizzing all around him, screeching and wailing of wounded men. It seemed like everyone was shouting orders.

The first rebel regiment closed within firing range and a volley slammed into their line. George could hear several minies zing by his head. Suddenly, he felt a burning sensation, like a bee sting in his side; however he didn't have time to see what happened. Just load and fire, load and fire. The ram rod was so slippery that he had a terrible time ramming the bullets down the barrel. To his amazement, he saw the rebel regiments moving back. A loud cheer went down the line.

George looked over and saw that Skeeter was OK and trying to load again. He was having the same problem as George did with the slippery ram rod. Finally, Skeeter, out of desperation took the musket with the ram rod half out and rammed it against a tree until the ball was seated. George took his ram rod and with a handful of grass, wiped the grease off, then used grass and dirt to wash his hands of the grease as best he could. During the brief lull, he had time to check himself over and to check the spot on his side which still burned. He saw the hole in his jacket and shirt, then pulled up his shirt which revealed just the slightest break of the skin where he had been grazed. The whole area was black and blue already. He was lucky this time, but the bullets were getting closer. Looking around to make sure nobody was watching him, George took out a small tube of the antiseptic ointment he always carried and smeared it gingerly on the flesh wound, to prevent infection.

* * * * * *

Jack thought he was going to pass out, the heat, humidity, and exertion were taking its toll on him and many of the other men. Runners scurried for water and the noncoms and officers urged the men to drink as much water as they could. The water helped, but right now Jack would give a $100 for a tall glass of iced tea with crushed ice. Jack's uniform and leather goods were saturated from perspiration. Looking at his hands, he noticed they were completely black and greasy. He wiped them on his wool pants. Jack removed his slippery ram rod from the musket and took a handful of grass, wiping it down, just like he saw the other men around him doing. There was still intense firing off to his right, beyond the railroad cut and now he could hear heavy firing down in front where the skirmish companies were. Jack wondered if his friend was still alive and hoped he would survive the day. Then, he thought of his wife and longed to see her again. He would never take her for granted again. His day dreaming was shattered as the firing increased by the railroad cut! The 150th wheeled to help the 149th and fell into the battle line, opening fire at another regiment of rebels directly in their front. They staggered the gray clad soldiers with a well-placed volley, but not for long. The Confederates re-grouped, and opened fire into the Bucktail ranks.

The two regiments stood their ground with only 50 yards separating them and fired volley after volley into each other. This is crazy, thought Jack. Finally the 150th charged bayonets and drove the remaining rebels from the field. Jack's mind was completely worn out by now and he was just loading and firing by rote. After the enemy in their front disappeared, the 150th marched back to their original line on the farm lane. Looking around, he could see the company was down to less than 20 men. His file partner, Jed was still with him, but Crackers was no where to be seen. Jack drank deeply from his canteen, trying to wash the terrible taste of black powder, sweat, smoke, and grease from his mouth. Nothing worked, however right now, nothing mattered, except that he was still alive.

Jack's body didn't feel like it could move another foot. In fact, he felt like he could just lay down and sleep, but that wouldn't happen. Another attack appeared to be coming from the northwest and the west, with very heavy cannon fire coming from Oak Hill and Herr Ridge! Shells hissing, screeching and moaning, appearing to come from every direction. And every shell seemed to be aimed directly at him. Shells were exploding everywhere and men were falling right and left. Jack could see scores of men being helped to the barn where the field hospital was set up.

* * * * *

The two rebels, Josh and Paul arrived at their regiment, the 26th North Carolina and waited for the axe to fall. Colonel Burgwyn[10] called them traitors, shirkers and everything else that came to mind. After the officer cooled down a little, "You came back on your own, that's your only saving grace. I'm going to put both of you in the skirmish company and you'll stay there forever. If I hear of shirking or skedaddling about either of you, I'll have you court-martialed as deserters and shot. Do you understand me?"

"Yes sir!" They both replied in unison.

The colonel turned to the first sergeant, "Put these two men in the skirmish company. Give Captain DeCamp my best regards and instructions to shoot these two men if they try to avoid their duty!"

The sergeant marched them to their new

----

[10]Known as the Boy Colonel, he was barely 21 years old.

230

company and on the way, he hissed at them, "You sunvabitches got me in hot water with the colonel. If I had my way, you two bastards would have every bit of skin ripped off your backs with a horse whip."

After joining the skirmish company, they waited for a while before advancing. Heavy firing could be heard ahead of them and the cannons were crashing out their deadly orbs of iron toward the yankee lines. It was extremely humid and they couldn't drink enough water. Shortly they were on the move. The skirmishers advanced ahead of the brigade and soon passed over Herr Ridge. The cannons on the ridge were firing hotly at the Federal positions. They could hear the enemy cannon balls passing overhead, heading for the advancing troops behind them. In their front, the skirmishers could hear Archer's Brigade heavily engaged, but for the moment they stopped and crouched down in the wheat, waiting for the word to move out again.

Josh called over to his file partner, who was about 15 feet from him, "Hey Paul, can you see anything?"

"Naw, can't see nary a thing, excepting them cannon balls going over!"

This was the worst part. Just waiting. Hearing the fighting close by and listening to the minie balls whistling overhead, along with the shells going in both directions. The day was getting hotter, more humid and laying in the sun in a dusty wheat field, didn't help matters at all. Josh wished they would move out and see some of the action, but he didn't dare get up and look around. That would be a good way of becoming a target. He knew one thing for sure, he was better off as a skirmisher. At least they wouldn't be shoulder to shoulder, battling it out at close range with the blue bellies. The last time he had done that, everybody around him was shot down, those damn minies and cannister shot tore up men pretty bad. The colonel thought he was punishing them by putting them in the skirmish company, but Josh knew he stood a better chance of surviving being spread out in a skirmish line.

At last they were given the order to move out. As they advanced in a crouch, their line swung slightly to the right and Josh could see they were heading toward some woods on the other side of a creek and a brush line. For some reason the line stopped and they retraced their steps and held the skirmish line again, this time a little closer to the toll road.

The corporal came by checking on the men and Josh asked him, "What's going on, are we gonna fight soon?"

"Don't quite know? Excepting we are being held in reserve for the time being," he replied. "But the old man is hopping mad. He wants to tear into those yanks. So we'll just have to wait here for a while."

"Corporal, our water's gettin' kinda low, can we get them filled at that creek down yonder?" Josh asked.

"The captain said you two boys were to stay put. I'll send someone around to pick up the canteens and get them filled at that thar farmhouse over yonder." And with that he was gone, leaving Josh wondering how long before they got some more water. His mouth was so dry his tongue felt like it was swollen.

After about 15 minutes a soldier came crawling along dragging about ten canteens by the straps and Josh gave his canteen to the waterman. Then the man crawled on to collect more. The cannons on the ridge behind him started firing heavily again and as he laid there, looking up, he could actually see the balls in flight, trailing a wispy trail of smoke from the fuze. About two seconds later, he could hear the explosions and feel the ground shudder from the impact. Josh was glad he wasn't on the receiving end.

Several cannon balls came from the other direction as the yankee guns fired back. After what seemed like hours, the man came crawling back with the filled canteens. When Josh got his, he pulled the cork out and drank deeply.

The water carrier cautioned, "Laddie, better take it easy on that water. We may be on the move soon and that may be the only water you'll get for some hours."

The firing on the ridge in front of them was getting very intense and he figured the blue bellies would soon be skedaddling back to wherever they came from. If the skirmishers didn't go soon, the fighting would be over and that would be OK with him. He didn't feel like fighting today, much too hot. Suddenly, he could hear men approaching and Josh got up and peeked over the top of the wheat to see who it was. Now what in the world is going on, Josh thought. It looks like Archers men and they sure didn't look like they were letting grass grow under their feet. As the first men passed through the skirmish line, he called out to a bedraggled man whose face was blackened and looked very drawn. "Hey, what happened up thar on the ridge? Why are ya'll coming back? Are the yanks gone?"

The man stopped and looked at Josh, with the look that only a man who had witnessed some God forsaken horror and slowly replied, "Hal no. Them yanks are fiten like banshees! Ain't never seen anything like it, we got wupped real bad like. We got surrounded and they poured volley after volley into us. They even captured the general hisself. Saw it with my on eyes. I just got out by the skin of my teeth. My whole company's gone and them fellers was wearing them black hats."

The demoaralized soldier moved off and out of sight, as other men straggled past. Some were wounded and bleeding, being helped by comrades. Oh damn, he thought, It didn't look good. Looks like we're gonna get to fighten real soon like. Danged if it wasn't too hot to fight. He laid there again, listening to the sounds of the battle. Still they weren't given the order to advance. It seemed a bit strange, but he wasn't no general, so he would just wait.

"Hey Paul, did ya'll hear what Archers men said? He said Archer hisself got captured!"

"Yea, I heard. Did he say them fellers were wearing the black hats?"

"Yup, that's shure enough what he said. Shure don't sound like no militia to me," Josh answered.

"Quit talking, we don't want the yanks to know we're here!" A sergeant ordered.

During this time, the battle would intensify, then wane for a while; then start again. This went on for over an hour. It was starting to get to him. Josh had no idea what was happening around him. From the sounds, it appeared to be many different battles, none at the same time. It just didn't make any sense to him. Wonder what the yanks are up to? And that feller said they were wearing those black hats. Danged if it didn't sound like the Army of the Potomac, it couldn't be. The general himself said there were only some cavalry and some local militia. And the yanks only had a few cannons from the sounds of it. So it couldn't be the Army of the Potomac. Well, he would just rest as best he could for now. He only wished he were in the shade and had some vittles to eat. Josh heard a "Psst" and he called, "Who's there?"

A voice came back, "It's me, Paul. I'ma comin over. Don't shoot." Soon Paul was next to Josh, "Ya'll know what's happening around here?"

Josh responded, "Danged if I know, but the fightin's been gone on awful long so far and them Archers fellows said they got whupped by the black hats. They must be mistaken. Why there's only some cav and militia up there. They ain't hardly got no artillery. So it can't be the army as I see it."

Paul stuck his head up for a second then ducked down and turned to Josh, "Yea, if that's so, then why is there all that shootin gone on up ahead."

"Soldier, what are you doin out of position? Git your arse back over there and get ready to move out!" The corporal demanded. Then looking at Josh, "You two better watch out, the captain will shoot you like a dawg! Now get ready to move. We're gonna feel out the enemy up ahead, and it looks like theys got piss in their veins."

Then he was gone and Josh started rechecking his musket. It was a good thing he did. Sometime while he was jostling around, his percussion cap had fallen off. So he reached into his cap box, retrieved a cap and inserted it onto the nipple of his musket. After he took a swig of water from his canteen, he was ready.

Josh could hear the sergeants and corporals calling out in hushed tones, "Skirmishers, up and move forward!" With the order, Josh stood up and he noticed all the skirmishers pop up like rats out of a hole. They started moving forward in a crouch. Ahead of them was a line of trees and a creek at the bottom of the small hill they were on. Several regiments of the South Carolina troops could be seen massed up, ready to attack across the stream. Josh's skirmish company wheeled right and headed on a line that would take them past the woods that ran to the stream. As they moved ahead, he could see the results of all the heavy firing he had heard earlier. There were bodies lying everywhere and there were blue and grey uniforms intermixed. They had to be careful not to step on the wounded men who were still lying there. Some begging for water. Others just asking for help, but the skirmishers couldn't stop. He was snapped out of his reverie by a musket ball which just missed his face. Danged if he didn't feel the push of air, as it whistled by, Josh thought. Instinctively, he ducked his head, then remembered his sergeant saying, "Don't worry about the ones you hear, they already passed you. You don't hear the ones that will get you!" As they were passing the woods on their left, they were coming under enfilade fire until they finally went into a swale which hid them from the woods. They were fortunate, no one was hit, as most of the fire went high. It was getting hotter and the dust they were kicking up was clogging his nose and getting into his eyes. Not to mention the sweat that was streaming down his face.

Soon they reached the end of the woods, then wheeled left again and came to the creek. The water was knee deep with a muddy bottom. The sluggish stream didn't carry away the silt and the water was a dark brown. Cautiously they crossed it and Josh reached down filling his canteen in the muddy, dirty water. Taking his hat off, he filled it to the brim, putting it back on his head. The water rushing down his face and back helped relieve the heat and humidity if only for a minute or two. When they were through crossing the waterway, they pushed on further along the enemy lines. Meanwhile, the enemy was sending harassing musket fire their way. Minies were still going high and they had no casualties. As they approached a low ridge, Josh could see a cupola of a large white building ahead of him. For some unknown reason they were ordered to stop and went to the ground, laying in the tall grass awaiting orders to move. Josh could hear the heavy sounds of volleys being fired around the woods they had just passed and he could hear the blasts of cannons spewing out the hated cannister shot in the woods. The fighting was intense and Josh was glad they weren't attacking there. The portion of the skirmish line Josh was in, had drifted to the extreme right because of a gully which they followed. While the rest of the skirmish line and main line smashed into the 24th Michigan, they unknowingly slipped to the side of the 19th Indiana and toward the Bucktail skirmishers.

The word whispered up and down the line to move out toward the enemy's line. They had no sooner started moving when a company of blue bellies stood up in front of them. They were about 50 yards out and fired a volley into the rebel skirmishers. Josh heard a loud crack and he was spun around, at the same time his musket was ripped out of his hands. He quickly bent over and picked up his gun and looked to see if it was damaged. To his amazement, a minie ball had ripped the hammer and lock plate clean out of the musket.

One of the corporals passed the order, "Charge them while they're trying to reload!"

So Josh charged with his disabled musket but the yanks didn't break and run. The lines sort of moved back a little, while they were reloading. He saw one of the other skirmishers charging a federal soldier, who was left behind by the others. The union soldier was down on one knee, with his head down. As Josh was still running, he saw an amazing sight. The skirmisher who didn't see the musket pointed at him, ran full onto the bayonet of the yankee soldier!

Josh was upon the hapless yank, as he was trying to pull the bayonet out of the lifeless body of the unlucky rebel. Josh raised his disabled musket, swinging it butt first toward the yankee soldier. As he was about to smash in the man's head, he saw the Bucktail on the man's hat. He immediately recognized the man from the night before. In his surprise, he pulled the blow as best he could, but still struck him with a glancing blow on the head and the man went down. Josh quickly threw down his broken musket and picked up the yankee's musket and started back with the others, as a volley was fired at them again.

He couldn't believe his luck but he had the Enfield he swore he would get. As he was running, he left out a loud "Whoopee," which could be heard above all the noise. After reaching the safety of his skirmish line Josh stopped. The men were hiding in the grass awaiting their next move. Although he was out of breath, Josh didn't understand but he was totally elated at getting this musket. But why, it was just a Enfield!

******

George could tell they were in trouble as more Confederate flags could be seen coming over the ridge. Looking over to his right, he could see a rebel regiment coming at an angle to their line. This would make the enemy hit the right side of his company first. As the whole Confederate line hit them, pandemonium broke out! There was total confusion as the right side of his company was rolled back. This in effect cut them off from the rest of the skirmish line. George could see the skirmishers from the 149th and 143rd regiments being pushed back to McPherson's ridge and there was no way to rejoin them. Confederate attackers were pushing the line back with determination. The 150th skirmish line started to sag backwards toward Herbst's woods, completely cut off from their Brigade. They leap frogged back by platoons, firing and loading as they were slowly pushed back to the Iron Brigade's battle line. Fortunately they had the cover of the tree line and brush which kept their casualties low.

The Confederates seemed confused and if they wanted to, they could have swooped up this small company with one good charge, but it never happened. George could only guess, maybe the rebels weren't sure how strong a force they were. Company B moved into the woods and fought at the right flank of the Iron Brigade for a short time. The 150th skirmish company still had quite a few men left, so an officer from the Iron Brigade came over to Captain Jones saying, "My colonel, would be forever indebted, if you would join our thinned out ranks."

George could hear the captain reply, "Why the Bucktails would be honored to lend assistance to your colonel." They were placed at the right of the Brigade for about a half hour. The Bucktails helped stave off increasingly intense attacks from the West. During one of the short lulls in the action, George was able to see an old man wearing a top hat and swallow tail coat with one of the skirmish companies to his front. Damn, he thought to himself, That's John Burns! I'll have to try later and talk to him. He could see the men around him talking to him and shaking his hand, but what stood out most was the man's height. He stood almost 4" taller than the men in the skirmish company. Add in that old silly looking top hat and the old veteran would be an inviting target for some rebel tree frog.[11]

After holding their position for a time, one of the brigade officers came over to Captain Jones. "It is desired by the colonel that you move your company to the extreme left of the brigade to protect that flank."

"As you wish. Sir!"

The order was passed, "Company right face," and they formed into a four-man column. The next order

---

[11]Sharpshooter or sniper

239

issued, "Forward march. Counter files by the left, march." The company moved through the woods toward their assigned position. As they pushed on, George could see the intense effects of the cannon projectiles and minie balls on the trees. There were trees cut in half and branches littered the ground everywhere. This made marching and staying in ranks very difficult. Every possible type of equipment imaginable littered the ground, interspersed with pieces of what had been men a short time ago, covered the ground. The carnage of the last several hours was everywhere. George was benumbed to it by now. His only concern was to make it through today, then worry about tomorrow.

The Bucktails came to a field and were ordered, "Column into line." They formed a two deep line of battle to the left of the 19th Indiana, where they formed the extreme left of the brigade. The men crouched down in the tall grass and waited. Soon the word was whispered down the line, "There's an enemy skirmish line approaching us. When the order is given, stand and fire." After waiting for a couple of minutes someone screamed, "Pour it into them boys!"

The company stood and fired a volley, but the enemy skirmishers were spread out and only a couple were hit. As the Bucktails tried to reload, the rebels charged them and they were forced back 20 yards.

George, completely overcome by the heat and exertion did not hear the command to fall back. His head felt light and vision was blurred. He felt like he was going to pass out as he went down on one knee. He tried to keep from falling by holding himself up with his musket butt placed firmly on the ground. Through the dimness of his mind, he heard a scream. To his horror he saw a Confederate soldier charging him with his rifle butt raised, ready to smash George's head in. To his astonishment the soldier slid onto his bayonet. The rebel soldier's eyes opened wide and his mouth formed a perfect "O" as he expelled his last breath in a loud "whoosh." He fell, wrenching the musket from George's hands.

George stood up and tried to pull out the bayoneted musket from the lifeless body. Suddenly he saw a flash of white, then nothing. George was dimly aware of being dragged by someone. Whom he didn't know. He was completely at the mercy of others and somewhere in the deepest recesses of his mind he could hear screaming and shouting. But it was surreal and far, far away.

As he started to come back to his senses, he heard Skeeter asking in a loud voice, "Pops, are you Ok?"

"Yea, but my head hurts like hell. What hit me?"

"Dangdist thing I ever did see. You run thru a reb like skewering a hog when another reb came along and beaned you on the head and took your musket. He did all kinds of whooperin and hollarin as he ran back into some trees. The company fired by files while you were down. It forced the rebels back to the cover of a ravine and gave me time to get to you. I came out and drugged you back with me. Can you stand up?"

George managed to get on all fours when he felt Skeeter grab him by the arm to help him to his feet. Damn if he wasn't dizzy. He hoped he didn't have a concussion. He gingerly felt his head where he had been struck. George had a large goose egg and a piece of his scalp laid open. He realized how lucky he was, it had only been a glancing blow. Pulling the flap of skin back in place, he put pressure on it until the bleeding stopped. Looking at his uniform he could see it was completely soaked down one side in his blood. You always bleed heavily from a head wound, he thought.

Meanwhile, the Bucktails resumed their original

241

position. Someone had picked up a discarded gun and the Corporal handed it to George with the admonishment, "See if you can hold on to this musket for a while."

George looked at the original Enfield and it was a beauty. The stock was polished with very few nicks in it. The metal barrel and hardware were highly polished. This musket was well-taken care of by its previous owner. He wondered what had happened to the owner. Was he dead or alive? George hoped he would be able to hang onto it. His head still hurt like hell and it really throbbed. At least he was sure he didn't have a concussion. He wondered who the rebel was and if it was that same one Bill Sloan had told him about. Everything the old man said had come true. The only thing he didn't tell him was, whether he would survive in one piece. Something wasn't right with this picture. He had lost the musket as predicted. So why didn't he go back to the future? Maybe the wrong person captured the musket. No, Bill Sloan was emphatic about it being taken from a Bucktail on the first day. Nothing made sense anymore. George wished he would go forward in time and real soon. He'd had enough of the Civil War to last a life time.

Again the rebels came back. This time in force, trying to drive the Bucktails back so they could flank the Iron brigade. They waited until the gray backs stopped to fire a volley into them. The Federals were given the order to fire by ranks. They did this with devastating results. The line in front of them just melted away and the rebels only managed to fire a few shots before they fell back. Off to their left, heavy firing could be heard and if he remembered correctly, it would be Biddle's men.

The respite didn't last long for Company B. The rebels came back once more. This time George's

Company fired just as they came over the rise. This volley staggered the Confederate line and there was confusion in the gray ranks. George could see one of the sergeants pointing to their left and he looked over and just about had a heart attack. As they fought off the rebels in front of them, another enemy regiment rapidly approached them on their flank, previously hidden from view by a swale. They were about 200 yards out and the Bucktails were in deep trouble. They would have to swing their line back and hope that the rebs on their right didn't slam into them at the same time. But time was running out on them!

The 26th North Carolina Regiment had 11 men including Colonel Burgwyn shot down with the colors on July 1, 1863.

The 26th NC lost approximately 550 men out of about 800 men on July 1, 1863.

As the bucktails left Seminary Ridge and advanced toward McPherson Ridge, an unknown bucktail shouted, "We have come to stay." The whole brigade took up the chant and before the day ended, many stayed for eternity.

CHAPTER TWELVE

As Jan sat on the bench with the reporter, she looked up and saw a mini van fly into the parking lot. She recognized the vehicle and Marge driving it. The car pulled into the first available slot. It hardly stopped moving, when both doors flew open and the two wives jumped out running toward them. Jan met them half way and embraced both of the wives and at least felt better that she was with friends again.

The barrage of questions started, Marge asking first, "Is Tim OK? Where are the others? You said only Tim came back."

"Did they find Jack or George yet? Where did they go? Did Tim say anything about our husbands?" Katey asked.

Jan put her hand up and was able to quiet them both for the moment, "Yes, Tim is OK, but we don't know the where abouts of George or Jack yet. I don't know what's happening. Not until we can talk with Tim, will we know anything else. Come with me, I want to introduce you both to someone." As they approached the bench where the reporter was sitting, Jim Craig stood up, "This is Jim Craig, he's a reporter."

"I don't like the idea of a reporter being involved!" Marge protested.

"He's a friend and if he hadn't alerted me this

morning, I probably still wouldn't know what was happening. He has promised not to write anything until after this whole mess is cleared up."

Her husband was safe which relieved Marge. But she feared for her friend's husbands who were still missing. "Jan, what do you know about what happened to our husbands? Did they go back in time or did something else happen to them?"

"Marge, I'm not sure what has happened. I haven't talked to Tim yet, only to our lawyer. He only knows what Tim has told him. He was going to go over the arrest report before he did anything further. In fact he's inside right now with the Park Service and the Deputy U.S. Attorney, seeing if he can get your husband released."

"Well I'm going inside right now and demand that I see my husband." Marge said as she stood up.

Stopping her Jan said, "I think it would be better to wait until our lawyer comes back out. He's one of the best and I could tell that the rangers were very uneasy when they saw him."

Katey was still sitting on the bench not saying anything, when suddenly, she started shaking uncontrollably and sobbing. Both Jan and Marge put their arms around her and tried to comfort her. In a torrent of tears Katey cried, "Where's my Jack, what's happening to him? Oh God! If anything happens to him, what am I going to do?"

"For the moment, we have to assume that he is OK and soon he will appear." Jan tried to reassure her. "After all, didn't Tim come back?" This managed to soothe her a little, but she continued to hold on to Jan and Marge for dear life. Jim Craig had moved a short distance and left the women alone out of respect for their distress. There would always be time to talk to them later, when emotions had settled down.

Ron Dustin finished going over the arrest report and a small smile crept over his face, he had them, plain and simple. The secret service blew the whole case by dancing around the lawyer issue before questioning Tim. According to the arrest report, the musket, ammunition and bayonet were over 20 feet from Tim and never under his control. Plus the fact he had told the arresting officer where they were. That charge should be dropped. The only thing they may have stand up in court was Tim being in the park after hours. Shortly he was called into the office with the U.S. Attorney and the superintendent. As he entered, he recognized U.S. Deputy Attorney George Atwell, whom he knew for several years and respected as being very fair and level headed. Ron sat across from Richard Jackson, as George Atwell stood by the desk. Ron asked them both, "Well, have you decided to drop charges and release my client?"

"Well sir, you know your client has broken a multitude of park rules." The Deputy U.S. Attorney informed him. "It could cost him a lot of money and maybe a little jail time. Now I've talked to the Secret Service and the agent in charge feels this is an extrodinary case. He also believes your client is telling the truth as he knows it. In the interest of fairness, we would be willing to say, just charge him with being in the park after hours. Maybe a little fine, say, $125.00 and costs. Would your client agree to that? We can put this whole thing behind us and he can go home."

They were only trying to save face, Ron realized, but it irked him. People always had to save face even if an innocent man had to plead guilty to a lesser charge. Ron stood up, then replied in a very even, hard voice, "Gentlemen, you know you don't have a strong case! In fact, if this is pursued at all, I can smell a very large law suit, not to mention a lot of ruined careers. So let's cut out the dancing around. Drop all charges and I will talk to my client and have him agree not to pursue this any further. Is that acceptable?"

George Atwell looked at him and asked, "Does that mean, your client will agree not to press charges against the park service and not go public with the arrest?"

"Let me talk to my client for a few minutes and see what I can do."

Ron was let into the room by a ranger standing guard where Tim was being held. As he entered, Tim stood up and crossed the room to hear what his lawyer had to say. "I've gone over the arrest report and the charge of being in the park after hours would probably hold up. They are willing to drop all charges as long as you agree not to hold them libel or go public."

"Does this mean I can't sue any of them for false arrest?"

"This whole episode is something out of the ordinary but it was not an illegal arrest," Ron explained. "And if you try to pursue this in court, yes, you may win with a sympathetic jury, but the cost might be high. Think about it, you would have to convince a jury that you had traveled in time. I don't think they would believe that possible, not even probable. True, they may find the Secret Service acted outside the law and in violation of your civil rights. In all reality they would probably only award a dollar in damages. I've seen it happen before. I'm only advising you, however I think you've been through enough and you do have to find your friends."

Tim thought for a few minutes Mr. Dustin was right. He might be able to sue, but he could become the laughing stock of everyone who knew him. Was it worth the time and aggravation? And for what? Sure he may destroy some careers, but under the circumstances, what else could they have done? They were only trying to do their jobs. No it would be better to put the whole thing behind him. Tim told Ron Dustin, "OK, I'll agree to everything, on the condition, that they give me all of my equipment back including the ammunition and primers. That is the only thing I have to prove to myself that it did happen."

Ron went back to the park superintendent's office and announced, "My client will agree not to press charges, but he wants all of his equipment back including the ammunition and primers."

The U.S. Attorney balked at the last condition. After conversing with the park superintendent, "Agreed, but the transfer of the musket, bayonet, cartridges and primers will have to take place off of park property, so that no laws will be broken again. Ron Dustin went outside to tell Jan Murray the good news, when he noticed the other wives had arrived. As soon as they saw Ron coming out of the building, they rushed over and hit him with a barrage of questions. "Mr. Dustin, are they going to release him?" "Does he know where my husband is?" "Is he OK?"

Ron put his hand up to quiet them, "Tim is being released without being charged. Let's go inside."

Jim Craig waited outside, hoping that Mrs. Murray wouldn't go back on her word about giving him the story and deep inside, he knew she would come through.

Tim was walking out of the holding room, when Marge spotted him she let out a scream and threw her arms around him, and she started to cry uncontrollably. After a few minutes, she slowly loosened her grip and stepped back, looked at him and simply said, "Phew, you stink, you need a shower, really bad."

Tim started to laugh, "If you slept in a barn and didn't have a shower in a week, you'd stink too."

With that, the whole entourage went outside to talk. Ronald Dustin briefed them on what had transpired earlier and that he would be on call in case the others showed up.

"Mr. Dustin, I'm not happy about not being able to bring a civil suit against the park service and the secret service," Marge voiced her displeasure.

He explained the reason they took that course of action. Ron ended with, "Don't you think it's time to put this behind you, not to mention the ridicule and embarrassment you would face, trying to fight the government."

"Marge, this was my decision," Tim interrupted, "I don't think they were trying to break the law. If you look at all the circumstances around this, what else could they have done. The Secret Service was only trying to protect the President. Now, why don't we go some place where I can get a shower and something to eat. Then I'll tell you everything I know."

The lawyer told them he would be going back to his office to write up what had happened, just in case things changed. He also told them he was not going to charge them for handling the case, but he would like to know the whole story when it ended.

Each of the women hugged the lawyer, thanking him for what he had done for Tim. Ron told them, "If you hear anything at all, I'm only a phone call away. I will keep your missing husbands in my prayers. I do have the feeling they will return OK."

The women agreed to call Mr. Dustin if they heard any news at all. Especially if their husbands showed up, which deep in their hearts, they wished would happen soon.

"Let's go to my motel room," Jim Craig suggested. "Tim can take a shower, while we send out for food. Then we can talk over what happened to Tim since he disappeared with his friends. Also I have a scanner, and just maybe, we'll hear something about your husbands. Also, I would like to hear all about that video tape that shows your husbands' disappearance."

Tim's head snapped around, "What tape showing us disappearing? What are you talking about?"

Marge explained to the disbelieving Tim all about the tape.

When she finished the story, Tim asked of no one in particular, "What time is it?"

Jan looked at her watch, which her husband, gave her the past Christmas and replied, "It's 4 p.m. already."

"No wonder I'm starved. I haven't eaten since last night, or was it 125 years ago. But I don't want any damn rabbit."

Puzzled Marge asked, "Why did you say that, about the rabbit?"

Tim replied, "It's a long story, I'll tell you all about it later."

They all agreed to go to the reporter's room and ordered a big feast. But no rabbit.

* * * * * *

At Secret Service headquarters, Tom Gallager finished the agents assignments for the next two days and went over all the reports from that day. He was satisfied that everything was in order and bar any unforeseen events, he was ready for the President's visit.

An agent on desk duty buzzed Tom and told him that Agent Stoner was on line one. He picked up the phone quickly and said "Bucky, what do you have?"

The voice on the other end had a touch of excitement in it. This was quite unusual for Bucky, as he was one of the coolest persons he knew. "Tom, you're not going to believe this, but honest to God, it's true. I went back to Bill Sloan's house and we went to his collection again. We were both standing in front of the slot, where the missing musket had been. I was trying to figure out some logical explanation for its disappearance. When, not more than five minutes ago, lo and behold, that damn musket appeared before my very eyes. One second there was a blank spot and the next, it was there. Just like that! I checked everything, there was no way it could have gotten there! We took it out of the case and Mr. Sloan said it was the missing musket. Tom I'm shaking so bad, I couldn't hold a cup of coffee even if I had to. Something has happened here that defies all logic!"

Tom allowed the words to sink in slowly and for once in his life, he was speechless. It appeared, that what the re-enactor told him might be true, but all his experience said it was impossible. When he was able to speak again, "Bucky keep looking. There has to be an explanation and call me back in the morning. Maybe I can try to piece this incredible story together!"

Tom spoke out loud to himself, "I hope those two men survive and return!" What the hell am I saying, he thought to himself. Picking up the phone, Tom called the park service. A voice on the other end asked, "How can I be of service?"

"This is Special Agent Tom Gallager of the U.S. Secret Service, I would like to speak with the superintendent?"

After a click of a line being transferred, a voice on the other end answered, "This is Richard Jackson. What can I do for you Mr. Gallager?"

"You can call me Tom. What do you know about

the fighting on the first day at Gettysburg?"

"Well Tom, I'm quite versed on the whole battle. What in particular were you looking for? Oh, by the way, you can call me Dick."

"Dick, something very weird has happened," Tom replied. "First of all, did the 26th North Carolina Regiment attack the 150th Bucktails on the first day?"

There was a slight pause before Dick answered, "Well, not exactly."

"What do you mean not exactly?"

"There's a possibility that a small portion of the 26th North Carolina skirmishers may have engaged Company B of the 150th Bucktails. Company B was the skirmish company. They wound up holding the left flank of the Iron Brigade, next to the 19th Indiana Regiment. The 26th North Carolina did attack the 24th Michigan in that vicinity. So it is possible. Why is that so important?"

"Just a hunch. Do you have any idea of the approximate time they may have been attacked?"

Dick was confused by the questions replied, "Just an educated guess, it may have been between 2:30 and a little after 3 p.m.. What is the importance of that?"

Almost in a whisper Tom said, "You know the story of those re-enactors. Well my man in South Carolina just called me a few minutes ago. Right around 4 p.m., that missing musket I told you about earlier, appeared right before his very eyes. But if it's like you say, the time doesn't add up."

There was total silence on the other end of the line. Finally the voice on the other end replied incredulously, "But they didn't have daylight saving time in the Civil War! Remember, spring ahead!"

On the first days battle there were eight Medal of Honors awarded. Seven were in the First Corps. Three medals were from the Bucktail Brigade. Two went to the 150th PVI and one to the 143rd PVI.
(Blue and Gray 11/87)

CHAPTER THIRTEEN

Jack turned to Jed, "Do you see Crackers anywhere?"

Jed just shook his head sadly and Jack could detect tears coming to his eyes as he spoke in a trembling voice, "Crackers is dead! He got hit right twixed the eyes when we was fighting that last bunch of heathen rebs! I have to try to find him later so I can give him a decent burial, like I promised."

Jack could feel his grief, even though he hadn't known Crackers very long. But, he had a funny feeling in his gut, knowing it may only be a matter of time before he would be killed or wounded. The way they were fighting at close range, there was no way he was going to survive this day. He wasn't a religious man, but he was going to pray like he never prayed before, hoping for deliverance from this hell on earth. Jack thought of his wife, Katey and what she must be going through, not knowing what happened to him. Oh how he wished that he could at least see her one more time, to tell her how much he loved her.

A loud voice, snapped Jack out of his daydream, "Here they come again, in our front!"

Looking toward the west, Jack could see the skirmish companies coming back, with the rebel skirmishers hot on their heels. Something wasn't right.

Where Company B should have been, there wasn't anything but open field. That meant George was either killed or captured. He felt himself getting sick. After the remaining skirmishers fell in with their regiments, they were given the order "Give them a volley boys, your fighting for your homes." The volley went off like one gigantic crash of thunder. While the smoke hid the rebels, they feverishly loaded as the enemy in their front fired blindly toward the Union line. The deadly minies could be heard whistling and whining close overhead. Over to their left next to the Herbst woods, two Union cannons were adding to the din, firing canister shot as quick as they could. Soon the Confederate pieces on Herr Ridge found the range of these cannons and more than twenty balls tore around the Union crew, forcing them to retire.

Thank God, Jack thought, The heavy smoke hid them from the enemy and they fired high with their volley. As the smoke cleared a little, they could see the enemy advancing, but there were many gaps in their lines.

Screaming, someone ordered, "Fire at will! Fire at will! Load quickly, men!"

It seemed to Jack that every man was taking his time, aiming and firing as the rebels were falling right and left. But on they came, reforming and advancing, firing, loading and firing. The Bucktails were receiving punishing blows with every shot fired by the enemy. It was an almost constant thud or thump as the minies struck home. The screaming of the wounded was so shrill, they could be heard above the battle sounds.

When the Confederates were about 50 yards from the Bucktail line, the order was screamed, "Charge bayonets!" As a roar went up the whole regiment charged at the double quick time. This totally unnerved the advancing enemy troops and quickly they turned and ran from the cold steel.

A cheer went up and Jack felt himself getting caught up in the fever of the moment, screaming at the top of his lungs.

Again the shouted orders, "About face without doubling. At the double quick step. March!" The Bucktails literally ran back to their original position on the farm road. Jack was out of breath again and his legs felt like they wouldn't hold his weight. He thought to himself, How in the world can these men hold up so well?

The artillery fire from both the west and the north was very heavy, with air burst, ground bursts and the bouncing solid shot tearing into the battered Bucktail Brigade. The only respite they had from the cannons was during the enemy infantry attacks, which wasn't much consolation to Jack. Another thing that Jack noticed was the low volume of cannon fire from the Union side.

"Here they come again on the right!" Sure enough, the gray backs were back with determination. This time a little further down the road. Jack could clearly see a regiment of gray clad rebs coming from the right.

Orders were screamed above the din of battle, "At the right oblique by the ranks FIRE," and the flames shot out of the barrels as each rank fired. Then it was load and fire as fast as possible. It seemed like everyone was screeching at once, "Load quickly! Load quickly!" And on the rebels came, taking the punishment the Bucktails were giving them; but the enemy fired back with deadly effect! The ranks on both sides were getting smaller and smaller. The man next to Jack fell to the ground, flat on his face. He could see the man was dead. The back of his head was completely blown away by a minie ball.

Jack was grabbed and shoved by a file closer and the sergeant was shouting "Close it up, close it up," as men fell like leaves. He could hear the minies striking home all around him, but he didn't have time to look around. He was fighting for his life. God, he thought, How long can this go on? There won't be a man left standing in a few more minutes. Jack's arms were so tired he could scarcely use the ram rod. The heat took its toll; but he had to keep on fighting just like the rest of the men.

The rebel troops smashed into them again from the west. Colonel Wister, his mouth and lower face swathed in a bloody bandage, unable to speak, raised his sword, leading another bayonet charge. After taking horrendous losses against this small Bucktail Regiment and not wanting to taste their steel, the Confederates started falling back.

Only this time, there was no cheering. The men were beginning to show exhaustion from the hours of combat in the open. Canteens were emptied, both to quench their thirst and also to pour down their hot barrels. They had to clean out the black powder residue, which was making loading extremely hard if not impossible. While runners ran back for more water, the soldiers were busily swabbing out the barrels and checking for ammunition. Quickly they checked fallen comrade's pouches for ammunition and as well as the pouches that littered the ground. The Bucktails were running low on ammunition and they still had a long way to go.

Time was running out, more enemy troops could be seen coming toward them. Jack could hear heavy firing from the position occupied by the 11th Corps. He realized that the fighting there was moving closer to town.

During the brief lull, Jack looked around the area.

He guessed that there was less than 200 men left in their regiment. Looking toward the 149th off to his right, Jack saw that they appeared to be in similar condition. Jack couldn't see the 143rd since they were closer to town on the Chambersburg Pike. The other thing Jack noticed was the lack of officers. Most had been killed or wounded and there was a steady stream of wounded going to or being helped to the barn.

Jack turned to Jed and he looked drawn, and Jed had aged considerably over the last few hours. In fact he had a vacant stare and Jack wondered if he looked the same way. "Jed, are you okay," he asked?

"I'm all fagged out. I don't know if I can go on. I think I'm a dead man."

"Jed, your gonna make it. I'll help you. Don't give up," Jack tried to console him.

Nodding his head, Jed with shaking hands took a long swig from his canteen. Looking past Jack his eyes got big as saucers and the blood drained from his face as he exclaimed, "Shit! Here they come again. They're coming from everywhere!"

Jack turned and looked. Sure enough there were Confederate battle flags approaching from the west, northwest and the north all at the same time. Damn, he thought, There's no way they could hold out against those odds. Hell, there were ten to one odds and they are all going to hit us at the same time!

A Lieutenant Colonel motioned for the Color Guard to advance the Colors. The Color Guard moved forward with no hesitation, into certain death. As the Colors moved so did the whole line of Bucktails. As soon as one of the rebel regiments appeared over the hill, Sergeant Peiffer started waving the colors defiantly at the advancing enemy. This was like waving a red cloth at a bull. It seemed as if every gray clad soldier zeroed in on the hapless Color Sergeant. Minies found their mark and the sergeant started to fall. With his last dying breath he kept waving the proud colors. Then he died! Never had Jack seen such bravery! The men of the regiment started to fire at the rebels with a vengeance after seeing their Color Sergeant cut down. Another man picked up the colors, held them for a couple of seconds before he too, was cut down. Each time the colors were picked up, the man would be cut down. Damn, Jack thought, These men are the bravest I've ever seen. They know they will be shot if they pick up the flags, but they do it anyway. The ferocity of their attack completely stunned the Confederates and they retreated. This break gave the battered Bucktails a short breather.

Suddenly a loud crash of thunder erupted on their right, startling Jack. Looking toward the sound, he saw a battery of cannons had been pulled up while they were beating off the last attack. Thank God, Jack thought, They should hold off the rebels for a while. However, it was not to be. The cannons were drawing heavy artillery counter fire from Oak Hill and Herr Ridge. The gunners started scrambling to hook up the horses. Several of the animals screamed in agony as minies and pieces of shrapnel tore into their bodies. Jack could see the men wrestling with the horses, however, the poor wounded animals simply thrashed around. Jack calmly watched as one of the cannoneers pulled a revolver and shot the injured animals in the head, dropping them on the spot. This enabled them to cut them out of their harnesses and pull the cannons out of harms way with the remaining horses. That's strange, he thought, Under normal circumstances he would have been appalled at someone shooting horses. Today, the horrors of intense combat had desensitized him to death!

CHAPTER FOURTEEN

In Herbst Woods the Confederates slammed into the Union line and the Iron Brigade started to give way under the overwhelming weight of the rebel attack. The 150th Co. B fought off the attack on their front and managed to wheel right checking the flanking gray backs. They only suffered light casualties with one dead and four men wounded. The whole line started to sag back. Slowly the entire line moved east, fighting every inch of the way. Relentlessly the rebel regiments kept pressure on the retreating line. However, in spite of the furious attacks, the Union line never broke. At every opportunity they would stop and fire a volley into the pursuing enemy. The retiring Union troops were inflicting such heavy casualties, that caution became the rule for the rebs. They kept just enough pressure to move the Union line, but not engage it heavily. They found it was very costly to get too close to these battle hardened Bucktails.

Gradually, the Federals fell back across the open area between the woods and the Seminary. The ground sloped down from the woods into a slight ravine then slanted up toward Seminary Ridge. George could see the Union troops falling back off to their right where the fighting was intense. Confederate waves of gray were swarming over the ground resembling a hoard of army ants on the move, pushing the 11th Corps off the field. Captain Jones formed his company of Bucktails into a column of fours as they reached the town where the Hagerstown Road forked. Here they found a long line of Union cannons and the remnants of the First Corps starting to form up for the final assault from the rebels. As they reached the line they fell into a battle formation facing West.

George watched a drama unfold in front of him like slow motion. A lone Union Regiment was falling back. It started climbing the swale to Seminary Ridge. Behind them a Brigade of Confederates pursued the little band of yankee troops, who bravely stopped and turned to fire at them. Everyone on the Union line was cheering the retreating band of soldiers on, and firing on the rebels. Just when it seemed that it was the end for the yankee soldiers, a tremendous blast erupted up and down the line. Over twenty cannons unleashed their double shotted canister loads into the unsuspecting enemy troops. George watched as the canister balls tore into the ranks of the men in gray. The bodies of men could be seen twisting and turning through the air before they crashed to the ground in twisted heaps. I never imagined it being so horrible, George thought. It was sheer slaughter and very few men were still standing when the smoke cleared. No matter where he looked, there were bodies and pieces of bodies lying where a Rebel Brigade had been only seconds before. The stunned survivors moved back to McPherson Ridge. Looking to his right, George could no longer see the 11th Corps. They were replaced by hoards of Confederate gray.

Musket and cannon fire up and down the Union line intensified. The noise was so fierce, that orders could not be heard. George and the other men in the company were firing as fast as they could load. Confederates were falling like flies everywhere he looked. The barrel of his musket was so hot that the stock was almost too hot to hold. Once when he reloaded, the barrel touched his neck as he reached into his ammo pouch. It sizzled like a steak being thrown on a hot grill. Damn, he thought, Don't do that again. It burns like hell. Still more waves of gray backs came over McPherson Ridge. They're going to run us out of ammunition, he thought.

The order came to withdraw to Cemetery Hill. George took one last look to his right, straining to see the Bucktails. He spotted one lone regiment in line fighting, while the last of the cannons could be pulled off. If he remembered correctly that would be the Bucktail Brigade. He couldn't tell for sure at this distance.

Company B marched though the town very quickly. There were only about thirty men left in the unit and George was thankful that he and Skeeter were among them. The men all around him looked drawn, dejected and extremely dirty. As they quick timed up the street the dust was rising and choking them. George could see civilians looking out windows and at one house the people stood on the porch cheering them on.

Captain Jones called over to them, "You good folks better get inside or you could get hurt. There are rebs hot on our heels!"

They came to an intersection and a rebel officer on a horse approached them, demanding their surrender; but George watched as one of the men at the head of the column raised his musket and shot the officer dead. The group double quicked across the intersection as a rebel regiment tried to cut them off. Now it was down to an old-fashioned foot race and they made it. Even though it was hot and humid, George found some hidden reservoir of energy. They were almost at a dead run trying to keep out of the reach of the Confederates. The firing was heavy in the town and off to his left he could hear the deafening blasts of the Union cannons firing near the square, covering the retreat. Soon they passed the Court House where they turned onto Baltimore Street. This street was choked with troops, wagons, ambulances, cannons and everything with wheels or legs moving in the same direction. The street was a sea of humanity scrambling toward the safety of Cemetery Hill. They could no longer stay in ranks. Joining this mob of fleeing men, the company hastened its bid to safety. Dust and smoke almost hid the buildings even though they were only a couple feet away. The noise along the escape route was overpowering! Cannons and muskets were firing constantly. Everyone seemed to be screaming orders.

There were galloping teams of horses, caissons, cannons and wagons bouncing over the road in their bid for safety. Occasionally you could hear men screeching as horses and wagons smashed them to death. The escaping troops had to stay as close as possible to the houses to avoid being trampled. These wagons and cannons stopped for no one. As George reached the intersection of Emmitsburg Road and Baltimore Pike, he stopped to look for Skeeter. But, he was no where to be seen in this mass of fleeing men. George looked to the corner and wished he could see the convenience store that was there in twentieth century. Dreams of a very large Coke with gobs of ice crossed his mind. Caught up in the crowd and pushed up the hill, George ultimately arrived at the cemetery gate house. Soldiers feverishly dug entrenchments for cannons while others tore up fences and built barricades. Troops from every regiment were in this mix. Many were on the ground, completely exhausted and drenched in perspiration. Scores of soldiers were wounded, treated at an aid station before returning to the fight. George spotted a Bucktail on a hat in the crowd and headed toward it through the crush of humanity. At last he found Skeeter and hugged him like a long lost brother saying, "Thank God you're alive. I lost you back in town."

"I didn't think I was gonna make it. Almost got run down by some officer on a horse. But I fixed him. I jabbed the horse in the arse with my bayonet. Now for shure that officer won't be able to sit for quite a spell!"

Above all the noise they heard shouts, "Bucktails, fall in by the tree." George could see a hat with a Bucktail being held up on the tip of a sword, so they moved toward it. As hard as George looked, he couldn't see Jack anywhere. He would keep looking.

* * * * *

After their encounter with the Bucktails, Josh and Paul took cover with the other men in a small ravine. They were trying to figure out where they were and the rest of the regiment. Extremely heavy firing could be heard just to their left and only 50 yards away. Josh looked at his war trophy and marveled at the good condition. He thought, That yank didn't even take the bluing off the barrel.

"Is that the same musket ya'll said ya'll were gonna get last night?"

"Yup, shure is. That shure is weird. Whata the chances of that ever happening out here on the field? It musta been meant to be. Do ya'll have any idea whar's the rest of the regiment?"

"Nope, but the shootin is purity heavy just over yonder whar all that thar smoke is."

A corporal crawled over to them, "We got to get back to the regiment. They needs us real bad like. Follow me!" The two men followed the corporal toward the sounds of hades through heavy thick smoke. Josh thought, My God, there's dead men everywhere, never saw such slaughter. Just ahead of him a tremendous amount of smoke was billowing out in all directions as volley after volley was being fired. Minie balls were whistling and whining all around him. As they moved through the killing fields, Josh spotted one of the men in the color company holding up an officer while trying to pull the bloody flag wrapped around the body. He ran over to help the soldier when he realized who the wounded man was. "Oh God, it's the colonel," he shouted to Paul.

"I shure liked the colonel. He was a good sort, hard sometimes but he is a good officer. Shure hope he makes it," Paul shouted back.

An officer screamed at them, "You there, go with the color bearer and guard the colors."

The corporal along with Josh and Paul ran after the color bearer, who was carrying the blood stained flag with the staff half shot off. Smoke was so thick they couldn't even see where their line was, even though it was only a matter of yards. As they approached the front line the noise intensified so loud, orders couldn't be heard. It was just the incessant crash of volleys, men screeching in agony, shouting and cursing. Josh fell in along with the color bearer and just fired blindly into the thick smoke ahead of him. Bullets were whining by his head one after the other. This is crazy, he thought, A man can't live long in this hail storm of lead. All-around, soldiers were going down, some just falling quietly where they stood, while others screamed God awful howls when hit. Their line surged forward and as he passed the enemy's front line, he saw they had suffered just as bad from the point blank volleys. Bodies were everywhere and Josh couldn't avoid stepping on them. As they were pushing the enemy back, Josh's leg tangled in what he thought were vines. He jostled and pulled but couldn't free himself. Finally he looked at his leg and realized it wasn't vines but someone's intestines. This was the final straw, Josh fell down and tried to crawl away screaming, "Get them off, get them off!"

Paul stopped, untangled Josh's legs and helped him get up. "Get a hold of yourself, we gotta advance with the colors."

An officer came up and pushed the two men shouting, "Get up with the colors, move it!" All they could do was head toward the heaviest sounds of firing while keeping a sharp lookout for yanks. The enemy line was falling back quickly now, but the fighting was just as intense as before. Soldiers were dropping rapidly all along the line. As they approached the end of the woods the regiment stopped and re-formed before advancing. Josh looked around and wondered, where was everyone? There was less than half the men they had started out with this morning. The brigade was ordered forward but the soldiers protested, they were fagged out but most of all, they were out of ammunition. When they left the woods the men simply laid down as fresh troops move through them in pursuit of the yankees. Josh wondered why the new troops didn't send out a skirmish line.

As Dorsey Pender's fresh division started down into a swale, Josh and his comrades watched the drama unfold before them. In front of him, Josh could make out a white building with a cupola through all the smoke. He could see a lone Union Regiment fighting its way back as Dorsey's troops were given the order to charge. Blindly they rushed down the slope and as they reached the bottom, the Gods of war descended upon them. The most intense noise Josh ever heard, crashed into his body as he and everyone else just watched in horror as a red mist rose over the battlefield. Josh could see arms, legs and other body parts being flung high in the air as most of the brigade in front of them simply disappeared. There were only a few men left standing, stunned at what just befell them.

He turned to Paul, "What in all hells tarnation happened?"

Pointing toward the Ridge, "All them cannons thar fired all at once. Them boys never had a chance, it was less than 100 yards. It was like shooten fish in a barrel."

An officer screamed, "Get down and outta sight before they load again." The men hugged the ground while listening to the intense firing near Seminary Ridge and the canister shot whizzing overhead.

How did this happen, Josh thought to himself? Damn, the skirmishers should have gone first. They just walked into a trap and them yanks are good at springing them. At least he still had his musket and he was still alive.

"Hey Paul. How much ammunition do you have?"

"I got my gun loaded and one spare bullet."

"See that yank officer over by that white building? Betcha I can drop him from here."

"Hey sarge," Paul called out, "Josh says he can dust the britches of that officer over yonder, but I only have one spare round."

"Well give it to him, I don't think he can do it, hell its got to be over 500 yards. What the hell, let him try."

Josh quickly loaded his musket, primed and adjusted the sights. The officer looked like a small dot silhouetted against the white building with the cupola. He wiped the sweat from his eyes, took careful aim and squeezed the trigger. Smoke billowed out in front of him hiding his intended victim.

After a couple of seconds the sergeant who was watching with binoculars swore, "Well I'll be a sunvabitch, you just dropped the yank with a minie through his head. I swear, I never saw a shot like that! Anybody that has ammo, pass it down to Josh and we'll see if he can do that again."

The legend of Josh and the mysterious musket just began.

*****

The small band of Bucktails stood their ground for a few minutes against the hordes of Confederates, but they began to give way against overwhelming odds. The 149th on their right was being pushed toward them by the heavy attacks from the north. As they stood their ground by the barn, the remnants of the 149th joined them. Even though the two regiments combined as one, they still had only the equivalent of two companies. Colonel Wister, who was still with his men, gave hope to everyone. This small band of men might be driven from the field of honor, however they wouldn't be beaten. As the survivors started to move toward town, the men stayed in ranks and fired as they slowly retreated.

Jack was extremely tired and could think of nothing more than lying down and saying the hell with it. This day Jack had gone through the greatest range of emotions he had ever experienced in his life. From fear, to exhilaration, horror, hopelessness, sheer terror and every other emotion that were possible. Now he felt total hopelessness. Jack resigned himself, I'm going to die soon. At the point of accepting his impending death, a strange calm came over him. It was a feeling that he had never experienced before in his life. Before, he was indestructible, now he fully realized the frailty of life. Jack had seen death up close and very personal today. This was truly the first test he had in life where failure could result in death. Somehow Jack would rise to the occasion. He would not give up! Knowing that if he survived, he would be a much better man for it.

He was brought back to reality as Jed pulled on his cartridge belt, hollering, "Jack, are you OK?"

"Yea, yea, I'm OK, I was just in a daze."

The horrendous thunder of battle deafened Jack's ears. Cannons on Herr Ridge and Oak Hill had clear shooting at the small body of retreating Bucktails. The only thing that saved them from being annihilated completely was dense smoke which blanketed the battlefield. There simply wasn't enough wind to clear the smoke away. Still the artillery shells exploding overhead took their toll. It could have been worse. They were taking most of their casualties from the heavy volleys of musketry. Every time they came to a barricade of rails they would stop and fire several volleys. This seemed to hold the rebels back.

As Jack gazed across the terrain where they had been, blue clad men with Bucktails could be seen littering the ground. The blood of the Union Soldiers stained the Pennsylvania soil. Everywhere he looked, there was carnage. Smoking holes showed where cannon balls had exploded, dead horses, smashed cannons, dropped muskets, clothing of all sorts, shattered trees and wounded men pleading for help.

The Union cannons on Seminary Ridge opened a tremendous fire to cover the retreating men in blue. The noise was so overpowering that Jack could no longer think.

When the remnants of the Bucktail Brigade reached Seminary Ridge, regiments of Confederates could be seen sweeping across the fields toward the town and them.

One of the officers yelled, "We'll make one final stand here. Then we'll head into town!" After the Bucktail survivors fired a couple of volleys into the advancing rebels, the men started falling back again. This was accomplished by leap-frogging by platoons. Firing, then running to the rear and loading on the run. As they approached a small orchard, Jack could see a battery of light artillery positioned there. Jack heard the guns firing earlier but hadn't realized where they were.

Jack could see an officer run to their captain asking, "Can your men stay long enough to cover us while we pull our pieces off the field?"

So the battered Bucktails hunkered down one last time and started pouring volleys to their front, then right oblique, fire, and left oblique, fire! The minies could be heard striking the fence rail breastworks they were behind. A man next to Jack screamed as a bullet ripped through a rail before tearing into his body. Blood spurted everywhere, literally covering Jack from head to toe with the dying man's blood. God, this butchery has to stop soon! God its got to stop! Jack thought he was losing his mind. His first instinct was to run and just get as far away as possible. What was keeping him here? He just knew he couldn't leave these brave men, even if he had to die.

As this small band of survivors was fighting for their lives, a tremendous blast of cannon fire erupted behind them. Jack watched as Confederates in the attacking formations simply disappeared as canister shot tore into their ranks. This was the Union Army's last hurrah. The enemy kept advancing relentlessly, facing certain death at the muzzles of the cannons. The battery the Bucktails were protecting, was at last limbered up and dashed off. At last the order was given to start falling back. However, this delay probably made them one of the last Union regiments to leave the field as the rebels pushed them from all sides. As they reached the edge of town, Jack saw Confederates everywhere. The remnants of the Bucktails dispersed and it was every man for himself!

Jack and his file partner Jed, cut down a side street and started running. They could hear firing behind them and as the minies whistled by his head caused Jack to run faster. The two fleeing men reached another corner and took cover for a minute. As they caught their breath, they tried to figure out how to escape capture.

"I know we have to go that way" Jack said, as he pointed in the direction of Cemetery Hill. "We'll have to keep to the rear of the houses because the rebs are everywhere."

Jed nodded in agreement. They both loaded their muskets and started toward Cemetery Hill, cutting through backyards. Dogs were barking everywhere as they made their way through gardens, past outhouses, over fences, and even through a pig pen. It took them almost an hour to make it to the other side of town. As they continued, they could hear heavy small arms fire behind them. The two men came upon a hay field and small orchard on the southern side of the town. Much to their dismay, there was a Confederate regiment in formation awaiting an order to advance. Men in the ranks were talking and joking among themselves. Jack and Jed were close enough to hear them speak, "We really whupped up on them thar bluebellies." There was some more laughter and another voice quipped, "Shoar enough did Jake and we're gonna run them plumb back to Washington!"

With that Jack and Jed slipped back to the last house they passed, in an effort to figure out what to do. When they reached the house Jack banged on the back door. He could see a curtain part as someone inside peered out.

The door opened and a young man came out and asked, "You yanks better get out of here. Rebs are coming down the street searching houses!"

Jack implored of him, "Can you hide us somewhere until we can sneak back to our lines tonight?"

The young man thought for a second, "I may just have a place to hide you out in the chicken coop, but it won't be comfortable. Come with me quickly." He led them inside the small structure pushing away the straw on the floor to reveal a small trap door. He explained to the two soldiers, "The man I bought the house from put a false floor in, so he could hide his whiskey from his wife! I store my garden tools down there in the winter." When he opened the trap door, it revealed an area 18 inches deep under the main floor.

The two men crawled in and Jack asked the young man, "Come out after dark and let us out."

"I'll do that. If I get chance, I'll bring some food and water."

As the trap door closed over them, almost instantly, Jack had wished he had taken his chances outside. It was very hot and dusty as only a chicken coop can be.

Jed asked Jack in a low voice, "Do you think we have a chance of getting though the reb lines tonight?"

"It's our only chance. We can't stay here for three days." As soon as he said it, Jack realized his mistake.

"How do you know how long we'll be here?"

Jack felt himself flush, "I don't know how long, I was just guessing." This satisfied Jed, but Jack knew he would have to watch what he said in the future.

As they lay in the stifling heat, they could hear the chickens over their heads scratching and clucking. Outside they could still hear sporadic firing all around them.

"Jack, are you scared?"

"Hell yes I'm scared. Not only that, this is a hell hole, the dust and heat is unbearable."

Jed lay there for a few minutes before he spoke again, "I have this terrible feeling, I'm not gonna make it. I'll never see my Ma and Pa again. Jack, do you have a girl friend or wife?"

"You're going to make it Jed, I'll see to that. Yes I'm married and have a loving wife. I do hope I'll see her again."

"Do you have a likeness of her?"

"No, I lost it with my knapsack the other night," Jack lied.

"I never had no girlfriend or nothing. Never had no time. Too busy working. I'm kinda glad that way I won't leave any grieving widow. Just my family."

"Jed, pull yourself together. You're not going to die yet, you're too ornery!"

"Yea, I suppose you're right about that" Jed chuckled.

The two men had been hiding about an hour when they heard voices outside, "Whacha you got in that thar hen house? Some real live chickens and some eggs I hope?"

The door opened and they could hear footsteps overhead and then the squawking of chickens as they were chased and caught. The pleading voice of the young man who hid them could be heard, "Don't take all of my chickens. I don't have much money and they help feed my family."

A gruff voice replied, "Now don't you fret none. We'll leave yu a cuple layers and we gots some good Confederate money to pay you."

A few minutes went by as they searched around, including the loft in the hen house, then the

Confederates left. Jack said a silent prayer of thanks. With all the commotion above their heads, the dust had started filtering down on them. Jack did all he could to keep from sneezing. He reached down, found his canteen and took a long swig to help wash the dust from his throat.

Jed whispered, "Damn, that was close, I thought I was gonna die. That danged dust almost made me sneeze."

Jack laughed quietly, "Yea, I know what you mean."

Several more times they heard soldiers come into the chicken coop. The second search party ensured there would be no more chickens left. Other soldiers would just look around and leave. All the two Federals could do for now was just wait and hope they could escape later. This was as bad as being buried alive. The two men just laid there in the overbearing heat, listening to the musket fire and occasional cannon roar, hoping that it would soon be dark. They were both out of water by now and Jack knew they would have to get some soon. This hot house was wringing every drop of moisture from their bodies. They couldn't do anything until dark because they could hear the Confederates nearby as they sought out Union soldiers who were cut off.

Occasionally they would hear a rebel prodding Union prisoners along with "Move smartly bluebelly, or I'll stick you with this toad sticker here."

"Hey Jed, how are you doing? Are you OK?"

"Oh I'm just honkey dorey, just love this heat and dust. Do you think we'll get out of here tonight?"

"Well we have to get out of here as soon as possible. We can't survive another day in here or we'll be cooked alive!" Jack answered.

According to General Doubleday, he considered Stones Bucktail Brigade held the angle in the line. "In truth the key-point of the first day's battle."
(Gettysburg Magazine 7/1/89)

CHAPTER FIFTEEN

George and Skeeter made their way through the throngs of men toward the upraised Bucktail and joined the men with Captain Jones. Only a hand full of troops where present when they arrived and the survivors formed into companies. As they waited, more Bucktails continued filtering in. It was the most bedraggled bunch of men imaginable. Everyone had black grime covering their hands and faces. Uniforms were torn, blood splattered, and grease covered. All the soldiers looked as if they were at the end of their endurance. After a half hour wait the Sergeants started counting the troops. Company B had the most, with almost thirty soldiers. They were the skirmish company and made it through town before the rest of the regiment. By the time the main body of the 150th Regiment entered town, the Confederates were everywhere. Many of the Bucktails were captured in the town. The other companies looked forlorned, seven here, five men there and on it went. The final count was less than 90 men out of the 397 the Bucktails started out with in the morning.

George couldn't see Jack anywhere and he felt dreadful. He believed his friend had been killed, wounded or captured. If he went back to the future, what would George ever say to Jack's wife, Katey. He felt responsible and was helpless to do anything for him. In

277

fact, both Tim and Jack were gone. For now, however, he had to survive and just hope for the best. Maybe they would show up. He received permission to see the survivors of Company A. The re-enactor asked one of the tired men if he knew what happened to his friend.

"The last time I saw Jack and his file partner, Jed, was when we was fighten, holding off them rebs whilst the cannons was being pulled off. By the time we got to town them gray backs was everywhere. It was every man for hiself."

As George slowly went back to his company, he passed the few men left in the color company and realized the regimental flag was gone. He remembered reading that the colors were captured in town. There was no longer any excitement about reliving history now. The re-enactor was too tired and dejected over his friends.

After an hour wait, the remnants of the Bucktails marched out and passed through the Evergreen Cemetery gate. On the way they passed scores of high ranking officers going into the gate house. There must have been thirty horses tied up nearby with orderlies attending to them. In fact, George thought for sure he had seen General Hancock ride by on a handsome Chestnut mare accompanied by two Sergeants. One carried the Second Corps flag. The remainder of the 150th PVI marched through the cemetery which was strewn with large boulders and through the area which would someday become the National Cemetery. Off to his left he could see the Widow Leister's house which would become the army's headquarters tomorrow.

Eventually they stopped and broke ranks in a rocky area which had many more rocks than he remembered in his time. In front of them, a little to his right, stood the copse of small trees. This would become the focal point of the famous Pickett's charge on July 3rd and it made the hair George's neck stand up. This is where they would bivouac for the night. It was a wheat field that had been completely flattened down by thousands of marching feet. The men started tearing down fence rails for fire wood for a company fire. The only problem was, there was nothing to cook. Only coffee. There was not even a piece of hardtack to be found. Suddenly, it occurred to George, how hungry he was. He hadn't eaten anything since the night before. In the excitement of the day's fighting it never crossed his mind that he was hungry. The men were so tired, most of them just laid down on the ground with their muskets and fell into exhausted sleep. George would like to have slept, however he had to keep a lookout for his friends. He had a cup of steaming coffee and it tasted like the most expensive gourmet brand that could be had. Everyone who had coffee in their haversacks dumped some in the pot. The only bad thing was the coffee grounds floating on top. They had just thrown the coffee grounds in loose. The soldiers had used a large cooking pot that someone had liberated from somewhere.

George felt his head and he still had a goose egg. At least the wound was not bleeding however it was extremely tender. One good thing, his headache was almost gone. He had forgotten all about the flesh wound in his side during all the excitement. The re-enactor started to examine the wound and thought, Damn I came awful close today. The burn on his neck hurt like hell too. It had blistered from the touch of the musket barrel. The blister had ruptured from all the activity and the salt from the perspiration irritated the open wound. As he sat there, he watched all the activity going on around them. Teams of horses pulled batteries into position and the gun crews unlimbered them. The caissons were positioned behind the cannons about 30 feet, unhitched, and the horse teams tethered nearby just in case they were needed. Men built breast works all along the line feverishly. Everywhere he looked, George saw thousands of soldiers. As darkness set in, George fell into a deep exhausted sleep, his back resting on a boulder and the musket nestled in his arms.

* * * * * *

Jed whispered to Jack, "How long do you reckon we been in here?"

"I'd say about four hours."

Maybe we should get out of here and stretch a little. If some rebs come, we can crawl back in here," Jed replied.

"Naw, how would we put the straw back over the trap door. We'll wait a little longer."

Another half hour went by and outside they could hear troops marching by and they could still hear an occasional gunshot as nervous troops fired at imaginary targets. Without warning the door of the chicken coop opened. The rush of fresh air hit them as the young man opened the trap door.

He whispered, "Hurry, there's several rebs in the house having dinner and I told them I had to use the privy. If I don't go back in soon, they'll come a lookin!"

Jack and Jed quickly crawled out of their prison and stretched their tired, cramped muscles. The young man had a jug of cold well water for them. After they filled their canteens, they polished off the remaining water like shipwrecked sailors.

The trio went outside and in a low voice, "Your army is up on the cemetery over yonder. You'll have to sneak through the Confederate lines. So be careful.

280 . -

They're everywhere!"

Turning to the dark form Jack said, "Thanks. You saved our lives. You took a terrible chance for you and your family. We don't even know who you are. What is your name?"

The young man simply replied, "No time for that. 'Sides if they catch you, you can't tell who was hiding you if you don't know. Now git outta here!" They both shook hands with their benefactor and quickly disappeared into the darkness.

They were back out on the dirt street and off to their right they could see 30 or 40 campfires with men standing in small groups talking. Jack knew they had to be Confederates and he motioned to Jed to head to their left.

Jed whispered to him, "Maybe they're our troops over there."

Jack simply replied, "Trust me, they're rebs for sure. We have to go to that hill over there."

In the moon light they could only see a black mass with many small dots of campfires and lanterns moving around. Cautiously they moved up a dirt road angling away from town. The two men kept in the shadows as much as possible. The stranded soldiers slowly approached another house with a large barn lit up with lanterns. Jed and Jack could clearly see the troops both inside and outside. That was when Jack realized he was looking at a field hospital. He could see doctors working on men laying on makeshift operating tables, while orderlies carried the dead from inside and laid them outside on the ground. Screams came from the barn, "God no. Don't take off my arm. Not my arm!"

Jack decided they should avoid the barn as there were too many troops standing around with lanterns. The two of them angled a little more to the right, to bypass the hospital. It was then that Jack realized that the town was over more to their left, about four or five blocks. It occurred to him that he was lost. This didn't look familiar, because in modern times it was built up and at night it was well lit.

He motioned for Jed to stop for a minute while he got his bearings. "Jed, I'm lost. I could have sworn we were at the edge of town." Then it dawned on him. They must be in the vicinity of the ball field. This meant they had seven or eight blocks to the Union lines. First they had to get through the Confederate lines. Warily they made their way, sneaking around groups of men who were sitting at campfires talking in low voices. The rebels here were not celebrating their victory today. They were exhausted from the day's marching, fighting and the damned heat.

"Jed, I've got an idea. Instead of sneaking along we'll take off our jackets, ditch them and put our hats in our haversacks! We'll just walk along like we know where we're going. In the dark they'll think we're fellow rebs."

"Hey I like that. You're a pretty smart feller for being a fresh fish."

"Now when we get to their pickets," Jack whispered, "We'll have to make a run for our lines. In the dark they won't get good shots at us."

"Don't worry, I'll be running so fast they'll think a rabbit ran by them," Jed laughed.

The two men continued walking, keeping out of the light of the fires. As they moved in the dark they passed several groups of men who paid no attention to them. After sneaking along for ten minutes, Jack and Jed could see the dull glow of someone smoking a pipe up ahead of them. Off to his left they made out the dark form of another man standing by a tree. As they stopped and looked around, Jack whispered, "I'm sure we're at the picket line. Somehow we'll have to figure out how to get across safely without getting shot by either side."

"Hey reb, you got any good tobacco with you?" A voice queried from the Union lines.

The dark shadow by the tree answered, "Yup, shur do Billy, I'll trade you for some yankee cuffee, shur am tared of acorn cuffee."

"OK reb, we'll have a truce. I'll meet you half way."

"Hey Tom bring me a bag of that good tabbaca. We're gonna get some real cuffee."

"Now's our chance." Jack whispered, "We'll sneak over there to that fella who's gonna trade. When he gets out to the center, we'll make a run for it right past them. Neither side will fire for fear of hitting their man."

Jack and Jed were in place as the reb soldier walked out unarmed toward the Union lines. In the dim light of the moon they could see the two men meet. The two stranded soldiers jumped to their feet and started running.

The noise of their running feet surprised the traders, and the rebel yelled, "What the hell? Damned yankees! Shoot boys! Shoot!"

As they rushed by the confused trading soldiers, they heard one of the rebel pickets cry out, "We can't shoot, we'll hit you."

They reached the Union picket line and strong arms grabbed and pulled them down. "Who are you men," a gruff voice asked?

"We're Bucktails, 150th PVI of the First Corps." Jed answered. "We've been hiding in town until dark to get out."

"Where are your hats and coats then," the voice demanded?

"Our hats are in our haversacks, but we threw our coats away so they couldn't tell we were Union soldiers in the dark," Jack replied.

One of the soldiers left out a, "Whew, you fellers smell like chicken shit!"

Another voice in the dark, "That's mighty good thinking. Now show me those hats."

They both pulled their hats out and gave them to a man, whom they still couldn't see in the dark. He gave the hats back saying, "OK Bucktails, head up that hill there. Somewhere on top you'll find what's left of the First Corps. You guys got chewed up pretty bad I hear. Oh and by the way, if you get challenged by any sentry on the way, the sign is bully and the counter sign is file. Good luck."

As they were about to leave, a voice from the rebel side called out, "Hey yanks, that was a dirty trick you played." Then they were on their way. Jack tried to figure out where they had come out, when they crossed the Emmitsburg Road. The two men walked through a wheat field which had been trampled flat earlier in the day. They had to pass through two post and hole fences where sections were removed for the movement of the troops. It occurred to him that they were coming up to the area where the Cyclorama would stand. Just off to their left stood the Bryant house and barn.

No one challenged them on the way up the slope until reaching a hastily constructed stone wall and a voice challenged them, "Bully"

Jack was caught off guard and couldn't remember the counter sign.

Jed saved the day, saying "File."

"Come over the wall you two! What regiment do you belong to?"

Again they explained who they were. With the sentries satisfied, they told the Bucktails, "What's left of the First Corps is over yonder, by that bunch of trees."

Everywhere they looked there were small campfires and men with lanterns tending horses, digging gun emplacements or just laying on the ground in small groups of 10 to 15 men. The two latecomers walked on a cow path which had been deepened and widened by thousands of feet, and hundreds of horses, cannon and wagon wheels. They passed groups of men around campfires and unknowingly passed the copse of trees in the dark.

Jack looked ahead at a campfire and not watching where he was walking when he tripped over the legs of a sleeping form.

"Damnit, watch where you step. You like to broke my ankle!"

Jack recognized the voice immediately, "George is that you?"

George awoke instantly and jumped up and hugged his friend shouting, "Thank God you're alive!" Then he stepped back and said, "Damn, you smell like chicken shit. Where in the hell have you been? I thought you were dead or captured!"

Before Jack told him about the day events, he introduced George to his file partner. George shook Jed's hand, "Thanks for getting my buddy through the day safely. Man you smell like chicken shit too!"

They all laughed and told each other what had transpired throughout the day. When they had finished, Jed told them he was going to the company and report in.

"I want to talk to my friend here a little. Would you muster me in? I'll be over in a short while."

"Don't be shocked when you find your company, there's only a couple men left," George warned Jed.

Jed let out a low whistle and disappeared into the dark. After Jed left, they started talking in earnest of their problems.

"Did you see or hear of Tim today?" George asked first.

"No, but I was hoping you may have."

"Did you get wounded anywhere?"

To his relief Jack answered, "I didn't get a scratch, I really don't know how I managed not to. Men were falling all around me all day. We would no sooner close ranks and someone else would get it. It was murderous, simply murderous!"

George detailed to Jack, "While we were on the skirmish line my camera was smashed by a minie ball. My big chance for some pictures is gone forever. Later I got creased by a bullet and I'm here to tell you, that was too close. Worse than that, I was nailed on the head by a rebel and lost my musket. In fact today, I killed several men. One man ran right onto my bayonet. I don't feel very good about that. In fact I feel rotten."

"Was it that same rebel who was in camp last night, who got your musket?"

"Hell I don't know. I never saw the blow coming. Just the flash of light. Then I was down for the count. Skeeter, my file partner saved my life."

"If you lost your musket to that reb like the old man said, why didn't we go forward in time?"

"Jack, I just don't know. None of this makes any sense at all. I can't figure it out. Everything that old man said has come true so far. I'm pissed at myself for not questioning him more. But at the time, I just didn't believe the story could be true. Maybe we're stuck here in this time forever. There's no logic to this whole thing."

"Well, nothing we can do about it now, except to do the best with what we have," Jack replied.

George told his friend about all the bullet holes in his clothes.

Jack started feeling over his pants legs, "Holy shit,

I've got a bunch of holes in my pants legs too. Damn that was too close. George, you've read the regimental history of the 150th. What happens in the next couple of days?"

George went over what he could remember with Jack. He told them that they had a good chance of surviving. Especially since that they made it through the terrible first day. When they finished comparing notes, they went over to the campfire to join the small knot of men sitting there.

As they approached the group, they could hear Jed telling them how they had hid out and how Jack had come up with, "The audacious idea of just marching through the whole rebel army. And then just prance between the lines to safety." Everyone laughed at the way they had fooled the rebs.

A voice in the dark stated, "I don't know where you two are sleeping tonight. I surely do know it won't be near me. You both smell like chicken shit!" Everyone broke out laughing again.

Noticing the commotion, Captain Jones came over and told them, "Men, you better get some sleep. We will probably have a hard day ahead of us come tomorrow."

"Capt'n, when are we gonna get something to eat?" A man asked.

"As soon as our supply wagons catch up, which I hope will be in the morning. Hell, where's Crackers? He always has a stash of hard tack?"

"Capt'n, he's dead!" Jed said sadly. Suddenly it grew quiet and the group slowly broke up to find a spot to sleep.

The 150th PVI lost almost all their line officers on the first of July. Captain Jones was the senior officer commanding the regiment on the evening of July 1 through July 3, 1863. The only other commissioned officer present through July 3 was Lieutenant Kilgore.

CHAPTER SIXTEEN

George woke at sunrise and discovered that he was soaking wet. What really woke him was the pain in the center of his back. Damn stone, he thought as he threw the rock to one side. He tried to figure out where he was. George had fallen into an exhausted sleep the night before. He could hardly move. Every muscle in his body was stiff and sore. As his senses came back, he remembered where he was. There was activity all around him. Wagons could be heard creaking along. The sounds of metal wheel rims striking rocks, horses snorting, mules braying, troops marching, were things he'd never heard at a re-enactment. Slowly he got up and looked around in the eerie light of the dawn. Everywhere he looked, he could see sleeping forms. Several fires blazed, with men around them, just looking into the flames. For the most part, the fires of the night before had died out, extinguished by the light rain that had fallen while they slept. Looking toward the stone wall of the angle, George saw cannons lined up with caissons and limbers behind them. Some of the cannoneers busied themselves working on their pieces, polishing and wiping them down. Others were just getting up from where they had laid down to grab a couple of hours sleep. The sky in the east was lighting up quickly now and George could see some light clouds. Dawn was an ominous red. Red sky in the morning, sailor take warning, he remembered from his sea faring days.

Jack was all curled up and George shook him, trying to wake him; he would just groan, then grumble, "Leave me alone." George rolled him over, which really disturbed Jack.

"You bastard, I'm tired. Leave me alone. I'm not going out for that re-enactment this morning!"

George shook him again and spoke in a hushed tone, "Damn it Jack, this is the real thing, now get up and watch what you say!"

Slowly Jack sat up, but every movement hurt. Stretched muscles that contracted while he slept refused to move. He had pushed them to the extreme the day before. The re-enactor gently stood up and stretched, God, how I hurt, he thought to himself.

George motioned for his friend to follow him where they could talk without being overheard. "You've got to watch what you say," he admonished him.

"Damn, I thought this had been a dream. When I woke up I realized it was worse, it was a nightmare." As he looked around, he was in total shock at the amount of men, cannons, horses and wagons that were on this hill. Soldeirs started fires all over the hillside. Men began to cook their coffee and waited hopefully for food, if the supply wagons showed up.

George told Jack, "Today, we should have it fairly easy, if I remember right. Tonight we'll be on picket duty over by the Codori house. But today, nothing much happens here. So keep an eye out for Tim, just in case he shows up."

After digesting George's comments, Jack replied, "Do you remember everything that happens here today and tomorrow to the 150th?"

"No. Like I said, it's been a couple of years since I read the regimental history. I've read so many books since then, everything runs together. But I do know one thing for sure, I know the first day's battle by heart now!"

Jack laughed, "Amen to that brother, and I think we'll know the second and third day by heart before too long!"

They took a walk over to the stone wall and looked toward the Confederate lines. Movement could be seen across the field as a courier rode along the tree line. The smoke of hundreds of fires could be seen hanging just above the trees in the Confederate lines.

"You know, it's totally awesome, the number of troops that are here. In re-enacting, a person gets some idea of what happened during the Civil War." Jack said. "But never the enormity of this battle. Some of the emotions I experienced yesterday were mind boggling. It went from exhilaration, to helplessness, to terror, then to a calm I have never felt before."

"Jack, my lad, you have "Seen the Elephant!"

"You know George, I don't care if I ever see that damn elephant again. I have never been as scared as I was yesterday. Especially when we were firing at each other at point blank range. In my whole life I've never ever seen such brave men. On both sides!"

George told Jack in a low voice, that was almost reverent, "Jack, I killed men yesterday! It didn't start out that way. In fact when I fired the first few times, I purposely shot high so I couldn't possibly hit them. Then as the fighting got heavier I just lost it. From that point on, I was picking them off right and left. It was a matter of survival. It does go against my medical background. I do feel very badly about it."

"George, you're being too hard on yourself. You had no choice. You're not a corpsman now, you're a common soldier. You have to do whatever it takes to survive. That's all that matters now. Hell, we don't have the foggiest idea what's going to happen to us. We have to roll with the punches."

Silently they walked back to where the regiment was positioned. When they arrived, everyone was up and moving around. The company fire was going and the pot of coffee was starting to steam as they went over to the fire. The men were strangely quiet as they thought back over the previous day, and of all the friends they lost. Some of the soldiers were cleaning their muskets, which had rusted with the light mist of the night before. Several examined their equipment, while others just sat and stared. George recognized those haunted stares. Many of these men suffered from battle fatigue. Having seen some of the most horrible sights imaginable, blood, gore, and the smell of death. Every man including George, had uniforms soaked with other men's blood mixed with grease, sweat and dirt. But these were very brave men and George knew they would go on, even if they would be the next to be blown apart. He had a lot more respect for them now and he was also proud of Jack and himself, they had survived. And Jack used his head to escape back to his lines last night.

When the coffee was finished brewing, the men waited their turns as coffee was dipped out. Skeeter and Jed came over to sit with the two re-enactors. Skeeter said, "Pops, you showed true grit yesterday and I hope you'll be my file partner until this war is over."

George thought to himself, I sure hope I'm not your file partner that long. Then he replied, "Thanks Skeeter. You did pretty good yourself."

Not to be undone, Jed remarked, "Well you shoulda seen what my possum did last night. Hell, he made a laughing stock of the whole Confederate army..."

He was cut off by Skeeter, "Now that's the third time I've heard that story." Everyone laughed. Then they heard the drum beat, calling them to assembly.

"150th Bucktails, FALL IN," shouted one of the corporals, "Tall men to the right, move quickly!" What remained of the 150th fell in facing the stone wall. Just off to their right was the Copse of Trees. After they were in ranks, they counted by twos again and George looked around. Some of the companies were in very bad shape. If you grouped all the remaining men together, they would scarcely equal one full strength company. A few stragglers showed up and the count had risen to 109 troops, including officers, noncoms and enlisted.

Captain Jones stood in front of the regiment and addressed them. "Yesterday, you've proved yourselves, standing to your duty against all odds. Today we don't know what will happen to us. You do know the whole Army of Northern Virginia is just over there," and with a sweep of his arm behind him, indicated west. "We lost a lot of good officers and men yesterday. They were not lost in vain. We will triumph in the end. However, we still have a hard fight ahead. I know that many of you haven't eaten for quite a while. I'm working on getting our supply wagon brought up. Also the Ordnance Sergeant will be inspecting arms and issuing ammunition. As soon as we finish with roll call, fatigue duties will be assigned." When he was finished, he turned the regiment over to Lieutenant Kilgore with a salute. The lieutenant turned the regiment over to the sergeant.

"Corporals, fall in on me," the sergeant commanded. Quietly he told them, "I want you to take roll call, but don't call out all the names. Just have the men give you their names. We must keep up their spirits. To hear their lost friend's names would be too much. Captain Jones wants us to get all the men on various work details, to keep them busy and not allow them time to think. You're dismissed."

George, Jack, Skeeter and Jed were assigned to help build breast works as soon as they finished breakfast. Supply wagons had just pulled up and they overheard a sergeant call out for rations for 107 men. As they broke ranks, designated soldiers from each company lined up to draw the rations of hard tack and salt pork. One enterprising scavenger from George's company had located a frying pan from somewhere and the men started cooking the salt pork. Another veteran took the top off of the hardtack box and they broke the hardtack into small pieces, mixing it in with the cooking salt pork and grease. As George watched the operation in progress he thought to himself, Man, that meal is loaded with cholesterol. However before this day is out, we'll burn every bit of it off. He was so hungry, that it was the tastiest meal he had ever had, except George was thirsty from the salt pork. Before the regiment was called for fatigue duty, George went over to Jack and Jed to see how they had made out for their meal. He noticed that several of the depleted companies had joined together to pool their resources in preparing the meal. As George approached he watched as Jack wiped his mouth on his sleeve. Jack said to no one in particular, but loud enough for every one to hear, "That was a meal fit for a King. Here King, here King," as he motioned as if calling his dog. Everyone broke out laughing. One of the soldiers got down on all fours and started barking and panting. The man portraying the dog ambled over to one of the non-coms, lifting his leg at the corporal's leg. The non-com played along and kicked at the actor cursing, "Get away from me you mangy cur!"

At this antic, several of the Bucktails were laughing so hard, it hurt their sides. In times of great stress, it doesn't take much to make a veteran laugh and these soldiers had seen the stress for sure.

Again the drums rolled, calling for the troops to fall in for work detail. They spent several hours digging up small rocks with their bayonets, cups, and anything else they could find. All along the line you could hear the clinking and clanging of cups and tin dishes scraping the rocks as they dug. They built low stone walls about 100 yards behind the cannons, just on the breast of the hill that went down to Taneytown Road. This would be the second line of defense if the first line was broken in an attack. On top of the stone wall they piled fence rails they pulled down from a farmer's fence. This was backbreaking work and made doubly hard by the humidity and the intense heat. A wagon pulled by two mules brought up several casks of water, which the men drank and filled their canteens for later. However, they weren't allowed to wash with it.

While they were working, George saw a regiment marching at the double quick north along the forward stone wall. If he remembered correctly this would be the 12TH New Jersey going to flush out sharpshooters from the Bliss Farm. All morning they had heard bullets flying overhead from that farm. Occasionally a soldier would grunt as the missile found its mark and the man would fall.

At last they had a little break. George and Jack sat by a boulder by themselves. The two talked about their families and how distraught they must be over their disappearance. He noticed that Jack was scratching. George felt like something was crawling on him also. The disgusted soldier exclaimed, "Aw shit, I don't believe this, we've got lice!"

Jack looked at him quizzically and asked, "We've got what?"

"We've got frigging lice," as George pulled one off and squeezed it between his fingers showing it to Jack.

"How do we get rid of them?"

"Unfortunately, we won't get rid of as long as we're here. So just get used to them. This was a problem during the Civil War. Everybody had lice, including the generals," George replied.

"I have a question George, my file partner called me a possum a little while ago. What does that mean?"

"In Civil War times, that meant good buddy or something like that. Actually it's a compliment. You must have impressed him"

"I hate to remind you, this is the Civil War. You seem to forget we are here now."

"Jack, one thing you can be sure of, I know exactly where we are and when."

Suddenly, from down near the peach orchard, they heard the unmistakable popping of muskets as a skirmish was being played out.

"What is that?" Jack asked.

"I don't know, the battle doesn't start until around four or so, but there must have been a bunch of little skirmishes all day. That's probably Berdan's sharpshooters tangling with the rebs in Pitzers woods."

Sarcastically Jack replied, "Well, there has been sporadic firing all morning, but that sounds like more than a skirmish. Just what time is it?"

George took out the watch from his coat pocket, "It's just about noon, my how time flies when you're having fun. I didn't think it was that late. We better get back to our companies, just in case we get called out to help or something." Both men went back to their units and waited to see what would happen.

George found Skeeter sound asleep. For something to do, George sat on a boulder and cleaned the new musket. He thought, If I go back to the future, will I be able to take this musket with me? Naw, don't think so dumb. I'll just be thankful if I can get back in one piece.

Skeeter woke up and looked over to George, "What's all that shooting about?"

Without thinking, he replied, "Oh, that's Berdan's sharpshooters tangling with some rebs in Pitzer's Woods."

Looking long and hard at George, "How do you know who's fighting way over there? And how do you know it's Pitzer's Woods?"

Frantically George thought of an answer, "Oh, when my friend and I were coming back over here, we heard some staff officer telling another officer what was happening."

Skeeter didn't fully believe George, but the answer did seem plausible. So he let it drop.

"Skeeter, I'm tired as hell. I think I'll stretch out and take a short nap." George laid down on the ground to rest and before he fell asleep, he thought, Better be more careful of what I say. I must be too tired. He promptly fell into a deep slumber. While he was napping, Jack came over to talk to George. He saw that he was dozing so he sat and laid against a large rock. He too fell into an fitful sleep in spite of the heat.

BA-ROOM, a battery exploded six times in rapid succession as the guns let loose with their load of solid shot. George and Jack who had been in a deep sleep not more than 100 feet from the guns, leapt straight up in the air as did many other men who had been resting. What the hell's going on George thought, his heart racing a mile a minute. Looking over to the cannon line, the next battery commenced firing, the flames darted out seven or eight feet. Voluminous amounts of white smoke blasted out of the barrels as the grass in front was laid flat. Barrels dipped down and the carriages rolled four or five feet in recoil, as each gun fired. From where they were standing, the infantrymen couldn't see what they were firing at.

A drum roll called the regiment into formation and the men fell in running, most carrying their accouterments and muskets knowing another fight could be at hand.

Jack ran to his company and on the way put on his cartridge box and buckled his belt that carried his bayonet and primer pouch. As the men were getting ready, they all looked around trying to figure out what was going on. They still couldn't see what the artillery were firing at. Again they were called to attention and they counted off by twos again.

Captain Jones hurried and addressed the troops, speaking as loud as he could, "If you're wondering what is happening, the cannon crews just spotted some rebels moving along the woods over yonder. We're not sure where they're heading yet, but it could be here. The gun crews are short men for passing ammunition. We'll detail some people to help them out." He turned to the sergeant to take care of matters as the lieutenant was not there.

The sergeant assigned George and Skeeter with several other men to help the cannon crews. They were assigned to help pass the ammunition from the caissons to the cannon crews on the line. Men were shouting everywhere as the cannons were quickly reloaded time and again. George couldn't figure out what was happening. The attacks should be coming much later in the day. He did notice they were only passing packets with solid shot and shells with their fuzes cut for a predetermined distance. They weren't passing any canister shells. This meant the enemy wasn't too close. This was hot, dirty work as the dust kicked up by the guns covered them along with the thick acrid smoke. George's eyes and nose burned and tears were running down his cheeks. He couldn't see the cannons anymore, just the man next to him who would hand a loaded round to be passed on.

After five minutes of continuous firing, they stopped at last. Their targets disappeared into the far woods. Perhaps they would get a little rest now. George's arms felt like lead and he was soaked by perspiration. However, it was now the Confederate's turn for counter battery fire on the Union lines. Enemy balls came crashing in on them. One of the pieces had a wheel knocked off by a solid shot. The explosive shells were the next to come in, exploding all around them. The shards of iron could be heard whistling and clunking as they slammed into rock, the ground, wood and bodies. Somewhere just behind them a caisson blew up, sending pieces of wood and burning material in all directions. Several men near the cannons were knocked down by the falling debris. Fortunately none were hurt seriously, until a explosive shell detonated directly overhead.

George felt the heat and the concussion drove him to the ground senseless. In the far reaches of his mind, he could hear screaming; but for the moment though, he was dimly aware of what was happening. After a few seconds George could start moving his arms. The first thing he did was feel all over for wounds. Other than ripped and torn clothing, he was unscathed, except for the wound on his head from the day before.

The blast reopened the gash and blood was running down his neck and face.

Skeeter came crawling over, "Pops, you're bleeding, are you hit?"

George replied, "No, that blast just opened my old wound, that was too close. Are you OK Skeeter? You're all covered with blood!"

Skeeter replied, "Naw it ain't mine. I just got the bejesus knocked out of me and my ears are ringing, otherwise I'm OK."

Slowly George got up and looked around him, and everywhere he looked he saw destruction. Two dead men hung over a cannon and several others were down and not moving. Two guns were dismounted off their carriages and behind them, the exploded caisson was burning.

Both Skeeter and George hobbled back to the regiment.

When the sergeant saw George's bloody face, he told him, "You better get to the First Corps aid station and get that wound taken care of."

George knew he had to stay away from there, so he told the sergeant, "I'm OK. That shell just opened my wound from yesterday and I'm only shaken up a little." George put pressure on the wound until the bleeding stopped. Then he washed his face as best he could with water from his canteen and a rag.

Jack came over to see how he was and was all excited, "Man, I got up to the wall and could see the Confederates moving along the woods by Confederate Avenue and they were in perfect formation. Even when the shells tore holes in their ranks, they just reformed and kept on moving. You never saw anything like it. I saw that shell go off over your head, about 30 feet up and I thought you were a goner! I'm glad you're OK."

"Jack, you're rambling! Slow down! Yes, that was

too close and my head hurts like hell again. How about doing me a favor and check my ears to make sure they aren't bleeding. Another thing, that's not known as Confederate Avenue quite yet!"

Jack checked both ears, "You aren't bleeding. Didn't your mother tell you to wash your ears, or you would grow potatoes? Well I hate to tell you this, but you have a nice crop growing."

George wanted to laugh, but it hurt his head too badly, so he just laid there resting. Sporadic firing was heard coming from the vicinity of the Bliss Farm. He figured it was probably the rebel sharpshooters and the 12th New Jersey taking pot shots at each other again. The remainder of the afternoon was relatively quiet with the exception of troops being deployed and redeployed. George dozed off in the heat of the afternoon.

Jack rested in the shadow of a boulder which afforded a little shelter from the blazing hot sun. Gazing down toward Taneytown Road, he watched as wagons moved up and down the road carrying supplies. The mules could be plainly heard braying as the mule skinners snapped their whips over the animal's backs. Someday, if he ever had children, what stories he could tell them about this place and time. Jed was lying down and sound asleep next to Jack. His body twitched and trembled as he slept. Jack imagined he was reliving the horrors of the day before. The re-enactor's head started to nod and soon he too was sound asleep.

Late in the afternoon a single artillery piece fired over near the Roundtops. No-one paid attention as it sounded far away. The sound was muffled by the hills and tree foliage. Several more cannons joined in, followed the popping of muskets. The resting soldiers stood up and looked toward the south where smoke could be seen rising above the trees. The artillery and infantry fire kept increasing in intensity as a major battle unfolded.

George knew this would be Longstreet's attack starting at the Wheat Field and would spread all the way around to the Cordri Farm. Cannon fire was increasing rapidly all across the line of battle as artillery crews on both sides saw targets of opportunity. The sky was filled with livid flashes then puffs of white from the aerial burst. It reminded George of the movies from World War Two showing the heavy flak over Germany. The only difference was white puffs instead of black smoke of the flak. Occasionally a shell wouldn't explode until it hit the ground and debris could be seen flying into the air. Fifteen minutes went by and the appalling inferno kept escalating until the noise was overpowering even at a distance of almost a mile.

A drum roll called the Bucktails to their posts. George and Skeeter hobbled as best they could to the formation. Both were stiff as they stood in ranks. George's head hurt along with a shoulder blade that he felt was probably knocked out of joint from the blast of the exploding shell.

The First Sergeant stopped in front of George, "You and Skeeter will stay here to guard the regimental equipment until we get back."

Another man in the formation asked, "Where are we going sergeant?"

"Don't know yet. The Capt'n went to a corps staff meeting. He just sent word back to have the regiment ready to move when he gets back."

The battle now extended from the Round Tops West to the Wheat Field. Very soon it would circle around to the Codori Farm. Batteries on Cemetery Ridge started firing on advancing troops in front of them. Palls of smoke surrounded them as the regiment waited to be deployed. The ground rolled with the concussion of scores of cannons firing around them.

Captain Jones returned to the regiment and tried to talk to the men, but the noise was so overpowering, he simply gave up. Drawing his sword, raising it over his head then swinging it in an arc and dropping it forward. The regiment immediately formed a column of fours and stepped off at a fast trot behind the captain, moving in the direction of the Trostle Farm.

George and Skeeter found a vantage point to watch the battle unfold before them. They looked on as the regiment moved down toward the Wheat Field. George actually felt bad that he wasn't going with the men. The sight unfolding in front of them was astounding. Waves of blue and gray crashing into each other, then recoiling back only to surge forward again. Even at this distance, the fields could be seen littered with dead and wounded men. Everywhere they could see, caissons were burning, smoke was billowing up from fires started by shell burst. Amidst all this pandemonium you could hear the fierce crackle of musket fire interspersed with the CRUMP of volleys. George watched as a horse and rider were going up and down the line encouraging the Union troops to hold the position. Suddenly the horse was emptied of its rider as a cannon ball hit the soldier. A man's torso was seen turning end for end, 20 feet into the air before falling to the ground. George could see the horse galloping toward him away from the battle. The mount disappeared in a hollow and never reappeared. He wondered what happened to the horse, maybe someone caught it. Off to his right at the angle, the musket fire intensified as rebels approached the Codori Farm. The batteries along the stone wall were firing cannister with a vengence at the attacking enemy close by. Soon the smoke of battle hid everything from George's eyes but not the cresendo of sounds.

Jack moved with the regiment at the double quick and the heat and smoke almost overpowering. At last they stopped about 100 yards from the main line and the noise was so intense, that it hurt his ears. The slaughter that lay in front horrified Jack, even more so than the day before. The battle appeared to be utter chaos as the opposing sides intermingled in the smoky haze. Reserve regiments including the Bucktails, waited to be called into action, if the line in front of them gave way. They all laid down to rest, to keep out of sight and not draw fire. Even so, a steady stream of minies whined overhead, interspersed with cannon shells. He watched in panic as a whole line of Union went down in a volley of musket fire from the rebels. It was almost as if everything around him revolved in slow motion as the two forces kept slugging it out at point blank range. A riderless horse, its eyes bulging from the butchery it had seen, came galloping right by them trying to get away from that inferno. The poor horse streamed blood from several bullets in its side. This intermixed with the heavy lather, soaking the horse. As it passed Jack, he could see the blood and gore on the saddle that the late owner left behind. It probably was a cannon ball that ripped him into the next life, he thought.

Gradually, after laying there for a half hour, the firing ebbed in their front. As the Confederates broke off the engagement, a loud "Huzzah" went up as the Union troops celebrated their victory. When it was apparent the battle was over on the southern battle line, the Bucktails and other reserve troops counter marched back to Cemetery Hill. On the way back they saw the same riderless horse, where it had collapsed and died. The men were greeted with a grisly sight as they passed the dead horse. A hand still grasped the reins. Nothing else to show that a man sat in that saddle, alive shortly before.

George could see the regiment marching back toward Cemetery Hill. It appeared to be intact since they had been held in reserve only and not engaged. A steady stream of wounded men came back from the battle. The less wounded were walking and the severely wounded being transported by the wagon fulls. Over near the Codori House, heavy musket fire continued, along with the singing of stray minies going overhead. Union soldiers at the stone wall were firing back at the sharpshooters. For the most part, the battle with Longstreet's Corp was now over.

After the regiment reached the First Corps area, they were able to rest for little while. The sounds of battle were muted as the sun sank lower on the horizon. George ambled over to Jack and Jed. "How bad was it down there? From up here it looked as the fighting was pretty intense."

"Well I'm here to tell you, it was one hellava ruckus," Jed replied.

"George, we were down at the base of Cemetery Hill. You never saw anything like it. That whole area has so many bodies all over, you could walk the whole area without touching the ground. I was scared to death while we were waiting. The bullets were so thick, to stand was to die. I stuck my head up once to see what was happening. The rebels fired a volley at point blank range and at least 50 Union soldiers went down in a line. They fired back and did the same thing to the rebels. When the cannons fired their canister, it was gruesome. Bodies and pieces of bodies were flying everywhere. It was worse than yesterday. George, I'm ready to go back to where we belong. I don't ever want to relive history again!"

Suddenly, to the surprise of most, the fighting started at the other end of Cemetery Ridge, on Culps Hill. Just about sunset, the drum rolled, calling the regiment to formation. This time the 149th and 150th Regiments formed together as one skirmish company. Again George and Skeeter were told to watch the equipment and recuperate.

The skirmishers left for Emmitsburg Road and the Codori farm. They were to drive out the Confederate sharpshooters, who were plaguing the Union line with devastating results. George wished he were going along, but he knew he wasn't in any condition to join them and just hoped Jack would be OK. The Bucktail Regiment formed by the wall with several other regiments from the First Corps and waited as a mounted general conferred with other officers. George knew that he was seeing General Meade as he looked just like the pictures he had seen. The general was pointing down toward the Codori Farm as he fired off orders. When he finished he turned the horse's head and galloped right past George and Skeeter as he headed toward the battle at the Evergreen Cemetery. The Bucktails disappeared over the stone wall heading toward Emmitsburg Road. The fighting on Culps Hill became fierce and the hill was blanketed in smoke. The cannons over by the Evergreen Cemetery fired constantly and the CRAAUMP of musket volleys told of the attack by the cemetery.

"Hey Skeeter," George called to his partner, "I wish we could go with the regiment."

"Well, you're a fool if you do. I don't care if I never go on a skirmish line again."

"I thought that seeing the elephant wasn't so bad," George chided.

"That was yesterday. This is today and tomorrow

is the rest of my life. What's left of it," Skeeter countered.

George let the conversation end. He really didn't feel like talking much anymore.

Everything imaginable, cannon wheels, spokes, pieces of wood, knapsacks, canteens and smashed caissons, some still smoking littered the ground around George and Skeeter. Then, there were the horses. Everywhere you looked, horses were down. Some of them starting to swell from the heat, producing a terrible stench.

George turned to Skeeter and said, "Let's take a walk over to the stone wall, so we can watch our boys go down to the skirmish line." When they reached the wall, they could see the skirmishers spread out and move forward in a crouch, in the open. Smoke suddenly erupted from the Codori farmhouse windows as the skirmishers came under fire from the sharpshooters. Several of the advancing troops stopped, took aim and fired at the windows. Then firing broke out around the fencing of the farm. This time all of the skirmishers fired and kept advancing while they reloaded.

An officer yelled at George and Skeeter, "Get down and away from the wall you fools! Do want your heads blown off!"

Reluctantly they moved back to where they had been resting earlier. George still worried for Jack's safety.

Meanwhile the fighting and artillery fire on Cemetery Hill and on Culps Hill seemed to be getting worse. The heavy smoke hid Culps Hill from the eye. They wanted to rest, but the ground just rolled from the thunderous blasts of the cannons. Regiments were double timing to the sounds of the battle at the cemetery. Mounted officers galloped to and from the headquarters at the Leister Farm. Occasionally a stray minie ball could be heard moaning overhead from the fighting at the Cemetery.

A gentle breeze blew up the hill from Emmitsburg Road and with it the stench of the dead from both horses and human left unburied over the past two days. George thought, God this smell is overpowering and it will be worse tomorrow.

Skeeter looked over and asked, "You seem deep in thought. Is there a problem?"

"No. I'm just thinking about the smell of death around here, it's sickening."

"Well, I'm afraid it will get more putrid as time goes on."

As the evening wore on, George watched the activity going on through the hours of the moonlit night. The area along Taneytown road was a beehive of activity through the entire night. He could see a solid line of wagons stretched along the whole road. Cassions and limbers were lined up awaiting their turn to replenish cannon ammunition used during the previous days action. Other men were unloading and carrying musket ammunition boxes up to the men on the line and passing out the contents to the soldiers. The whole area by the wagon trains was lit up by hundreds of lanterns. George thought, Boy I hope no one knocks over one of those lanterns, if one of those wagons catches fire, it will be disastrous. Also during the night he watched troops moving all over, as they shifted to newly assigned positions. The whole scene looked surreal to George in the light of the full moon. He would liked to sleep, however they had to watch over the remnants of the regimental equipment. Foraging soldiers would not feel guilty helping themselves to the provisions if the guards were unwary or asleep.

CHAPTER SEVENTEEN

After the soldiers had moved through the troops manning the stone wall, they started spreading out in a skirmish line. The skirmishers moved through the knee high grass and down the hill toward the farm house. The Federals hadn't gone 200 yards, when they started drawing heavier fire from the farm house and from the barricades the rebels had thrown up. Bullets were whizzing by Jack and occasionally one would strike a rock, making a wicked whining noise as they went overhead. Slowly, moving in a crouch, the skirmisher line moved another 200 yards and started shooting back at their tormentors. The musketry intensified as they approached the farmhouse. However, their return fire was starting to take effect on the enemy. Two artillery pieces, positioned between them and the farmhouse, started blasting at them. However the skirmishers being spread out, made poor targets. While the artillerist were trying to reload, the Union troops made a full charge. Before the crews reloaded, they were among them. The fighting was hand to hand and furious for less than thirty seconds. Jack put his bayonet to the throat of a Rebel and the man just put his hands up in surrender. Then it was all over. They just recaptured two Napoleons that were lost earlier to the Rebels. Two squads of men were detailed to watch over the prizes as the remainder of the skirmishers moved toward the farmhouse firing at every movement or flash of a musket. Jack was amazed at the ferocity of his attack moments before. Maybe he would make a good soldier yet.

Jack saw movement in a second story window and fired. A musket fell out of the window, the only indication that he had hit his mark. The skirmishers hid behind anything they could find. A stump here, a tree there and traded fire with the rebels who were less than fifty yards away. Jack knew that their accuracy was having a severe effect. As the minies struck home, the sound of wounded rebels could be heard. This contest lasted almost 15 minutes and surprisingly, very few of the Federals were even wounded. Soon the enemy had enough and moved back, allowing the Bucktails to take over the farm. Darkness set in quickly now and the Union soldiers spread out from the farmhouse. Their line bent backwards toward town and touched the Emmitsburg Road. Once in place, the men found whatever cover they could and settled down for a night of watching and waiting. It had grown fairly quiet around them, with only sporadic musketfire. But behind them, they could hear the terrible fighting on Culps Hill. As Jack looked to the sounds of the distant fighting, the clouds of smoke could be seen glowing an eerie orange, as the artillery fired.

Out in front of him in the darkness, Jack could hear the groaning and crying of wounded men. The sounds were nerve wracking, especially the men calling out and pleading for water. Slowly through the night, the wounded men grew silent one by one. That night was one of the longest in Jack's life. Staying awake was extremely hard, but he managed to keep his eyes open. Throughout the night, he could see men moving about the previous day's battlefield with lanterns looking for fallen comrades. Strangely, neither the Confederates nor the Union troops fired on these angels of mercy. After midnight the fighting had died down on Culps Hill. The moonlit night just dragged on.

Jed called to Jack, "Did you hear that?"

"Did I hear what?"

"The Whippoorwills calling!"

"I didn't hear anything," Jack replied.

Jed, with fear in his voice said, "If you didn't hear them and I did, it means I'm gonna die soon!"

"Dammit Jed. Stop talking so foolish. You're not gonna get killed. Nothing much more happens to us during this battle."

"How do you know what's gonna happen in this battle?"

Oh shit, Jack thought, I've slipped again. "I don't know what's going to happen. I just have this feeling that we've seen the worst of it."

As the night passed slowly, Jack could hear movement in front of him and several times he swore he saw someone. Jack held his fire, but several times other men would fire at the sounds. One time when a man fired a voice screeched out, "Damn it! I'm wounded. Don't shoot at me yank!"

The soldier replied, "Sorry Johnny Reb. Didn't mean to scare you. Are you OK?"

"Hell no I ain't OK. I'm gut shot and it hurts like hell. Just let me die in peace."

Dawn came, then sunrise and the heat started to build once more. At last fresh troops came down to relieve the skirmishers. The Bucktails formed up into columns of fours and started marching back to the Union lines.

As they started marching, Jack turned to Jed, "Last night was too damn long. I'm glad we're outta there. I'm hungry and tired."

Jed, who seemed very lighthearted for some reason, replied, "Yea it was. But today is going to be a glorious day. I'm going home!"

"What do you mean, you're going home?"

"It's just like I told you last night. I've resigned myself to my fate. I made peace with the Lord and I'm ready."

"Dammit, Jed, I'm tired of that kind of talk. Nothing is going to happen to you. So quit talking that way!"

Unfortunately, the marching column proved to be a very inviting target to some far away Confederate cannon crews, who lobbed some shells at the departing Bucktails.

Jack was in the column and never heard the muffled boom of the battery. Suddenly, he heard the shell cutting the air. He saw a white flash and felt unbearable heat. His body slammed into the ground, then total darkness. As Jack came to, his first awareness was of men screaming and someone leaning over him shouting, "This one is still alive!"

Jed heard the same shell swishing through the air, saw the flash and felt a quick, sharp pain in his shoulder blade. He felt his body spinning as the hot, searing pain tore into his chest. The pain only lasted for a split second. Hardly enough time for the brain to even register that something catastrophic had just happened to the body. Jed felt himself floating and looked below. That's odd he thought, Look at the men down there scattered all over. Hey, that's me laying there! He looked up and saw himself being drawn to a bright white light!

Slowly, with the help of a soldier, Jack raised on his hands and knees. He started checking his body for wounds. Luck was with him. Other than his hat being burned along with his neck, he was unhurt. His head hurt, his ears were ringing and when he tried to move his legs, he just stumbled around like a tipsy man. As Jack looked around, he could see men gathering a couple of bodies and getting ready to carry them back up the hill. He looked around for Jed, but he was nowhere to be seen. A chill went up his back.

Jack moved over to one of the bodies being carried away and peered into the man's face. He immediately broke down crying. His file partner Jed, was that lifeless body in the gum blanket. Falling to his knees, Jack screamed, "O God no! Not Jed! Why him?" Weeping he cried out, "Jed, Jed, you said you were going to die and I didn't believe you!" Grabbing the one man by the arm, he told him, "I'll help carry Jed's body. He was my friend!"

"Are you in any condition to carry anyone?"

"I'm going to help carry my friends' body. I'll make it. Now get the hell out of my way."

The soldier just shrugged his shoulders and gave the corner of the gum blanket to Jack.

Slowly they made their way up the hill, carrying the dead and seriously wounded. Jack's heart was heavy. This brave young man had helped him survive. Probably even saved his life several times. And young man's life was snuffed out in a flash. Somehow he would try to keep Jed's promise to Crackers. To try to find Crackers and give him a proper burial.

During the fighting of those three days at Gettysburg, the 150th PVI lost 57 men killed or mortally wounded.

During their entire service, the 150th PVI lost 112 men killed or mortally wounded. They lost an additional 95 men to disease.

CHAPTER EIGHTEEN

George watched a new skirmish company heading down to relieve the Bucktail regiment on the skirmish line. He went to the stone wall and peered over to watch the men come back. The Bucktails stood, formed up and started marching back up the hill. Off in the distance he saw the flashes and smoke as several cannons fired. A small dot loomed larger and larger as it headed straight for the marching men. "God no, it's heading right for them! They don't know it's coming," he screamed. Watching in panic as the shell burst right over the men, George felt like someone kicked him in the stomach, as he saw the men go down. He prayed that Jack survived the shell, but they were too far away to recognize anyone. He watched as they carried two men in gum blankets, the arms and heads just dangling down told George these two were dead. There were several others being transported, but George could see their arms moving, which meant they were alive. It seemed it took forever for them to come back up the hill. To his relief, he could see Jack helping to carry the second body. As they reached the stone wall, helping hands reached across to bring the bodies over the wall. George went over and helped Jack with the corpse. From the look on his friend's face, he knew it had to be Jack's file partner, Jed.

When they reached the First Corp area, the soldiers gently laid the body down. Just as George suspected, it was Jed.

Jack shaking his head, "We were talking, he was sure that he was going to die. I didn't believe him. I just finished telling Jed that he wasn't gonna die. That's when I heard this weird noise. The next thing I remember was getting up, my head hurting and my ears ringing. In that instant, Jed was dead. He never knew what hit him! Last night he said he heard a whippoorwill and that he was gonna die. In fact, when we were stuck in the chicken coop Jed had the same feeling and I didn't believe him then!"

George checked Jacks eyes and ears, then checked his neck. It was burned like a bad case of sunburn. "Well Jack, you were lucky, you don't have a concussion, nor ruptured ear drums." George looked quickly at Jed's body and when he rolled him over, could see where the single piece of shrapnel had entered just above the right shoulder blade. He could tell from the lack of bleeding, that the shrapnel had ripped into Jed's heart, stopping it forever, almost instantly. George put his hand on Jack's shoulder and quietly said, "I'm very sorry. Just be thankful it wasn't you. If it's any consolation, Jed probably never knew what hit him"

Jack sat on the ground and started weeping uncontrollably. "He saved my life several times. Hell, I only knew him three days. I wish it were me who died, not Jed. He had his whole life ahead of him."

George put his arm around Jack, "You know, I've seen death many times and I've lost several good friends in war. The first one is always the worst. And don't feel guilty about being alive. It wasn't your time. God has other plans for you."

"It just occurred to me. I don't even know his last

name. All I ever knew him by was Jed. I'll be right back." Jack went over to another man in his company, "What was Jed's last name?

"His name was Jediah Walsh. His family lives in Philadelphia."

"Thanks. Does anyone have a pencil and some paper?"

Another soldier searched in his haversack and pulled out an oilskin pouch, removing a piece of paper and a small wooden pencil.

Jack thanked the man and sat to write, "Jediah Walsh, My Possum. A brave man. 150th PVI Co. A." He pinned the paper to Jed's shirt and helped load the body on a wagon, which had just stopped to pick up the dead. Jack stood and watched as the wagon lurched and bounced as it headed down the hill toward Taneytown Road.

The men of the regiment found places to rest and fell asleep. Jack stayed up and went to talk to George for a while. Sitting on a rock, Jack asked, "George, did you know about that shell that hit us this morning?"

George shook his head no, "I told you it was a while since I read the book and I thought it was going to happen this afternoon. I'm sorry I didn't remember."

"It doesn't make any difference, it's too late now."

As the two sat there, the whole area was a bee hive of activity. Regiment upon regiment moving back and forth, finding positions in case an attack came. George could see that several of the regiments had recently arrived. Their uniforms and faces not covered with blood and grease like the men around them. They didn't have the vacant stares. Just looks of amazement as they passed the troops who carried the brunt of the attacks the previous two days. Several Bucktails taunted the new comers, "You dandies sure do look sweet. Just wait till Bobby Lee teaches you a lesson."

One of the fresh troops countered, "If you soldiers knew how to fight, why, there would be no reason for General Meade to send his best troops. Us!"

The only thing that averted a brawl, was an alert officer who screamed, "You soldiers stay in ranks and keep marching. As for you men over there," as he pointed to the Bucktails, "You men shut your mouths. Now!"

The soldiers quieted down and the two re-enactors decided to find a place get a little rest. Less than five minutes went by and their rest was interrupted by a call to fall in again. This time George and Skeeter joined the ranks in their company.

Captain Jones addressed them, "Boys, we had some more losses this morning, but our job is not yet done. I know you were on the skirmish line all night. So I'll make this short so you can get some rest. The Commanding General said, Lee tried both our flanks and has been repulsed. General Meade feels that sometime today, Lee will hit the center of our line. Gentlemen, this is the center of the line! We are being held in reserve here just in case the enemy breaks the first line of defense. So I don't want anyone wandering off. Stay close to your company at all times. If you go to the company sink, let your sergeant know. Good luck and may God bless you."

The exhausted soldiers found shade wherever they could to get out of the glaring hot sun. As George sat there, he looked over towards the Bliss Farm and thick black smoke could be seen rising. Damn, George thought, the Union Army burned that house and barn down on purpose. He remembered reading about it in one of his books. The last three days, he had seen enough history for two lifetimes. As he looked around almost everyone in the regiment was lying down and sound asleep. It sounded good to him and he too dozed in the sweltering heat.

In the distance two cannons fired. No one stirred until they heard the boom, boom of two aerial bursts nearby. George bolted up and looked around, "Damn, I hope I wasn't asleep that long" as he heard the rapid succession of cannons going off. He knew what was coming next. "Everyone down and hug the dirt," he screamed, as he dove behind the biggest rock he could find.

Jack rolled over to him, "Is this it?"

George couldn't answer as the noise of Union cannons was deafening and the ground just rolled and tossed like some large creature in its death throes. Smoke was everywhere, shells exploded, and the air was alive with the sounds of whirring pieces of iron. They both lay face down in the dirt with their hands over their ears trying to keep out the terrifying sounds of this cannonading. It never stopped. The sulfurous smoke was so bad that it hurt the lungs when they drew their breath. George thought, God, this is going to go on forever. How will we last through this?

After an hour, they were still huddled by the rock. Several more men crawled over to join them in the shelter of the small boulder. No one spoke, you couldn't talk loud enough to be heard anyway. They never saw it happen. A caisson about a hundred feet from them suffered a direct hit by a Confederate shell, spewing exploding shells in all directions. George felt the thud of one of these shells from the caisson as it hit the ground near them. There was a tremendous explosion as the shell went off! Both George and Jack saw the flash, but they never felt any pain, nor heard any sound as total blackness engulfed them!

The 150th suffered 139 wounded during those three days in July. Most on the first day. An additional 49 men were captured on the first day's battle. This was due to the town being overrun by Confederates before they retreated through Gettysburg.

CHAPTER NINETEEN

Janet Bullock was addressing a group of tourist at the copse of trees known as the high water mark. "Before Pickets famous charge, there was a tremendous cannonading. Most of the Confederate shells overshot the Union cannons, hitting behind us in the supply area and where the reserve troops were held." And with that she turned around to point to the area, when she heard a bloodcurdling scream.

A hysterical woman was pointing, "What is that? It just started appearing before my eyes!"

There on the ground by a large rock, a heavy mist was forming. The fog seemed to be revolving around something. Janet thought, That's weird, how can fog form like that on a hot July afternoon?

As the strange fog disappeared, the forms of two men dressed in Union uniforms lay there, bleeding and groaning. One soldier was on his back and was raising an arm up. Dropping it, then raising it up again. He was whimpering, "It hurts. It hurts, it hurts!"

She thought to herself, Oh no, this can't be happening again! Running over she noticed they both appeared seriously injured. She pulled out her radio and called for immediate assistance and asked for a medivac. The one man raising his arm and dropping it, was completely soaked in blood and the blood was pooling under his body. The other man was bleeding rather badly from one arm which had the sleeve ripped from the shoulder to the wrist. His neck appeared to be severely burned. "Everybody stand back. Give these men some room," she commanded. "Is there a doctor or medical technician here?"

A woman spoke up, "I'm a registered nurse!"

Ranger Bullock called her over and asked her to help give the men first aid.

The nurse swiftly looked over the extremely dirty men. Their faces and hands were greasy black and their uniforms were filthy and blood soaked. She whispered to the ranger, "I did a tour in Vietnam and if I'm not mistaken, these are shrapnel wounds and flash burns. This man also has a head wound that looks to be over a day old but has reopened. Does this make any sense to you?" she asked the ranger.

Janet Bullock shook her head No, but deep down she knew these were the two missing re-enactors. "Will they live?" She asked the nurse.

"I really don't know, their vital signs are reasonable, considering the wounds. The one fellow appears to be bleeding a lot, however it's not as bad as it looks. A head wound always bleeds heavily. The other one has a nasty laceration down his arm and as long as I keep pressure on this artery, he won't bleed to death. They both appear to have shrapnel in their bodies and without x-rays we won't know if any vital organs have been hit." Then they heard the Medivac flying in.

* * * * * *

George wasn't fully conscious, he was aware of raising and dropping his right arm and repeating, "It hurts!" He wasn't aware of any pain, but for some reason, he couldn't wake up and he didn't know where he was. He heard the unmistakable sound of helicopter blades cutting the air. Damn, this must be a dream, I hear a Dust Off[12] coming in. I must be back in Vietnam, he thought just before blackness set in again.

Jack wasn't aware of anything until he felt himself being lifted and placed on a stretcher. He couldn't hear anything except the damn ringing in his ears. But he couldn't open his eyes either. It was like being in a nightmare and you just can't wake up. Jack could feel a vibration and then the sensation that he was flying. Later, Jack was cognizant that he was in a hospital and being rushed somewhere on a gurney. And darkness again.

* * * * * *

The General Hospital in Harrisburg was alerted to an incoming Medivac helicopter racing toward them with some seriously injured men. Doctor Broder was on duty in the emergency room as he listened to the EMT in the helicopter describe the men's conditions. He turned to his nurse and asked, "Is there a military exercise in the area using live ammunition?"

---

[12] Term used for a medical evacuation Helicopeter used in Vietnam

Cindy Martin, who had been a nurse in the emergency room for over ten years replied, "No Doctor, why do you ask that?"

"Years ago when I was a doctor in the army in Vietnam, I heard the same descriptions of wounds as the dustoff helicopters would bring in wounded."

The EMT's rushed the injured re-enactors to the emergency room and the doctors and nurses started cutting away their blood and grease soaked clothing.

Dr. Broder started barking orders in rapid fire, "Start cleaning them up. Check their vital signs? Check for bleeding. Start IVs. Get Radiology, have them stand by."

Nurse Martin stated, "Doctor, their vital signs are stable and luckily the major bleeding was stopped by the EMT's. They appear to have some type of tearing wounds and flash burns, as if they were in some kind of explosion."

"I know that Nurse. Get these men to x-ray now. Keep watch on their vital signs. Interns, go with them. At the first sign of problems, call Code Red. Now go. I'll be in OR2 waiting for the men with the rest of the Trauma Team." As the team rushed out of the room, Dr. Broder scratched at something crawling on his neck and picked it off with his fingers. He looked closely at the critter between his finger and exclaimed, "Oh shit, lice!" Turning to a nurse, he ordered, "Bag those clothes tightly for the police and put them in the closet. Fumigate this room!"

* * * * * *

Tim and Marge Fretz along with the other wives, managed to get rooms at the same motel, as Jim Craig the reporter. As they were sitting in Tim and Marge's room as they heard a helicopter fly low over the motel. It sounded as if it was landing.

Katey looked over to Jan, "That sure sounds like a helicopter landed over on the battle field somewhere. Wonder if somebody is hurt?"

"There's so many people here, somebody probably got hit with a car or something."

About 5 minutes later the chopper could be heard coming back and they rushed outside as the Medivac passed low over head.

Jan spoke first, "That's odd. They just bypassed the hospital here and seems to be heading toward Harrisburg. They must have someone hurt real bad."

The four of them heard a door slam hard against a wall with a loud crash. They turned to see what the commotion was. It was Jim, running toward them screaming, "They found them! They found them!"

The trip to Harrisburg took over an hour. Thanks to the state police escort, it wasn't as bad as it could have been. The traffic in the area was horrendous this time of the year. On arriving at the hospital, they dashed toward the emergency room door, as if it was a race. As they rushed through the automatic doors, which almost didn't open fast enough, a doctor stopped them.

Dr. Broder put up his hands, "Ladies and gentlemen, slow down. I heard you were on your way. Please come with me into this room here."

Upon entering the room, the ladies fired off a barrage of questions at the doctor.

"How's my husband? Is he alive? Is he hurt? Where is he?"

"Settle down, please. Your husbands are going to be OK, and I'll make arrangements for you to see them. But they are both sleeping right now in the recovery room. I'll tell you what we found. Mrs. Myers, your husband has a nasty gash on his right arm, but no nerves or tendons are affected. We repaired the damaged artery and it appears to be OK. We did take out a couple pieces of shrapnel out of his back and legs. Again, he was lucky, nothing major.

Mrs. Murray, your husband had a nasty head wound which appears to have been opened a couple of times. He also had some shrapnel in his back. He too, was lucky, nothing major. I do have one question for both of you. They were both dressed up as Civil War re-enactors. How in the world did they get those wounds?" Neither wife could give an answer. No-one would believe them anyway.

* * * * *

"Good evening ladies and gentlemen, this is the channel 69 news. Our main story this evening centers around the town of Gettysburg! An amazing story about some missing re-enactors being found today on the battlefield. We have a news team standing by to give you a report by people who were there! We also have a news team standing by in Harrisburg to give you the rest of the story!"

* * * * * *

George was beginning to regain consciousness and he could smell the antiseptic aroma, realizing he was in a hospital. He was dimly aware of someone holding his hand and talking to him. Gradually it came to him, it was Jan's voice he heard. The wounded re-enactor was confused, where was he and what happened to him? It seemed like a dream, but he actually fought in the Civil War! At last he opened his eyes and the first thing he saw was his wife's face and tears were streaming down her face.

"Thank God you're awake, you've been out for quite a while."

"Why are my hands tied to the bed rail, where am I?"

"You're in the hospital in Harrisburg. The nurse tied your hands so you wouldn't roll onto your back."

"Oh God, my back is tight and sore. What happened to me? I had this dream that I was in the Civil War."

Relieved, Jan told her husband, "Honey I don't know what happened to you, I was hoping you could tell me. Your back and backside was full of shrapnel, not to mention that terrible gash in your head."

Everything started coming back to George, "Now I remember, Jack and I actually fought in the Battle of Gettysburg. Where's Jack, is he OK? And Tim, have you seen or heard of him? We lost him and have no idea what happened to him."

"Jack is alright, in fact he's in the next bed, but he's still asleep. Actually Tim showed up a couple of days ago. He told us what happened to all of you, until he came back. The whole thing sounds impossible, but there doesn't appear to be any other explanation. I'm just thankful that both of you are safe and back with us. You should rest now and later you can tell us what happened."

George closed his eyes and tried to piece together everything that had happened the last few days. At least everyone was back and safe. He felt much better now. As he dozed off he murmured, "I love you!"

Jack was aware of a terrible pain in his arm and the ringing in his ears. He heard a voice he recognized, Katey was talking to him.

"Jack, oh Jack, wake up. I love you. Please wake up."

"How can anyone get any sleep around here with you blathering like that," Jack surprised his wife.

"Damn you. How long were you awake. If you weren't so banged up, I'd smack you. Thank God you're Ok. I love you, you big oaf. You had me scared to death for days."

"Where in the hell am I? Is George here? Where's Tim?"

"You're in the hospital. George is in the next bed and just fell asleep. Tim is outside waiting to see both of you. You've been very lucky. A nurse saved your life up on the battlefield where you two showed up. You had a cut artery and she stopped the bleeding. If she hadn't been there, you may have bled to death. I think you and George have a lot to tell us about what happened to you. It can wait for a while, until you both feel up to it. You need your rest so just close your eyes. I'll be right here with you. I'm never letting you out of my sight again."

Later that night after the two men were alone, George said to Jack, "Are you awake over there?"

"Yea I'm awake, I was just laying here thinking what happened to us."

"I was too. You know Jack, after all we were through, I'm sorry we didn't stay long enough to see Picketts Charge."

"I was thinking the same thing. Now that we are back, I'm glad that I did re-live history. At the time I didn't like it one bit. Thank God that Tim is OK. Did you notice he seemed a little weird? Like he felt guilty about something."

George replied, "He did act a little funny. Maybe he just feels bad about being so close to the battle and not seeing it. I wonder if Skeeter survived the war. I'll have to check the regimental records. I sure hope that he made it. I'm happy that we survived, but I sure and hell don't want to do that again. One thing I do know for sure, I have nothing but the deepest admiration for those soldiers on both sides. Their courage and steadfastness in the face of certain death is totally amazing. The other thing that strikes me is the savagery and butchery in war. All you do is change the date, uniforms and arms. There is no difference between the Civil War and the Vietnam War. They're both horrible and the suffering is the same. I feel deep remorse for taking lives during the fighting. I do from the bottom of my heart, thank God for sparing us and allowing us to return to our families. God had to have a hand in this for some reason. There's some plan for our experience but I have no idea what it is. I guess we better get some sleep now. We're supposed to get out of here tomorrow. Maybe we can get some more answers then. Good night Jack."

"Good night George. Tomorrow is another day."

* * * * *

Tad was the first to speak after Tom had told the story, "Pop-Pop, did this really happen?"

"Yes Tad, it did happen, I don't know how or why, but as far as I'm concerned, it happened!"

"There must be some logical explanation to this whole story. It has to be a hoax," Matt stated.

"Matt, I've checked every angle in this phenomenon and I couldn't find any inconsistency, none whatsoever. We even had the shrapnel taken out of those two re-enactors analyzed at the lab. Those pieces of iron came from the Civil War, everything matches."

"Whatever happened to those two men?" Tad

asked.

"Well, they survived. Fortunately their wounds weren't really bad. I have been in contact with them ever since, trying to figure this out. Surprisingly, two of them are still re-enacting, but they don't look at the re-enactments quite the same. The two that went through the battle, are hard of hearing though. The fellow who came back before the battle. He gave up re-enacting but never told why. Maybe it's because of his guilt for what he was thinking when he came back. That's basically the story and like I said earlier, this event has no beginning and possibly no end!"

"Pop-Pop," Tad asked, "What do you mean there's possibly no end to the story?"

"Well Tad, I did some research on the 26th North Carolina Regiment and there was a soldier named Josh Akers who survived the war. His story is quite amazing also. Since then I've become good friends with George Murray. And that Parker-Hale Enfield that is a part of this story, well it's back with Mr. Murray. About a year later, after it reappeared in Bill Sloan's collection, he gave that musket back to George. Sloan said the musket had made the full circle and it belonged to Murray."

"Tell us about those stories, please Pop-Pop."

"No Tad, it's almost time for dinner. I'll tell all of you those stories some other rainy day, as they will take awhile."

NEVER, NEVER say or think, "I wish I could go back in time and relive history . . . " You may just get your wish!

SUGGESTED READING

150th Pennsylvania Volunteers 1905 by Thomas Chamberlin

The 149th Pennsylvania Volunteer Infantry Unit in the Civil War by Richard E. Matthews 1926 and 1994

Gettysburg July 1 by David G. Martin 1995

Gettysburg A Journey In Time by William A. Frassanito 1975

Early Photography At Gettysburg by William A. Frassanito

The U.S. Army War College Guide to the Battle of Gettysburg Edited by Dr. Jay Luvaas and Col. Harold W. Nelson 1986

Civil War Letters Of The National Guards The 19th & 90th Pennsylvania Volunteers Edited by James Durkin 1994

Hard Tack And Coffee by John D. Billings 1887

They Met At Gettysburg by Edward J. Stackpole 1956

Gettysburg The Second Day by Harry W. Pfanz 1987

The Guns At Gettysburg by Fairfax Downey, Reprinted 1987 by Olde Soldier Books Inc.

Morning At Willoughby Run July 1, 1863 by Richard S. Shue

Upon The Tented Field Edited by Bernard A. Olsen 1993

All issues of The Gettysburg Magazine

All issues of The Blue and Gray Magazine

The Forgotten War by Clay Blair

Pennsylvania At Gettysburg Vols. I & II 1904

The Mifflin Guard donned bucktails to fill the Bucktail ranks re-enacting July 1, 1863 at McPherson Ridge. This would have been an approximate size of a Union Regiment at Gettysburg.

Bucktails from the 1st Pennsylvania Rifles, 149th and 150th PVI re-enact Color Sergeant Samuel Peiffer's heroic actions at Gettysburg when he is mortally wounded and flaunts the flag at the Confederates on June 1, 1863. This picture was taken at the 135th anniversary of the battle of Gettysburg on July 3, 1998. (by Dianne Conroy)

Confederate dead and wounded in front of the Bucktails. Picture taken July 3, 1998 at 135th anniversary of the Battle of Gettysburg. (photo by Dianne Conroy)

Bucktails in center of the line fire a volley. July 1998, 135th anniversary of the Battle of Gettysburg.

Smoke and haze cover the battle lines as the Bucktails start to advance.
July 1998, 135th anniversary of the Battle of Gettysburg. (by Dianne Conroy)

ABOUT THE AUTHOR

John has resided in the Upper Perkiomen Valley in Southeastern Pennsylvania since he retired from the U.S. Navy. He has a lifelong interest in history and in the Civil War in particular for over thirty years. He has lived in Florida, South Carolina and Virginia where he started delving into the War between the States.

The author is re-enactor with the 150th PVI Co. F, 5th Alabama and 7th Tenn. Co. B. He is an associate member of the 150th Co. C. He is a member of the 150th PVI in the N-SSA, a Friend of the 51st. PVI, Civil War Roundtable of Southeastern Pennsylvania, member of Pennwriters Inc., and member of the Montgomery County Historical Society.

He is also a speaker at various functions on the Civil War. His main topics are, The Common Soldier, Firearms of the Civil War and how topography affects the outcome of the battle. John also writes articles on history for local newspapers.